F
\
O

A TIME TO REMEMBER

A TIME TO REMEMBER

Margaret Pemberton

Severn House Large Print
London & New York

This first large print edition published 2009
in Great Britain and the USA by
SEVERN HOUSE PUBLISHERS LTD of
9-15 High Street, Sutton, Surrey, SM1 1DF.
First world regular print edition published 2008 by
Severn House Publishers Ltd., London and New York.

Copyright © 1988, 2007 by Margaret Pemberton.

British Library Cataloguing in Publication Data

Pemberton, Margaret
  A time to remember. - Large print ed.
  1. English - China - Hong Kong - Fiction 2. Hong Kong
  (China) - Social life and customs - Fiction 3. Love stories
  4. Large type books
  I. Title II. Pemberton, Margaret. Multitude of sins
  823.9'14[F]

  ISBN-13: 978-0-7278-7757-4

Printed and bound in Great Britain by
MPG Books Ltd, Bodmin, Cornwall.

For Mike
Again, as always

Defeat cries aloud for explanations, whereas success, like charity, covers a multitude of sins.

ADMIRAL MAHON

Prologue

The immaculately uniformed doorman, bearing the gold-crested insignia of the Victoria Hotel, Hong Kong, swung open the vast glass door leading on to the street and saluted respectfully. Elizabeth Harland gave a slight smile in acknowledgement of the service rendered and stepped out into the pale light of early morning. It was barely dawn. The noise and tumult, so inherently a part of Hong Kong's street scene, were temporarily subdued. The city of Victoria was taking a brief rest, pausing before it launched itself into another frenetic, fevered, adrenalin-packed day.

The sleek, low-slung sports-car she had hired the previous evening had been brought round to the front of the hotel and was waiting for her. A bellboy opened the door for her, ascertained that she had everything she required, and sincerely wished her a good day. As she turned the key in the ignition, firing the engine into life, he stepped back, watching as she pulled away from the kerb, the same expression of admiration in his eyes as that still lingering in the eyes of the doorman.

Lee Yiu Piu was sixty-two years old and he had been a doorman for over twenty years. The Victoria Hotel was one of the most prestigious in the world, and Lee Yiu Piu knew class when he met it. Elizabeth Harland, tall and slender and graceful, her wheat-gold hair coiled into a thick knot at the nape of her neck, her white linen suit starkly simple, her only jewellery the ring she wore on her left hand and the small pearl studs in her ears, reeked of it.

'Where can she be going at this time of the morning?' the bellboy asked curiously as he stepped back into the hotel's flower-filled lobby.

Lee Yiu Piu shrugged. He didn't know. It was certainly strange, especially so if the rumours he had heard were true. An airport taxi throbbed to a halt beneath the *porte-cochère*, and a party of flight-weary newsmen and cameramen spilled out. Lee Yiu Piu stepped forward, opening the massive glass doors for them. Their conversation as they entered the hotel indicated that the rumours *were* true. In which case, the beautiful Englishwoman's lonely dawn departure was even more puzzling.

Elizabeth's hands shook slightly on the wheel as she turned into Chater Road and past huge hoardings announcing the televised concert that was to take place that evening. She had known her return to Hong Kong would be traumatic, but she hadn't expected such a physical onslaught on her senses; such a searing sensation of having been whisked back in time, of never having left.

She had flown into Kai Tak Airport late the previous evening, the island a dark hump in the silk-black sea, glittering like a Christmas tree with a myriad twinkling lights. She had never approached it by air before and she had been grateful. It brought back no memories. No visions of the island as it had been on the sun-filled afternoon twelve years ago when she had first sighted it from the rails of the *Orient Princess*, its mountains soaring silver-grey, silver-tawny, silver-green, gashed by ravines and tortuous valleys, the lower slopes dense with vegetation and thick with flame trees and vines and deep-scented hibiscus. So long ago. Before the war. Before the Japanese. Before Raefe.

As she sped through the narrow gaudy streets the unmistakable, indefinable smell of Hong Kong assailed her, ripping wide the intervening years and sending them scattering. She was twenty-five again. Twenty-five and so deeply in love that the mere memory of it made her gasp for breath.

With her knuckles white on the wheel, she turned inland, skirting the Happy Valley Racecourse and zig-zagging up the mountainous road that led to the Wong Nei Chung Gap, the centre of the island. Behind her were stupendous views of the city and the harbour and Kowloon; and in front of her, as she neared the Gap, were glimpses of the bays and rocky inlets of the island's southern shore, milk-white beaches merging into an indigo sea. There was no other traffic, no other traveller in view. She drew to a halt, opening the car door and stepping out on to the roughly made road. Wong Nei Chung Gap. Peaceful, serene – and the scene of a bloody carnage that had left scores of men dead and countless others wounded.

A sparrow-hawk wheeled high above her head,

9

disturbing the silence. No familiar landmarks remained. There was no sign of the Brigade Headquarters that had once nestled in a fold of the hills. No sign of the shelter that had been erected lower down, closer to the road. For Hong Kong, the war was over, forgotten. And for her? Her delicately featured face was sombre. Despite the huge hoardings that lined Chater Road, and despite the newspapermen already gathering, how could it ever be forgotten? How could she ever even wish to forget?

The sparrow-hawk, sighting prey, plummeted. She watched the large wings flutter against the scrub and rock, and then it soared high, wheeling into a ravine, a small unidentifiable mammal imprisoned in its talons. There was silence. In the distance, the sea shimmered, outlying islands insubstantial as shadows in the early morning heat. There was no one to be seen. On the most crowded island on earth she was, as she had wanted to be, alone.

She sat down on the grass, hugging her knees, knowing that before she returned to the teeming streets of Victoria the past would have to be faced and the most important decision of her life taken.

Chapter 1

Snow fell steadily over the bowed heads of the mourners as they gathered at Serena Kingsley's graveside. The autumn of 1924 had been chill and bleak; and now, in January, an Arctic frost showed no sign of giving London relief. As the familiar words of the Anglican burial service were read, more than one elegantly gloved hand surreptitiously lifted the cuff of a mink or vicuña coat to glance at a wristwatch and estimate how much longer it would be before the service was over and they could decently leave. There would be heart-warming French Cognac and a lavish buffet awaiting them at Jerome Kingsley's Belgravia home, and a chance to indulge in the social gossip that was their meat and drink.

The mourners were fewer in number than they would have been if Serena had died at a more suitable time of the year. Winter, for the Kingsleys' friends and acquaintances, was a time of migration. They either sought refuge in the milder climate of the Riviera or sailed south to the more exotic retreat of Madeira. Apart from the Kingsleys' only child, a daughter, there was no family present. Serena's parents had died in a yachting tragedy many years previously, and Jerome Kingsley's antecedents were a mystery.

If he had a family, it was one he never acknowledged. He had appeared on the London scene in 1905, polished and assured, and the possessor of a talent for financial manipulation that amounted to near-wizardry. By the time he was thirty-two and had proposed marriage to Serena Hughendon, one of the most eligible heiresses of the season, he was able to be accepted with society doing little more than raise a delicate eyebrow. Self-made millionaires cannot, with impunity, be accused of fortune-hunting.

The marriage was a remarkably happy one. If Jerome Kingsley was unfaithful to Serena, he was so discreetly, and there were those of his friends who doubted if, in fact, he ever did more than indulge in a little light flirtation. He was forty-five now, a tall, powerfully built man with a strong assertive jawline, his massive shoulders hunched beneath his beaver-trimmed overcoat. He had loved her deeply and now, at thirty-two, she was dead.

'Glory be to the Father, and to the Son, and to the Holy Ghost,' the priest said concludingly.

The mourners breathed a sigh of relief and stamped their feet on the snow-covered ground with as much energy as good manners allowed. Jerome Kingsley released his daughter's hand and stepped forward, staring long and silently down at the coffin. All her life Serena had hated the cold and the dark, and now he was leaving her here, alone. Tears blinded his eyes, and a muscle twitched convulsively at the corner of his jaw as he gently dropped a long-stemmed, perfectly formed white rose on to the coffin, and then a handful of the earth that was to cover her. Ashes to ashes, dust to dust. He didn't believe in a resurrection. This was their final parting. And he would not try to replace her.

His daughter squeezed his hand comfortingly as he returned to her side; and then, heartbreakingly vulnerable in a black velvet coat with a black velvet tam-o'-shanter perched on top of her pale gold hair, she, too, stepped forward, a posy of winter violets clutched in her hand. 'Bye, Mummy,' she whispered, and with all the grace that had been so characteristic of Serena she let the delicate blossoms fall lightly on to the coffin deep at her feet.

Adam Harland swallowed, chasing away the lump in his throat. His friend's ten-year-old daughter had always held a special place in his heart; and now, seeing her dignity at this most traumatic moment, he felt both pride and pity. She would miss Serena terribly. Jerome's financial interests took him to many different parts of the world, and his frequent absences from home had forged a deep bond between his wife and his daughter. School would, no doubt, fill part of the void her mother's death would leave. School and her music.

As they began to walk out of the cemetery towards the gates and the waiting Rolls-Royces, Hispano-Suizas and Lanchester Fortys, he wondered how much comfort her music would be to her. It had always played an important part in her life. He could remember calling in at Eaton Place before continuing with the Kingsleys to the opera or theatre and a chiffon-clad Serena trotting Elizabeth out of the nursery in order to sing and do her party piece for him. She could have been only two or three years old at the time and already she had had excellent intonation. It was a talent inherited from Serena, who had a great love and respect for music; not from Jerome, who was tone deaf, and who viewed his daughter's musical talent with indulgent forbearance.

He paused at the door of his Austin Swallow, watching as the chauffeur opened the rear doors of Jerome's Daimler and Elizabeth stepped inside. He could see her chin begin to wobble suspiciously and knew that once the Daimler drew away her tears would fall, fast and free. Jerome seated himself next to her, his strong-boned face white and pinched. He was a man unaccustomed to ill fortune. Adam wondered how he would come to terms with his loss.

He slid behind the wheel of his Austin, removing his black Homburg with relief and running his fingers through his thick shock of unruly hair. It had been Serena who had encouraged Elizabeth's ear for music. There had been piano lessons as well as singing lessons. He followed the chauffeur-driven limousines away from the cemetery and down the Harrow Road back to West London, remembering his amusement at lifting her on to a piano stool when she was barely old enough to walk. By the time she was four she had learned to read music and had started to compose her own pieces. Serena had been thrilled, but he had always suspected that Jerome was less so. That he would have preferred his daughter's precociousness to have taken a different form: one that he could more easily identify with.

He turned left, motoring with extreme care down Edgware Road and into Park Lane. The snow was beginning to settle, and driving conditions were hazardous. Several motor-cars had been abandoned, and only the stout-hearted were persevering with their journeys. A horse-drawn cart, undeterred by the weather, rattled in his wake, delivering ale to public houses. On his right a lone nanny determinedly pushed a perambulator across the icy fastness of Hyde Park.

He smiled to himself. He liked London. He liked the noise and the bustle. He liked the flower-sellers at Piccadilly Circus, their giant baskets at their feet, their cockney cheerfulness warming the greyest of days. He liked the unchanging stability of the gentlemen's clubs in Pall Mall, lunching at Quaglino's, driving down to Goodwood for the races. The war and all its hideousness was over, a slight limp his only legacy from the years of fighting. Life, for a bachelor of independent means, was good.

He skirted Palace Gardens, turning left for Eaton Place, narrowly avoiding a tramp carrying a board emblazoned with the words 'HELP THE UNEMPLOYED'. His mouth tightened. Life might be good for him, but it was hell on earth for the million and a half who were unemployed. Most of them were ex-soldiers. Men who had fought at Ypres and the Somme. Men who had expected a little more from victory than the misery of the breadline.

He skidded to a halt outside the imposing façade of the Kingsleys' London home, wondering if the socialists really did have the answer to the age-old problem of poverty and if it wasn't about time he became one. He grinned as he stepped out of his car. Jerome would have ten fits. 'Bloody reds,' he called them, shuddering with distaste whenever they were mentioned. Yet, as with most of Jerome's pronouncements, Adam had a shrewd idea his words were more for effect than a reflection of his true feelings.

As he crossed the snow-covered pavement he saw that many of the chauffeur-driven vehicles had not yet arrived, their drivers being more cautious on the icy roads than he himself had been. The Kingsleys' Daimler was there, and he wondered how Elizabeth would cope with the funeral-party that was to follow. In his experience, they were never sedate affairs. It was as if the shadow of death, touching uncomfortably close, had to be banished with loud laughter and determined gaiety.

The butler opened the door to him, wearing a suitable expression of sombre gravity. Adam suspected that it was not just a matter of appearance. Serena had been a considerate mistress, and her household staff had been with her since the early days of her marriage.

'Mr Kingsley is in the drawing-room, sir.'

Adam nodded, aware that more mourners were hard on his heels. There was already the sound of muted laughter, nervous tension seeking release in jocularity. He walked through into the long, wide, high-ceilinged room that Serena had insisted be decorated in cool tones of ivory and pearl grey. The only colour was in the bowls of flowers that graced the Adam fireplace, the exquisitely carved occasional tables, the two handsome Louis XV chests, magnificently inlaid and topped with marble. It was impossible to think of Serena in a room without flowers. Adam felt a catch in his throat. It was impossible to think of her as being dead.

'Thank God you're here,' Jerome said, clasping his hand tightly. 'The motions have to be gone through, but I'll be damned glad when this charade is over.'

They had been friends for a long time. Jerome was fast-living, selfish, the possessor of deadly charm. Adam was quiet-spoken, reserved, with none of his flamboyance or charisma, yet the friendship was firm. When Adam had returned from the Western Front with a Military Cross for bravery in action, many of those who did not know him well had been surprised. Jerome had not been. He was well aware of the steely strength that lay beneath Adam's unassuming manner. No matter how famous, how illustrious his other friends, it was to Adam that he turned in time of need.

'What are you going to do when it is?' Adam asked, aware that in another second Jerome would be surrounded by people offering sympathy and that all private conversation would be impossible.

'Leave,' said his friend tightly. 'There's no home for me in this house without Serena. Most of my business affairs are conducted from Paris or Geneva. I shall move into the Georges V for a few months.'

'And Elizabeth?' Adam asked, shocked. 'She's just lost her mother, Jerry. If you move to the Continent, she's going to feel totally abandoned!'

A slight smile touched Jerome Kingsley's harrowed mouth. 'Don't worry Adam. Elizabeth will come with me. There's no point in her staying on in London alone.'

Adam stared at him. 'But her music ... the Academy...'

Jerome's green-flecked eyes were uncomprehending. 'A piano can be played anywhere,' he said bleakly. 'I need Elizabeth with me. I'm going to be lonely enough without Serena. I don't want to be separated from my daughter as well.'

'Hang on a minute, Jerry. I don't think you've thought this through,' Adam began urgently, but it was too late. The mourners who had been close behind him when he entered the house now surrounded them.

'Darling Jerome, what a terrible, *terrible* tragedy for you,' a pretty young woman with bobbed dark hair said, kissing him effusively on the cheek. 'I was simply *devastated* by the news, darling. Completely *shattered*.' She clung to his arm as if for physical support. Adam eyed her ringless left hand cynically. Jerome was once more a prize in the marriage market. Perhaps a retreat to the Georges V was not such a bad idea after all.

He looked around the now crowded room for a glimpse of Elizabeth, but she was nowhere to be seen. Cloche hats clung to sleekly waved hair, daringly short skirts emerged from beneath minks and sables, cigarette smoke curled upwards from long ebony holders.

'...and so we're going straight from Nice down to Rapallo...'

'I dropped a thousand at roulette and another thousand at the baccarat table. Ferdie was *furious*...'

'My dear, they were lunching together quite openly and it was *obvious* what their relationship was...'

He moved away. Serena had loved gossip, too, but Serena's gossip had always been laced with impish humour and peals of affectionate laughter.

The doors leading into the dining-room had been opened, and he saw that the long dining-table was laden with both cold and hot dishes; kedgerees and sweetbreads; cold salmon and hams; black and red caviare and oven-hot blinis. The mourners moved towards the refreshments, and he knew that, for most of them, Serena was already forgotten, her funeral just another event in a busy social calendar.

The butler stepped across to him, saying discreetly: 'I believe Miss Elizabeth is in the upstairs sitting-room, sir.'

Adam thanked him, grateful that at least one other person was anxious as to her welfare. The noise of talk and laughter followed him up the sweep of the stairs. How to explain to a ten-year-

19

old that the party taking place was not meant to be disrespectful, but was normal funeral manners? He sighed. Even worse, how was Jerome going to explain to her that he was going to take her away from her school and her home? He knew what Jerome's lifestyle was when he travelled. An itinerant round of hotels, restaurants, nightclubs, parties. How could he possibly imagine that Elizabeth would fit in with such a life? He sighed again, feeling suddenly much older than his thirty-four years, and far older than Jerome.

She was sitting hunched up on the window-seat, her arms hugging her legs, her eyes huge in her white face. 'Hello, Beth,' he said, entering the room and closing the door quietly behind him. 'Has everything got too much for you?'

She nodded mutely, tears spilling down her cheeks and on to her black velvet dress. He was reminded of a stray kitten he had once taken home as a boy. She had the same look of bewildered helplessness. Of utter vulnerability. He sat down beside her, wondering what the devil he could say to comfort her. He had no young sisters, no nieces, no previous experience with children at all. He took her hands, saying awkwardly: 'Your mother would hate you to cry so, Beth.'

It was the diminutive he had always used for her. The name she had used for herself when she had been too small to pronounce 'Elizabeth' clearly. Her hand tightened in his, and she drew in a deep, shuddering breath.

'But it's all so h ... h ... horrid, Uncle Adam,'

she gasped, a fresh flood of tears coursing down her cheeks. 'All those people downstairs are I ... I ... laughing and t ... t ... talking as if Mummy hasn't died at all!'

A fresh gale of laughter floated up the stairs, and Adam's good-natured face tightened. 'They know your mother has died, Beth,' he said, choosing his words carefully. 'And they are all sorry, but they are also frightened. Your mother was young and she was ill for a very short space of time. They are frightened that if pneumonia could strike her down so suddenly and so fatally something similar could also happen to them. And because they are frightened and don't want to think about it they are laughing and talking and trying to pretend it has never happened.'

'Then, they're s ... s ... silly,' she said, a sob catching her breath, 'and I don't l ... l ... like them.'

'Nor do I,' he said, rising to his feet and drawing her to hers. 'Let's go for a walk and forget about them, shall we? If we borrow a couple of tea-trays from the kitchen, we might even be able to find a hill in the park that we can toboggan down.'

'Do you think we ought?' she began doubtfully.

He bent down in front of her, looking her straight in the eye. 'It's the sort of thing your mother would tell us to do,' he said firmly, hoping that he was right, and not caring if he was or not when he saw the burden lift from her eyes. 'Now, come on, find some wellingtons and a thick coat and some gloves. I haven't tobogganed in years, and the snow won't stay for ever.'

'And so the concerto I played last year at the Academy I'm now going to play with the London Symphony Orchestra at the Central Hall in Westminster,' she said with shy pride as they ploughed for a third time back up the hill with their tea-trays. 'It's a very great honour ... Mummy was thrilled...' Her voice faltered. 'I don't think Daddy knows yet. Mummy was going to tell him when he came back from Geneva, but by the time he came back she was ill. He'll be pleased, though, won't he?' Her eyes were anxious, but he was relieved to see that the sting of the cold and the exertion of their climb had put some colour back into her cheeks. 'The London Symphony Orchestra!' Her voice was awed. 'I can hardly believe it!'

They had reached the crown of the hill and were placing their tea-trays strategically for the descent.

'And when is this concert to take place?' Adam asked, a frown furrowing his brow.

'Oh, not for ages. I have masses of practising to do. Miss Rumbatin says I have to learn to think orchestrally at the piano. That when I play a piece I have to imagine Furtwängler conducting a fantastic orchestra, or perhaps Toscanini. I'm going to every orchestral concert that I can now, not just to piano recitals. All my pocket money goes on tickets.'

Adam stared down at her, his frown deepening. 'If you were to go away for a while, would it mean you wouldn't be able to play with the LSO?'

She settled herself on her tray and turned to look up at him. 'No, of course I couldn't. But I'm not going anywhere. You'll come and hear me play, won't you?'

He wondered if he should tell her. If he should gently break the news that Jerome intended taking her away from the Academy and disrupting her musical studies. 'Beth...' he began and then hesitated. Jerome had told him of his plans only minutes after burying Serena. He had been understandably distressed and no doubt not thinking clearly.

'Yes, Uncle Adam?' she said expectantly, pale blonde strands of hair escaping from her woollen beret, her green-gold eyes wide and trusting.

'Nothing,' he said with a grin. Jerome was insensitive, but he wasn't so callous as to brutally disrupt her life even further. 'Beat you down to the bottom!'

She giggled with laughter, pushing herself over the lip of the hill and down, temporarily free from the weight of her grief, finding solace in the company of her father's friend, who was her friend as well.

By the time they returned to Eaton Place it was dusk. The house was quiet, only desultory cliques of mourners remaining.

'Ah, there you are,' a weary-looking Jerome said, coming out into the hall to meet them. 'I wondered where you had both got to.'

'We've been to the park,' Elizabeth said, the flush in her cheeks dying, her voice suddenly

23

uncertain. 'Tobogganing.'

Jerome looked at the tea-trays in their hands, the melting snow that had been kicked from their boots. 'Of course,' he said with a vagueness that irritated Adam. It was obvious that Elizabeth needed reassuring that she had not been disrespectful to her mother's memory, and it was equally obvious that Jerome was unaware of her need and was going to say nothing to set her mind at rest.

'Can I have a word with you, Adam?' he said, taking Adam's arm and steering him towards the now empty drawing-room.

'Of course, Beth...' He turned round to indicate to her that she should follow them, but Jerome's voice cut across his.

'Change back into your black coat and shoes, Elizabeth,' he said as they entered the drawing-room, and she remained standing alone in the hall 'We'll eat out quietly tonight. I've booked a table at the Savoy.'

'Yes, Daddy.' The exhilaration of the afternoon had deserted her. Her shoulders sagged, her hair hung wispily to her shoulders, and her voice was small and lost.

'I want you to do a favour for me,' her father said, oblivious of her need for comfort, closing the door on her and turning to Adam.

Adam checked his rising impatience. Jerome had been his friend for fifteen years. He had many virtues but sensitivity was not one of them, and it was useless to expect him to begin exercising it now.

'Yes, what is it?' he asked, pouring himself a

warming brandy and moving towards the blazing fire.

Jerome seated himself in a winged leather chair, resolutely ignoring the sight of the over-full ashtrays that his guests had left behind and that his household staff had not yet had the opportunity to remove.

'I want you to take roses up to Serena's grave for me while I'm away. I know I can easily pay for the service, but I don't want some faceless minion taking them for me. She'd hate it. Will you do it?'

Adam swirled the brandy round in his glass, glad that his friend's insensitivity was not yet total. 'Yes,' he said, 'but if you're still adamant about leaving London I think I should tell you that Elizabeth won't wish to accompany you. The Academy has arranged for a repeat of the Mozart concerto she played last year, only this time with the London Symphony Orchestra at the Central Hall.'

Jerome's shoulders lifted imperceptibly beneath his hand-stitched Savile Row suit. 'I'll have to get in touch with the principal. Apologize. They'll easily be able to find a replacement for her.'

'For God's sake, Jerry! Don't you understand? Elizabeth won't *want* them to find a replacement!' Adam said explosively. 'She's been asked to play with the London Symphony Orchestra, for Christ's sake! Can't you understand what that must mean to her? It's exactly what she needs right now. Months of hard work and total commitment that will ease her over Serena's death.'

'I appreciate your concern for Elizabeth,' Jerome said tightly, and Adam felt his heart sink. When that particular note of determination entered Jerome's voice, then nothing on earth would dissuade him from whatever course of action he had decided upon. 'But she can study piano just as easily in Paris as she does here. I think you'll find she will leave the Academy without a moment's hestitation when she knows how much I want her to be with me.'

Adam groaned. He had no doubt that Jerome loved Elizabeth, but he was showing no understanding of her need for stability. The George V in Paris would be no substitute to Elizabeth for Eaton Place and the reassuring routine of the Academy.

'You're making a mistake, Jerry,' he said tensely. 'Elizabeth needs you, but she needs you here, in London. She needs you to be in the audience at the Central Hall when she plays with the London Symphony Orchestra. She needs the day-to-day routine that she has always known.'

Jerome rose to his feet impatiently. The house was unbearable without Serena in it. He had no intention of staying a moment longer than was necessary. And he wanted Elizabeth with him. And what he wanted he always got.

'We're leaving first thing in the morning, on the boat-train,' he said abruptly. 'Do you want to have dinner with us? I thought the Savoy would be quieter than the West End.'

Adam shook his head. 'No,' he said shortly. 'Elizabeth needs you to herself this evening. Say goodbye to her for me.'

26

He was at the door before Jerome said conciliatorily: 'Try to understand, Adam. I'm bitterly regretting every business trip I ever took that robbed me of time with Serena. I'm not going to make the same mistake again. From now on, wherever I go Elizabeth goes, too.'

Adam looked at his friend: rich, successful, powerful, and at that moment almost as vulnerable as his daughter had looked only a little while earlier. His anger disappeared. There were worse sins in life than wanting the companionship of a daughter.

'It's OK, Jerry,' he said with an affectionate grin. 'Have a good trip across the Channel and send me a postcard from Paris.'

Upstairs in her bedroom, Elizabeth heard the distant thud of the front door closing. She pulled a hairbrush through her hair with a pang of disappointment. It would have been nice if Adam had stayed and accompanied them to the Savoy. Almost immediately she felt a rush of guilt. It would be nicer still to be alone with her father. They had hardly had a minute together since her mother's death. There had been arrangements for him to make, his friends had descended in droves, and when he had been alone he had seemed almost dazed. She put the ivory-backed hair-brush down on the glass tray on her dressing-table and picked up her hat and coat. Black velvet. She hated the touch and sight of it, but her father had insisted it be worn.

She sighed, slipped her arms into the sleeves, and set the tam-o'-shanter on top of her gleaming gold hair. When she grew up she would never wear black. Not ever. It would always remind her of the loss of her mother. Of standing in the bitterly cold cemetery and knowing that she would never see her again. Never be cuddled by her or kissed by her. Tears sprang to her eyes, and she dashed them away fiercely with her knuckles. She musn't cry. Her father was alone, too, and he needed her to be brave and comfort him, just as she needed him to comfort her. From now on it would be just the two of them together. He would stop spending so much of his time in France and Switzerland. He would be at home when she needed him. He would be able to attend her concerts, perhaps even go with her to the Albert Hall, and the—

There was a light tap on the door, and Mrs MacBride, their middle-aged housekeeper, came into the room. 'Are you all right, dear? Your father asked me to tell you that he's ready to leave.'

'Yes, thank you, Mrs Mac.' Her small pointed face was white and strained, but her tears were held firmly in check.

Mrs MacBride regarded her with affection and compassion. If she had cried over her mother's death – and by the dark rings carved beneath her eyes she had done so long and hard – then it had been in private. There was a strength in her that her ethereal looks belied. A determination of character that was wholly her father's. At the thought of Serena Hughendon's fragile blonde beauty being coupled with Jerome Kingsley's reckless zest for life, Mrs MacBride shuddered.

It would make a lethal combination when she grew older.

'I'll make sure there's hot chocolate waiting for you when you get back,' she said, glad that she couldn't see into the future.

'Thank you, Mrs Mac.'

Mrs MacBride watched her with pursed lips as she buttoned her coat. The Savoy indeed! There were times when she wondered if her employer was in his right senses. The child was only ten. It wasn't the Savoy she needed, especially not on the day that her mother had been buried. It was scrambled eggs on toast, a milky drink, and an early night.

Her father was waiting for her at the foot of the stairs, and Elizabeth noticed with shock how the grief of the last few days had aged him. The lines running from his nose to his mouth had been gouged deep, and there was a sprinkling of grey at his temples that she had never been aware of before. She slipped her hand into his and squeezed it tight. She loved him and she wasn't going to lose him as she had lost her mother. She was going to look after him and see that he didn't worry, or drink too much, or smoke too much. She was going to make sure that he lived for years and years and years.

'I'm glad we're going to the Savoy,' she said, aware of how silently disapproving Mrs Mac-Bride had been. 'I like to look out on the river at night.'

They walked outside to the parked Daimler. 'I've booked a window table,' her father said, grateful for her understanding. 'You can look out at the river all you want.'

Her hand remained firmly in his as the chauffeur carefully negotiated his way through the icy streets. Trafalgar Square was eerily empty, the biting cold and drifts of snow deterring even tramps.

'I love you, Daddy,' she said, nestling close to him as they left the Square and entered the Strand.

Jerome Kingsley's rich dark voice was thick as he patted her hand. 'I love you, too,' he said, glad that it was dark in the rear of the Daimler and that she could not see the tears that had sprung to his eyes. 'From now on we're going to be together, Elizabeth. We're not going to be apart. Never again.'

They slid to a halt outside the Savoy's palatial entrance, and as Elizabeth stepped out on to the snow-cleared pavement, he felt the first stirrings of comfort, of grief eased. He had lost his wife, but he was still luckier than most men. He still had his daughter.

For once, he decided against his customary *aperitif* in the American Bar and went straight through into the River Restaurant. Many people claimed it to be the most beautiful restaurant in London, and Jerome was in agreement with them. The long, deep windows, heavily swathed in damask, looked out in the daytime over the Embankment gardens and the wide majestic sweep of the Thames. As they were seated Jerome asked that the curtains behind them be drawn back. There was a slight hesitation on the part of the *maître d'hôtel*, and Jerome smiled.

'My daughter likes to look out at the river, even though it is dark,' he explained, and the *maître d'hôtel* inclined his head.

'Of course, sir.' Mr Kingsley was a valued client. If his daughter wished to have the balance of the room disturbed by having one set of curtains drawn back, then one set of curtains would be drawn back. Besides, hadn't her mother just died? He noted the black velvet dress, the brave set of her mouth, and saw to it that her chair was moved a few inches further to the left so that her night-time view of the river was unimpaired.

'Lobster, terrine of duckling, and a bottle of Montrachet 1914,' Jerome said, seeing no reason why mourning should spoil his appreciation of a fine wine.

'And for Madame?' the waiter enquired discreetly.

Jerome looked vaguely surprised. It was the first time they had dined out together alone, and it had not occurred to him that she might need help with the menu.

'I'll have lobster, too,' Elizabeth said, determined not to let her father down by choosing something childish. 'And the duckling, but not the Montrachet.'

The waiter suppressed a smile. 'Lemonade, perhaps?' he enquired helpfully.

Elizabeth hesitated and then shook her head. Lemonade did not sound very sophisticated. 'No, thank you,' she said with grave dignity. 'Could I have a pineapple juice, please?'

The waiter nodded, enchanted by the silk-gold fall of her hair, the medieval severity of her black velvet frock, and her natural gracefulness.

The restaurant was not very full, the bad weather having kept all but the Savoy's residents firmly indoors. With relief, Jerome saw that there was no one he knew at the nearby tables. He was tired of listening to well-meaning friends sympathizing with him on his loss. Their words brought him no comfort at all. They were platitudes, politely uttered but revealing that the speakers had no idea of the depth of his grief. Only Elizabeth had any understanding, and only with Elizabeth did he gain any comfort.

Looking across the table at her, he pondered on what Adam had said to him. Did her music really mean so much to her? She was talented, certainly. Everyone told him that. But, then, it was to be expected. She was, after all, his daughter. He regarded her with pride. There were music schools in Paris. No doubt better schools than they were in London. He would fix something up for her. Something a little more convenient than the rigid demands of the Academy. The lobster arrived, and as he began to eat he began to feel the first stirrings of well-being. From now on she would be his companion, as Serena had been whenever they had been together. His brows pulled together slightly. Serena had loathed travelling and had seen no necessity for it. Though Jerome always pleaded business commitments, both he and she knew that it was not strictly true. If he had wished to remain in London, he could have done so quite easily. As it was, he was a restless man, happier in hotels than in a permanent home; and Serena, loving him, had colluded quite happily in the fabrication that his many absences were necessary for their financial well-being.

'You have never been to Paris, Elizabeth, have you?' he asked as the remains of the lobster were removed and the duckling was placed before them.

'No. Mummy said she would take me as a treat when my French improved.'

Jerome stared at her curiously. He hadn't known she had been studying French. Nor that Serena had intended a trip to France with her. He wondered how many other things concerning his family's day-to-day life he had been ignorant of.

'Well,' he said, slightly disconcerted, 'it's a beautiful city, even in winter. I've booked tickets for tomorrow's boat-train. We should be there in time for lunch.'

Her eyes widened, and her mouth rounded on an 'oh' of pleasure. He felt himself relax. Adam was a well-meaning idiot to have thought Elizabeth would be dismayed at the prospect. 'It's a good place to buy clothes, too,' he added, thinking how adult she looked in the black velvet, and what a pleasant change it was from her school uniform.

'That will be lovely, Daddy,' she said enthusiastically. 'Can we go to the Salle Pleyel and the Théâtre des Champs Elysées?'

'I don't see why not,' he said, pleased with her response. Previously it had always been Serena who had taken her to concerts. From now on he would have to undertake the task. He had no ear for music himself and found it neither pleasurable nor relaxing. However, if Elizabeth wished to attend one or two concerts, he would endure them with good grace.

'We can drive down to Nice if it gets too chilly,' he continued affably. 'March and April are beautiful months on the Riviera.'

'I don't understand.' She looked bewildered. 'I thought you said we were leaving right away. Tomorrow.'

He nodded, helping himself to another glass of Montrachet. 'We are.'

Slowly she laid down her knife and fork. 'For a holiday? And then later, in the spring, we're going again?'

Her voice had lost its eagerness and was small and unsure. Jerome was unaware of her apprehension. The wine was excellent, and he was anticipating the brandy that would follow.

'No,' he said easily, signalling for the waiter. 'We'll make our base the George V in Paris. At the end of the month I have a meeting to attend in Geneva. It's only a three-hour train ride. You can boat on the lake while I attend to my meeting, and then we could stay on in Switzerland and do some skiing if you wish. Later, at the end of March, or the beginning of April, we'll move down to the Negresco in Nice. It's just as easy a base to work from, with all the advantages of milder weather and the prospect of some cruising.'

Her face was ashen beneath the bright lights of the chandeliers. 'But, Daddy, I can't take such a long holiday. There's school...'

'That's no problem,' Jerome said confidently.

'I'll write to the principal tonight. Explain the circumstances...'

Her knuckles were clenched white on the starched linen table-cloth. 'You can't do that, Daddy,' she said, her voice tight and shaking. 'I've been asked to play at the Central Hall with the London Symphony Orchestra. I'm going to have to rehearse very hard and...'

He leaned across the table, taking hold of her hands and imprisoning them in his own. 'I'm sorry,' he said, and his voice was sincere, his eyes pleading. 'I know that it's a disappointment to you, Elizabeth, but it can't be helped. There'll be other concerts for you later. Lots of them. At the moment what's important is that you and I are together.'

'Can't we be together in London?' Her hands grasped his tightly. 'Please, Daddy. You can stay in London, and I'll look after you and —'

'No.' Gently he released her hands, turning to the waiter and requesting two lemon sorbets and a bottle of Château Yquem, 1921.

Her mouth was dry, her heart slamming against her chest. She wanted to be with him more than anything else in the world. The thought of Eaton Square with only Mrs Mac for company was horrific. Yet they couldn't leave London. They couldn't live in France. There was her music. Miss Rumbatin. The concert.

'You don't understand, Daddy,' she said, trying to keep her voice steady, trying not to let her panic show. 'If I leave the Academy now, they won't take me back. I have to stay on there and I have to work...'

'I'll arrange piano lessons for you in Paris,' Jerome said, a trace of irritation creeping into his voice.

'I need to go to the Academy,' she said again, her voice desperate. *'Please*, Daddy! It's the best school of music in Europe, and...'

The Château Yquem was very good, and he wondered why he had not had the foresight to lay some bottles of it down. Her eyes were pleading with him across the table. A smile touched his lips at her naïvety. 'There are other schools,' he said reassuringly. 'Other teachers. Don't worry about your music, Elizabeth. Just think how marvellous it will be for us to be together.'

He didn't understand. He was her father and he was absolutely wonderful, but he didn't understand about music. He never had. Her throat tightened. He needed her. He wanted her with him. And it would break his heart if she refused and remained in Eaton Square with Mrs Mac. She shuddered. That was as bad as the prospect of being torn away from the Academy and continuing her studies elsewhere. Her father was talking of being in Geneva at the end of the month. Of being in Nice for March and April. What school could possibly tolerate such absences? As she looked across the table at him, loving him with all her heart, she knew that any future lessons would not only be inferior in quality but would also be terrifyingly sporadic. And she also knew that she had no choice. No choice at all.

'Paris will be lovely,' she lied bravely, and he did not see the glitter of unshed tears in her eyes or hear the anguish in her voice. He was smiling to himself, thinking how wrong Adam had been, anticipating with relish the fine French brandy that was to follow the Château Yquem.

Chapter 2

'And will Madame require a buffet breakfast for the guests?' the rose-buttonholed deputy manager of the famed Negresco Hotel asked deferentially. 'Kedgeree and scrambled eggs perhaps? Smoked salmon and champagne?'

Madame hesitated, shining soft shoulder-length blonde hair held back from her face with a ribbon, her cotton dress demurely collared in white piqué, her feet shod in ankle-socks and buckled sandals. Her father relished his parties, but by five in the morning he was usually happy to sink into a chair with a large brandy and conduct a witty and often malicious post-mortem on the proceedings with Adam Harland. An organized breakfast for the hundred guests he had invited to his forty-fifth birthday party would mean no such early-morning reprieve.

'It is customary...' the deputy manager murmured.

'No, thank you,' Elizabeth said with the quiet confidence of one accustomed to making decisions and unawed by the deputy manager's status. 'I would like the last drinks to be served at three a.m. and the musicians to leave half an hour later.'

The deputy manager nodded. He was not in the

habit of discussing arrangements with little girls still in the schoolroom, but this one was pretty and charming and certainly knew what she was about.

'And the flowers, madame?'

'Orchids and franciscea and bird-of-paradise,' she said unhesitatingly. They were not her favourites, being too sub-tropical and lush, but they were her father's favourites, and as always she ordered what he would like and what would bring him pleasure.

The deputy manager nodded. The Kingsleys had a permanent suite at the Negresco, and if Elizabeth had asked for African lilies they would have been flown in without demur.

'Perhaps if you just cast your eye over the menu again, madame?' he said, proffering the menu that she had agreed earlier with the chef.

Elizabeth did as she was asked and handed it back to him, satisfied. Everything was in order. It was going to be a lovely party. Adam was motoring down from London. Friends of her father's were coming from Paris and Geneva and even Rome. There was a gorgeous white chiffon gown hanging in her wardrobe, specially designed for her by Schiaparelli. And in three days' time she would have her father entirely to herself. They were going to Venice where he had promised her she could indulge in concerts for a whole week. She sighed rapturously. There would be the choir in St Mark's Cathedral, starlight concerts in the courtyard of the Doge's Palace, opera at the Fenice...

'Will there be anything else, madame?' the

deputy manager asked, aware that he no longer had her attention. A slight flush touched her cheeks at being caught so flagrantly daydreaming.

'No, thank you,' she said in her charmingly accented French. 'I am sure everything will be perfect.'

'Enchanté, madame.' There was a gleam in his dark brown eyes as he inclined his head and took his leave of her. She was like a beautiful flower in perfect bud, just about to blossom. And when she did... 'Une belle femme,' he said beneath his breath as he closed the door of her suite behind him. 'Une très belle femme!'

Elizabeth poured herself a glass of iced fruit juice from the carafe standing on a glass-topped table and carried it out of the opulently furnished sitting-room and on to the balcony that looked out over the Promenade des Anglais and the shimmering blue of the Mediterranean. Despite her father's promises to the contrary, there had not been many concerts in the three years since he had taken her away from Eaton Place. Nor had there been many music lessons. Certainly there had been nothing to compare with the tuition she had been receiving at the Royal Academy of Music in London.

Despite her pleasure at the prospect of the forthcoming party, her heart hurt and she suppressed a sigh. She now knew that it would never be any different. Her father loved her, spent money lavishly on her, adored her company, yet he was insensitive to any but his own needs. Music was unimportant to him, and so he could not conceive of the importance it played in her own life. She loved him too much to reproach him for his failings. Whenever she could, she sought out lessons in whatever city they happened to be in. It was better than nothing, but she knew that such haphazard coaching would never develop her talent to the full.

The local piano teacher in Nice had been amazed when he had first heard her play. 'And you want to take lessons from me, mademoiselle?' he had asked her bewilderedly. 'You are not in full-time attendance at a college of music? An academy?'

A shadow had darkened her eyes, and then she had smiled and he had wondered if he had imagined it. 'No,' she had said, and for the first time he realized that she was not French but English.

'Then, I will be delighted to accept you as a pupil. Shall we start now? With a Hanon exercise?'

As her lessons increased in number, he had become more and more puzzled. She had extraordinary talent and a self-discipline rare in a girl so young. Money was not a problem for her. It had taken him less than a week to discover that her father was a wealthy financier and that she was resident at the Negresco. Why, then, was she not enrolled at one of the major music schools in Paris? It made no sense to him, and neither did her frequently cancelled lessons. He could have sworn that they were the most important thing in her life, yet she often cancelled them, her voice strained and apologetic. With any other pupil he would have lost patience, telling them that they must find tuition elsewhere. With Elizabeth he made an exception. She was different from any other pupil he had ever had, striving for perfection with dedicated single-mindedness. There were often times when he suspected that he learned far more from her than she did from him.

'Tell me how you memorize,' he had asked her at her third lesson. 'Explain your method to me, please.'

She had frowned a little, finding it difficult to analyse and to put into words. Her hair was pulled away from her face, secured with a ribbon at the nape of her neck as it always was when she played. She tucked a stray strand behind her ear, saying: 'First of all, I sight-read and then I look at the structure of the work, and work on the fingering and write it in.'

He was sitting opposite her and he leaned towards her, his hands clasped loosely between his knees. 'And do you *always* write it in?' he asked, intrigued.

She nodded.

'And then what do you do?'

She gave a slight shrug of her shoulders, as though it should be obvious. 'Then I memorize the piece from a visual point of view, and then the harmonies.' Her voice grew more confident. 'In a sonata, for instance, first you have the exposition, then the development, then the re-capitulation, and so you have a union, a connection you can build on.'

'And how old are you?' he had asked, wondering if, when she had told him previously, he had misheard.

Her mouth had curved into a dimpled smile. 'Thirteen.'

He had shaken his head in disbelief and had asked her to return her attention to a Czerny *étude*.

She looked out across the promenade, suppressing a small sigh. Her lessons had continued but they were formal and routine, possessing none of the inspirational quality that had been so much a part of her lessons at the Royal Academy.

A white Lamborghini slid to a halt beneath the *portecochère* far below her. A smile touched her lips as she saw a stunningly dressed, olive-skinned woman step out of the car, a large circular hat on her head, two chihuahuas skittering around her ankles. Princess Luisa Isabel Calmella, her father's latest woman friend. The thirty-year-old princess was a fervent patron of the arts, and it was to her urgings that Elizabeth owed the coming trip to Venice.

She glanced at the slim gold watch on her wrist. It was nearly one o'clock. The princess was obviously visiting the Negresco for lunch. She put down her glass and hurried back into the sitting-room, grabbing a blazer and a school-bag. It was also time for afternoon classes at the *lycée* she attended a half-dozen streets away.

The lift came directly, and a pageboy, little older than herself, greeted her with a polite inclination of his head. Seconds later she hurried through a reception hall of Versailles splendour, acknowledging the doorman's salute as she stepped out on to the sun-drenched promenade.

Within minutes she was in the maze of narrow streets at the back of the hotel, no longer 'Madame', arranging a de-luxe birthday party for a hundred guests with poise and flair, but a schoolgirl sadly lacking a knowledge of French history.

The *lycée* was not the kind of school to which Jerome Kingsley would normally have sent his daughter. It was a little local school neither academically famed nor exclusive. However, other more suitable schools had refused to accept a child whose father insisted that she only attend lessons when it was not inconvenient to him that she do so. The *lycée*, too, was not over-pleased by Jerome's *laissez-faire* attitude towards his daughter's education.

'C'est une crime!' her despairing French-history teacher had exclaimed when Jerome had breezily announced that Elizabeth would not be able to do the extra work set for her in order that she reach a satisfactory standard in the subject. That, instead, he had need of her to organize his dinner-parties, accompany him to cocktail-parties, be his companion at late-night suppers on the yachts of visiting friends.

Even Adam had protested. 'Beth is still a child,' he had said, horrified at Jerome's intention of taking her with him on a yacht cruise with a party of people more famed for their indiscretions than for their good sense.

'Nonsense. Elizabeth hasn't been a child for years,' Jerome said airily, with no sign of guilt for the fact. 'If I don't take her with me, I shall be seduced by my host's wife, and you wouldn't

44

want that to happen to me, would you, *mon brave*?'

They were in the casino in Monte Carlo, relaxing in the Salon Rose after both losing badly at baccarat. Jerome leaned back in his wine-red velvet-upholstered chair, resplendent in a dinner-suit hand-made for him in Savile Row. There was more grey in his hair than there had been when Serena had died, but he was still a formidably attractive man. Large, expansive, delighting in the good things of life. Adam regarded him with despair.

'If Elizabeth hasn't been a child for years, then the fault is yours, Jerry. All this spending time with you and your friends is robbing her of her childhood. She needs friends her own age; she needs someone looking after *her* needs, not to be continually looking after yours. She needs to be back at the Royal Academy again, studying music.'

'Rubbish,' Jerome retorted, one leg crossed nonchalantly over the other. 'She would be bored to death in London after the life she has been living these last few years *and* she would be bored to death with friends her own age,' he added, as Adam began once more to protest. 'This mother-hen attitude of yours is becoming tedious. Why don't you marry, for God's sake, and get it out of your system by fussing over a wife and a brood of children?'

Adam grinned, amused at having succeeded in rousing Jerome to irritation. 'I may just surprise you and do that one day. Meanwhile, when are you going to stop using Beth as protection

45

against predatory females?'

'When females stop being predatory,' Jerome said with a return of good humour. 'I have no desire to marry again, Adam. And no desire for any relationship that taxes the emotions. A little light diversion now and again is very welcome, but nothing more strenuous.'

'Is Princess Luisa Isabel strenuous?' Adam asked, his good-natured face sombre for a moment as he considered the prospect of Beth coming to terms with a stepmother. 'I understand she's very much in favour at present.'

'Ah, yes,' Jerome almost purred with satisfaction. 'Luisa regards music as being of monumental importance to the well-being of mankind and so, naturally, Elizabeth adores her.'

'And you?' Adam asked curiously. Jerome's women friends all had three things in common. They were beautiful, well bred – and their reigns were of short duration. The princess was showing surprising signs of durability.

'Luisa is perfect for me,' Jerome said with disarming honesty. 'She adores my bank balance, is admiring of my prowess in the boudoir and, as my antecedents feature nowhere in the *Almanach de Gotha*, would no more dream of marrying me than of marrying her chauffeur.'

Adam didn't know whether to be relieved or sorry. An indulgent stepmother, sympathetic to her needs, would transform Beth's life for the better. There would be a stable home, instead of a hotel suite, disciplined schooling instead of her haphazard attendance at the *lycée*. He ran his fingers through his thick shock of sun-bleached hair. It was obviously an event that was never going to come to pass. Jerome had discovered he was a bachelor by nature, and he was enjoying living like one. He could only be grateful that he was, in his way, a responsible parent. He rose to his feet, mentally calculating his current bank balance.

'Come on. Jerry, I'll have to see if I can win back some of my losses or I'll be thumbing a lift home.'

He had won back enough to be able to enjoy an illicit week in Paris with the wife of one of Jerome's business friends. It was an enjoyable diversion but nothing more. At thirty-seven he had never yet been seriously tempted to marry, though he regretted the fact that he had no children.

It had been six months since his last visit to the Riviera. Jerome and Elizabeth had cruised the Adriatic with the friends he had been so disapproving of, Beth's postcards to him indicating that the only harm to befall her was a mild attack of boredom. They had been to Deauville for the polo, Lausanne for the flower festival, and Oporto for the wine pageant.

'I'm looking forward to seeing Uncle Adam again,' Elizabeth said when she whirled in from school. 'Has he arrived yet?'

'No.' Jerome was amused by the way she clung to the appellation of 'uncle' to a man who was no blood relation at all. 'He's driving down, and I don't expect he'll be here till nearer seven.'

'Then, there'll hardly be time to have him to ourselves before the party starts,' Elizabeth said, throwing her bulging schoolbag on to a satin-upholstered Louix XV chair and shrugging herself out of her regulation blazer. 'Have the buffet-tables been laid yet?'

'They're doing it now,' Jerome replied with a slight gesture of his hand towards the adjoining room.

Elizabeth could hear the clink of silver and the low murmur of the maids' voices as they prepared the room for Jerome's guests. 'Good.' She knew it would never have occurred to him to have gone next door and checked that everything was to his liking. Such details had become her responsibility. As had his business arrangements. She booked restaurants for him, remembering which merchant banker was a vegetarian, which a fish fanatic. She had a card-index file of birthdays and anniversaries, and Jerome's friends remarked with pleasure how much more thoughtful he had become as they received cards and flowers, all with his best wishes, all sent by Elizabeth.

He had already showered and was dressed and sitting on the balcony, sipping a dry sherry, languidly surveying the early-evening strollers on the palm-lined promenade below him.

'I'm going to have a bath and change,' she said, dropping a kiss on his temple, wondering if she could also manage to do the homework that was required of her and doubting it. She would need to check the food when it was brought up, make sure that the musicians knew which of Jerome's favourite tunes to play, ensure that his surprise birthday cake was brought into the room on cue.

She hurried out of the room and down the wide, thickly carpeted corridor to her own suite. She had to write an essay on Napoleon's victory at Borodino, the task made no easier by the requirement that it be written in French. Once in her own smaller, but no less opulent suite, she ran a deep bath, taking her schoolbooks into the bathroom with her. 'On 7 September 1812, Napoleon faced the Russians at Borodino on the outskirts of Moscow,' she began to write with one hand, feeling the temperature of the water with the other. By the time she was describing the heavy losses that the Russians sustained under General Kutuzov she was in lace-trimmed lingerie, about to step into the white chiffon creation that had been designed for her by Elsa Schiaparelli.

'Kutuzov lost nearly half his men,' she scribbled hurriedly, hoping that the water-splashes decorating the page would dry with no tell-tale marks. The white chiffon dress hung tantalizingly on her wardrobe door. '*Damn* Napoleon,' she said under her breath, pushing the book to one side and slipping the froth of chiffon off its padded hanger with a shiver of delight.

Two hours later, when Adam belatedly arrived to find the party already under way, he, too, surveyed her with pleasure. 'You look absolutely fabulous, Beth,' he said as she flung her arms around his neck and he hugged her tight. 'I can hardly believe it's you! What happened to the little girl in short socks?'

She laughed delightedly, a slight flush touching her cheeks as she drew away from him. 'Do you really like my dress? It's a Schiaparelli. Daddy took me to Paris specially to be measured and fitted for it.'

Her sun-gold hair fell softly to her shoulders, held away from her face with a pale blue velvet ribbon.

'Madame Schiaparelli has done you proud,' Adam said, aware of a curious tightening of his stomach muscles as he released her. The dress had not been designed to make her look any older than she was. Yet for the first time he realized that she was no longer the child he was accustomed to. There was a flowering sexuality about her, the more disturbing because it was artless and innocent. The wide curving neck of the dress and the puffed full-blown sleeves gathered into a ribboned band a fraction above her elbows emphasized her natural fragility. The bodice was plain, almost medieval, but there was no mistaking the rounding swell of her budding breasts, the minuteness of her waist as her skirt fell in a soft swirl to her white satin-clad feet.

He felt strangely uncomfortable as she guilelessly took his hand, leading him into the crowded room and introducing him to the people she knew he had not met before.

By midnight he was happily intoxicated on champagne and casting his eyes over the single ladies with no apparent escorts. His attention was caught by a petite blonde, a backless dress of shimmering coral silk dancing softly over her honeyed skin, a mischievous light in her eyes. He grinned to himself, confident of his ability to attract, hoping there would be no tiresome husband to evade.

There wasn't, and he found the remainder of the party highly enjoyable. Her name was Francine; she was a Parisienne, in her mid-twenties, and had been invited because she was a house guest of Jerome's close friends Frank Jay Gould and his wife. In the early hours of the morning he drove her back to the Goulds' luxurious home in Juan-les-Pins, kissing her goodnight with zest, arranging to see her again that evening.

The hood of his Austin Swallow was down as he motored back along the curving coast road to Nice. The sun was rising golden over the Mediterranean, the dew-fresh air fragrant with the tang of the pines, and in a couple of hours' time he would be breakfasting with Jerry and Beth. He swept through Antibes at high speed, whistling cheerfully.

'God knows I don't ask much of you,' Jerome grumbled when he returned to the Negresco. 'Just a little company when the junketing is over. Where the devil have you been?'

A score of maids were busy removing all signs of the junketing, and Jerome was ensconced in his bedroom, clad in an elegant silk dressing-gown, a brandy in his hand.

'Escorting a young lady home,' Adam said, kicking off his shoes and sinking down into a comfortable chair.

'Selfish bugger,' Jerome said, looking pained. 'The last guest went an hour ago. I've been sitting on my tod ever since.'

Adam tried to look suitably sympathetic and

51

failed. 'Where's Beth?' he asked, ignoring the brandy on the glass-topped coffee-table and pouring himself a fresh orange juice instead.

'In her room. She insists she has to attend the *lycée* this morning and that she has an essay to finish before she does so.'

'This morning?' Adam said incredulously.

Jerome shrugged his massive shoulders. 'I've told her she doesn't have to. I fancied a drive up to La Colombe d'Or for lunch, and if she goes to the wretched *lycée* she won't be able to come with us. There are times when I suspect that child of selfishness.'

Adam ignored the ridiculousness of such a statement and said again, unbelievingly: 'She has to finish an essay *this morning*?'

Jerome regarded him with irritation. 'Yes. I've said so twice. Quite clearly.'

'But she can't have had any sleep! The party didn't finish till five!'

Jerome's strong-boned face was querulous. '*I* haven't had any sleep. I was looking forward to a chat with you when the last reveller had been evicted. A long leisurely breakfast with you and Elizabeth; a reviving snooze and then a drive up to Saint-Paul-de-Vence for lunch. You let me down by careering off God knows where, and Elizabeth lets me down by forgoing breakfast in order to write about Napoleon!'

'For heaven's sake, Jerry,' he said relentlessly, 'you should have squared all this with the *lycée* days ago.'

'The *lycée*', Jerome said heavily, 'is *very* unco-operative. Now, as it doesn't look as if Elizabeth will be breakfasting with us, have we to order it now? I'm famished.'

Adam was tempted to give breakfast a miss and instead knock on the door of Beth's suite and ask her if she needed any help with Napoleon. He suppressed the urge. A thirty-seven-year-old man knocking on the door of a thirteen-year-old girl at half-past six in the morning would look definitely suspect. Especially a thirteen-year-old as tantalizing and desirable as Beth.

He set down his glass so savagely that orange juice spilled on to the glass top of the table. Desirable! God in heaven, was that really how he had seen her? The answer came thundering back at him and he rose abruptly to his feet, feeling sick and disorientated.

'What the devil's the matter?' Jerome asked in concern. 'Are you feeling ill?'

'No, I'm fine. Let's have breakfast,' he said tersely, the blood pounding in his temples. 'I think I'll sit on the balcony for a while and get some air.'

Jerome watched with raised eyebrows as he strode from the room. Adam was the most emotionally stable person he knew, yet something had violently disturbed him. He wondered if it was the pretty French girl he had escorted home, and followed him out on to the balcony. 'Women are the very devil, but it's not like you to allow one of them to needle you,' he said sympathetically, seating himself on one of the wicker chairs and regarding his friend with interest.

Adam gave a barely perceptible shrug of his shoulders and said with an air of forced ease:

'You're on the wrong track, Jerry. I'm not needled, just a little tired.'

'That's OK, then,' said Jerome, not for one moment convinced. 'We'll breakfast out here. The sun is already warm; it's going to be a hot day.'

Adam stared out over the Baie des Anges, his back rigid, his fists driven deep into his trouser pockets. God. Did all men have moments like these? Moments when their sexuality turned traitor on them, taking them by surprise and filling them with horror?

'I'm thinking of doing a little cruising this year,' Jerome said as a waiter set scrambled eggs and smoked salmon and apricots down on a glass-topped cane table. 'Do you fancy coming along?'

If he had been asked twenty-four hours ago, Adam's immediate reaction would have been positive. Now he firmly shook his head. Beth, clad in a bathing suit or a sun-dress might face him with more home truths than he could handle.

Jerome shrugged and turned as a shadow fell across the table. 'Ah, there you are Elizabeth,' he said with satisfaction. 'Has Napoleon received his just deserts?'

'Not yet,' Elizabeth said with a tired grin. 'He's still cock-a-hoop after thrashing the Russians at Borodino.'

'Never mind,' he said as she sat down. 'The retreat from Moscow lies in wait for him.'

She turned to Adam. 'Did you enjoy the party?' she asked, a smile dimpling her cheeks. 'I saw you with Francine. She's very pretty, isn't she?'

'Very,' he said, aware of an overwhelming

feeling of relief. She was wearing a cotton school-dress and short socks and sandals, and he felt for her what he had always felt – a love untainted by anything base.

'We're going to La Colombe d'Or for lunch,' Jerome said, crumpling his napkin on the table and rising to his feet. 'Are you going to come with us?'

Her smile faded, and Adam could see the fatigue in her eyes. 'No, Daddy, I told you. I have to go to school.'

'Then, Adam and I will lunch without you,' he said, not concealing his irritation. 'I'm going for a lie-down now,' he continued, addressing himself to Adam. 'Let's meet in the bar at twelve-thirty.'

Adam nodded, more than ever annoyed by Jerome's cavalier attitude towards Beth. He was going for a sleep. She was going to the *lycée* after no sleep at all, not even a kind word.

He had already determined to leave Nice later in the day. His carnal reaction to Beth, however fleeting, had shaken him too profoundly for him to want to stay. As he saw the tiredness on her face and the unhappiness Jerome's dismissive words had caused her, he determined that before he left for Cannes or Menton he would do what he had intended doing for years. He would give Jerry a dressing-down that he would *have* to take note of.

As Elizabeth ignored the covered hot dishes and reached for an apricot, he said concernedly; 'You look exhausted, Beth. Have you had any sleep at all?'

Despite her weariness she grinned. 'I dozed off once or twice as the Russians were routed.'

Although still furiously angry with Jerome, he laughed. 'Do you get your French history a little one-sided at the *lycée*?'

Her dimples deepened. 'If you mean do we concentrate on French victories and ignore French defeats, then the answer is yes.'

His own smile faded. She was sitting with the half-eaten apricot in her hand, her wheat-blonde water-straight hair skimming her shoulders, her green-gold eyes full of laughter despite her tiredness. He remembered Serena lying in a hammock at their holiday cottage in the country, sewing in an enormous hat, laughing and welcoming and golden. Beth had inherited all her beauty, all her sparkle. His throat tightened. He had loved Serena, but he had never been in love with her. Yet if Beth were older...

'Why are you looking so morose?' she asked suddenly, leaning across to him and taking his hand. 'Aren't you happy to be back in Nice with us?'

He squeezed her hand tightly and then released it. 'I'm leaving for Cannes later this afternoon,' he said, hating himself as disappointment flared through her eyes.

'But why? Do you have to?' she asked bewilderedly.

He looked down at her and felt something terrible tremble within him.

'Yes,' he said, his voice hard and queerly abrupt. 'I have to. Goodbye, Beth.' He didn't see her again for two years.

His affair with Francine had deepened to the point where he was seriously considering marrying her. She possessed a china-doll prettiness that turned heads wherever they went, an impish sense of humour and, despite the diversions of living in Paris, he knew that she was faithful to him during their frequent separations.

They were on holiday in Rome and had just strolled out of the Hassler after a late breakfast and were walking down the Spanish Steps towards the Via del Corso when Francine said suddenly: 'Isn't that Jerome, *chéri?* Standing at the foot of the steps?'

Adam shielded his eyes against the sun. The baroque stone staircase was massed with tourists, smothered in fragrant pink-blossomed azaleas. At first he could distinguish no one between the clutch of souvenir-hawkers and jewellery-vendors crowding the bottom dozen steps, and then Jerome moved, stepping out of the way of a young priest, and Adam grinned. 'It's Jerry all right. Come on.'

Taking Francince's hand, he began to quicken his pace, running lightly down the sun-warmed steps, calling 'Jerry! Jerry!'

Jerome turned his head, betraying not the slightest surprise at seeing them. He was wearing a double-breasted grey silk suit, carefully tailored to disguise his increasing weight, a grey silk tie, and sported a white carnation in his buttonhole.

'Adam, old chap. Nice to see you,' he said warmly as they ran up to him. He caught hold of

Francine's hands, gave her a long and appraising look from the top of her sun-gold curls to the tips of her elegantly shod feet, and then kissed her with relish on both cheeks.

'Where are you staying?' Adam asked, as Jerome reluctantly released a laughing Francine from his embrace.

'We're not,' Jerome said with no sign of regret. 'We're simply passing through on our way to Capri and lingering only because Elizabeth insists it would be sacrilege to be in Rome and not visit the Raphael Rooms at the Vatican.'

Adam felt a rush of heat to his groin. Beth. Still loyally and lovingly accompanying Jerome wherever he chose to go. He looked beyond Jerome across the crowded Piazza di Spagna.

She was striding gaily towards them, her ivory-pale hair sweeping her shoulders, a scarlet cotton skirt swirling around naked sun-tanned legs. Her sandals were high-heeled and delicate, her white blouse silk and Parisian. For years Jerome had been trying to hurry her into womanhood, and now, at fifteen, effortlessly and without help, she had left the gracelessness of childhood behind her.

He was aware of an overwhelming feeling of relief. She was breathtakingly beautiful, inno-cently sensual, and pleasure surged through him at the mere sight of her. But it wasn't perverted pleasure. He no longer felt like a paedophile. The emotion he felt now he could come to terms with, even though it would still have to be sup-pressed.

She saw him and her face lit with joy. 'Uncle

Adam! Francine!' she cried, breaking into a run, throwing herself into his open arms. He hugged her tight, feeling again all the love he had always felt for her, ever since she had been a baby. All too soon she drew away from him, her eyes shining. 'It's so wonderful to see you again!' She turned to Francine, kissing her affectionately on both cheeks. 'He's been hiding away from us ever since Daddy's forty-fifth birthday party, Francine! *We* can't persuade him to join us in Nice, but maybe you can.'

'I will do my best,' Francine said, her corn-flower-blue eyes sparkling. The South of France was always fun. Nice, for a few weeks at the end of the summer, would be a very good idea.

'Let me take advantage of this *very* fortuitous meeting,' Jerome said, taking Francine's hand and placing it firmly in the crook of his arm 'We have five hours before we leave for Naples. Five hours in which Elizabeth was intent on dragging me round as many museums and art galleries as possible. Now I no longer need to do so.' He smiled benignly. 'Adam is far better equipped than I to suffer the rigours of the Vatican Museum. He can escort Elizabeth, and we...' – he looked down at Francine and patted her hand – '...can enjoy a long cold drink at the Hassler.'

Adam gave Francine a quick glance and saw that she was perfectly happy to keep Jerome company for a few hours.

'OK,' he said, suppressing the elation he felt. 'We'll meet up at two o'clock at Il Buco on the Via Sant' Ignazio.'

'Ah,' Jerome said with relish, 'Tuscan *cam-*

pagna and *crostini* and those delicious little almond biscuits that you dip into the wine. Benissimo!'

With Francine prettily decorating his arm, he took his leave of them, sauntering back up the Spanish Steps to the Hassler, his equilibrium restored.

Adam looked at Beth and grinned. 'Where to first?' he asked, aware that in her high heels she was nearly as tall as he was. 'Do you want to go to the Raphael Rooms first, or take a stroll?'

'A stroll, I think,' she said, happily linking her arm in his, quite unaware that the action added another two or three years to her age, making her look more like a girlfriend than a daughter or niece.

They wandered into the maze of narrow cobbled streets that led away from the Piazza, a not very tall, toughly built man who moved with the ease of a useful-looking middleweight, in spite of his slight limp, and a tall slender girl carrying herself with natural grace and pride, burnished gold hair swinging glossily to her shoulders.

'It's a pity you aren't staying in Rome,' Adam said, aware of the number of heads that kept turning in their direction. Italian male eyes flagrantly admiring of her, envious of him.

There was a pang of regret in her voice that went far deeper than disappointment that their holiday could not be shared as she said: 'Daddy doesn't like sightseeing holidays. He'll be much happier at the Hotel Quisisana in Capri. Lots of his cronies will be there, and he'll be able to swim and sunbathe and gossip to his heart's content.'

'And you?' Adam asked, his honey-brown eyes darkening. 'What will you do?'

'Oh, I will swim and sunbathe as well,' she said with a little laugh and a shrug of her shoulders.

Adam's mouth tightened. He knew what she would do. She would sit quietly in the background while Jerome enjoyed himself, flirting and exchanging scandalous stories with his cronies about mutual friends.

They crossed the Via del Tritone heading in the direction of the Fontana di Trevi 'What about your music?' he asked brusquely. 'Do you still play?'

She averted her eyes quickly from his before he could see the flare of unhappiness that flashed through them. 'I still play,' she said. 'I have a Steinway concert grand in my suite at the Negresco.'

There was a strange note in her voice that he couldn't define. It was almost a note of defiance. He wondered how hard a battle she'd had to fight before Jerome had agreed to her having the Steinway.

'What about your tuition?' he asked relentlessly. 'Are your teachers good?'

'I don't have tuition any longer,' she said, her eyes still avoiding his, her voice carefully controlled. 'We're very rarely in the same place more than two or three weeks at a time, and so it isn't possible.'

They had reached the fountain. Spray blew

softly against their cheeks, the breeze from the water coolly refreshing. Her hair was pushed away from her face with tortoiseshell combs; her profile, as she kept her face stubbornly averted from his, so lovely and pure that he felt his breath tighten in his chest. There was no bitterness in her voice. He doubted if she even admitted to herself that Jerome had let her down. Yet he could sense and feel the unhappiness that his insensitivity was causing her. His jaw hardened.

'Let me speak to him,' he said as a group of tourists laughingly tossed coins into the fountain to ensure that they would one day return to Rome. 'He has to be made to see what a thoughtless bastard he's being.'

She shook her head vehemently, the sunlight dancing in her hair, meshing it to silver. 'No, you musn't do that, Adam. His feelings would be terribly hurt. He sees himself as giving me a marvellous life, and he does. I live like a queen. Sumptuous hotel suites, yacht cruises, dresses from Schiaparelli and Worth. How can you possibly accuse him of being thoughtless or uncaring?'

'Because the hotel suites and the yacht cruises and the clothes mean nothing at all to you, and your music does. It isn't too late for you to return to the Royal Academy in London. Jerry has his princess for company now. There is no reason why you should feel guilty or that you are letting him down.'

She shook her head again, this time resignedly. 'No, Luisa is a darling, but Daddy isn't the most important person in her life, and she isn't in his. He would be dreadfully lonely if I returned to London without him.'

'Then, he can return with you,' Adam said with unconcealed exasperation. 'The house in Eaton Place is still fully staffed, though God knows why. Jerry can't have spent more than half a dozen days there in the last five years.'

'Neither of us wants to return to Eaton Place,' she said, her eyes clouding. 'It holds too many memories.'

'Then, let Jerry do what he always does. Move into a hotel suite. The Dorchester is only five minutes from the Academy. It would be ideal.'

He could see the longing in her eyes, but then she said with finality: 'No, he would hate it. Perhaps if things change between him and Luisa and they decide to marry, then I will. If not...' She gave a philosophical shrug of her shoulders, saying with determined gaiety: 'Let's toss coins into the fountain and then walk across to the Vatican. The popes were very astute when it came to art, weren't they? Fancy having Raphaels on the walls of your dining-room, Botticellis on the walls of your bedroom, and Michaelangelo above your head when you prayed!'

He knew better than to continue talking about music and London. There had been the same note of determination in her voice when she had rejected his suggestions that he had heard so often in Jerome's. Her mind was made up and, no matter how unhappy her decision privately made her, she would not change it. Not until she could do so with a clear conscience.

They strolled in easy intimacy over the Ponte Sant' Angelo, tourists among a stream of other tourists, all making their way to St Peter's Square.

It was one of the most perfect mornings Adam could remember. They refused to be side-tracked by the other marvels in the museum, feasting their eyes on Raphael and Raphael alone. When they emerged once more into the sunlight, they bought ice-creams, walking along the banks of the Tiber until Adam realized with a shock that it was nearly two-thirty and that Francine and Jerome had already been waiting for them for thirty minutes. Flagging down a taxi, they arrived at Il Buco's as the waiter was serving Jerome his dessert.

'I thought you'd both disappeared into the bowels of the Vatican, never to be seen again,' he said unperturbedly, helping himself to a lavish spoonful of cream.

'We forgot the time,' Elizabeth said, her cheeks flushed and her eyes sparkling. 'We've had the most glorious morning, Daddy. I didn't want it ever to end!'

The *maître d'hôtel* handed Adam a leather-bound menu, eyeing Elizabeth admiringly, and Jerome said to Adam: 'Try the *pasta con porcini*. Its's delicious.'

None of them saw the expression on Francine's face. She had been delighted to see them return, about to chastise them playfully for their lateness. As Elizabeth innocently said what a glorious morning she and Adam had shared, she sat suddenly very still, as if she had been slapped, fettucini slithering from her fork.

Adam had the same glow about him as Elizabeth. He was grinning broadly at something Jerome was saying to him, his thick shock of auburn hair bleached almost blond by the sun. But his eyes weren't on Jerome. They were on Elizabeth. As were the eyes of the *maître d'hôtel* and the eyes of the businessmen enjoying lunch at a nearby table. For the first time Francine realized that Elizabeth was no longer a child. She was only fifteen, but because of her lifestyle, because of the sophistication Jerome had thrust upon her, she was a woman. And it was as a woman, a highly desirable woman, that she was now being looked at by the *maître d'hôtel* and their fellow-diners. And by Adam.

Francine's eyes narrowed. Nice no longer seemed such a good idea. She was quite sure that Elizabeth's remarks had been guileless. But for how long would they be guileless? With a Frenchwoman's hard-headed common sense, Francine judged it best that Adam and Elizabeth did not meet again too often. One could never tell, *n'est ce pas*? And it was better to be safe than to be sorry.

They did meet again over the next years, often. Adam now regarded the lust that Beth inflamed in him as normal, if not desirable. He no longer felt like a dirty old man or a sexual pervert. These things happened. Sometimes it was a cousin or an aunt that aroused emotions that had to be suppressed and that, eventually, died. It was nothing he need be ashamed of. As long as no one but himself knew of it.

In the autumn of 1931 he asked Francine to marry him, and both Jerome and Beth attended the lavish engagement-party held at the Savoy Hotel in London. Francine, with a Parisienne's reluctance to live anywhere but in Paris, spent the winter and spring trying to persuade Adam to lease a house in the sixteenth *arrondissement*, telling him that he could easily conduct his business affairs from Paris. Adam showed no sign of being persuaded. His directorships were with London companies, he was London-based, and he had no desire to spend two days out of every seven travelling backwards and forwards between Croydon and Le Bourget.

It was Easter when Francine said that she had found the perfect house and that, once he had also seen it, all his objections would be overcome. He had seen it. And he had known he was not going to take it. If Francine wished to marry an Englishman, then she would have to accommodate herself to the idea of living in England. Tempers had been fraught on the drive back from Chantilly to her Montmartre apartment. He knew that Jerome was staying at the George V over Easter and he was tempted to abandon Francine to her ill-humour and enjoy dinner with him there.

There was something about the set of Adam's jaw and the quality of his silence that prompted Francine to think that she had probably gone too far. The wedding was to be in June, and whether they lived in Paris or London, or Timbuktu, she did not want him to change his mind about it.

'I am sorry *chéri*,' she said conciliatorily, slipping her arm through his as they drew up outside her Montmartre apartment. 'It was too big a house anyway. What does it matter? We will forget it.'

Adam, who had no desire to prolong the quarrel, gave her an affectionate grin. 'OK,' he said, knowing that he had won the battle and could afford to be magnanimous. 'Pax.' With his arm around her shoulders, he led her past the concierge and into her elegantly furnished apartment, and bed.

Jerome was feeling unusually tired. He liked Paris, spending nearly as much time there as he did in Nice, but he was beginning to think that Easter was too early in the year for him to enjoy it to the full. The air was damp, the breezes chill.

'We'll go back south tomorrow,' he said to Elizabeth as she came into his room to see if he was ready to go down for dinner, her cream silk dress rustling around her knees in a myriad of tiny pleats, her hair falling in a long smooth wave to her shoulders. As he spoke, the diamond cufflink he had been in the act of inserting into his shirt-cuff fell from his grasp, rolling across the pale beige carpet.

Elizabeth bent down and scooped it up. 'The Prince of Wales is attending Luisa's party on Friday. I thought you were looking forward to meeting him?'

'Not enough to suffer another three days of cold and damp,' Jerome said, making no attempt to take the cufflink from her and to finish dressing. 'I feel so cold that I doubt if I'm ever going

67

to be warm again.'

Elizabeth looked at him with concern. A light rain had fallen for most of the afternoon, but it wasn't cold. She suddenly realized how overpoweringly warm it was in his suite and realized that he had turned the central heating up to maximum.

'Are you feeling unwell?' she asked, a slight frown puckering her brow as she slipped his cufflink into his shirt-cuff and fastened it for him.

'No,' Jerome lied. Illnesses were tedious, and he had no intention of succumbing to one. 'Let's go down for dinner. I shall ask reception to make reservations for us at the Mamounia. Tangier. We'll travel down to Marseilles by train tomorrow and make the crossing tomorrow evening.'

'But if you're not feeling well,' Elizabeth began, undeceived by his lie. His face was white and pinched and there were lines of strain around his eyes.

'I am *perfectly* well,' Jerome said indignantly, rising to his feet and slipping his arms into the dinner-jacket she held out for him. 'All I need is a little North African sun.'

She knew better than to argue with him. She would telephone his Paris doctor and ask him to make a visit early next morning. Her father would be furious with her, but at least then she would know if he was fit enough to travel.

'Perhaps Adam and Francine will join us in Tangier,' Jerome said as they sat at a window table, overlooking the darkened terrace garden.

'I shouldn't be too hopeful.' Elizabeth smiled

as the waiter took their orders. 'The wedding is only two months away, and they are being very busy house-hunting.'

'*Francine* is being very busy house-hunting,' her father corrected, a twinge of pain darkening his eyes. 'Adam has no intention of living anywhere else but where he is living now.'

'Daddy! Are you all right?' Elizabeth asked, forgetting all about Adam and Francine, aware only of the effort the last few words had caused him.

He tried to smile, but it was more a grimace. 'No,' he said, and there was a look almost of fear in his eyes. 'I'm sorry, Elizabeth, but I feel most odd...'

She was already halfway round the table to him when he pitched forward, sending cutlery and glasses flying.

'Daddy!'

He was still seated, the top half of his body prone on the disarranged table, his arms hanging limply at his side. She clutched hold of him, her eyes wide with terror. 'Daddy! Daddy! Can you hear me?'

The *maître d'hôtel* and an army of waiters were running towards them. His chair was being pulled back. Someone was easing him to the floor, undoing his collar. She could hear the words 'Un docteur! Une ambulance! Vite!'

'Oh God! Don't die, please don't die!' she sobbed, kneeling at his side, her hands still clutching at his powerful shoulders, tears pouring down her cheeks. He was inert. His eyes closed. His face waxen. She stared up at the circle of waiters and diners who had gathered round them. 'Oh, where is the doctor? Why doesn't he come?' she gasped, distraught.

The *maître d'hôtel* knelt down at her side. 'He has been sent for, mademoiselle. Please, sit down ... a brandy...'

She ignored him, bending once more over her father. 'Daddy! Daddy!' she pleaded, her voice desperate. 'Can you hear me? Can you open your eyes?'

Above her head the waiters looked at each other, lifting their shoulders in barely perceptible shrugs. It was obvious that Monsieur Kingsley was dead. That there was nothing anyone could do.

She was keening now, cradling him in her arms, knowing that he would never hear her again. Never open his eyes and look at her with love and amusement.

'The doctor is here, mademoiselle,' the *maître d'hôtel* said in a voice of relief as the crowd parted and a pinstriped-suited gentleman knelt competently at Jerome's side.

'Daddy ... Daddy ... I love you so ...' she sobbed, knowing that the doctor had arrived too late. That there was nothing that could be done. That in a matter of seconds, in the restaurant of one of the sumptuous hotels he had loved, she had lost him.

The doctor knelt swiftly at Jerome's side and for several minutes attempted to reactivate his heart. At last he leaned back on his heels. 'It is over,' he said regretfully. 'I am sorry, mademoiselle. There is nothing that I, or anyone else, can do.'

There were gentle hands at her elbows, encouraging her to rise. A stretcher was laid at Jerome's side.

'Please, mademoiselle,' the *maître d'hôtel* was saying in concern, and she knew that they were waiting for her to release him so that he could be put on the stretcher and carried from the room. She felt as if she herself were dying. It was impossible to hurt so much and live.

'Mademoiselle,' the *maître d'hôtel* said again, and this time the pressure beneath her elbows was more insistent.

She pressed her lips to his still warm cheek. 'Goodbye, Daddy,' she whispered, her breath ragged. '*Au revoir*, my darling.'

She was helped to her feet, her ivory-pale hair spilling in dishevelled disarray around her shoulders, her eyes bleak. It was all over. There would be no more good times together. He had left her as once, long ago, her mother left her. She was seventeen, and she was alone.

Chapter 3

The manager of the George V telephoned Francine's apartment an hour later. There had been no other telephone number that Elizabeth could give him. Jerome's body had been discreetly taken from the hotel to the morgue. The dining-room was again functioning perfectly, as if the regrettable incident had never taken place.

The elegantly dressed hotel manager pursed his lips as he waited for an answer to his call. Monsieur Kingsley had been like many other rich men he had known. Surrounded by an army of so-called friends and acquaintances in life, strangely lonely in death. If Monsieur Harland could not be contacted at the telephone number his charming and distraught daughter had given him, then he could envisage difficulties ahead. Princess Luisa Isabel Calmella, Monsieur Kingsley's mistress, would certainly not relish undertaking his funeral arrangements. There were no relatives. No sons or nephews. No one but the sobbing girl who had given him the telephone number he was now ringing.

Adam was appalled. At first he thought the telephone message was a cruel practical joke. It wasn't possible for Jerry to be dead. He was only forty-nine, for Christ's sake.

'Mademoiselle Kingsley would very much appreciate it if you would come at once,' the hotel manager finished smoothly. 'She is very distressed.'

Adam understood. He crashed the telephone receiver back on its rest, grabbing for his clothes as Francine sat up in bed, her hair tousled, her eyes wide.

'What is it, *chéri*? What has happened?'

His handsome face was bone-white, his lips tight. 'Jerry's dead. He collapsed in the George V restaurant an hour ago!' He didn't bother to button his shirt, ramming it down the waistband of his trousers, snatching hold of a tie and a jacket.

'*Mon Dieu!*' Francine pressed the back of her hand against her mouth. 'Oh, but that is terrible!' Horror flared through her eyes. 'Was Elizabeth with him?'

Adam nodded, stumbling in his haste as he put on his shoes, blaspheming viciously.

'*La pauvre petite!*' Francine gasped, scrambling from the bed, searching for her négligée. '*Quelle horreur...*'

She was still slipping her arms into the gauzy sleeves when the apartment door slammed behind him.

His heart jack-knifed in his chest when he saw her. She was sitting on the edge of her father's bed, her shoulders hunched, her hands clenched tightly in her lap. The doctor was still there. He had given her a sedative and had no intention of leaving her, not until she was more composed or until someone arrived with whom she could be safely left. An under-manager stood uncomfortably at the door, making sure that no curious undesirables entered the suite. A maid was removing an untouched tea-tray from a bedside table and depositing another in its place. The hotel manager was offering her his condolences, saying what a fine man Jerome had been, and how sadly missed he would be by them all.

She was wearing the cream silk dress she had gone so happily down to dinner in, little more than an hour earlier. Her head was bowed over her hands, and her hair hung forward at either side of her face, the light from the chandeliers sparking the gold to silver. She looked terrifyingly fragile. Heartbreakingly alone.

'Beth,' he said, his voice catching in his throat as he stepped towards her.

Her head whirled in his direction, and she sprang to her feet, running towards him, hurtling into his arms.

'Oh, Adam! Adam! Daddy's dead! He's dead, and I can't bear it!'

Tears poured down her face unchecked. The maid slipped unobtrusively from the room. The hotel manager withdrew a discreet distance, waiting until he could intimate to Monsieur Harland that he would like to speak to him about the various arrangements that would have to be made.

'Oh, Adam! I loved him so, and now he's gone!'

He held her tight, giving her what comfort he could as she clung to him, her body racked by sobs.

The hotel manager cleared his throat. 'Monsieur Kingsley's body has been taken to the morgue,' he said quietly. 'His lawyers have been informed of his death and — '

'Thank you,' Adam said, cutting him short, disconcerted by his French practicality. 'I'll speak to you later, if I may.'

The hotel manager bowed his head. 'Of course. I can be found in my office. Good night, Monsieur Harland. Good night, Mademoiselle Kingsley. Once again, you have my most sincere condolences.'

He left the room, and the under-manager followed him. A bellboy could replace him on duty at the door of the Kingsleys' suite, this time standing on the outside of the door. It was a mark of respect that the manager favoured.

'Sit down, Beth,' Adam said gently. 'Tell me what happened.'

As she leaned against him, no longer sobbing but crying quietly, the doctor judged that the time had come when he could decently leave. He placed a small bottle containing two tablets on the bedside table, saying to Adam: 'I am leaving two sleeping tablets for Mademoiselle Kingsley. If more are required for tomorrow night and the night after, I will prescribe them, but they will only be dispensed one night at a time, you understand?'

Adam nodded. The doctor checked Elizabeth's pulse. 'Are you sure you wouldn't like a nurse to stay with you?' he asked.

Elizabeth shook her head. 'No,' she said,

drawing in a deep ragged breath. 'Thank you for your kindness, Doctor.'

The doctor picked up his bag, grateful that the Englishman he believed to be her uncle was both sensible and sympathetic. 'I have left my telephone number on your night-table in case it should be needed,' he added, walking towards the door. *'Bonsoir, mademoiselle. Bonsoir, monsieur.'*

The door closed behind him, and Elizabeth sank down on to one of the chairs, her face deathly white. Adam poured her a cup of tea from the still hot teapot, stirring in two generous spoonfuls of sugar.

'Here,' he said, placing the cup and saucer in her hands and squatting down on his heels Indian-fashion before her. 'Drink this, Beth. It will do you good.'

She sipped at the tea with childlike obedience, and he said compassionately: 'Now, tell me what happened, Beth.'

Her breathing had steadied, and she said, her voice full of pain: 'He was getting ready for dinner and he said he was cold.' Her eyes were anguished. 'I thought perhaps he might be starting with flu, but he wasn't feverish and I thought the doctor could wait until morning.' Her voice broke, and she began to cry again. 'If only I'd realized! If only I had rung for the doctor there and then!' Tea slopped over into the saucer, and he removed the cup from her hands.

'It would have made no difference, Beth,' he said with certainty. 'A heart attack, or an embolism as severe as the one your father suffered,

76

couldn't possibly have been averted. There was nothing you could have done.'

'But I could have *tried!*' she said, her face ravaged. 'It was so awful, Adam. We were having dinner and making plans. He wanted to leave Paris and travel south, to Morocco. Suddenly he said that he felt most odd and then he ... he just keeled over on to the table.' Her voice was barely audible. 'He never spoke again,' she said, her eyes wide and dark and tragic. 'He never said my name. He just lay there, and people came running and someone – the *maître d'hôtel*, I think – loosened his collar and tie, but it was no use.' Her voice was disbelieving. 'He was dead, Adam. Daddy was dead.'

He stayed the night with her, sleeping on the sofa while she slept deeply, mercifully sedated. He had left her for only a few moments, and that was when he had paid his visit to the hotel manager and discussed with him the arrangements that would be made. To the hotel manager's relief, Elizabeth had no desire for any arrangements to be made at the hotel for family and friends. There would be no reception after the funeral. No wake. Other hotel guests would have no further reminders as to the frailty of human existence. The body would remain at a funeral parlour until the funeral service. After that, it would be shipped back to England for burial next to Serena in Kensal Green Cemetery.

A maid had stayed with Elizabeth during his

absence, and he was relieved to see, when he returned, that she had persuaded Elizabeth to eat some scrambled egg and toast.

'I must telephone Luisa Isabel,' she said tiredly to him. 'Other people can wait until morning. I've made a list of everyone who should be informed, and their telephone numbers, and also a list of all those who must be cabled.'

He took a list from her, determined to save her the anguish of such a task and to undertake it himself.

'Telephone Princess Luisa Isabel,' he said, hoping that the Princess would not be histrionic in her grief. 'I'll send down for a pillow and blankets and make a bed up for myself on the sofa.'

'Thank you.' Her voice was thick with relief, her eyes telling him how very grateful she was that she was not to be left alone.

If the under-manager regarded it as odd and unseemly that a single, middle-aged gentleman should ask for bed-linen in order that he might share the room of a bereaved seventeen-year-old girl, he gave no indication of it. A death on the premises was anathema to all hotel staff. It disquieted the clients and created a host of minor and sometimes major difficulties. If all that had to be endured as a result of Monsieur Kingsley's sudden death was the irregularity of his friend sleeping on the sofa in Mademoiselle Kingsley's room, then the irregularity could, just once, be overlooked.

Jerome had been a non-practising Anglican, and

the funeral service was held at St George's Church in the rue Auguste Vacquerie. Princess Luisa Isabel wore black sable with a tiny hat and a wisp of black veiling to cover her eyes. She had been Jerome's mistress for four years and, though she had not been so heedlessly in love that she would have forgotten her position and married him, she had been deeply fond of him.

Other friends were there: business friends from London and Geneva; fashionable friends from the Riviera; titled friends that he had met as a consequence of his affair with Princess Luisa Isabel. It was a simple service, short and dignified, and Adam was vastly relieved when it was over. Francine clung to his arm, weeping into a diminutive lace-edged handkerchief. Elizabeth stood a little apart from them, her face as still and pale as a carved cameo, her silver-blonde hair wound into an elegant chignon at the nape of her neck, her narrow-skirted black wool suit emphasizing her pallor and her willowy slenderness.

He had been terrified that she would break down. That she would find the service and the sight of the coffin, submerged beneath its blanket of flowers, unendurable. She had not done so. Jerome would have wished his funeral service to be conducted with style and good taste, and she was determined that his wishes would be carried out. Her grief was a private thing and not for public display.

Later that day Adam left Paris with her, as she accompanied Jerome's body back to England. The next morning, in the large impersonal cemetery in which they had stood seven years previously, when Serena was buried, Jerome was laid to rest. Adam was unashamed of the tears that stung his cheeks. Jerry had been a good friend, and he had died, like Serena, too young.

When they left the cemetery the hired Rolls took them, not to Eaton Place, but to the suite that Elizabeth had reserved for herself at the Savoy. Beneath the weight of his grief, Adam was vaguely amused, wondering if she intended to live as Jerry had lived.

'Will you be moving into Eaton Place or returning to France?' he asked her as they entered her suite and she flung her coat on to a chair.

'Neither.' Tea was waiting for them on a silver tray. She crossed the room towards it, pouring Earl Grey into two wafer-thin cups and handing him one. 'I'm going to sell Eaton Place and buy something smaller and more manageable, something in the country. Kent or Sussex, I think. Somewhere that has no memories.'

Her dress was a narrow sheath of black wool crêpe with long arms and a high neck, the skirt stopping just short of black suede shoes, her hair once again in a glossy chignon. She looked incredibly chic, more French than English.

'Won't you be lonely?' he asked, moving abruptly towards the window and the view of the Thames.

'I shall be lonely wherever I live,' she said quietly.

He didn't say anything, but the muscles at the corner of his jaw clenched.

He heard her put down her cup and saucer, and then she said: 'I shall never be able to thank you enough for all that you've done, Uncle Adam. I truly don't think I could have managed without you.'

The childhood appellation made him wince. She rarely used it now, and she had chosen to do so just when he had been about to make an almighty fool of himself. When he had been about to say that she needn't be lonely. That she could live with him in London. That he would adopt her, marry her. Anything, as long as he could keep her with him.

'I'll send you the address of wherever I move to,' she said, crossing the room towards him and slipping her arm through his. 'And in June I shall be in Paris for your wedding. I wouldn't miss that for the world.' Her voice was warm and loving.

She was not to be a bridesmaid. Francine had apologetically explained to her that she had an army of young nieces all eager for the honour. What she had not put into words was that Elizabeth, as a bridesmaid, might be considered by some people to be more beautiful than the bride, and that was a risk Francine was not prepared to run.

Adam forced a smile. There was no further excuse for him to stay. Jerry had left her abundantly provided for, and there was a score of lawyers and business advisers to shield and protect her. Even so, turning to her and saying goodbye to her was the hardest thing he had ever done.

She had walked with him along the thickly carpeted corridor to the lift. 'I shall miss you,' she had said, squeezing his arm.

'I shall miss you,' he had said, and his lips had brushed her hair-line and then he had stepped into the lift, a handsome man with a thick shock of hair who looked much younger than his forty-two years.

The metal-meshed doors closed between them, and five minutes later he walked out into the rain-washed Strand, trying not to think of how fragile and vulnerable and achingly beautiful she had looked as they had said goodbye, but of how in eight weeks' time he was to be married. And how little he was looking forward to it.

Elizabeth walked slowly back into her suite. Now she was really alone. Adam could no longer act as her support. She had to learn to live by herself, and she had to learn to do so bravely.

She stood in the middle of the luxurious room. Silence. No Jerome asking her to book him on a last-minute flight to Zurich; to arrange a luncheon-party; to find him his collar-stud, his cufflinks. No one to care for. No one to fuss over. No one to love.

The chill April day was drawing to a close. The daffodil sky of evening paling to dusk. She stared out through the windows to the broad grey sweep of the Thames. She was luckier than most people, and she knew it. She had money. She had financial security, even if she no longer had emotional security. Jerome's lawyers had explained to her the terms of his will, the value of his estate. Until she was eighteen she would be under their guardianship, and there would be restrictions that could not, by law, be lifted until she was twenty-one. However, any of her requests, providing that they were reasonable, would be acceded to, and that included the selling of Eaton Place and the purchase of an alternative residence in southern England.

She sat on the sofa, curling her long legs beneath her. She wanted a house of her own. Somewhere she could lick her wounds like an injured animal and adjust herself to a new way of life. Somewhere she could plan her future and come to terms with her loss.

She drew the mass of literature that had been sent by London estate agents towards her. She knew exactly what she wanted, and only hoped that she would be fortunate enough to find it.

Adam walked down the Strand into Trafalgar Square, staring glumly at Landseer's enormous bronze lions. Francine would be waiting anxiously for him. Her genuine sympathy for Elizabeth had not been deep enough to override the dismay she had felt when he had told her that he would be accompanying Elizabeth back to London.

'But *chéri*, is that necessary?' she had asked, with a Gallic lift of her shoulders. 'Surely Jerome's lawyer will be with her and perhaps Princess Luisa Isabel, and—'

'For God's sake, what comfort will Jerry's lawyer be to her?' he had shouted. 'She's going to bury her father! She can't possibly do it alone!'

They had parted on bad terms. Francine was sorry for Elizabeth but had seen no reason why

Adam should have stayed with her in her hotel suite the night Jerome had died. It wasn't his place to do such a thing. A nurse could have stayed with her. A woman friend.

'Beth doesn't have any woman friends,' Adam had said, white-lipped. 'She's never been able to make any friends of her own. The only people she ever met socially were Jerry's friends, and they're all twenty years older than she is!'

'As you are,' Francine had said, her china-blue eyes flashing ferally.

He had sucked in his breath sharply, as if she had slapped him. 'Yes,' he had agreed between clenched teeth. 'As I am!' And had spun on his heel, striding from the room, slamming the door behind him.

Dusk closed in around him. Red motor-buses and Austins and Fords and taxi-cabs vied for supremacy as they roared along the side of the square and down Whitehall. On his massive stone column, Nelson looked out with an indifferent eye over the darkening streets. Adam turned his coat-collar up and flagged down a taxi-cab. 'Victoria,' he said without enthusiasm. 'The boat-train.'

Francine greeted him with delight, secure enough now that he was back with her to indulge in her pity for Elizabeth. *'La pauvre petite,'* she said, as she curled up against him, a mug of hot chocolate in her hands. 'Was it very bad for her, *chéri*? Were there no London friends at the cemetery? No one to give her comfort?'

Adam shook his head. It was late the next evening, and a log fire was burning in the grate of Francine's apartment. They had made love, eaten a bedroom picnic of hot cheese on toast, and were now sitting half-naked in front of the fire.

'No,' he said as Francine rested against him and he gazed over her head and into the flames. 'Beth did not want another funeral service in London. There were only the two of us there, and the priest.'

Francine shivered. '*Alors*, it does not sound very nice,' she said, snuggling closer against his chest. 'And now what will Elizabeth do? Live in London and become a débutante?'

Despite his inner turmoil Adam grinned. 'No, she's going to buy a house in the country and, though she didn't say so, I suspect she's going to resume her piano lessons under the very best teacher that she can find.'

'*Mon Dieu!*' Francine said, an expression of horror on her face. 'She is crazy! She is young and pretty and rich. She could be having a wonderful time in London!'

'Maybe she will,' Adam said, his grin fading. 'Later, when she has had a breathing-space to adjust to life without Jerry.'

He needed a breathing-space himself. Time alone in which to reassess his feelings for Francine. He had believed himself to be in love with her. He enjoyed being with her more than he enjoyed being with anyone else, except for Beth. She made him laugh; she made him feel good. Her petite, high-breasted, slightly plump body gave him more pleasure than he had ever before experienced. She was sweet-natured and, for most of the time, even-tempered. She adored him and she wanted to marry him and bear his children. And he knew, with pain, that though he was deeply fond of her he was not in love with her and never would be. The decision he had to make was whether to tell her so and break her heart by calling off the wedding, or keep the knowledge to himself and settle for the kind of marriage that most practical-minded Frenchmen would envy.

The decision grew harder with each passing day. A wedding dress was bought, a trousseau. The cake was ordered, the invitations sent.

'I have never been so happy, *mon amour*,' she whispered to him in the warmth and darkness of her Montmartre bedroom. 'Another three weeks and I shall be Mrs Harland.' She giggled, nestling close to him. 'Do you think I will begin to look like a Mrs Harland? Will I become very English with twin-sets and pearls?'

He had not answered her. She was loving and generous with her love, and he knew that she was being cheated in return. That she was not receiving the single-minded passion that was her due.

When the steady rhythm of her breathing indicated she was asleep, he eased himself away from her, dressing quietly, knowing that he had to make up his mind one way or the other, and that, whatever decision he made, there would be no going back. He let himself noiselessly out of the apartment, walking quickly down the curving stone stairs, past the concierge's empty cubicle and out into the deserted moonlit street.

It wasn't that he wanted to marry anyone else. There was no other woman in his life, except Beth, and he had long ago rejected that idea as being impossible. If he married Francine, all his creature comforts would be taken care of. He would have a pretty fun-loving companion. He would have the family life he had always wanted, and he would, no doubt, be happy, because being happy was in his nature. He crossed the cobbled street, walking beneath the chestnut trees towards the rue du Printemps. He would also be living a lie and denying Francine the right to be loved as she deserved to be. He dug his hands deeper into his pockets, walking down the dark shuttered street towards the milky-pale dome of Sacré-Cœur, knowing that when he returned to her his decision would have to be made.

She looked at him as though he were mad. *'Je ne comprends pas!* Why can we not be married in June? Have you to go away somewhere on business? Is there an emergency?'

She was sitting at the breakfast-table in her tiny kitchen, her blonde curls tousled, a pale-blue chiffon négligée over her lace-trimmed nightdress, her eyes wide and uncomprehending.

'It has nothing to do with business,' he said gently, hating himself for the pain he was about to inflict. 'I'm sorry, Francine. I should never have asked you to marry me. I'm not the sort of man that should be married.'

'That's not true!' He was sitting opposite her, and she flew from her chair, kneeling down at his

87

side, clutching his hands. 'You will make a wonderful husband, *chéri*! You are sweet and kind and understanding...'

He looked down into her frantic eyes and knew that there was no way of sparing her the truth. 'I don't love you, Francine,' he said gently. 'I'm sorry. I thought I did. I thought we could have a good life together, but...' He raised his shoulders in an expression of despair.

She gave a little sob, pushing herself to her feet as if she were suddenly old. 'You don't love me and you're *sorry*!' she choked. 'Sorry!' She raised her hand and slapped him across the face with all her strength, tears raining down her cheeks. 'It is Elizabeth, *n'est ce pas*? It is Elizabeth you love! Elizabeth you wish to marry now that Jerome is so conveniently dead!'

He rose to his feet, shocked at how much she knew of feelings he had thought were secret. 'No,' he said tightly, sick that their affair was ending on such a note. 'It has nothing to do with Beth, Francine. I—'

'Liar!' she howled, flying at him with her nails, gouging at his face. 'You have always loved her! Always wanted her! Ever since she was a little girl! I've seen it in your eyes!'

'You're wrong.' His hands were clenched, the knuckles white.

'I'm not wrong!' Francine spat, her breasts heaving beneath the flimsy covering of her nightdress. 'When did the little bitch seduce you? The night Jerome died? Was that why you stayed in her room all night? Was the "comfort" you gave to her the comfort you never dared give her while Jerome was alive? Is "comfort" a new prissy English word for *fuck*?'

His hand caught her across the mouth, and she fell against the table, stunned incredulity in her eyes.

'You're wrong and you know it!' he blazed, appalled at the violence she had unleashed in him 'For Christ's sake. her father had just died! I stayed with her because I'm the nearest thing to a relative that she's got!'

'You stayed with her because you're in love with her!' Francine screamed as he stormed into the bedroom, dragging his suitcase from the top of the wardrobe, yanking suits and shirts from hangers and stuffing them inside. 'You stayed with her because she's a whore! A slut!'

He slammed the lid of his suitcase shut, not trusting himself to speak to her.

'I hate you!' she sobbed as he strode past her out of the bedroom and across the living-room to the door. ' *I hate* you! Hate you! Hate you!' The door crashed on its hinges behind him and she flung herself on the sofa, battering it with her clenched fists, sobbing as if her heart would break.

Elizabeth was stunned when he telephoned her and told her. 'But what went wrong, Adam? I thought you were both so happy together.'

'We were ... for a time. She's going around with a friend of Bendor Westminster's now. It will probably end in marriage. He's been crazy about her for years.'

'Poor Adam,' Elizabeth said sympathetically,

and he said nothing to disillusion her. It was easier for Francine if it was believed that she was the one who had broken off their engagement.

'How is the house coming along?' he asked, changing the subject.

She had bought a small manor-house near Midhurst in Sussex, only an hour from London by train, but deep in the countryside, the old English garden looking out over a magnificent view of the South Downs and the distant sea.

'It's fabulous.' There was undisguised pleasure in her voice. 'Parts of it date from the fourteenth century, and there's even a tiny minstrel gallery and a solar!'

'And the music lessons?'

'The Academy have taken me back.' There was so much whole-hearted relief in her voice that he laughed.

'Is it very hard-going?'

'Excruciating,' she said, laughing with him. 'My Steinway has finally arrived from Nice, and the house had to be nearly taken apart before it could be fitted in. However, it's sitting prettily in the drawing-room now and looking perfectly at home.'

'And you're happy there?'

There was an infinitesimal pause, and then she said, a little too brightly: 'Yes, it was the right thing for me to do, Adam. I couldn't possibly have lived in Eaton Place alone, and I have had enough of living in impersonal hotel suites. I wanted somewhere of my own, and Four Seasons is mine. You must come down and see it now that you're not travelling to Paris every weekend.'

'I'd like that,' he said, the strong lines of his face softening. 'Bye, Beth. God Bless.'

He had purposely restrained himself from visiting her. He had written to her, had long conversations with her on the telephone, but he had not seen her since the day they had parted at the Savoy. Now that he was no longer spending the best part of every week in Paris, he had no excuse for not visiting her.

He drove down the following Saturday. Once out of London there was very little traffic on the roads. It was a scorching-hot May day and the top of his Austin Swallow was down, the light sweet scent from the Sussex hedgerows thick as smoke in the sunlight. Feeling more lighthearted than he had done for weeks, he motored south through Guildford and Godalming, enjoying the sight of Georgian houses, their windows sparkling in the sunlight; thatched cottages, their gardens full of lupins and honeysuckle and Michaelmas daisies; and greystone Norman churches, their lychgates casting pools of shadow in the sunshine.

She was waiting for him in the driveway when he arrived. Her hair was loose around her shoulders, and she was wearing a red silk shirt and a white linen skirt and summer sandals. Her legs were naked and honey-toned, her toenails varnished a rakish scarlet. She began to run towards him as he stepped out of the car, her arms wide. 'Uncle Adam! It's so marvellous to see you again!'

His arms were round her, and he breathed in the clean sweet scent of her, never wanting to let her go. The silky fall of her hair brushed his face, and she withdrew, taking his hand, her eyes shining.

'Well,' she said with pride, turning towards the house. 'This is Four Seasons. What do you think of it?'

It was exquisite. Built of mellowed stone, it stood amongst its gardens as it had stood for centuries, as much a part of the surrounding countryside as the trees that sheltered it. Clematis clung to the walls, spilling clusters of purple blossom along window-sills and lintels. Roses, in bud but not yet in bloom, edged up the doorway promising splendour to come.

'It looks perfect,' he said truthfully as she led him inside into the drawing-room that had once been the great hall of a Norman knight.

'This is the oldest part of the house,' she said as he stared upwards at the hammer-beamed ceiling in amazement. 'The two wings that give it its H-shape were added on much later, some time in the late sixteenth century.'

'Quite modern, in fact,' he said with a grin.

She laughed back at him, leading him through into the dining-room and then into the kitchen. 'The last owner was an American who spent lashings of money on it and restored it with a great deal of love and care.'

'I take it he died,' Adam said as they walked out from the kitchen into a herb garden. 'No one in their right mind would ever leave such a house voluntarily.'

'Yes.' A small shadow darkened her eyes. 'He died about six months before Daddy. The house only went on the market the day I began looking for one.'

He caught the note of sadness in her voice and he knew she was thinking of Jerome. He also knew that Jerome would not have thought the house exquisite at all. It would have been too far from London for him. Too quiet. Too secluded.

'Are you happy, Beth?' he asked, no longer smiling, his eyes holding hers steadily. 'Have you become used to living on your own?'

Her hair glistened in the sunlight, skimming her shoulders as she turned her face slightly away from him and said: 'I don't think living alone is a thing anyone gets used to, not when they've been happy with someone. I know that you thought Daddy was selfish and that he shouldn't have insisted on my being with him all the time, but it was because he *needed* me. And because he needed me I didn't mind.'

A bee hovered, buzzing, over a clump of sage. In the distance, beyond the rich sweep of the Downs, the sky merged into the bright glitter of the sea.

'Why did you break off your engagement with Francine?' she said suddenly, turning to face him. 'She isn't in love with that friend of Bendor Westminster's. Luisa Isabel rang me yesterday to invite me to her summer party and she told me that Francine was heartbroken and still in love with you.'

The bee transferred its attentions to a tuft of purple-blue salvia with scented grey leaves. The sun was fierce, and he took his blazer off, hooking it with his finger over his shoulder. 'Because I discovered I was in love with someone else,' he replied, his free hand deep in the pocket of his sporting flannels. 'Because it would have been grossly unfair of me to have married her.'

She had stopped walking and was staring at him. 'But who is it you are in love with?' she asked, bewildered.

He was a yard or so ahead of her. He turned round slowly, facing her in the age-old garden, the bee still skimming the salvia. The sun was hot on his back.

'You,' he said, and knew that his Rubicon was crossed. That there could be no going back. Not ever.

Chapter 4

She continued to stare at him. The bee, replete, winged up and away. He sucked in his breath, his nostrils white and pinched, the pain behind his eyes almost unbearable.

'Now you know, I don't expect you to continue offering me hospitality,' he said harshly, wondering how, in the name of all that was holy, he could have been such a fool. 'I'm sorry for the offence I've caused...'

'Adam...'

'I don't know what possessed me.' His voice was stiff, controlled, embarrassed. 'I would appreciate it if you would –'

'Adam!'

'– forget what I said. I'm truly sorry, Beth. Goodbye.' He turned on his heel, striding quickly from the garden, sick at the expression of numbed incredulity he had seen on her face; sick at his folly, which had ruined the happy relationship between them.

'*Adam!*' She was running after him, her cheeks flushed, her eyes agitated. 'Adam, wait...' She caught hold of his arm, but he did not halt in his purposeful stride. He had to get away. He didn't want her sympathy or her pity.

'Adam, please...' she panted, trying to keep

pace with him. 'I don't *want* to forget what you said!' Her eyes were urgent. 'I never imagined ... never considered...'

He had reached the car. He flung his jacket on to the rear seat, slamming open the door, sliding behind the wheel and punching the engine into life. 'No. I don't suppose you did!' he said. 'It isn't what a girl expects from a man she regards as an uncle, is it? A man she's always believed she could trust. I don't blame you for how you feel, Beth.' He rammed his foot down hard on the clutch.

'You don't *know* how I feel!' she shouted over the roar of the engine. 'I don't *mind*, I tell you! In fact, I'm *pleased*!'

He stared at her, one hand on the wheel, the other on the gear-stick, smoke from the exhaust billowing into the air.

Her hands gripped the car door. 'I'm glad that you're in love with me! I'm not offended at all, Adam! I'm *glad*!'

Smoke continued to plume into the air. He couldn't move. He stared at her, transfixed, and she began to laugh. 'Why are you so surprised? I'm eighteen now. I'm not a little girl any longer. I think you being in love with me is flattering and incredible and quite, quite wonderful!'

He snapped the engine off, his hand trembling slightly, not trusting himself to speak. She stood only inches away from him, a light breeze stirring the glossy sheen of her hair, her eyes warm and untroubled, far more in command of the situation than he was.

'Jesus God,' he blasphemed softly, and then he

96

vaulted from the car, seizing hold of her hands. 'I'm forty-two,' he said abruptly, 'and I'm not just in love with you, Beth. I want to marry you!'

Her eyes flew wide with shock, and his hands tightened on hers with bruising intensity. 'Is that an idea you could learn to come to terms with, Beth?' he asked tautly. 'If not, I won't mention it again, but...'

She gasped, her eyes still open wide, still incredulous. 'I ... I think it's an idea I could come to terms with very easily...'

He felt as if his chest were encircled with a band of steel. It couldn't be happening. It was too wonderful, too marvellous.

'I love you, Beth,' he said again, huskily, and this time his arms slid round her, drawing her close. Her body swayed lightly against his, trembling in uncertainty and expectation. Gently, letting all the love he felt for her show in his eyes, he tilted her face to his. 'Dearest Beth,' he murmured, his lips brushing her temple, moving tenderly, slowly, to her cheekbone, the corner of her mouth. 'Dearest, beautiful Beth.' He could feel a moment of doubt flare through her and gently, deliberately, overcame it, bending her in to him, kissing her with tenderness and then, as he felt her doubt fade and she yielded willingly against him, with rising passion.

It was a long deep kiss and when at last he raised his head from hers her cheeks were flushed, her eyes sure and certain. 'Yes,' she whispered, her arms still around his neck. 'If you want me to marry you, Adam, then the answer is yes.'

He grinned down at her. The gossips would have a field day. They would say he was marrying her for her money. That he was abusing his position as a family friend. He didn't care. He loved her. He had always loved her. And now he was going to marry her.

Later, sitting in the tiny solar that she had massed with plants and cushions, Elizabeth said anxiously: 'You won't want me to give up Four Seasons when we marry, will you?'

They were sitting on the window-seat, sharing a bottle of ice-cold Sauterne. Adam put down his glass. For him to move into Four Seasons would do nothing to silence the gossips who would say he was marrying her for her money. He had his own, extremely comfortable home in Kensington.

'No,' he said, drawing her closer to him. 'But we'll keep on my house in Kensington for when we're in town, and it will be easier if we are married from there.'

'At Kensington Register Office?' she asked, a smile tugging at the corner of her mouth.

A slight frown furrowed his brow. They had agreed on a quiet wedding, but she was only eighteen. It would be understandable if she wanted a church wedding with all the trimmings.

'Not unless you want to,' he said, lifting the bottle of Sauterne from its ice-bucket and topping up her glass. 'We could get married at St Mary Abbots, or even St Margaret's, Westminster.'

She giggled, snuggling close to him. 'No, thank you. The Kensington Register Office will

98

do very nicely. At least if we get married there I shan't have to scout around for someone to give me away!'

They were married a month later. Her tutor from the Royal Academy of Music stood as one witness and Princess Luisa Isabel as the other. She wore a cream satin dress, high-necked with short belled-cap sleeves, the mid-calf-length skirt swirling lushly around her legs. Her hair was swept high, smoothed into a glistening figure-of-eight knot, her only jewellery a single strand of pearls and matching pearl earrings, her bouquet a delicate cluster of white roses and dew-fresh freesias.

Adam drew his breath in on a whistle when she walked down the staircase of his Kensington house towards him. 'My God, you look lovely,' he said reverently. 'Like a princess in a fairy-tale.'

She had slipped her hand into his, suddenly shy. The previous night had been the first they had ever spent beneath the same roof, and she was suddenly conscious of the night that was to come. A night that would not be chaperoned by Princess Luisa Isabel, as the previous night had been.

The Princess, who was staying as Adam's guest, had been appalled at Elizabeth's decision to marry from Adam's home and not her own. 'People will think you have been living together!' she protested, aghast. 'It really isn't done, Elizabeth. You must either leave for the wedding from your home in Sussex or from a hotel or a friend's house.'

'I have spent enough of my life in hotels and I don't want to leave for my wedding from one,' Elizabeth said gently but firmly. 'And I don't have friends of my own in London. All the people I know here were Daddy's friends. I can't very well presume to stay with them when I haven't even asked them to the wedding!'

Princess Luisa abandoned good sense as an argument and tried superstition. 'It is *terribly* bad luck to meet your husband on the day of your wedding, before you meet him at the altar.'

'But there's not going to *be* an altar,' Elizabeth had said in amusement. 'We're being married in a register office, not a church, Luisa.'

The Princess had thrown up her hands in despair. A first marriage for both bride and groom, and it was to take place in a register office. It offended her to the very depths of her Catholic soul.

'I, Adam Harland, know not of any lawful impediment why I may not be joined in matrimony to Elizabeth Helena Kingsley,' Adam said to the registrar in a strong sure voice.

Luisa Isabel sighed and dabbed at her eyes with her handkerchief.

'...I call upon these persons here present', Adam continued, 'to witness that I, Adam Harland, do take thee, Elizabeth Helena Kingsley, to be my lawfully wedded wife.'

The registrar turned his attention to Elizabeth. 'Please repeat after me,' he said gently.

There was a slight pause before she spoke, and

Luisa Isabel wondered if she was suddenly realizing what it was she was doing: marrying a man who had always been a surrogate father to her. A man twenty-four years her senior. A man who, until four weeks ago, she had never in her wildest dreams visualized as a lover.

'I, Elizabeth Helena Kingsley ...' she began in a low husky voice, and Princess Luisa Isabel lifted her shoulders fractionally in a gesture of resignation. It was over now. With God's good grace they would be happy. That Adam loved her and was in love with her was beyond question. Perhaps it would be a long time before Elizabeth discovered that, though she, too, loved Adam, she was not in love with him. And perhaps by the time she discovered it the difference would cease to matter. She hoped so. She kissed them with much affection, laughingly accepting the gift of Elizabeth's bouquet, showering them with confetti as they left for a simple wedding breakfast at the Café de Paris.

They had told no one where they were going to spend their honeymoon. The Princess assumed it would be on the Continent. Florence, perhaps, or Venice or Rome. Her tutor, if asked, would have surmised somewhere quiet and scenic: Cornwall or the west of Ireland.

They told no one their secret. When the wedding breakfast was over and their two guests waved them off from the front entrance of the Café de Paris, Adam drove not in the direction of Victoria Station and the boat-train, or in the direction of the roads leading west to Cornwall or to the ferry for Ireland. Instead he drove south, out through the London suburbs to Leatherhead and Guildford, motoring down leafy country lanes to Haslemere and the rolling countryside beyond. To Four Seasons and its quietness, its serenity and its uninterrupted peace.

She sat close beside him in the open-topped Austin Swallow, blissfully happy. She had been lonely and bereft, and now her whole world was transformed. She had someone to love again, someone to care for. Someone who loved her.

'How does it feel to be an old married lady?' Adam asked with a grin as the house came into view and they swooped down through a tunnel of trees towards it.

'It feels very secure,' she said laughing, her arm hugging his. 'Now you can't run away from me. Not ever.'

Adam pressed his foot down on the brake, sliding the car to a halt on the gravel that fronted the house. 'I can't imagine there was ever much danger of it,' he said in amusement, slamming the driving-seat door behind him and walking round to her side of the car to open the door for her.

'It's better to be safe than sorry,' she said, her cheeks dimpling as he swept her up in his arms and carried her over the threshold.

Her arms were around his neck, his thick brown hair springy as heather beneath her fingertips. She rested her head next to his. 'I love you, Adam Harland,' she whispered softly as the oak door swung closed behind them and he walked with her across the wood-panelled hall to the staircase.

His arms tightened around her. 'I love you, too,' he said huskily, 'and in another few moments I'm going to show you how much, in every way that I can.'

The bedroom was golden, filled with afternoon sunshine. He laid her gently on the large brass-headed bed and walked across the room to close the curtains. They had never been alone in such intimacy before. Ever since he had asked her to marry him, he had courted her with the restraint and propriety of a Victorian suitor, painfully aware that she had no parent to keep a watchful eye on her, determined that no one would ever be able to accuse him of taking advantage of the fact.

She was still wearing the cream silk dress she had been married in. She lay where he had placed her, watching him as he drew the curtains and the room was plunged into muted light. She had very little idea of what to expect. She had never had a lover before. Never enjoyed even the most casual of friendships with members of the opposite sex. Her life with Jerome had been a strange one. It had made her worldly-wise in many ways; assured, sophisticated. At home in the grandest of surroundings, unimpressed when confronted by titles or fame. Yet it had also left her curiously innocent.

She had never had any girlfriends her own age to discuss boys with, to laugh and giggle with. She had never enjoyed the easy-going camaraderie that comes from being a member of a group. Jerome had always been at her side, shielding her by his presence. She had seen things and witnessed a way of life that many people twice her age had never seen or were even aware of, but she had experienced very little. And nothing at all of love.

He took off his jacket and tossed it on to a chair, saying with obvious tension in his voice: 'Would you like some champagne?'

She pushed herself up against the pillows. 'Yes ... No...' And then, with disarming frankness; 'Is everyone so scared when they're finally left alone?'

His tension evaporated, and a smile tugged at the corner of his mouth. 'Not many would admit to it, but I'm damned sure they are. I think the champagne is essential. I told the daily help to leave some to chill in the refrigerator before she went home. I'll be back with it in a jiffy.'

When he had gone she rose slowly from the bed and walked across to the dressing-table, looking intently at her reflection in the mirror.

There's nothing to be scared of, she chided herself. It's Adam I'm going to bed with, not a stranger.

She raised her hands and unclasped the pearls, laying them down on the glass tray of her dressing-table. The drawn curtains were summer curtains, and the room was still full of soft light. She took off her earrings and laid them beside the necklace. Adam, who loved her. Who made her feel safe and secure. She remembered Francine, chic and sexy and uninhibited. He had very nearly married Francine. And, if he had done, she knew how different the consummation of his marriage would have been. He was forty-two. He was accustomed to women who were sexually knowledgeable. Was she going to allow him to be disappointed in her?

She raised her hands behind her neck and slowly drew down her zip fastener, letting the cream silk slip from her shoulders to her waist, to her hips, till it slithered into a milky pool about her ankles. Carefully she stepped out of it, picking it up and laying it on the chair next to his jacket. She couldn't remember a time when she hadn't been happy in his company. When she had been very small he had listened to her sing, throwing her up in the air afterwards while she had shrieked with delight and her mother had looked on indulgently. Then, when Jerome had been travelling abroad, he had become a surrogate father to her, taking her to the zoo, the park, the circus. And now she was going to go to bed with him.

Her hands shook slightly as she stepped out of her cream kid pumps, lifting up her lace-trimmed underslip and unfastening her suspenders. A month ago she had been disappointed that she was not to be a bridesmaid when he married Francine. She had never been jealous of Francine. It had never occurred to her to wish to be in Francine's place. She slid the sheer silk of her stocking down her leg. Yet now she was. How had it happened? How had he moved so smoothly from being the Adam of her childhood to the Adam who was now her husband? She let the stockings fall to the floor and stared at herself in the mirror. Would her father have approved? A slight smile touched her mouth. He would have been too astonished to approve or disapprove. He had always lived his life exactly as he had wanted, taking no thought of other people's desires or wishes. He could hardly be disapproving if she showed the same streak of wilfulness herself.

The door opened behind her and Adam stepped into the bedroom, a bottle of Moet et Chandon in one hand, two champagne glasses in the other. On seeing her dressed only in her slip, her breasts rising cream and pale from the lush lace that covered them, he halted abruptly, as if he had been punched hard in the chest.

Through the mirror her eyes met his. His hair was rumpled, as if he had run his fingers through it several times on his way down to the kitchen. His handsome good-natured face was showing signs of strain. She could see tension in the lines around his mouth, uncertainty in the honey-brown depths of his eyes. Her doubts fled. He was Adam. Adam, whose generous compassionate nature had been her strength and support ever since she had been a little girl. Adam, to whom she was now married, and to whom she was going to give her love.

Her eyes continued to hold his, and a smile curved her lips. 'We don't need the champagne,' she said huskily. 'I'm not scared any more.'

Her reward was the relief in his eyes. He put the champagne and glasses down on the bedside table and walked towards her, sliding his arms around her, holding her tight. She leaned against him, looking at their reflection in the glass. He was not much taller than she, a toughly-built

106

man who, despite his slight limp, moved with easy strength and confidence. A man whom women admired and other men liked. A man she was going to spend the rest of her life with.

She turned round in his arms to face him, her hands sliding up and around his neck, her body pressing, soft and warm, against his.

With a groan, he lowered his head to hers, kissing her with infinite tenderness, his hands moving reverently over the thin silk of her slip.

'Oh God, Beth ... I love you ... love you ...' he whispered hoarsely.

She was pliant and willing in his arms, pressing so close against him that he had to exert all his will power not to lower her to the floor and take her there and then.

'My darling ... my love ...' he groaned, scooping her up in his arms and carrying her towards the bed. For years he had restrained his desire for her; now, at last, it could be expressed. The thought of caressing her small, uptilted breasts, her private places, filled him with awe. She was so young, so pure, so immeasurably precious.

He laid her gently down on the bed, his heart hammering in his chest as slowly, carefully, he peeled away the delicate straps of her silk and lace underslip, revealing the satin smoothness of her flesh, the rose-tipped perfection of her breasts.

Excitement raged through him like a forest fire, but he held it firmly in check. She loved him and she trusted him, and he was going to do nothing to alarm or dismay her. He was going to be gentle and patient. Carnality had never had any place in their relationship, and he did not want it to have now. The thought of seeing shock or disgust in her eyes made him physically tremble.

'You are so beautiful, Beth. So perfect ...' he whispered, refusing to give in to his body's demand that he release his engorged penis from the tight constraint of his wedding-trousers.

Lightly, barely touching her, he ran his fingertips down the curve of her throat, marvelling at the beauty of her milky-pale flesh, her splendour as she lay half-naked beneath him.

Her arms slid up around his neck, her lips soft and yielding as his mouth came down on hers. His hands closed caressingly over her breasts, her nipples brushing his palm, erect and taut. He could feel her heart beating under his moving hand. Her tongue hesitantly met and slipped past his, and he knew that he could endure no more.

'I want you!' he gasped, his voice choked. 'Oh God, Beth! How I want you!'

He rolled away from her, standing by the side of the bed, pulling off his shirt with shaking hands, kicking off his shoes and socks, unzipping his trousers.

She watched in shy fascination. She had never seen a grown man naked. The muted sunlight cast golden shadows on the strong muscles of his chest and arms. His belly was flat, a line of crisply curling auburn hair running down from his navel. The blood rose hot in her cheeks.

'Adam, I ...' she began hesitantly.

The bed rocked beneath his weight as he lay beside her, taking her lovingly in his arms.

'I won't hurt you ...' he promised fiercely, seeing the sudden apprehension in her eyes. 'I promise I will never, ever, hurt you.' His mouth closed once more over hers, and as he felt her relax against him he very gently slid her underslip down to her hips, to her knees, tossing it free of the bed.

'We have all the time in the world,' he whispered reassuringly, as only a wisp of lingerie shielded her from his view. 'There's nothing to be afraid of, my love. Nothing.'

She clung tightly to him, her eyes closed as he lifted her beneath him, reverently removing the last remaining barrier of lace. The spring of her pubic hair, crisp and golden, brushed the palm of his hand like an electric shock. Beth. Toddling to meet him in the drawing-room at Eaton Place. Beth. Her face pale, her eyes wide and dark as they tobogganed together on the day of her mother's funeral. Beth. Her hand sliding guilelessly into his as they left Francine and Jerry on the Spanish Steps and set off towards the Vatican Museum. So many memories. So much love. So much longing.

He hardly dared breathe as he straddled her, taking his weight on his elbows, easing his legs carefully down between hers.

'I'm going to be careful, Beth. Careful ...' he breathed, as slowly, gently, he eased himself into her soft sweet centre.

She stirred against him, her fingers tightened in his hair. His hands on her breasts had stirred something deep and dormant in her. She wanted him to touch them again. To bite and suck them.

To kindle her newfound feelings and make them burst into flame.

He scarcely moved when he had entered her, his entire body rigid as if he were terrified of hurting her.

'It's all right,' she whispered encouragingly. 'It's all right, Adam.'

His face was contorted in an expression almost of torment. He could bear no more. She was so small, so tight, so unflinching beneath him. With a single thrust and a deep groan he came, his sperm shooting into her in an agony of relief. As he shuddered and gasped for breath her arms tightened round him. No spasm rocked her own body, her breathing was calm, steady. She felt curiously on edge, as if she had been taken to a wonderful party and, having got there, had found the doors closed against her.

'Did I hurt you, my love?' he asked, looking down at her, his eyes dark with anxiety.

She raised her face to his, lovingly tracing the line of his brow, the curve of his cheekbone.

'No,' she said with a smile. 'You didn't hurt me, darling.'

It was true. She had felt comfort and gentle pleasure and a hungry, almost frightening feeling when his hands had skimmed her breasts, but she had not felt pain. Nor any other emotion.

'I love you, Beth,' he said again drowsily, as his breathing deepened into the slow rhythm of sleep. 'Only you. For ever.'

She turned her head, kissing his shoulder. She had pleased him. He was happy. Everything was all right.

'Good night, my love,' she whispered, curving her body against his. 'God bless.'

Their lives fell into an agreeable pattern. From Monday to Friday they stayed in Kensington. The Royal Academy was only a few minutes' drive away and, no matter what his plans for the day, Adam always drove her there himself. On Friday evening they left London early, motoring down into the heart of Sussex, to Four Seasons. They seldom shared their weekends with any guests. Occasionally, Princess Luisa Isabel would join them with her new lover, a Brazilian millionaire whose only occupation was polo. Other than that, they remained alone, content with each other, needing no other diversions.

To Princess Luisa Isabel's dismay, Adam had become a socialist, staunchly supporting Ramsay MacDonald, who led the National Government.

'I don't understand it,' she said to Elizabeth with a pretty lift of her shoulders. 'Adam is a wealthy man. Why is he a socialist? Surely a socialist government will take all his wealth away?'

'They will take some of it away, Luisa, and it is only fair that they should do so,' Elizabeth said as they lay in hammocks waiting for Adam and Luisa's lover to return from a polo match at Windsor.

The Princess sat upright in her hammock. 'My goodness, have you become a socialist, too?' she asked, sincerely shocked.

Elizabeth laughed. 'I think I'm becoming a pacifist. I like the idea of the League of Nations,

111

and of disputes being settled by international collaboration instead of by armed force.'

'It hasn't been very successful in stopping Japan from invading China,' the Princess said tartly, lying down once again and closing her eyes. 'And I don't suppose it will be any more successful in curbing the new German Chancellor if he should begin casting his eyes on the Rhineland and complaining that the 1919 peace treaty was unfair to Germany.'

'He won't stay in power long enough to complain,' Elizabeth said confidently. 'He's far too unpleasant to last.'

A year later she was having to reconsider. The Oxford Union had passed the motion that 'This house will in no circumstances fight for its king and country' yet Hitler was growing increasingly obnoxious in Germany, and Mussolini was being equally abhorrent in Italy.

'You can't have patriotism *and* pacifism,' Adam had pointed out to her in amusement when she had been indignant at the motion. 'Churchill's got it right. The League of Nations needs military power to back it if it is going to act effectively for peace.'

By the summer of 1935 she had begun to agree with him. Italy had invaded Abyssinia and the League had stood by, powerless. In Germany, Hitler was adopting conscription in defiance of the Treaty of Versailles, and it seemed as if Princess Luisa Isabel's fears had been well founded. Elizabeth was concerned, but it wasn't the growth of fascism that was filling her with

112

increasing anxiety, but her failure to become pregnant.

'Do stop worrying, darling,' Adam said to her when another month went by and she was disappointed yet again. 'There's no hurry for a baby. You're only twenty-one. We've all the time in the world.'

She was about to protest that, though she was only twenty-one, he had just celebrated his forty-fifth birthday when she saw the faint lines of strain around his mouth and decided against it. He had been pushing himself very hard lately, painfully aware of the large workforce dependent on his company's success. Of the long line of the dole queue waiting for them if he should fail them. His curly brown hair was as thick and as unruly as ever, but it was heavily sprinkled with grey, and the laughter-lines at the corners of his eyes and around his mouth had deepened.

'I think I should see a gynaecologist,' she said, reaching across the breakfast-table for another slice of toast. 'I don't *want* to wait any longer, Adam. I'm impatient for motherhood!'

He grinned. 'Have you considered how bulky you will look on the concert platform, pregnant and playing Bartók?'

'The Bartók recital is in two months' time,' she said, feeling a quiver of anticipation at the mere thought of it. 'I could hardly be bulky by then!' She glanced at her watch, her concentration moving from motherhood to music as he had intended. 'Goodness, is that the time? I have a rehearsal class in thirty minutes! Please hurry, darling.'

* * *

The Bartók recital at the Albert Hall was an overwhelming success. Frank Howes, the music critic of *The Times*, wrote that it was 'an outstanding performance, glowing with vitality.' At the end of the year she was chosen to represent Great Britain in the third International Chopin Competition in Warsaw. The competition was held in the concert hall of the National Philharmonic Society in Warsaw, and to her amazement she came first in the preliminary stages, only losing her position in the finals. It was a tremendous achievement, and from then on she knew, with dizzying certainty, that she was on the verge of becoming what she had always dreamed of becoming. A concert pianist of international repute.

Adam's pride was touched with alarm. He knew how important her music was to her and he had gained pleasure from allowing her to indulge it, but he had never foreseen the extent to which it would affect their lives. The Chopin Competition in Warsaw was followed by other competitions. In Brussels and in Vienna. It wasn't always possible for him to travel with her, and he hated the separations her music brought, resenting the long hours she spent alone practising at the keyboard.

In May of the following year, she was invited to undertake an eight-week tour of the United States.

'*Eight weeks?*' Adam stared at her in horror. 'But it's impossible, Beth. I can't possibly absent myself from London for eight weeks!'

'I know,' she had said, slipping her arm through his. 'I shall miss you terribly, darling....'

His eyes were unbelieving. 'You can't mean you intend to go?'

It was her turn to look astonished. 'But of course I must go! It's a wonderful opportunity! Two recitals at Carnegie Hall! One in Chicago, one in Toronto; goodness knows how many more in smaller cities.'

He felt cold. He knew that if she went she would not miss him. Not as much as he would miss her. There would be other tours. Longer estrangements. He closed his eyes, remembering how he had charged Jerome with selfishness for wanting her with him at the cost of her studies. If he refused to sanction the New York tour, he would be doing exactly the same thing. And, if he didn't, he knew that she would begin to be lost to him. That their lives would grow increasingly further and further apart.

They were in the drawing-room at Four Seasons. It was a Saturday morning, and Princess Luisa Isabel and her latest boyfriend were coming for lunch. They were flying in from Paris, and he was due to meet them at the airport in an hour's time.

For the first time in his life, he was fiercely, burningly jealous. She could not have spent more time from him if she had been having an affair with another man. His knuckles clenched. God damn it. If it had been another man, at least he could have socked him on the jaw. But a piano couldn't be socked on the jaw. He moved abruptly away from her, walking across to the windows, standing with his clenched fists thrust deep into his pockets, so jealous of the time and passion she lavished on her music that he thought he would choke with it.

She bit her lip, acutely aware of his distress and suspecting the reasons for it. He didn't want her to go, and he didn't want to have to ask her not to go. Disappointment surged through her so acute that she almost cried aloud with it. Two concerts at Carnegie Hall! They would have been the most wonderful, most momentous concerts of her professional life! And she knew, as she looked across at his rigid back, that she would not go. That the cost would be too high. As she walked across to him, she wondered how much of her sacrifice was due to her growing guilt at her lack of passionate response to him in bed. For the first few months of her marriage, she had been undisturbed, certain that it would come in time. Now she knew that, though she loved him with all her heart, it never would come.

'You're quite right, darling,' she said softly, slipping her arm once more through his. 'Eight weeks is far too long. I'll decline the offer. Maybe we could go away on holiday for a week or two instead? France perhaps, or Spain?'

Relief surged through him, and for a moment he couldn't speak, then he said gruffly, 'Not Spain,' ashamed of not being able to overrule her decision. At not being able to tell her that eight weeks was not too long and that, of course, she must go. 'The whole country is about to be plunged into the most hideous civil war. Luisa

Isabel must be distraught at the thought of what is happening there.'

'France, then,' Elizabeth said, glad that his eyes were still avoiding hers and that he couldn't see the misery she felt. She forced enthusiasm into her voice. 'Perhaps we'll be able to make a baby there. The gynaecologist said that, as there was nothing physically wrong with me, it could be that I needed to relax more. We'll go down to Antibes and stay at the Eden Roc. It's the easiest place in the world to relax in!'

They swam and sunbathed and laughed and talked, but both of them were aware that a shadow had been cast across the happy surface of their marriage and neither of them was able to dispel it. Adam made love to her with tender frequency, but no baby resulted.

'Does it really matter so much, Elizabeth?' Princess Luisa Isabel asked when they visited her in Paris on their way back to London. 'It would interrupt your musical career and make life very difficult for a while. What if you received an invitation to tour America? You couldn't possibly undertake it if you were pregnant. It would be far too gruelling.'

'Yes,' Elizabeth said, her voice oddly flat. 'Of course it would be. Do you think it's true what the French magazines are saying about the Prince of Wales and Mrs Simpson? There's nothing in our newspapers at home. Only the occasional discreet mention, "Among the Prince of Wales's guests was Mrs Wallis Simpson". That sort of thing. Nothing any stronger.'

Princess Luisa Isabel was glad that she had changed the subject. The lack of a baby was obviously beginning to distress Elizabeth.

'The French say that the prince is in love with her and that he wants to marry her. Perhaps he is. If so, I feel sorry for him. He will not be able to marry her.' Princess Luisa Isabel spoke with all the authority of her title. 'Not if he wishes to keep his crown.'

A month later the prince had become king, and Elizabeth watched with avid interest as he struggled to make Wallis Simpson his queen. She had thought that the Government would make a compromise, enabling him to marry her and remain king, though without bestowing on Wallis the title of queen. She had been wrong. The Government and the king had not compromised, and on 11 December he had abdicated.

'At least it's a relief from reading about the fascists,' Adam said wearily, tossing a log of wood on to the drawing-room fire. 'How our government and the French government can opt for non-intervention in the war in Spain is beyond me. Especially now that Hitler and Mussolini have officially formed an alliance. God help the rest of Europe if those two start hunting as a pair!'

'Will it lead to war?' Elizabeth asked, putting down the music score she had been reading.

Adam's face was grim. He had fought in one war and had believed, for a time, that it had been the war to end all wars. Now another was looming. One in which he would, most likely, be too old to participate.

'It will if no one puts a curb on Hitler,' he said as the wood took hold and the pungent smell of pine filled the room. 'His marching into the Rhineland is only a beginning. That's obvious from his rhetoric.'

They were silent, each thinking of the rhetoric that was bringing terror to thousands of European Jews. His statements that Jews born in Germany were no longer entitled to German citizenship. That marriage between Jews and non-Jews was illegal.

'Horrid little man,' Elizabeth said, shivering depite the heat from the fire. 'How I wish someone would put a stop to him.'

They didn't. All through 1937 the swastika rampaged triumphant. By 1938 war was becoming not just a possibility but a certainty. In September the British government mobilized its navy. Hitler shouted that Czechoslovakia was the last territorial demand he would make, and the Prime Minister, Neville Chamberlain, flew to Munich to try ineffectually to make peace.

Adam watched events with growing rage. 'Can't Chamberlain *see* that he's being taken for a fool? Dictators like Hitler don't honour their word or respect peace agreements! The only thing they respect is force!'

By February of the following year Hitler, not content with Czechoslovakia, was casting lustful eyes on Poland.

'That's it,' Adam said decisively. 'Another few months, weeks even, and we're going to be at war with Germany. I went to the War Office today. I'm too old for active service. The most I will be able to expect is a desk job.' He looked more distressed than she had ever seen him. 'I'm damned if I'm going to reconcile myself to sitting behind a goddamned desk!'

She had spent all day at the keyboard. She had a Mozart recital in a month's time, a Bach recital in April, and she had mentally been going over one of the scores she was to play, her left hand moving to the notes and phrases and harmonies that she could hear in her head. With a suppressed sigh of regret she relinquished them.

'Then, what are you going to do?' she asked, sensing his inner tension and certain that, whatever it was, he had already made up his mind.

'I don't know.' He had been pacing the room, and now he stood still and looked at her and she knew that he was lying. 'Beth....' He took her hands. 'Beth, would you mind if we were to leave England before we become trapped here by the war, and before I become billeted behind some bloody useless desk?'

'Leave?' The last strains of Mozart and Bach abruptly fled. She stared at him, the blood leaving her face. 'You mean go to America? Run away?'

His eyebrows flew together. 'Good God, no! I don't want to run away! I want to be involved!'

'But where can you be involved?' she asked, bewildered. 'I don't understand.'

His hands tightened on hers. 'The threat of war isn't only coming from Germany, Beth. Japan has been at war with China for five years now, and it's my belief that if we declare war on

120

Germany the Japanese will take advantage of the fact and move towards Hong Kong and Singapore.'

The breath was tight in her chest, the blood drumming in her ears. He couldn't mean what she thought he meant. There was the Mozart recital, the Bach recital, the Brussels Competition in four months' time.

'I'm sorry, Adam,' she said, praying that her fears were groundless. 'I don't understand.'

His thumbs pressed hard on her wrists. 'I want to go to Hong Kong,' he said fiercely. 'I want to be in a position to fight when the fighting comes!'

Chapter 5

She stared at him, her disbelief total. 'Hong Kong?' she repeated, her voice cracked, not sounding as if it were her voice at all.

He nodded, running his hands through his hair. 'One of our subsidiary companies is based there. Leigh Stafford, the chap in charge, says that, though the vast majority of people out there ridicule the thought of attack by the Japanese, he thinks it a distinct possibility. He wants us to wind down our business interests and hold over our investments until the situation is more settled.'

She continued to stare at him. In all of the seven years that they had been married, they had never had a serious row. The nearest they had ever come was when she had been offered the eight-week concert tour of America. She had known then that, if she had gone, the very foundations of their marriage would have been shaken. And she had not gone. She had fought her disappointment, determined that there would be other opportunities, opportunities that would not drive a wedge between them. But now Adam was suggesting the impossible. He was suggesting that she leave the Academy; that she leave London; that she abandon her musical career as she had been forced to abandon it once before, many years ago.

'No ...' she whispered, her nails digging deep into her palms. 'Oh, no ... no ... no!'

He said, as if she had not spoken: 'Japan is on good terms with both Germany and Italy. She'll be able to count on support from both of them if she should need it. And she's an aggressor. Look at the way she's been pounding China. Stafford says that Japanese troops are pushing south now, a large contingent have landed at Amoy three hundred miles north-east of Hong Kong. If they have, it puts them in a very favourable position to attack Hong Kong if they should choose to.' His eyes held hers tensely. 'It's Stafford's belief, and mine, too, that if war breaks out in Europe that is exactly what they will do.'

She had been sitting in one of the deep-cushioned chairs by the side of the fire. Now she rose unsteadily to her feet, the lamplight gleaming on her hair. 'And you want to be there if she does?' she asked, her voice low and barely audible, with a strange note in it that he had never heard before.

He thought her strained reaction was because of his age, and a tide of colour stung his cheeks. 'Yes,' he said abruptly, delving in his jacket pocket for his pipe and his tobacco-pouch, furiously stuffing the pipe's bowl, his eyes avoiding hers. 'It isn't half as crazy as it seems, Beth. I'm an army man by nature. I should have realized it years ago and made the Army my career, but in the days when it would have been feasible there was no need for me to think of a career. Besides,

I thought I'd had enough after the last shindig. By the time I realized differently, it was too late.' He lit his pipe and drew on it deeply.

She leaned against the mantelpiece, her face pale, realizing with sick disbelief that her music and her future professional life were the furthest things from his mind. Even now, it had not occurred to him that her incredulity was anything other than that he was, perhaps, too old to contemplate active service once more. She moistened her lips with the tip of her tongue, instinctively knowing that if she cited her musical studies as a reason for their not going to Hong Kong the battle would be lost before it was begun. He would see it as proof that her music meant more to her than he did. They would be at an impasse, and her earlier sacrifice, in not touring the States, would have been in vain. She said carefully, trying to make him see how impractical his proposal was: 'You're forty-eight, Adam. Surely you can't want to see active service again?'

She had known, even as she said it, that it was the wrong thing to say. The uncomfortable colour in his cheeks darkened.

'God damn it, Beth! You're talking like the Army Board! Of course I'm not too old! I'm as fit as any of the runny-nosed youngsters they're so busy recruiting! And I'm experienced! It's men like me the Army should be rounding up! Men who have proved themselves on the battlefield and know what they're about!'

She had never seen him so furious. Her heart began to slam in thick heavy strokes against her chest. His proposal that they go to Hong Kong wasn't a whim. It was something he had thought about long and hard. Something about which he had already made up his mind. A wave of panic surged through her, and she controlled it with difficulty, saying with what she hoped was sweet reasonableness: 'But if you are right, and the Japanese do attack Hong Kong and Singapore, what will happen to the civilian population? Won't it be terribly dangerous for them?'

He frowned, as if he didn't understand what she was saying, and her panic gave way to impatience. She dug her nails deeper into her palms. 'You want me to go with you, don't you, Adam.' It was a statement of fact, not a question.

He nodded.

She drew in a deep steadying breath, certain that she had found his Achilles heel. He would not expose her to unnecessary danger. He loved her far too much ever to put her physically at risk. 'But if I go with you,' she said quietly, 'and the Japanese *do* attack, won't I be in a very vulnerable position?'

His frown cleared. 'Good heavens, no!' he said, amused. 'Darling Beth, you didn't think I would take you anywhere where I thought you would be in the slightest danger, did you? The Japanese may *attack* Hong Kong and Singapore in order to further their ambitions against the Malay Peninsula and the Philippines, but they will never, in a hundred years, succeed! Any fighting that occurs will be on the mainland, in the New Territories. You'll be far safer in Hong Kong, my darling, than you will be in London if

Hitler's bombs begin to rain down!'

She leaned back against the mantelpiece, her last hope of avoiding a confrontation gone. Her hair fell silkily to her shoulders, and the line of her thigh, as she balanced one foot on the fender, was unknowingly provocative.

'Cheer up, sweetheart,' he said, his voice thickening as he stepped lovingly towards her, resting his hand on her shoulder. 'It will be an adventure. Stafford says the climate out there is magnificent, the social life unrivalled. We'll have a whale of a time.'

'No,' she said, and though her voice was low and husky, as it always was, there was no trace of apology or weakness in it. 'No, Adam. I'm not going to Hong Kong. How can I? I have the Mozart recital in a few weeks' time, the Bach recital in April. I have been working for months preparing for the Brussels Competition in June. I'm on the threshold of achieving everything I have always dreamed of. I can't turn my back on it now. It isn't possible.'

If she had struck him, he couldn't have looked more stunned. His hand dropped abruptly from her shoulder, and he stepped away from her, saying tightly: 'I've explained my reasons for wanting to go. Surely you can understand them?'

The impasse she had always feared was opening wide at their feet. She did understand, but he did not understand her, and she knew with despair that except on a superficial level he never would. Her music, and her craving for recognition and success, was a closed world to him. Despite his many protestations to the contrary,

126

he had no more understanding of it than her father had had. For him, as for Jerome, her music was an indulgence, something he could take pride in when it suited him to do so, but something that was all too expendable when it came into conflict with his own desires.

'I do understand,' she said quietly, stepping away from the fireplace and moving towards him. 'But it isn't practical, Adam. Even if there is a war in the East, civilians will play no larger part in it than they will do if there is a war in Europe.'

His jaw cleanched, and he said with a savagery that was totally alien to him: 'Whether civilians will play a major part in the war or not isn't really what is at issue, is it?'

In the silence that fell between them she could hear a clock ticking and the hiss and spurt of flame as burning logs settled in the grate behind her.

'No,' she said, and the firelight danced on the glossy sheen of her hair, and he was struck again, as he had been when she was a child, by the strength in her delicately boned face. Beneath the loving gentleness that he found so attractive was a will as resolute as Jerome's had been, a toughness that enabled her to impose on herself long gruelling hours of daily practice and study. He turned away from her, filled with impotent frustration at what he saw as his lack of power over her, knowing, though he would never have admitted it, that one of the reasons Hong Kong had so appealed to him was because it would take her away from the Academy and from her studies. In Hong Kong she would have more time for him. His growing resentment at the long hours she spent alone at the piano would cease. He knew, defeatedly, that he couldn't browbeat her. That he could only plead.

'I have never before asked anything of you, Beth,' he said, his voice full of sudden weariness. 'Please don't let me down, my darling. I couldn't bear it.' And without turning to look at her he walked from the room, his shoulders hunched, every line of his body dejectedly middle-aged.

She knew that he had hoped she would run after him and she did not do so. She turned slowly and faced herself in the large gilt-framed mirror that hung above the fireplace. She had been confronted once before with the same sort of selfishness from someone she had dearly loved. Then she had been a child and she had had no option but to fall in with the plans that had been made for her.

She stared into the mirror, and smoke-green eyes, thickly lashed, stared back at her. She was a child no longer. The decision was hers and it was a simple one. She could refuse to go to Hong Kong and to abandon her career, just when it was on the verge of taking off. Or she could put Adam first in her life and regard their weeks or months in Hong Kong as nothing more than a short sabbatical.

The fire had begun to die down, hissing and spitting desultorily, and she bent down to the basket beside the hearth, lifting a log from it and tossing it on to the glowing embers. If she did not go to Hong Kong. Adam would go there alone.

And their marriage would be over.

'Oh God!' she said, with a venom that would have startled Adam. 'Oh shit! Oh hell!' And leaning with one hand on the mantelpiece she stared down into the flames, knowing that if she was to be able to live with herself, then she could not allow Adam to travel obstinately east alone. All through her life he had been there when she had needed him. Now he needed her. Her decision was made, but she did not follow him upstairs to their bedroom. She loved him too much to want to hurt him with her bitterness and resentment. She did what she always did when seeking peace of mind. She turned to her piano. When Adam woke, hours later, it was to the taut, savage notes of a Prokofiev concerto.

'My God! Is he serious?' Princess Luisa Isabel asked her as they sat over tea and cakes in Fortnum & Mason's elegant tearoom.

Elizabeth nodded. She didn't want to discuss Adam's decision to travel east, or hers to accompany him, only to appraise Luisa of it. They had been shopping, and lavishly wrapped parcels bearing the labels of Harrods, Hatchards, Swaine, Adeney, Brigg and Fortnum & Mason's were piled high around their feet as she said briefly: 'He says that, as he is forty-eight, if war does break out, the Army will take no notice of him at all. That the most he will be able to hope for is a desk job.'

Beneath the lavish veiling of her saucily tilted hat, Princess Luisa Isabel's eyes rose expressively heavenwards. 'But, goodness gracious, if there *is* a war – and your Chamberlain is quite adamant that there *isn't* going to be one, – why should Adam *wish* to be involved? He fought in the 1914 war, did he not? Wasn't he awarded the Military Cross for outstanding bravery? Why on earth should he wish to be physically involved again?'

Elizabeth sighed, knowing that she had been overly optimistic in thinking that Luisa would be satisfied by her cursory explanation. 'I'm sure I don't know,' she said truthfully. 'But he does. And he thinks his chances of involvement are much higher in the East than they are in Europe.'

Princess Luisa Isabel regarded her with concern, a lush pelt of double red fox furs draped around her shoulders, the heads dipping forward over the bodice of her Worth suit, the tails swinging flamboyantly down her back. 'But what about your music?' she asked forthrightly. 'What about your career? He doesn't, surely, expect you to go with him?'

Elizabeth flinched and remained silent. The princess rarely lapsed into her mother tongue and very rarely swore. Now she did both. *'Mae de Deus!'* she said explosively. 'How can he be so crazy? So blind? Naturally, you will not go?'

Elizabeth poured herself a second cup of tea, her face white. 'Adam has always been very kind to me, Luisa. I can't refuse him this, not as it is so important to him. Please try to understand.'

The Princess opened her mouth to say that she understood perfectly, and then closed it again. What she understood was something that Elizabeth would not want to hear.

For seven years she had observed the Harland marriage closely. There had never been one hint of unhappiness or discord. She had even begun to wonder if she had been wrong in believing that Elizabeth had married Adam because he so ably replaced her father in her life and not because she was as deeply in love with him as he was with her. Now, trusting her sixth sense, she wondered no longer. If Elizabeth was prepared to accompany him to Hong Kong, just when she was beginning to make a name for herself on the London concert platform, then it was not because of love. It was because of guilt.

She wondered when Elizabeth had realized the truth. Or even if she realized it at all. Looking across at her, she knew that she could not ask. Despite the twenty-year age-gap between them, Elizabeth had never treated her as a mother figure. It was too late now for her to try to behave as one. She said abruptly, feeling grossly incompetent: 'My God, but I miss Jerome!'

Elizabeth ground out her cigarette in a glass ashtray. 'Yes,' she said tightly. 'Me, too, Luisa. Me, too.'

'There's a sailing on the seventeenth of next month,' Adam said to her. They were in the bedroom of their Kensington house. She was undressed and brushing her hair at the dressing-table; he was in bed, a notebook and pencil and half a dozen sailing schedules scattered around him. She put down her hairbrush slowly. 'The seventeenth is three days before the Mozart concert,' she said, her eyes meeting his through
131

the mirror.

'I know.' There was a defiance in his voice she had never confronted before.

She turned round on the dressing-table stool to face him, overcome by a feeling of *déjà vu*, once more in the River Room Restaurant at the Savoy, hearing her father say: 'There'll be other concerts for you later. Lots of them. At the moment what's important is that you and I are together.'

There hadn't been other concerts. Not for a long time. Adam had called him a selfish bastard for disrupting her studies, yet now he was doing the exact same thing himself. She wondered if he was aware of it and, as her eyes continued to hold his, knew that he was. And that he was ashamed of it.

His hair was rumpled, his pyjama jacket open at the neck. 'I need you, Beth,' he said with boyish simplicity, as if reading her thoughts.

She felt a surge of compassion for him. He needed her and loved her and had always treated her with infinite kindness and patience. Now, just once, he needed something for himself. He needed to feel younger than his forty-eight years. He needed to feel that he was contributing something to the defence of England and its outposts. He needed to escape the ignominy of being assigned a desk job while younger, fitter men donned uniforms.

She walked slowly across the thickly carpeted room towards him, and he slid his hand around her waist, pressing his face against the smooth flatness of her stomach. She cradled his head against her, feeling as if she, not he, were the

132

elder.

'We'll sail on the seventeenth,' she said huskily.

Relief jarred through his shoulders, and then he drew her down on the bed beside him, his voice choked with love and gratitute. 'I love you ... love you ... love you, Beth,' he whispered as his hands slid up beneath the delicate silk of her négligée and he rolled her gently beneath him. 'I'll make it up to you, my darling. I promise. Now, let me show you how very much I love you...'

When he was asleep, she edged carefully away from him, slipping from the bed and wrapping her discarded négligée around her shoulders. It was only a little after midnight, and the moon was bright, filling the room with silver light. She went downstairs and made herself a cup of tea, sitting with it in the kitchen, hoping fiercely that at last she was pregnant. Knowing that if she was it would mean an early return to England. A return to normality.

Professor Hurok had been her tutor for the last six years. Russian-born, he was a fierce disciplinarian with an explosive and volatile nature that had, at first, terrified her. Now, as she came to the end of the piece she was playing for him, he nodded his head in approval.

'That is very good,' he said. 'The octaves were faster and louder and much more satisfying.' He gave her one of his rare smiles. 'And now for the Brahms. I absolutely forbid you to evade him any longer.'

Elizabeth groaned in mock despair. The Brahms first and second piano concertos had become something of a joke between them. When he had first suggested that she play the B-flat Concerto she had been aghast, protesting that her hands were much too small even to attempt it. 'Nonsense!' he had said, dismissing her protestations with a wave of his hand. 'The notion that Beethoven's Fourth Concerto and the Schumann Concerto are "ladies'" concertos, and that the Brahms B-flat is a concerto that can only be played successfully by a man, is ridiculous. Myra Hess has hands that are no bigger than yours. If she can play the Brahms B-flat – and she does so magnificently – then so can you.'

She had gone away, fired with determination, and for two weeks she had wrestled with a score that was the most difficult she had ever attempted. 'Look creatively at the text. Distribute things to make it more comfortable,' Professor Hurok had advised her, and she had done so. When she had not been playing it she had been listening to it, convinced that it was the most beautiful piece of music that she had ever heard.

'Are you ready?' he asked, sensing her nervousness. 'Then, please begin.'

She knew that he would not correct her, would not even speak to her, until she played the concerto through, without guidance. Summoning up all her fortitude and all her stamina, she lifted her hands and brought her fingers down on the keys. The music was titanic in scale. She became lost in it, obsessed by it. A small trickle of perspiration ran down her temple. She had thought

134

she had played difficult music before, but the architecture of the score she was now playing was something that was outside all her previous experience. It was like a cathedral with no top to it. It reached up for ever, demanding more from her than she had ever thought it possible to give. When at last she finished, she was wet with sweat, shaking with exhaustion.

'You see,' Professor Hurok said in calm satisfaction. 'It *can* be played. You have just done so.' And as their eyes met across the piano elation surged through her, intoxicating in its intensity. He sat down, taking a cigarette case and a lighter from his pocket. 'Tomorrow we will approach it again, from the first three uprising notes of the *allegro ma non troppo.*'

Her elation died. At the thought of the news she had to break to him she felt physically sick.

'What is it?' he asked, seeing the expression in her eyes and frowning in concern. 'Is it the Brahms? Was it too much for you?'

She shook her head, turning round on the piano stool so that she was facing him. 'No,' she said stiffly, her hands clasped tightly in her lap. 'I have something to tell you...'

He stared at her in disbelief, listening, immobile, as she told him that she would be unable to fulfil her coming concert engagements. That she would not be in Europe when the Brussels Competition took place. That she did not know when she would be in Europe again.

'It is not possible!' he kept saying. 'I do not understand! It is incredible! Unbelievable!'

'I am sorry, Professor,' she said at last, her

voice tight with pain.

'Sorry?' He pushed his chair away from him violently, jumping to his feet. '*Sorry? Don't you realize what you are doing? The chances you are forsaking? Good God, girl! You are one of the most gifted pupils I have ever taught! You are almost certain to win the Brussels Competition. Even before the International Piano Competition promoters will be hammering on your door!*'

She rose unsteadily to her feet, her face so white that he thought she was going to faint.

'I know,' she said bleakly, unable to bear any more 'Goodbye, Professor Hurok.'

'Elizabeth, wait!' He jumped from his chair, concern replacing his rage. 'Are you ill? Is there something terrible that you are not telling me?'

She shook her head, finding his concern far more distressing than his rage. 'No,' she said, her voice choked. 'Goodbye, Professor.' And before he could restrain her she hurried from the room, running down the corridor, half-blinded by her tears.

Two weeks later they left Four Seasons under the care of a housekeeper and closed the Kensington house. They left the keys with Adam's London solicitor, and without any farewell party, any goodbyes to anyone at all, left London for Southampton and the docks.

'You don't mind about not having a crowd coming down to the docks to see us off, do you, Beth?' Adam asked as they sat in the rear of their chauffeur-driven car, driving across Waterloo Bridge towards Waterloo Station.

'No, of course not.'

He took her hand in his. 'Luisa wanted to come, but she's at a christening in Derbyshire and there was no way she could cry off. It would have caused too many hurt feelings.'

Luisa was the only person Elizabeth would have liked to say goodbye to, but Luisa had already explained to her about the family christening.

It was late afternoon when they reached Southampton, and in the mellow sunshine the *Orient Princess* looked magnificent. For the first time in weeks Elizabeth felt her spirits stir. She had never been on a long sea voyage before, and a shiver of expectation ran down her spine as they walked up the gangplank and were greeted by the purser.

'She's a magnificent ship, isn't she?' Adam said enthusiastically as a steward led them towards their cabin. 'We're going to have a wonderful time on board her.'

Elizabeth, her hair falling softly to her shoulders, her figure slim and *svelte* in a biscuit-beige suit with wide fashionable shoulders and a chocolate-brown mink wrap over one arm, smiled in agreement. The steward had just turned round in order to tell them that all the bars on the ship were already open, when he caught sight of her smile and his voice faltered. My God, but she was lovely! He glanced hurriedly down at his passenger list. She was surely much too young to be Mr Harland's wife. Perhaps she was his daughter ... his niece. He found their names, and his hopes of a romantic diversion fell.

'Here is your cabin, sir,' he said to Adam, throwing open the door for them and envying him for a lucky devil. 'I hope you have a good voyage, sir. Madam.'

The cabin was large and spacious, with beds instead of bunks, a small bathroom, and ample cupboard space for their luggage.

'Three and a half weeks at sea,' Adam said to her exultantly. 'It's going to be a second honeymoon!'

She laid her mink wrap on one of the beds, and he stepped towards her, sliding his arms around her. 'I love you, Beth,' he said, his mouth closing over hers, warm and demanding. She knew that he was about to make love to her, and she knew that she did not want him to. Not now. If he made love to her now, she might not be able to pretend. He might realize that, though his caresses were agreeable, even stimulating, she did not crave for them in the way that he did hers. He would be dreadfully distressed, and their three-and-a-half-week cruise would be ruined.

'Let's go up on deck until she sails,' she said coaxingly. 'I want to feast my eyes on England while I can!'

He grinned. 'The only bit of England you'll see at the moment are the grubby docks of Southampton!'

'The docks will be quite satisfactory,' she said, sliding her hand into his. 'Come on, we're missing all the fun.'

They walked back along the mahogany-lined corridors and up the wide central staircase to the ship's lounge. A huge fanciful mural of Father

Neptune decorated one wall, and the room was full of passengers and their visitors, all saying noisy, exuberant and sometimes tearful good-byes. Up on deck the breeze was chilly, and Elizabeth shivered, wishing she had remembered to bring her wrap.

'The last of the luggage has been swung aboard,' Adam said to her, pointing out the crane that stood on the dockside, its big empty net hanging limp.

'All visitors ashore, please!' a loudspeaker blared out, and they leaned against the deck-rail, watching as the visitors disembarked and the gangplank was lashed into place.

'Only another few minutes now before we up anchor,' Adam said with boyish enthusiasm. As he spoke a taxi-cab hurtled on to the cobbles, squealing to a halt. The door flew open, and an elegant figure stepped out, her long legs clad in sheer silk stockings, her shocking-pink wool suit unmistakably Parisian, her fox furs swinging, her little hat of feathers perched at a preposterous angle over one eye.

'It's Princess Luisa Isabel!' Elizabeth cried, waving furiously. 'Luisa! Luisa!'

The Princess ran towards the ship, saw that the gangplank was up and laughed up at them with an expressive gesture of her hands and a shrug of her shoulders. 'It is too late for me to come aboard,' she called, 'but good luck, Elizabeth! Good luck, Adam! *Bon voyage!*'

The siren hooted, drowning their answering shouts, the thick hawsers were cast, and slowly the ship eased herself away from the dockside.

'Goodbye, Luisa!' Elizabeth cried, waving furiously. 'Goodbye!'

She waved until her arm ached, until they were so far away that the Princess was no longer discernible. Tears stung the back of her eyes as she finally turned away from the deck-rail and accompanied Adam below decks. She would miss Luisa. Apart from Adam, Luisa was all that remained to her of the past.

The only piano on board was in the first-class lounge. The ship's resident pianist was delighted to allow her to use it, and every morning, early, before too many people were about, she played Chopin and Mozart and Bach on an instrument that had previously only pounded out Irving Berlin and Duke Ellington.

The majority of their fellow-passengers were expatriates, returning to Hong Kong after leave in England. She soon discovered that Leigh Stafford had been correct when he had said that no one in Hong Kong regarded Japan as a potential threat.

'Japan!' an elderly colonel had said to her when she had tentatively suggested that it was a possibility. 'Japan! Who on earth has been filling your head with that idea? It's one thing for the Japanese to fight the Chinese, my dear, but they would never dare to presume to come into contact with British steel!' And he had laughed heartily at the very idea.

Even Adam seemed to have given up all thought of impending warfare. He relaxed visibly as the *Orient Princess* steamed her way

140

through the Mediterranean towards the Suez Canal, sunbathing on deck, playing tennis and deck quoits, dancing with her in the ballroom till late every night.

It was a casual remark from one of their fellow-passengers that made her wonder if she had discovered, at last, the real reason for Adam's obsession with being part of any action, if war broke out.

Mrs Smythe was elderly and partially disabled, and Elizabeth often joined her on deck, sitting in an adjoining deckchair and keeping her company. One day, as they approached Port Said, Adam joined them in his tennis whites. 'So pleased to meet you, Mr Harland,' Mrs Smythe had said. 'Your daughter is such a pleasant companion. I shall miss her immensely once we reach Hong Kong.'

Elizabeth had smiled, taken Mrs Smythe's arthritic hand and said unperturbedly: 'Adam is my husband, Mrs Smythe, not my father.' And as Mrs Smythe began to make hasty apologies, she had looked up at Adam, laughing, expecting him to be as amused as she had been.

He was not amused at all. The lines around his mouth were white, his jaw clenched as he said tightly that he was on his way to a tennis match and would see her later.

'Oh, my dear, I do hope I haven't caused any offence,' Mrs Smythe said agitatedly as he strode away from them. 'Whatever could have possessed me to think that you were father and daughter? Of *course* you are married, anyone can see that. What a silly *stupid* mistake.'

'Of course you didn't cause any offence,' Elizabeth said soothingly, but as she gazed after Adam there was a small furrow between her brows and her eyes were thoughtful.

Adam was such an emotionally well-adjusted person that it had never occurred to her that he might be sensitive to the difference in their ages. It was an intriguing thought. And it might explain why he was so eager not to be classified as being too old to fight for his king and his country.

That evening, as they dined, she caught sight of their reflections in one of the wall mirrors. Over the last few months Adam had gained weight, and his tough body had begun to take on middle-aged contours. His hair, though still thick, was heavily sprinkled with grey, and the lines around his nose and mouth had appreciably deepened. She was wearing an eau-de-nil silk dress, the skirt draped into a river of tiny, impeccably executed pleats, the neckline softly cowled. Her hair was held back from her face with two tortoiseshell combs, falling softly and smoothly to her shoulders. She was twenty-four and she didn't look a day over eighteen.

Next morning, when she brushed her hair, she didn't leave it loose. She swept it all off her neck, piercing the neat twist she created with long ivory pins, determined that Mrs Smythe's mistake would not be repeated.

Despite all her feelings at leaving London and not fulfilling the prestigious concerts that had been arranged for her, she enjoyed the passage to Hong Kong. Once they were beyond the Bay of

Biscay the sun shone steadily, and aboard the *Orient Princess* there were no rumours of war or depressing daily newspaper bulletins about Hitler and his bully boys, or Mussolini and his blackshirts. British expatriates returning to Singapore and Hong Kong were reassuringly adamant that nothing would happen to disturb their way of life out there.

'Your husband is quite wrong about the Japanese, my dear,' Mrs. Smythe said to her. 'Whatever happens in Europe, it won't have any repercussions in the East.' She had smiled serenely. 'Life will go on in Singapore just as it has done ever since Raffles snatched the island from under the noses of the Dutch in 1819, and in Hong Kong just as it has since Captain Elliot annexed it from the Chinese in 1841. You will have a lovely time there, my dear. Hong Kong is a magic island. There is nowhere else quite like it anywhere in the world.'

At the end of March they steamed into the Indian Ocean, and a week later Elizabeth woke to the knowledge that within hours they would be in sight of the island that Mrs Smythe regarded as so magical.

She sat on deck, binoculars in her lap, as the *Orient Princess* threaded its way through hundreds of deserted islands, the offshore breeze heavy with the fragance of flowers. Adam joined her, watching with her as hills and mountains began to take on distinctive shapes.

'This is the way to approach Hong Kong!' he said with relish, standing by the deck-rails. 'In another hour or so we're going to hit her slap on the nose!'

'Can you smell the flowers in the air?' Elizabeth asked him with pleasure. 'Isn't it the most marvellous smell? Mrs Smythe says that the words "Hong Kong" mean "fragrant harbour".'

Adam grinned. 'From what Stafford tells me, there'll be lots of other smells when we draw nearer shore. Not all of them quite so pleasant!'

Elizabeth laughed. The strain that had existed between them for their last few weeks in England and their first days aboard ship had now dissipated. She was quite sure that their stay in Hong Kong would be short and that within a few months they would be on their way back to England. Adam's restlessness would be satisfied, and she would once more be able to concentrate wholeheartedly on her music. In the mean time she was determined to be patient and to enjoy the experience as much as possible. 'I have it on very good authority that the more unpleasant smells are nothing more than the tang of burned sugar,' she said mischievously.

Adam's grin deepened. 'I will allow you to keep your illusions,' he said. 'Just look at those mountains! I'd never imagined them to be so magnificent. That one over there must be five thousand feet at least!'

A tall well-built man strolled across the deck and joined Adam at the rails. 'That is Victoria Peak' he said in amusement. 'The highest mountain on the island, though there are some others that come very near to it. That's Mount Butler over there to the west, and that one over there, on the right, is Mount Nicholson. I always like to believe it was named after an ancestor of mine. My name is Tom Nicholson.' And he held out his hand, his handshake firm.

'Adam Harland,' Adam said, and then turned, introducing him to Elizabeth, 'and my wife, Elizabeth.'

'I'm very pleased to meet you, Mrs Harland,' Tom Nicholson said sincerely. He had been aware of her ever since the *Orient Princess* had slid out of Southampton Water and into the Channel. It would have been impossible not to have been aware of her. She had the kind of beauty that was luminous, that turned heads in the most crowded of rooms. He wondered where Harland had met her. She didn't look much older than twenty or twenty-one, and Harland was easily in his late forties, and lacked the sophisticated glamour that was usually the attraction in such marriages.

'Is this your first trip out here, or are you an expat?' Adam asked, and reluctantly Tom Nicholson turned his gaze from Elizabeth to her husband.

'An expat,' he said with an easy grin. 'I've been out here since 1932. I'm a minor government official, for my sins. My major worry in life is how to avoid being posted anywhere else!'

Adam's interest quickened. 'This is our first trip out here. What's the government's line towards the Japanese? I've heard they're casting their eyes towards the Philippines and Malaya.'

'They've been doing that for centuries,' Tom Nicholson said dismissively. 'It won't get them anywhere. If they want to enlarge their empire, they'll have to be content with appropriating what they can from the Chinese.'

Adam would have liked to discuss the matter further, but they were nearing land now and the deck-rails were becoming crowded. 'Isn't it fabulous?' Elizabeth said, leaning her bare arms on the rails. 'Can you see all those boats? What are they? Sampans? Junks?'

'The small ones are sampans, the three-masted ones are junks,' Tom Nicholson said, smiling across at her. 'A vast majority of the population lives, eats, sleeps and dies aboard them. I've never understood where the Chinese get their reputation for being impassive from. They live as noisily and gregariously as Italians!'

Elizabeth laughed, and he felt his interest in her deepen. She had a low husky laugh that was as entrancing as her looks.

'Where are you staying?' he asked Adam, wondering how long they were visiting for and what the purpose of their visit was.

'The Peninsula Hotel, though as we intend to be here for an indefinite length of time I shall be looking about for a suitable property to rent.'

'The Peak is the most popular residential district,' he said, sensing that money for the Harlands was not a problem. 'My own house is up there.' He took a gilt embossed card from his breast pocket and handed it to Adam. 'Perhaps you would join me for dinner when you have settled in? Next Thursday, or Friday perhaps?'

'Friday will be fine,' Adam said agreeably, pleased that the social ball was rolling even before they had stepped on dry land. 'We would like that, wouldn't we, Beth?'

But Elizabeth wasn't listening to them. She was gazing rapturously at the sight of Hong Kong, its thickly foliaged steep slopes rising almost sheer from the sea, its glittering harbour massed with junks and sampans and a hundred different coloured sails.

Adam felt a surge of satisfaction as he looked across at her. Here, in Hong Kong, they would be together in a way that hadn't been possible in London. There would be no concert schedules to prevent her from spending time with him. No long hours of arduous practice. His decision had been the right one. Hong Kong was going to be good for them. He breathed in deeply. He was looking forward, with zest, to the next few months.

Chapter 6

She awoke next morning to the sharp white light of a Hong Kong dawn. She stretched luxuriously in her twin bed and then, being careful not to make a noise that would wake Adam, swung her feet to the thickly carpeted floor and slipped her arms into the sleeves of her chiffon négligée. It was barely five-thirty and, as she opened the french windows leading out on to the balcony, the air was cool and fresh, thick with fragrance.

The Peninsula Hotel was situated in Kowloon, on the Hong Kong mainland, overlooking the harbour. Across the shimmering wedge of water lay Hong Kong Island and the bustling teeming city of Victoria and, over and above it, the great granite rock that Tom Nicholson had referred to as 'the Peak'. She could see the houses clinging to its slopes, spacious white mansions surrounded by carefully tended, lush gardens. Tom Nicholson had suggested that was where they should look for a house to rent, and she felt a ripple of pleasure run down her spine. She was exiled from London and London's rich musical life, but it seemed there were going to be compensations. She couldn't think of a more wonderful place to live than the dizzy exotic heights of Victoria Peak.

'Are you all right, darling?' Adam asked an hour later, padding out towards her in his pyjamas.

She turned round to him and smiled – the slow, unknowingly sensuous smile that always made him catch his breath as if he had been punched in the chest. 'Yes. I couldn't sleep any longer. I feel like a child at Christmas. I've never seen anywhere so beautiful.'

He slid his arm around her waist, looking with her out over the harbour at the flurry of sampans and junk masts and patched sails and beyond them to the towering mountains of Hong Kong Island and the tortuous valleys and ravines that gashed and scarred their slopes.

'Impressive, isn't it?' he said with satisfaction. 'Let's have breakfast and get out there and see it properly.'

'I thought you had a meeting with Leigh Stafford this morning?'

'Not till lunchtime,' Adam said, picking up the telephone and dialling room service. 'We can have the morning together and then later, after I've talked to Stafford, we can perhaps do a bit of house hunting.'

They ate breakfast on their balcony: scrambled eggs and bacon, and papaya with limes and mango juice as well as coffee. By the time they walked out through the Peninsula's glass-fronted doors and on to the street, the delicious coolness of the early morning had given way to scorching heat, and Elizabeth was grateful for the light breeze that blew in off the water.

'You'll soon get used to it,' Adam said with a

grin. 'And the houses are air-conditioned. Haven't you seen all the fans?'

She had. The sound of their soft whirr had lulled her to sleep the previous night, and she understood now why Tom Nicholson had suggested that they look for a house on the Peak. It would be much cooler up there.

'Let's go across to Victoria on the ferry,' Adam said as they weaved their way between scores of Chinese women in black trousers and jackets, flat straw hats on their dark plaited hair. 'There will be a strong breeze off the water and it will help you to acclimatize.'

The ferry was packed with laughing, talking, jostling Chinese, and Elizabeth remembered Tom Nicholson's observations about them and grinned. He was quite right. They were more like boisterous Italians than the impassive Orientals she had been led to expect.

They landed at the Star Ferry Pier on Hong Kong Island only a few minutes later.

'That has to be the shortest, most spectacular channel crossing in the world,' Adam said as he extricated her from a throng of surging Chinese all eager to be the first to set foot on dry land. 'Let's find somewhere to take it easy and have a drink.'

For half an hour they sat in the coolness of a traditional tea house, sipping jasmine-scented tea, adamant that they would not lose face by asking for milk or sugar, or even lemon.

'When in Rome ...' Adam had said with a grin when the traditional Chinese teacups, without handles and with small lids, had been set down before them. It had tasted nicer than they had expected, and they each drank two cups before they left in search of a rickshaw and a leisurely tour of the city.

As their rickshaw-boy trundled them away from the harbour, the noise and clamour nearly took their breath away. It seemed as if the whole world was trying to squeeze into the narrow bustling streets. There were bicycles and trams and taxis, street-hawkers and sailors, delicately built Chinese women carrying their babies on their backs, old people pushing hand-carts, shop vendors touting their wares, their goods spilling out of tiny dark shops on to the street. The air was pungent with the smell of spices and dried fish and the sweetness of flowers, deafening with the cries of hawkers.

'A bit different from Bond Street, isn't it?' Adam said with relish.

'Much more fun,' she agreed, her hand affectionately in his. 'Oh, goodness, look at that jade, Adam! Is it real? It looks too good to be true!'

They bought a jade necklace, an exquisitely carved ivory horse and a rose-quartz paperweight, returning with their treasures to the Peninsula Hotel and lunch with Leigh Stafford.

He was a broadly-built, stocky man in his early fifties, with an affable smile and an easy manner.

'I must say, I was surprised to hear you were coming to Hong Kong to judge for yourself whether we should pull our horns in or not,' he said when initial introductions were over and the soup had been served.

'I had other reasons for coming out here,'

Adam said easily. 'Personal reasons.' He didn't expand on what they were. 'My fellow directors don't agree with you that there is any danger to the company at present. The general consensus of opinion is that there is to be no immediate pulling in of assets.'

Leigh Stafford shrugged. It was no more than he had expected. What he hadn't expected was someone coming out from London to judge the situation for himself. And bringing his wife with him. He tried to stop himself from staring across at Elizabeth. If Harland was to stay for any length of time, she would certainly cause a flurry in the dovecotes. The expatriate British clung together in a small exclusive social circle. Entry would be easily and eagerly given to a man of Adam Harland's standing, but it would be his wife who would attract attention. Her ivory-blonde beauty would be head-turning in any country, but in Hong Kong it was sensational.

'I have to tell you that I am not in agreement with them,' Adam was saying to him.

'Er, what? Sorry...' Stafford dragged his attention away from Elizabeth and once more towards Adam.

'I'm not in agreement with them,' Adam repeated. 'I personally think that your assessment of the situation out here is correct. The Japanese *are* casting covetous eyes on the Philippines and Malaya, and if war breaks out in Europe, then I think you're right. The Japs will try to take advantage of it.'

Leigh Stafford's interest quickened. It was a welcome change to meet someone whose ideas accorded with his own. 'Damn right they will!' he said forcefully. 'But tell that to the civil servants and they'll laugh at you! No one is taking Japanese aggression seriously. It's the usual story of complacency and facile optimism, and it's grossly misplaced. The Japanese aren't a joke. They're ruthless and fanatical. Anyone in doubt of that should have a word with the Chinese. The Japs are biting deeper into China every day, and they won't be content with China. Not when there are rich pickings of rubber and tin to be had in Burma and Malaya. Take my word for it, when the time is right they'll make their move, and when they do we're not going to like it!'

The impassioned authority in his voice sent a shiver down Elizabeth's spine. She had begun to believe that Adam's prediction of war in the East was groundless. That Mrs Smythe and the Colonel were right. The thought of Japanese aggression directed towards Great Britain was ridiculous and not to be taken seriously. Now, after listening to Leigh Stafford, she was no longer so sure.

'What signs have there been of their intentions?' she asked, tilting her head a little to one side, her green-gold eyes grave.

Leigh Stafford was grateful for the excuse once more to return his attention towards her. Her voice was as lovely as her face. Low and warm, with a faint trace of huskiness that he found entrancing.

Watch it, old boy, he said to himself chidingly. You're too old for this caper now. But as he answered her query he knew that it was too late. He already adored her. She had a serene, almost untouched quality about her that appealed to his old-fashioned notion of what a woman should be.

'They are widening their grip on south China, moving uncomfortably close towards us, and they are flauntingly gleeful of the fact that Hitler's Germany has recognized them as the rulers of Manchuria. Other than that, they're playing a waiting game. They won't make any move until our attention is centred elsewhere.'

'On Germany?'

He nodded, and then grinned. 'And I bet there are plenty of people back home who are still complacent and optimistic about *him*!'

They had all laughed, and the tension had ebbed. As they were lingering over their coffee, Adam said to him: 'Where is the best place to start house-hunting.'

'Hobson's in Chater Road. They generally have a good list of what's available. Who is it that's on the lookout?'

'We are,' Adam said, amused at his assumption that it was someone else.

Leigh Stafford stared at him. It had never occurred to him that Adam Harland intended staying in Hong Kong permanently. Damn it all. Only minutes ago he had been agreeing with him that it would very shortly come under attack by the Japanese! And the man had his wife with him!

He said carefully: 'Wouldn't it be wisest to forgo that sort of commitment? Considering what we have just been talking about?'

The smile lines around Adam's mouth deepened. 'We're here for the duration, Leigh. When, and if, those little yellow devils attack, I shall be in the forefront, driving them back where they came from! It's a confrontation I wouldn't miss for the world!'

Stafford drew in his breath sharply. Harland was a director, and he couldn't very well tell him that he was a fool. Nevertheless, he was staggered by his naïvety. For over an hour they had discussed Japanese aggression, and he had assumed Harland understood the seriousness of the threat. He hadn't. He thought it a game. A game that, like a little boy, he wanted to take part in. 'You must excuse me,' he said abruptly, rising to his feet. 'I have to be going now. I understand you are chairing our supplies meeting tomorrow? I'll see you then.' He nodded courteously and turned to Elizabeth, his fury that her safety should be valued so lightly by her husband white hot. 'Goodbye, Mrs Harland. It's been a pleasure meeting you. I hope we meet again.'

'Goodbye,' she said, but though her smile was warm her eyes were curious. Leigh Stafford was ragingly angry, and she wondered why. Was it because Adam had stated his intention of remaining in Hong Kong for some time? Was he afraid that his position as company manager would be usurped by Adam's seniority?

'Nice chap,' Adam said, oblivious of the undercurrents as Stafford strode quickly from the dining-room.

'He's not afraid that you've come out here to

check up on how he is running things, is he?' Elizabeth asked, frowning slightly.

Adam laughed. 'Good God, no! I've told him I'm here on a sabbatical, not a business trip. After tomorrow I doubt that I'll go near the office. Whatever put an idea like that in your head?'

'Nothing,' she said, carelessly dismissive, not wanting to spoil the day by reflecting too deeply on the alternative reason for Leigh Stafford's sudden flare of rage. It was far too disturbing and thought-provoking. She would think about it later, when she was alone.

They found a suitable house to rent on their very first trip to Victoria Peak. Hobson's had supplied them with details of three houses, but they only needed to see the first. It was a long, low, stately white mansion that had been built in the early years of the century by a prosperous merchant. The garden surrounding it was vast and lush, the views stupendous. A swimming pool had been installed by a later owner, and from the terrace surrounding it could be seen the distant harbour and Green Island and Peng Chau Island to the north, Lantau Island and Macau to the west. The furnishings were a pleasing mixture of modern comfort and Chinese elegance. Deep creamy-white sofas and chairs, silk Chinese carpets, jade cabinets, and ivory-framed mirrors. The houses of their affluent neighbours were hidden by forests of bamboo and fern, stunted Chinese pines, hibiscus and vines, so it seemed as if they were alone in a tropical paradise.

'Tom Nicholson lives only fifteen minutes away. He seems to be about the only civil servant here that Stafford has any time for,' Adam said as they walked in from the garden, both knowing that they were going to take the house.

'Does Leigh Stafford live on the Peak as well?' Elizabeth asked, mentally planning her first dinner party.

'No.' Adam was about to say that no company manager could afford the sky-high prices of Peak property when Elizabeth seized his arm.

'Look! Over there, in the trees! It's a monkey, Adam! I'm sure of it!'

'Then, I would prefer it to keep its distance,' Adam said with equanimity. 'Let's drive back to Chater Road and tell Hobson's that we'll take the house as soon as possible, with or without wild-life!'

On Friday evening they drove up to the Peak once more, this time for dinner with Tom Nicholson.

'Whatever sort of civil servant he is, he certainly isn't a minor one,' Adam said drily as they drove along exclusive Plantation Road, catching glimpses of colonial-style mansions hidden behind thick screens of bamboo and pine.

'Perhaps he's the governor,' Elizabeth said impishly. She was wearing an ice-coloured blue dress which hung silkily from her shoulders and danced softly over her skin. It was a halter neck with a low V in the back, and her silver-blonde hair was swept high into an elegant knot, revealing aquamarines at her ears and throat. She looked sensational, and Adam grinned, knowing full well the effect she would have at the Nicholson dinner table. He began to whistle beneath his breath. He was feeling more relaxed and fit than he had for a long time. The change of climate and scenery was doing him good. He no longer felt as if he was hurtling fast towards a wheelchair and decrepitude. The lifestyle of a wealthy expatriate suited him. There was plenty of sport: tennis and swimming were a part of daily life, as were the cocktail-parties and dinner-parties. The thought came from out of nowhere that it was a way of life Jerry would have loved. He felt a pang of loss as he drove up the wide drive of Tom Nicholson's home. It had been seven years since Jerry had died, and he still missed him like hell. His hand closed over Elizabeth's and tightened. 'I love you,' he said thickly as the car slid to a halt. He had lost Jerry but he would never lose Beth. She was the central point of his life and always had been, always would be.

She leaned across to him, kissing him gently on the cheek, the aquamarines dancing softly against her neck. He resisted the urge to draw her into his arms. There would be time, later, for that. For the moment he would be content in showing her off, enjoying the looks of envy in the men of his own age group, the vain hope in the eyes of those who were younger. He knew very well that Nicholson was attracted to her and he also knew that he had nothing to fear. His only rival for her affections was her music and, for a little while at least, he had put that firmly in the background.

A Chinese maid opened the door to them, and

then Tom Nicholson strode towards them, his arms welcoming. 'Good to see you!' he said expansively, greeting them as if they were old friends and not relatively new acquaintances. 'Let me introduce you to everyone.'

He led them into a vast white-carpeted drawing-room, long high windows looking out over the dark hillside and the distant glittering lights of Victoria.

'Helena, Elizabeth and Adam Harland. We met aboard the *Orient Princess*. Elizabeth and Adam, Helena Nicholson, my sister-in-law.'

Helena Nicholson shook hands with them warmly. She was a tall well-built girl with a beautiful square-jawed, high-cheekboned face and a mass of auburn hair falling untidily to her shoulders. 'It's lovely to meet you,' she said and then, with disarming directness, to Elizabeth: 'Tom tells me that you play the piano.' Tom Nicholson made an exasperated sound in the back of his throat, and she laughed. 'Sorry, he said that on *no* account was I to ask you to play. That you were a Bach and Beethoven performer, not an Irving Berlin party player.'

'If Irving Berlin is what you want, I'll happily play it,' Elizabeth said, liking Helena Nicholson instantly, and wondering just when her brother-in-law had eavesdropped on her early-morning practice sessions.

There were five other guests: Major Alastair Munroe, a soft-spoken Scot in his early thirties, who had been stationed in Hong Kong for over three years; Sir Denholm and Lady Gresby, who had also been resident since 1936; and a tall

159

languid American, Ronnie Ledsham, and his red-headed French wife, Julienne.

'We could do with a bit of decent piano-playing,' Ronnie Ledsham said as they all moved out of the drawing-room and on to the coolness of the veranda where cocktails were being served. '"Land of Hope and Glory" is all Tom can play, and he can't play that very well!'

'I understand you've moved into the Sumnor house?' Sir Denholm said to Adam as Tom Nicholson's Chinese houseboy served them with wickedly dry Martinis. 'Splendid views from there, if I remember rightly. A marvellous house for parties.'

The small talk continued. By the time they went in for dinner Elizabeth had gleaned that Helena Nicholson was a widow and that her escort for the evening was Major Munroe; that Ronnie Ledsham was a flirtatious rogue, and that Sir Denholm was a respected member of the Colonial Government. He talked knowledgeably of the East, discounting all suggestions that the Japanese were a force to watch.

'Certainly they are behaving belligerently,' he said to Adam as deep-fried prawns were served, 'but their sabre-rattling isn't to be taken seriously. It's just so much hot air. Nothing more.'

The conversation turned to more important matters. To last Saturday's race meeting, polo, the Royal Scots' chances in a forthcoming army boxing championship.

'I shall certainly not be there to cheer you on,' Julienne said to Alastair Munroe in prettily accented English. 'It is an ugly sport, the boxing.

160

I do not understand your enthusiasm for it at all.'

'And I don't understand your enthusiasm for mammoth shopping sprees,' her husband said to her amid much laughter.

Julienne looked up at him from beneath her luxuriant eyelashes, saying with obvious mischief: 'It is a pity that Raefe Elliot is not eligible to box for the Royal Scots. The result would be a foregone conclusion, would it not?'

Her husband's face tightened, and a tide of angry colour stained Sir Denholm's thin cheeks. 'My God!' he said explosively, oblivious of the mixed company. 'I couldn't believe the verdict when I heard it! "Accidental death!" Accidental, my foot!'

Elizabeth looked enquiringly at Tom Nicholson for enlightenment. There was a moment's uncomfortable silence in which Julienne continued to smile as she toyed with her prawns, well satisfied with the furore she had caused.

'We had an unfortunate incident here some months ago,' Tom Nicholson said to Elizabeth at last, trying to sound dismissive about it and failing. 'There was an ugly fist-fight and one of the men suffered a severe brain haemorrhage and died. The case came to court last week. Medical evidence showed that he had an abnormally thin skull, and the verdict was "accidental death".'

'It was murder!' Sir Denholm said harshly. 'Elliot should be hanged! He defamed the character of his wife in order to save his neck! It was a disgraceful unforgivable exhibition!'

'But what if it were true?' Julienne murmured provocatively, ignoring the silencing glare her husband shot her. 'If Melissa *were* taking drugs, and if the gentleman that Raefe found in her bed *was* a drug-pusher...'

'Stuff and nonsense!' Sir Denholm barked, pushing his plate to one side, all interest in his food forgotten. 'I've known the Langdon family for over twenty years! Melissa Langdon is a dear sweet girl who should never have married a rogue like Elliot! The man's a blackguard! He's ruined her life! Done his best to ruin her reputation! And he has the effrontery to pose as the injured party!'

'Some injured party,' Ronnie Ledsham said drily. 'He walked into the Hong Kong Club the night he was acquitted, with a Malay girl on his arm.'

'I hope he was shown the door!' Sir Denholm said savagely. 'Insolent young pup!'

'I imagine it's a little hard to show the door to a man of Elliot's wealth and background,' Alastair Munroe said quietly. 'No doubt he will be asked to resign his membership and honour will be satisfied.'

Elizabeth shot him a quick look, wondering if she was correct in detecting a faint note of contempt in his voice, certain that, if there were, it was directed towards the élitist policies of the club, and not towards the scandalous Raefe Elliot.

'And no doubt he will refuse,' Helena Nicholson said, looking across at her brother-in-law. 'Personally I don't blame him. There are surely worse sins in life than escorting a Chinese or Malay girl into the hallowed halls of the all-

162

white Hong Kong Club!'

To Elizabeth's surprise she saw that Tom Nicholson's face had hardened and that a nerve had begun to throb at the corner of his jaw. He cleared his throat to speak, but before he could do so Lady Gresby said coldly: 'You are, of course, entitled to your own point of view, Helena. But I must tell you that it is a singularly naïve one. If Mr Elliot wishes to parade his native mistress in public, then he may do so. But he will not do so in the Hong Kong Club. Not now, nor at any time in the future.'

'He shouldn't be in the damn club himself!' Sir Denholm expostulated. 'There's more than a touch of the tarbrush about Elliot, and no one can tell me any differently!'

'A touch of a tarbrush?' Julienne asked, her cheeks dimpling. 'I am sorry, I do not understand.'

'The fellow's got wog blood,' Sir Denholm said bluntly. 'Must have. Hair black as his isn't natural.'

'But I thought Raefe Elliot's pedigree was impeccable!' Julienne said, her eyes widening. 'Isn't he descended from the Captain Elliot who first annexed the island from the Chinese?'

'That's what the fellow would *like* us to think!' Sir Denholm spluttered. 'Personally, I have my doubts. And, even if he is, it doesn't mean there's no mixed blood in his veins! Elliot's grandfather lived up-country for forty years. You can bet your life that his grandmother was a native!'

Before Julienne could bait him any further, Tom Nicholson said smoothly: 'Is your horse going to run at Happy Valley on Saturday, Ronnie? Julienne tells me that you have a new jockey. Is he any good?'

Later, when they were sitting drinking coffee in the spacious drawing-room, Ronnie Ledsham leaned over to his wife and whispered chastisingly: 'You were *very* naughty, darling. I thought old Denholm was going to have an apoplectic fit!'

Sir Denholm was sitting at the far side of the room talking to Helena Nicholson and didn't hear him, but Elizabeth did. Julienne, aware that she had overheard, turned towards her. 'We are not really so ill-behaved as we seem. It is just that Sir Denholm loses his temper so quickly and so magnificently, and there are times when I cannot resist provoking him.'

'And mention of Elliot *always* provokes him,' her husband murmured, taking care that Sir Denholm did not overhear him.

'Who on earth *is* this Raefe Elliot that he arouses such passion?' Elizabeth asked as Adam moved away from her to look at some ancient Chinese scrolls that Tom Nicholson was eager he should admire.

Julienne's eyes danced. 'He is *very* handsome, *very* exciting; an American who lives by no rules but his own. He is also a part of Hong Kong in a way that Sir Denholm and his friends can never be. It is this, I think, that so enrages them.'

'He's dangerous,' Ronnie said, looking across at his wife with a curious expression in his eyes. 'Especially to women.' The conversation on the far side of the room between Helena Nicholson

164

and Sir Denholm and his wife continued; Alastair and Adam were engrossed in examining Tom Nicholson's antique scrolls. Ronnie settled himself comfortably on the arm of Julienne's chair and with a proprietorial arm around her shoulders said: 'The Elliots are an old New Orleans family, though the rumour that they are descended from the Captain Elliot who first hoisted a Union Jack aloft and claimed Hong Kong for the British remains. Old man Elliot, Raefe's grandfather, made a fortune by trading. Raefe's father consolidated it with rubber estates in Malaya and a tin mine in Sumatra. Whatever else they've been accused of, they can't be accused of being bad businessmen. The whole lot of them were, and are, as sharp as needles.'

'And just what have the Elliots been accused of?' Elizabeth asked, intrigued.

Ronnie Ledsham grinned. 'Whoring seems to have been their main vice. It's said that old man Elliot kept two concubines, aged fifteen and eighteen, when he was well into his eighties. Hence the rumours that abound about Raefe Elliot's ancestry. Raefe's father was no better. He snatched a high-ranking government official's daughter from her home only hours before she was due to be married to another man. By the time her father and his friends retrieved her, she was pregnant with Raefe and compromised beyond all hope. It is said that her father wept all through the wedding ceremony.'

'The bride's father may have wept, but if the groom was as handsome as Raefe, then the bride would not have done so,' Julienne said with a

165

wicked chuckle. 'She would have been a *very* happy lady!'

Ronnie gave her a playful cuff on the side of her chin. 'Don't cast your eyes in that direction,' he warned laconically. 'Raefe Elliot is far too dangerous a man for your little games. You would get very badly burned, my love.'

Julienne's chuckle deepened, but she took his hand, twisting her fingers lovingly through his as Helena Nicholson looked across at them and said: 'Can we have some music now, Elizabeth? Just for a little while.'

The piano was an old Bechstein, its surface crowded with family photographs in silver frames.

'I'm afraid it isn't played very often,' Tom Nicholson said apologetically as she sat on the piano stool and opened the lid. 'It's probably grossly out of tune.'

She ran her fingers experimentally over the keys. It wasn't what she was used to, but it was still a very lovely piano.

'It's fine,' she said. 'What would you like me to play?'

He smiled down at her, the expression in his eyes changing from one of easy camaraderie to one which told her how very lovely he thought she was. 'Play anything,' he said, his voice thickening. 'But don't play for a little while. Play for a long while.'

His admiration didn't ruffle her. She was accustomed to seeing heat in men's eyes when they spoke to her. And she was accustomed to not being disturbed by it.

Sensing the taste of her audience, she didn't play any classical music. To Tom Nicholson's surprise and pleasure, she played delicate blues and then straight jazz, finishing off with a medley of tunes by Jerome Kern, Cole Porter and Irving Berlin.

'Heavens!' Helena said rapturously, when she refused to be pressed into playing any longer. 'I would never have believed that old piano could possibly sound like that!'

'A magnificent performance!' Lady Gresby said. 'I'm afraid that from now on there won't be a party in Hong Kong at which you won't be asked to play, my dear!'

As they were all about to leave, Helena Nicholson took Elizabeth discreetly to one side.

'Just a quick little word, Elizabeth. I would hate Sir Denholm to have left you with the impression that Raefe Elliot is an unconscionable blackguard. He does have *some* redeeming features.' Her mouth quirked in a naughty smile. 'He's the most damnably attractive man on the island, and that's saying something! What drives Miriam and her friends wild is that he pays not the slightest attention to their marriageable daughters. Or to them. It's an insult they can't forgive. Julienne has been madly in love with him ever since she first saw him and, for once, I don't blame her. Where Raefe is concerned, I could nearly forget my quiet lifestyle and live very dangerously myself!'

'It's hard to believe it's only our first week here,' Adam said to her as he lay in bed later that night, watching her as she undressed. 'We're having lunch with Sir Denholm and his wife tomorrow, on Sunday we're lunching with Alastair Munroe and Helena Nicholson, and going to a party at the Ledshams' in the evening. We're playing a doubles of tennis on Monday with Tom and Helena, going on to a polo match with them, and dining with Leigh Stafford in the evening.'

She sat down in her négligée at the dressing-table and began to brush her hair. She was going swimming with Julienne in the morning, shopping with Helena in the afternoon. The social life in Hong Kong was proving as full and relaxed as Adam had promised it would be. And she wasn't remotely interested in it. She didn't want an endless round of parties and dinners. She didn't want to fill her days with swimming and shopping. She wanted to be working. To be practising hard for the International Piano Competition, to be extending her range, coming to terms with the new composers Professor Hurok had introduced her to – Vaughan Williams and Busoni and Pfitzer.

She put down her hairbrush, walking across to the large double bed and slipping in between the cool sheets beside him. His arm automatically slid round her shoulders, pulling her close, and she said tentatively: 'Sir Denholm is a member of the government out here, and *he* doesn't think there's the slightest possibility of an attack by the Japanese. Wouldn't it be wisest to go back to England? Julienne says that foreign newspapers are full of reports of how war between Great Britain and Germany is only weeks away. I know

168

you don't want to be relegated to a desk job, darling, but desk jobs *are* vital and—'

'No!' His voice was adamant as with his free hand he switched off the bedside lamp, plunging the room into semi-darkness. 'If the reports in the foreign press are true, then it would be far too dangerous for you in London. You are much safer staying here where, if there is a confrontation, it will be miles away up-country.'

His lips touched the side of her mouth, his fingers gently pulling the straps of her nightdress down, revealing the creamy white smoothness of her breasts, the rose-pink perfection of her nipples.

'Forget what Sir Denholm said,' he whispered hoarsely, rolling his weight on top of her, sliding her nightdress up to her waist, revelling in the delicious feel of her flesh against his, savouring her softness and fragrance. 'Stafford says the government is blind – that they haven't a true grasp of the situation.' Tenderly his hand parted her thighs as he gently eased himself into her. 'God, that's good, Beth!' he panted. 'Hold me! Hold me tight!'

She held him tight and she thought about Sir Denholm and wondered how on earth she could get Adam to agree to a return to London. With a groan he reached a climax, his hands tightening on her shoulders, his mouth closing lovingly over hers. She hugged him tight, telling him how much she loved him, remaining in his arms until he fell asleep and then, as she always did, gently disentangling herself. Perhaps Tom Nicholson could persuade him that he was wasting his time in remaining in Hong Kong. Perhaps, soon, the novelty would wear off. She lay on the far side of the bed, gazing up at the moonlit ceiling, hoping fervently that it would do so; that they would soon be back in London.

She went swimming at the prestigious Hong Kong Sports Club with Julienne the next morning.

'Isn't Tom Nicholson a sweetie?' Julienne asked as she came up from a dive, her dark hair sleeked close to her head, her long eyelashes sparkling with water.

'He's very nice,' Elizabeth agreed, striking out for the far side of the pool, Julienne swimming along beside her.

Julienne giggled. 'Don't be so English and reticent, Elizabeth! It's obvious that he is crazy about you. Tom doesn't fall in love easily, or often, so it's quite a compliment.' She looked across at Elizabeth naughtily. 'Do you think you could fall in love with him?'

'I'm married,' Elizabeth said, laughing at Julienne's ridiculousness as they reached the far side of the pool and hung on to the edge, recovering their breath.

Julienne laughed with her. 'Marriage!' she said expressively. 'What difference does marriage make?' And with a kick of her heels she executed a professional racing turn, not breaking the surface of the water until she was nearly thirty yards away.

Later, as they sat over cold drinks in the bar, Julienne said to her, incredulously: 'Do you mean that you have *never* had an affair?'

'Never,' Elizabeth said, amused by the expression of horror on Julienne's pretty, kitten like face.

'But that is terrible!' Julienne protested and then collapsed into giggles. 'Oh dear, what must you think of me? But really, Elizabeth, I cannot imagine it. I adore Ronnie, but not to have any little adventures now and again? *Non, je ne peux pas l'imaginer!* You must be very much in love with your Adam!'

Elizabeth's answering laugh indicated that she was, but as she continued to sip at her gin and tonic she knew that her love for Adam was not the kind of love that Julienne was meaning.

As they continued to talk, and as Julienne continued to be indiscreet, telling her about her present lover, who was a major in the Royal Scots, Elizabeth remained unenvious. The love that she and Adam shared was worth far more than the love Julienne enjoyed with her major or with her other boyfriends. It wasn't a very exciting kind of love, but it was deep and enduring and was surely of far greater value.

'Excuse me a moment,' Julienne said, breaking off her laughter-filled account of her latest affair. 'I promised Ronnie I would ring him and let him know where to meet me for lunch.'

She slipped down from her bar stool, blowing a kiss to a gentleman in the far corner of the room who obviously knew her, hurrying away towards the telephone booths.

Elizabeth remained at the bar, reflecting on how different social mores were in Hong Kong and London. In London she would *never*, not

171

even for an instant, have remained at a bar alone.

'Another gin and tonic, madame?' the Chinese barman asked courteously.

'No, thank you. I'll have a lemonade this time, please.'

As the barman turned to fulfil her request, two casually dressed men entered the room and approached the bar. 'I've never heard such a tirade of rubbish!' one of them said darkly as they sat down next to her. 'Straight off the boat from England and he believes he knows all there is to know about fighting off the Japs if they should attack! Christ! He believes they'll be fought up-country and that life here will go on as normal! One thing is for sure: he's the kind of middle-aged fool we can well do without! What did you say his name was?'

The barman handed Elizabeth her frosted glass of lemonade.

'Harland,' replied his companion.

Elizabeth gasped with shock and indignation, her fingers slipping on the ice-cold glass. It crashed to the floor, its contents gushing down the trouser leg of the man who had called Adam a fool. He spun round savagely. 'What the hell...?' he began, his eyes blazing.

His hair was black, straight and sleek, tumbling low over winged eyebrows. His skin was bronzed, his face harsh with high lean cheek-bones and a strong nose and jutting jaw. He looked like a man to be reckoned with, a man who could be a very nasty customer indeed.

'I'm sorry,' she said furiously, his masculinity coming at her in waves. 'It was an accident!'

172

His eyes were brown. Not the soft honey-brown of Adam's eyes, but a brown so dark it was almost black. 'Allow me to buy you another one,' he said, and she could see flecks of gold near his pupils and a small white scar curving down through one eyebrow. 'What was it? A gin and tonic?'

'A lemonade,' she said between clenched teeth. 'And I would *not* like another one! It may interest you to know that the man you were talking about with such a gross lack of respect is my husband!'

A flare of shock passed through his eyes and was quickly suppressed. 'Then, I must *insist* on buying you a drink,' he said and to her increased fury she could hear amusement in his voice. 'Li, a lemonade for Mrs Harland, please.'

Elizabeth rose to her feet, shaking with anger. She had no need to wait for him to introduce himself. She knew who he was. Sir Denholm's description of him had been searingly accurate.

'No, thank you!' she said, spitting the words. 'Goodbye, Mr Elliot!' And she spun on her heel, marching from the room, her head high, her back rigid.

Chapter 7

The doors slammed behind her, and she strode full tilt into Julienne.

'Steady on,' Julienne said, laughing. 'There's no need for us to leave yet. I'm not meeting Ronnie for another hour.'

Elizabeth drew in a deep steadying breath. 'Sorry, Julienne. I have to be going. I'll see you later.'

'Oh, come on. Just one more gin and tonic,' Julienne coaxed, looking genuinely disappointed.

Elizabeth shook her head. There wasn't money enough in the world to tempt her back into the bar and Raefe Elliot's obnoxious presence. 'Sorry, Julienne, I really must be going. We're lunching with the Gresbys, and I'm going to be late.' As she spoke, she continued to walk briskly, hurrying across the lobby and out into the sunshine.

Julienne gave the doors to the bar a last, regretful look and then followed her. There would be other opportunities to waylay Raefe. And next time he might not have a friend with him. 'Well, as you're in a hurry, and I've got time to spare, let me give you a lift,' she said, surmounting her disappointment with her usual bouncy optimism.

'I wouldn't mind a lunch-time drink at the Pen. The barman there mixes the most wonderful Manhattans.'

As they stepped into Julienne's little Morris, Elizabeth felt her anger begin to subside. Raefe Elliot was an ill-mannered bore, but the friendliness of Julienne and her husband, and Helena and Tom Nicholson and Alastair Munroe, more than made up for it. They didn't think Adam a fool. They liked him, and it was *their* opinion that mattered, not the opinion of an arrogant ne'er-do-well like Raefe Elliot.

As if reading her thoughts, Julienne said suddenly; 'Did you see the two men who walked into the bar just before you came out? One of them, the tall dark one, was Raefe Elliot. I saw them when I was on the telephone to Ronnie. I must say he doesn't look very ruffled by his court appearance – or by the new rumours that are beginning to fly around.'

Elizabeth knew she shouldn't ask, but curiosity overcame common sense. 'What rumours?' she asked as Julienne swung the Morris recklessly out on to the busy road.

Julienne's black-lashed eyes sparkled. 'That he's banished Melissa to one of his farms in the New Territories. That he's refusing her a divorce and is keeping her a prisoner, not even allowing her father to know where she is.'

'But, my goodness, can't the police interfere?' Elizabeth asked, shocked.

Julienne giggled. 'He *is* her husband, and the judiciary won't want to interfere with Raefe again in a hurry, not after he made them look

175

such fools over the murder charge that was brought against him. You can bet your life that Colonel Langdon, Melissa's father, would have been far less eager for charges to have gone ahead if he had known in advance that Raefe's defence would depend on revealing that Melissa was a heroin addict! *Mon Dieu*! You should have heard the intake of breath when Raefe was forced to part with *that* little piece of information!'

'And was it true?' Elizabeth asked, remembering Sir Denholm's impassioned avowal that it was a monstrous slander. That Raefe Elliot had grossly defamed his wife's reputation in order to save his own neck.

Julienne sped down Chatham Road with scant regard for other traffic and none at all for the pedestrians who leaped hurriedly out of her way.

'Who is to say?' she said with a Gallic shrug. 'Raefe says that she is; her father and everyone else who knows her say she is not. But the jury *did* believe that Raefe was speaking the truth when he said that he returned from a business trip to Singapore and found Jacko Latimer in her bed, and Jacko *was* a well-known pusher of drugs among the European community in Hong Kong. For myself, I believe Raefe. What other reason would Melissa have for being in bed with an unpleasant unprepossessing little man like Jacko? He was the kind of man that has to grovel for sex, not the kind that has it showered on him by a woman as beautiful as Melissa. No, if Melissa allowed Jacko Latimer into her bed, then it was not because she wanted him there. It was because she was paying him for something, and that something could only have been heroin.'

They drew up outside the Palladian-style splendour of the Peninsula Hotel.

'But as to why he is refusing her a divorce and is keeping her a prisoner in the New Territories, *je ne comprends pas.* That I cannot understand. I would have thought he would be glad to be rid of her. Certainly I do not believe he is still in love with her.'

She giggled naughtily as they walked into the coolness of the Peninsula's lobby. 'If he had still been in love with her, the blow that killed Jacko would not have been an accidental one, and would never have been mistaken for an accidental one! He would have torn Jacko limb from limb, and been magnificently unrepentant!' She gave a delicious shiver. 'Can you imagine how superb a man like that must be in the bedroom, Elizabeth? If only he didn't prefer his Chinese and Malay girls.' She ran the tip of her tongue suggestively over her full lower lip and said, her voice full of laughter: 'If only he would give *la belle France* a chance to show what she can do instead!'

After lunch with the Gresbys, Elizabeth excused herself and went to her room to lie down. She still found the humid heat enervating, and the scene with Raefe Elliot had disturbed her far more than she had been willing to admit.

She slipped out of her blouse and skirt and closed the rattan blinds, plunging the room into cool shade. 'Damnable man,' she muttered as she

177

lay down on her bed and closed her eyes. How *dare* he speak of Adam like that? And how *dare* he suggest that she share a drink with him? Her cheeks flushed as she remembered the way he had looked at her; the naked appraisal in his dark eyes; the lazy amusement in his voice; the sensual, confident, *arrogant* demeanour that had so unnerved her.

'Damnable man!' she said again savagely, turning her pillow over and thumping it with her fist. Julienne was welcome to her daydreams of him. In Elizabeth's eyes she was displaying a gross lack of judgement and taste. Raefe Elliot was *not* an admirable, sexy man coping with an unfaithful and drug-addicted wife. He was an insolent, ignorant, loud-mouthed braggart who was not only a flagrant womanizer and brawler, but possibly even a murderer as well.

She thumped the pillow again for good measure and tried to sleep. It was impossible. It wasn't only her unfortunate confrontation with Raefe Elliot that was disturbing her; it was her own increased knowledge of the geography of Hong Kong and the conclusions she was drawing from it.

When she had sailed from Southampton aboard the *Orient Princess*, the only thing she had known about Hong Kong was that it was an island off the coast of China, under the jurisdiction of Great Britain. Whatever Adam had told her about it she had believed. That Japan was aggressive towards it, would eventually attack it; that there would be fighting in which he would be able to take part and which would take place

178

'up-country'; that when it was over he would be able to return to England and, though not able to don a uniform and join in any fight against Hitler that might take place, his pride would be intact; that he would be able to say he had helped give the Japs a bloody nose in the East. That he would have nothing to feel ashamed of and, more important, he would not feel as if he was an old crock, too ancient to fight for his country. All this she had understood. But now, after only a few days in Hong Kong, she understood far more.

It wasn't the diverging views as to whether the Japanese would or would not attack that disturbed her. It was the overwhelming consensus of opinion that, if they *did* attack, they would soon be sent packing.

She had been shocked when she had first seen a map of Hong Kong. She had thought it was a large island, several miles off the coast of China, with an impressive harbour and a fleet to match. It wasn't an island in the way she had thought, at all. It lay – only eight miles wide and eleven miles long – a mere stone's throw from the mainland. Across the narrow channel of water lay the Kowloon peninsula and an area of over 360 square miles known as the New Territories. This was the area that Adam was presumably referring to when he spoke of fighting taking place 'up-country'. The only defence that the island and the mainland had against the Japanese warring across the border in China was two Regular Army battalions. The 2nd Battalion Royal Scots, in which Alastair Munroe served, and the 1st Battalion, the Middlesex Regiment.

There was no air force to speak of and only a handful of ships in the harbour.

'Is that it?' she had asked Alastair Munroe in amazement when he had answered her questions regarding the island's defences.

'It's more than enough to see off the Japs,' Alastair Munroe said with amusement. 'No point in having a surfeit of men and ships out here when it looks as if they're going to be needed elsewhere against Hitler.'

Elizabeth had said: 'No, possibly not.' But she hadn't been convinced. It seemed to her that it would be exceptionally easy for the Japanese to pour over the border into the New Territories whenever they wanted to. And that, once they did, the narrow channel of water between the mainland and Hong Kong Island would not deter them for long.

Later that afternoon they picked up the keys to the house, and the next morning they moved out of the Peninsula Hotel and into their new home on the Peak.

'Household staff is no problem,' Helena Nicholson said when she came round to help Elizabeth measure up for new curtains and blinds, bringing her two children aged two and five with her. 'Hobson's will supply them for you, but tell them you only need houseboys and a cookboy and a wash-amah. Tom's houseboy has a sister who is looking for a position. She is only seventeen, but Lee says she is very efficient, and it would be nice for them if they were in neighbouring households.'

She wrote down the measurements of the last

window and pushed her untidy mane of auburn hair away from her face. 'You didn't mind me bringing Simon and Jennifer with me, did you? Since Alan's death they hate me to be out of their sight, poor lambs.'

'Of course not,' Elizabeth replied. 'It's lovely to have them playing out in the garden.' Her eyes had lit up at the mention of the children. 'It makes the house seem already a home.'

Helena looked across at her curiously. 'I would have thought you and Adam would have adored parenthood,' she said in her blindingly forthright manner. 'Do you just not want any, or is there a problem?'

'There's no problem,' Elizabeth said, rolling the tape measure into a very tight ball. 'They just haven't arrived as yet. There's plenty of time.'

'Oh, yes, of course,' Helena said easily, but her eyes remained curious. There was something odd about the Harlands' marriage, but she could not for the life of her think what it could be. They seemed happy enough, and she couldn't, for one moment, imagine Ronnie Ledsham or anyone else luring Elizabeth into an extramarital affair.

The children's voices could be heard, laughing and shrieking as they played hide-and-seek in the garden. She looked out of the window towards them, her blue eyes clouding. It seemed such a little time since they had been playing in front of their house in Singapore. Since Alan had been striding up the path, and they had toddled to meet him.

Elizabeth said quietly: 'Is it still so very bad, Helena?'

181

She nodded. 'Yes, even after a year it still seems ... impossible. There's a part of me that can't truly believe it. Sometimes, in the morning, before I'm fully conscious, I think he's there beside me, or that he's away on a trip and will be coming home, and then I wake properly and I remember, and it seems too monstrous to be true. How *can* he be dead when I loved him so much?' She wiped the tears quickly from her eyes and gave a self-conscious laugh. 'Sorry, I didn't mean to come on the poor-little-widow bit. I don't usually talk about it at all. It was just seeing the children in the garden, and remembering...'

They were silent for a little while, and then Elizabeth said tentatively: 'Alastair Munroe is a very attractive man...'

Helena grinned, her grief once more under control. 'He is, and what you mean is that he seems to be in love with me and why don't I marry him.'

Elizabeth laughed. There was no way of coping with Helena's forthrightness except by being equally forthright. 'Something like that, yes.'

Helena sighed. 'He *is* an attractive man, Elizabeth, and I'm terribly fond of him, but I don't love him in the way I loved Alan. I don't feel ill with worry if he's late, or faint with excitement at the thought of seeing him. I don't want to die with pleasure when he touches me, or feel sick with fear at the thought of losing him. I don't want to marry him and him to know he's only second-best. I want to be in love with him as I was in love with Alan. As you are in love

182

with Adam. And I don't think I ever will be. Not with anyone, ever again.'

That night, lying beside Adam in the darkness, Elizabeth felt curiously restless. It was foolish to allow Helena's innocent words to perturb her. There were more ways than one of being in love. Helena's way certainly wasn't Julienne's way. Helena had loved one man faithfully and whole-heartedly in a way that Elizabeth doubted Julienne had ever done. So why did it matter if her way of being in love with Adam was different from their way of being in love?

Adam's rhythmic heavy breathing deepened into a slight snore, and she eased herself away from him and rolled over on to the far side of the bed. She knew the answer to her question. It was because, though Julienne and Helena loved differently, they both loved with a physical passion that she was incapable of. She knew the word that described her sexual responses, and it was an unpleasant one. For the thousandth time she wondered if Adam were aware of her frigidity, and if he ignored it and accepted it out of his very deep love for her. There was no way of knowing. In many ways he treated her as if she were still a child. A frank discussion between them about sex would be as unthinkable to him as it would be difficult for her.

She sighed and slipped out of bed, walking barefoot on to the balcony, looking out over the silk-black mountainside to the distant lights of Victoria. She was suffering increasingly from insomnia. Night after night she found herself making cups of tea while Adam slept, reading the latest Agatha Christie novel or browsing through her sheet music. She picked up the score of Busoni's 'Turandot' Suite that she had been reading earlier in the day. He was an exciting composer, and Professor Hurok had been eager that she familiarize herself with his work. She felt a surge of determination. Lack of work was surely the main reason for her restlessness and dissatisfaction, and lack of work was something she could rectify herself. She would buy a piano tomorrow. Helena would tell her where a suitable one could be obtained. And she would set six hours a day aside for practice. If Adam wanted to swim and sunbathe and play interminable tennis, then he could do so with the new friends they had made. She would accompany him to parties and dinners as she had always done, but through the day she would have her music. And her restlessness and dissatisfaction would surely disappear.

'It's going to take them at least six weeks to ship in the kind of piano you require,' Helena said to her as they came out of Lane Crawford, Victoria's largest department store. 'In the meantime, why don't you appropriate Tom's piano? It isn't exactly concert-platform quality, but it's better than nothing.'

'That would be super,' Elizabeth said gratefully, 'but wouldn't Tom miss it?'

Helena laughed. 'Until you arrived in Hong Kong, that piano was only played at Christmas and birthdays – and then always appallingly.'

She opened the door of her little open-topped Morgan. 'And, if time is hanging heavy on your hands, there's another favour you could do for me.'

Elizabeth slipped into the passenger-seat next to her. 'What's that? Arrange for a cooling breeze? An English shower?'

Helena shook her head, her mane of untidy hair bouncing around her shoulders. 'No, nothing so easy. The dog I bought Simon for his birthday isn't a dog at all. It's a bitch and she's just had puppies. I've found homes for two of them, but I'm left with the runt. Will you take it? If I don't find a suitable home for it soon, I'll have to have it put down.' She pulled out into the main stream of traffic, heading towards the Parisian Grill where they were meeting Tom for lunch. 'It's a sweet little dog, but a little ... indeterminate. The mother is a golden cocker spaniel and the pups seem to have inherited mainly spaniel characteristics. Will you take it?'

'Of course I will,' Elizabeth said, smiling across at her. 'Does it have a name?'

'No. The christening can be your privilege, but try to be a little more imaginative than my son. He calls ours "Boy", and every time Tom calls the dog the houseboy scurries into the room to ask him what he wants!'

Tom Nicholson was already sitting at a table, sipping a Scotch and soda, when they arrived. He looked up at them appreciatively as they entered. They were both tall girls. Elizabeth slender and graceful in a white linen suit and open-necked scarlet silk blouse, her wheat-gold hair swept into a glossy knot. Helena magnificently Junoesque and brimming with health and good humour.

He was excessively fond of his sister-in-law. He knew Alastair Munroe wanted to marry her and he wished that she would encourage him. Alan was dead, and she had to build a new life for herself and the children. She didn't possess Elizabeth's head-turning beauty or Julienne Ledsham's flirtatious femininity, and it wasn't every man who would want to take on the responsibility of two small children. If she didn't encourage Munroe, there might be a long wait before another suitor appeared on the scene, and that would be a pity. His nephew and niece needed a father, and Alastair Munroe would fit the bill admirably.

'Were you successful in your hunt for a piano?' he asked as they sat down.

'No, Lane Crawfords say it will take at least six weeks to ship one in, and so I've arranged for Elizabeth to borrow yours,' Helena said with her usual directness. 'I've also arranged that she will take the last pup off our hands.' She turned to the waiter hovering at her side. 'A large ice-cold gin and tonic, please,' she said, pleased with her morning's work. 'I've also got some more news. I've decided that I've presumed on your hospitality long enough, Tom. There's no sense in returning to England with the children until we know what that nasty man, Hitler, is going to do. And we can't possibly stay with you *ad infinitum*. So I've been to Hobson's and arranged to take a three-bedroom garden flat in Kowloon. I'm moving there tomorrow.'

'But there's absolutely no need!' Tom said explosively. 'Good God! You can stay with me for as long as I'm posted here, and that could be years!'

'No, I can't,' Helena said with unusual gentleness. 'I'm on my own now, Tom, and I have to learn to live on my own.'

Beneath the gentleness her voice was firm, and he knew that it was useless to argue. Also, he had a sneaking suspicion that she was right. Her own flat in Kowloon would be far better for her than continuing to live with him. It would give her greater freedom in her personal life. If she wished Alastair Munroe to stay the night with her, then it would be easy for him to do so and no embarrassment to anyone would be caused.

'OK,' he said with a broad grin. 'I give in. When's the house-warming party?'

All through lunch he was aware of male heads turning in their direction and knew that it was Elizabeth who was attracting them. He now knew why Adam Harland always looked so pleased with himself. It was a highly pleasant sensation being the envy of every man in the room. 'When are you going to take a trip into the New Territories?' he asked her as they were served with *filet mignon lili*. 'That's where you'll see the real China. The unspoilt China.'

'Soon, I hope.' The low husky note in her voice sent a flare of heat through his groin. On board the *Orient Princess* he had intended, if she were

187

willing, to have an affair with her. It had taken him very little time to realize that extramarital affairs were not part of her lifestyle, and in a way he didn't regret it. His personal life was complicated enough as it was, and he had begun to value her friendship too much to squander it on an affair that could have no long-term happy outcome.

'Adam *had* planned that we would drive up there this weekend,' she said, a smile touching the full generous curves of her mouth, 'but Ronnie is adamant that we attend the race meeting at Happy Valley. His horse is running, and he has a new jockey and he is convinced he is going to win. He has the celebration party all arranged!'

'He's an eternal optimist,' Tom said with a grin, wondering if Ronnie had propositioned her yet. A refusal would be unlikely to offend in that quarter, although it was something he suspected that Ronnie didn't experience very often. Not for the first time he wondered how a marriage that seemed founded on mutual light-hearted adultery could thrive as happily as the Ledsham marriage apparently did. 'But, if you're not going to the New Territories this weekend, perhaps I could join you when you do go? The country is pretty wild up there, and for anyone who isn't familiar with it it's best to have a guide.'

'My goodness, yes,' Helena said feelingly. 'There are still leopards on the prowl up there, and anteaters and cobras, and a score of other hideous things. The children think it's wonderful, but it scares me half to death. Take my word for it, Happy Valley, and even Ronnie, are much safer!'

Elizabeth had laughed, determining that if the New Territories were as full of dangers as Helena had indicated, then she would be only too glad to postpone the trip until Tom could accompany them. Adam hadn't been in agreement with her. 'There are two well-made roads running from Kowloon to the border. Whichever one we take, we'll be safe enough as long as we don't leave it.'

'What about Ronnie's party?'

'There'll be another party next week, and another one the week after that. A trip north will be far more interesting than seeing Ronnie's horse trail in third or fourth or last. We can accept Tom's offer to act as a guide another time. When we want to explore off the beaten track.'

They had set off early Saturday morning, driving out through Kowloon and taking the Taipo road towards Fanling and the Chinese border. As soon as they left the crowded garish streets of Kowloon behind them, Elizabeth was aware of being in a remote and distant country in a way she had never been while on Hong Kong Island. There was no trace of westernization. The countryside was bleak and barren, rising on either side into inhospitable mountains clothed with forests of fir. There was little cultivation, the villages they passed through were poor and sparsely populated with a few rice-fields surrounding them and very little else. As they drove by black pyjama-clad villagers paused from their tasks to watch them, large circular coolie-hats shielding their heads from the sun, their feet bare and caked with dirt.

'It doesn't look very prosperous, does it?' Adam said, shocked at the difference in living standards between the Chinese working the fields and those living in Kowloon and Victoria.

'There must be *some* prosperous farms,' Elizabeth said, remembering Julienne's reference to Raefe Elliot having banished his wife to a farm in the New Territories.

'If there are, I haven't seen any.' A frown furrowed his brow. 'Have you seen that old woman bent double working that rice-field? She must be a hundred if she's a day!'

They crossed the Shin Mun River, the water eddying in muddy swirls towards the sea. 'Is that a sparrow-hawk?' Elizabeth asked, pointing to a bird of prey hovering over the far bank in the still, hot air.

Adam squinted his eyes against the sun. 'Could be. Leigh Stafford told me that this place was a heaven on earth for birdwatchers. There are cockatoos, mynah birds, pelicans, the lot.'

At the small town of Sha Tin they stopped to pay their respects at the Buddhist monastery. Hand in hand, they walked up the hundreds of stone steps that led to the Man Fat Temple, reaching with relief the temple's veranda and shaded courtyard. Hundreds of small gilt statues of Buddha lined the wall, standing in niches and in crevices, a handful of Chinese meditating solemnly before them. On the far side of the courtyard rose a nine-storey pagoda, its walls a delicate shell-pink, its oriental up-turned roofs a rich coral red.

'Missy climb. Missy see wonderful view,' an ancient Chinese woman said, beaming toothlessly at them.

Adam groaned. 'Not more steps!'

'I'm afraid so,' Elizabeth said relentlessly. 'Come on, the view will be worth it.'

Breathing heavily, they climbed the cool circular stone steps that led to the top of the pagoda and emerged, gasping, into the sunlight.

It was like looking out over a painted landscape. Far to the north were the rolling forest-covered hills of China; to the west was the sea and Tolo Harbour and a flurry of junks, their square sails looking like a cloud of great brown and golden butterflies as they skimmed the silky blue water; and to the south lay the Kowloon Peninsula and Hong Kong Island and the soaring peaks of Mount Victoria and Mount Butler and Mount Nicholson.

'Oh, wonderful!' Elizabeth breathed rapturously, leaning her arms on the edge of the parapet and gazing down at the panorama spread before her. Down at the foot of the hill she could see their Riley, looking like a small black beetle, and a hundred yards or so away, half-hidden by a clump of pine trees, another European car indicating that they were not the only tourists exploring the pagoda and temple. As she looked down at the squares and courtyards and the black-clad Chinese that had come to worship, she saw a tall familiar figure stride out of the temple. She seized Adam's arm. 'It's Tom! Look! Down there!' She was just about to wave and call his name when Adam said suddenly: 'Who is that with him?'

Her waving hand faltered.

A small delicate figure was walking with tiny hurried steps at his side. Her hair was black and sleek, coiled heavily at the nape of her neck; her cheong-sam was richly embroidered, the slits at the side only modestly high. And her hand was very firmly in Tom's.

'Is it a girl from one of the nightclubs, do you think?' Elizabeth asked bewilderedly.

Adam shook his head. 'I don't think so. She doesn't look like a bar-girl. Even from this distance, she looks very respectable and demure.'

The two figures were beginning to walk down the hundreds of stone steps that led to their car. As they did so, Tom's arm slid round the girl's waist and they could hear the distant sound of her laughter as Tom stood still, turning her round to face him, drawing her close.

'That's no casual date,' Adam said decisively as they kissed. 'They're in love. Who the devil can she be?'

'I've no idea,' Elizabeth said wonderingly, watching as the two embracing figures finally drew apart and continued to walk, hand in hand, down the remaining steps. 'He's never mentioned her to me but, then, he wouldn't, would he?'

'Why the devil not?' Adam asked as they turned away from the parapet and began to make their way back down the stairs.

'Remember our first dinner at Tom's? Remember the remarks Sir Denholm made about Raefe Elliot and his Chinese girlfriend? Chinese girls

192

are regarded as perfectly all right in the bars and nightclubs of Wanchai, but they are most definitely *not* regarded as all right in European clubs and at European dinner tables. Poor Tom. I wonder how long it has been going on.'

Adam shrugged. The girl had looked beautiful and well bred. It seemed a nonsense that Nicholson had to keep his liaison with her a secret. 'Goodness knows, but I shall have a word with him when I see him again. I don't want him to think that we would disapprove. Life's too short for prejudices of that kind.'

She squeezed his hand tightly. 'I do love you, Adam. You're the *kindest* man I've ever met in my life.'

He grinned. 'I hope I'm a lot more than just kind!' he said, pulling her close against him as they ran down the remaining steps.

They continued their journey up as far as Fanling, returning to Kowloon on the Castle Peak Road, past ancient Chinese fishponds and duckponds and the medieval walled village of Kat Hing Wai. It was early evening by the time they crossed to Victoria on the ferry.

'Do you still want to catch up with Ronnie's party at the Jockey Club?' Adam asked as they docked.

She shook her head. 'No, I don't think so. We're seeing Ronnie and Julienne and Helena and Alastair for lunch tomorrow at the Repulse Bay Hotel. Let's have an early night tonight. I'm tired.'

That night in bed she tried to overcome her tiredness and imagine that she was Julienne or

193

Helena. It was no use. Adam's hands on her body were warm and familiar and even pleasant, but they did not inflame her or fill her with passion. She responded to him as she always responded to him, lovingly and patiently, holding him tight in her arms, wondering what it was that was wrong with her and how she could possibly put it right.

As they lay together afterwards, she rested her head against his chest and said tentatively: 'I'm sorry if I'm not very sensuous in bed, darling. Do you mind very much?'

His arms tightened round her. 'What a silly thing to say,' he said gently. 'I don't want you to be any different. I love you just as you are; I always have done.'

She twisted on to her elbow, her pale blonde hair tumbling around her shoulders as she said with sudden vehemence: 'But I don't *want* to be as I am! I feel such a failure!'

He laughed indulgently, pulling her down once again beside him. 'You're not a failure, darling. Sex isn't a competition. You make me very happy. Now, go to sleep and stop worrying about something that isn't important.'

Sunday lunch at the Repulse Bay Hotel was becoming a regular fixture for them. The hotel lay on the south side of the island, long and white and low, overlooking the most beautiful of Hong Kong's bays. The sand stretched in a perfect crescent of silver, lapped by gently creaming waves and backed by lush green mountains.

The Ledshams were already sitting on the veranda when they arrived, Ronnie resplendent

194

in white ducks and an open-necked white shirt, his blond hair slicked and gleaming, his grin triumphant. 'You missed a sensational day yesterday,' he said gleefully as they sat down. 'My horse romped home. Julienne lost a fortune because she didn't believe me when I told her it would win and the silly girl put all her money on an old wreck that barely tottered from the starting gate!'

Julienne said something extremely rude beneath her breath, and he leaned across to her, kissing her beneath her ear. 'I *told* you it would win, darling. Why, oh, why do you never trust me?'

Julienne began to giggle. 'Because you are utterly untrustworthy, *chéri*, and utterly adorable.' She gave him a kiss on his nose as Helena and Tom and Alastair strolled out to join them.

'What's this?' Tom asked teasingly as he sat down. 'I thought you two wouldn't be on speaking terms after yesterday.'

'I have a forgiving nature,' Julienne said impishly as he leaned over and kissed her on the cheek. 'Besides, I want to make quite sure Ronnie tells me when his horse is going to run again. I lost a *fortune* yesterday!'

'Old Denholm's got a new jockey,' Alastair said as the waiter served them with ice-cold Martinis. 'Swears he can outstrip yours any day of the week. He's entering him for the race next week.'

A friendly quarrel began to develop as to whether Ronnie's win had been occasioned by his new jockey or was nothing more than a freak stroke of good fortune.

'It was the jockey, blast you!' Ronnie was saying indignantly for the umpteenth time when they became aware that the tables around them had fallen suddenly quiet.

Elizabeth looked up and saw that Raefe Elliot was walking through the lounge towards the veranda, a diminutive Malay girl at his side.

'*Tiens!*' Julienne said admiringly. 'How *dare* he when he knows his father-in-law lunches here?'

Several other people were obviously thinking the same thing, their heads turning round to see if Colonel Langdon was present and, if so, what his reaction to his son-in-law and his companion would be. They were disappointed. The corner table normally patronized by Colonel Langdon was empty. Elizabeth, unable to help herself, watched in mesmerized fascination as he neared their table, certain that it was a matter of supreme indifference to him whether his father-in-law was there or not.

'Hello, Tom,' he said, and his dark rich voice sent a tingle down her spine. His lean, hard muscled body was taller and broader than she had remembered, and she forced her eyes away from him and down into her glass, furious at the response he aroused in her.

'Hello, Mrs Harland.' The amusement in his voice was blatant. 'Be careful with your drink. Martini stains far more lethally than lemonade!'

She was aware of Julienne looking at her with raised eyebrows and Adam looking at her in surprise.

196

She lifted her head, her eyes meeting his. 'Then be careful what you say, Mr Elliot,' she said coolly, and was aware of Adam's surprise deepening into incomprehension.

Raefe Elliot grinned down at her, his eyes bold and black and frankly appraising. 'Allow me to introduce my companion. Alute, Mrs Adam Harland.'

Elizabeth rose and shook the Malay girl's hand, seeing with relief that she had no need to feel sorry for her. The almond slanted eyes were full of confidence. If Raefe Elliot was behaving badly, his companion was happily uncaring.

He introduced her to Julienne and Helena and Ronnie and Tom, and Tom said easily, 'I don't believe you've met Adam Harland yet, Raefe,' and performed the introductions while Ronnie eyed Alute with open lasciviousness and Julienne tried desperately to catch Elizabeth's eye.

'Did you watch my horse run on Saturday?' Ronnie asked him. Elliot was an expert on horseflesh, and it was nice to be able to let him know that he, too, knew a thing or two about it. 'Won by a mile.'

'Congratulations,' Raefe said, his eyes no longer on him but on Elizabeth again.

'I owe you a fuller apology than the one I made earlier,' he said, and she was aware of the blue sheen on his hair and the disturbing sensuality of his finely chiselled, well-shaped mouth. 'Perhaps we could have lunch together so that I can make amends?'

Elizabeth heard Alastair Munroe's quick intake of breath and knew that they were being looked at with shocked eyes.

'I don't think so,' she said with an indifference she was far from feeling. 'Goodbye, Mr Elliot.'

The snub was obvious. A smile tugged at the corner of his mouth, and the broad shoulders shrugged philosophically beneath the linen of his well-cut jacket. 'Goodbye, Mrs Harland,' he said and, nodding in Tom and Ronnie's direction, he slid his arm around his girlfriend's waist and strolled off with her towards a corner table.

'My God! The bloody nerve!' Alastair Munroe said incredulously. 'What the hell will happen if Langdon walks in here?'

No one answered him. Adam said, an odd note in his voice: 'I didn't know you'd met him before, Beth. What on earth was he talking about? Why the devil does he owe you an apology?'

A faint flush touched Elizabeth's cheeks. 'It's nothing. There was an accident at the club. My glass fell and sprayed him with lemonade, that's all.'

Julienne's eyes sparkled. So, the day she had wanted to stay on at the club and speak to Raefe, Elizabeth had already been speaking to him. So effectively that Raefe Elliot had suggested they lunch together, *and* he had asked in front of Adam. It was all *most* intriguing.

'Even Elliot can't expect to get away with squiring a coloured round so openly,' Ronnie Ledsham said, unwilling admiration in his voice. 'Not in locales that Melissa frequents as well.'

Tom Nicholson's face had hardened at Ronnie Ledsham's words, and his sister-in-law said hurriedly: 'Melissa hasn't been seen anywhere since the end of the trial.'

'That's because Raefe is keeping her a prisoner,' Julienne said with relish. 'Ronnie overheard Colonel Langdon fuming about it to Sir Denholm. Apparently Melissa is on one of the Elliot farms in the New Territories, but Colonel Langdon doesn't know where and has had no contact with her since the trial ended.'

'He'll need to be keeping her a prisoner if he's going to continue squiring his Malay girlfriend around so openly,' Ronnie said drily. 'Melissa Langdon's temper is nearly as vicious as Raefe's. We could all be witnessing another murder trial before too long.'

'I'm going for a walk,' Tom Nicholson said, rising abruptly to his feet.

Elizabeth hesitated for a moment and then said: 'Would you mind if I came with you, Tom? I've never been out into the gardens at the rear of the hotel. Helena tells me they're gorgeous.'

She rose to her feet, uncomfortably aware that Raefe Elliot's eyes were still disturbingly on her.

'You didn't mind me asking to come with you, did you?' she asked Tom as they walked from the veranda.

He grinned down at her. 'Heavens, no. Were you suddenly feeling as claustrophobic as I was?'

She gave him an answering smile. 'Yes, the atmosphere was pretty tense, wasn't it? You would think Mr Elliot would have more sense than to dine with his girlfriend in a hotel frequented by his father-in-law.' As soon as she had uttered his name she was furious with herself. Why speak of Raefe Elliot? He wasn't of the remotest interest to her.

They walked out of the lobby and into the gardens. 'You'd think he'd know better than to bring her here, father-in-law or no father-in-law,' Tom agreed drily.

'Because she's Malay?'

He nodded, the lines around his mouth tightening. 'Yes, it's not the done thing. There are plenty of places in Hong Kong where you can take Malay or Chinese girls, but there are some places where you can't. Not without causing talk. And the Repulse Bay Hotel on a Sunday lunch-time is one of them.'

She said carefully: 'Adam and I didn't go to the race yesterday. We drove up to the New Territories instead.'

'Did you enjoy it?' he asked, making an effort at civility, only his eyes revealing that his thoughts were elsewhere.

'We went to Kam Tin.'

He stopped walking. 'Oh,' he said, understanding immediately. 'You saw?'

'Yes. She looked awfully pretty, and you looked to be very much in love.'

He grinned ruefully. 'We are. Her name is Lamoon. Her father is a property baron. If he knew she was in love with a European, he'd have her married to a suitable Chinese within twenty-four hours.'

'Is that why no one knows about the two of you?'

'Helena knows. There are times when I feel she

200

is a little disappointed in me. You know how direct Helena is. She doesn't see why I don't squire Lamoon around openly, as Elliot does his girlfriend.'

'And why don't you?' Elizabeth asked curiously. He wasn't a man she would ever have accused of cowardice, or of caring overmuch what other people thought.

'Because the minute I did, the minute it became known that it was a serious liaison and not just a romp in the hay, my career would be at stake. I would find myself conveniently posted to India or Africa or even Outer Mongolia. And Lamoon would suffer even more. She would be forced into a marriage of her father's choice. At least this way we still see each other. And we can still hope.'

They walked back into the hotel, and Elizabeth was relieved to see that the corner table on the veranda was empty. Raefe Elliot and his Malay girlfriend were presumably disturbing the Sabbath elsewhere.

'What did you think of Raefe Elliot?' Elizabeth asked Adam as they drove back home up the mountain road towards Wong Nie Chung Gap.

Adam shrugged dismissively. 'Not much. An arrogant devil, I should imagine. I thought it was a consummate nerve his asking you to have lunch with him.'

Elizabeth stared reflectively out at a bank of wild blue irises. 'Would you mind very much if I accepted?' she asked at last.

The car swerved slightly. Adam righted it and

looked across at her in stunned amazement.

'Of course I would mind! He's a married man and a notorious womanizer! Your reputation would be in shreds if you were out alone with him!'

She took his arm, immediately repentant. 'I'm sorry, darling. Of course I don't want to have lunch with Raefe Elliot. I can't think why I even contemplated it.'

They sped down the curving road that led towards Happy Valley and the racecourse, and into Victoria. A small smile touched Adam's mouth. 'Perhaps you suggested it because you want me to be jealous?'

Her eyes darkened, and she tightened her hold on his arm. 'No, Adam,' she said fiercely. 'I never want you to be jealous. I shall never do anything that will make you unhappy. Not ever!'

Chapter 8

Alastair Munroe pressed his foot sharply down on the brake of his battered old Austin, swearing volubly. There were times when negotiating a way through Kowloon's crowded streets was next to impossible. Taxi-cab horns blared as a bevy of rickshaw-boys blocked the street. A squawking hen, chased by a small Chinese boy, darted between the temporarily halted cars, a flurry of feathers in its wake. A hawker, his wares dangling from both ends of the bamboo pole that arched across his bony shoulders, took advantage of the lull in the traffic and accosted Alastair through the open window of his car.

'Fresh prawns, fresh mussels. You like?'

Alastair shook his head. 'No, thank you,' he said, averting his eyes from the grimy pails of shellfish.

The hawker persisted, and Alastair shook his head, pressing his palm down on the Austin's horn. Why the devil Helena had moved from the privileged peace and quiet of Victoria Peak to the mayhem of Kowloon was beyond him. The protesting hen was caught. The rickshaw-boys dispersed. Traffic began to move again, and the hawker philosophically trotted off to tout his wares elsewhere.

Alastair took a left turn into Nathan Road. At least the flat was near to a park. It would be easy to take Jeremy there for a game of football. Beneath his trim moustache his mouth tightened. He wanted to do far more for Jeremy than act as if he were merely a benevolent uncle. He wanted to become a father to him, and to Jennifer, and he knew that he would make a damned good father.

He swerved to a halt outside a block of recently constructed flats. There had been rumours that the Royal Scots were to be stationed elsewhere. If it were true, then he wanted an official understanding between himself and Helena before they were separated for months, or even years. Not for the first time he wished that she had been widowed for longer than fourteen months. If she had been, he would have felt able to be far more forceful in his demands that she marry him. As it was, it was only reasonable that she wanted to wait a little longer. She was still grieving for Alan, still in love with him. And he knew she felt that to marry again so soon after his death would be an act of disloyalty.

She had only been in the flat a week, but already it looked like a home. He walked into the large sunlit sitting-room, noting the silver-framed photograph of Alan that held pride of place on a lacquered cabinet. The children ran up to him gleefully.

'Can we go to the park, Uncle Alastair? Can we play football?' Jeremy asked, barrelling into him.

Alastair swung him high on his shoulders, taking Jennifer's podgy little hand and walking with them out into the garden where Helena was busy transferring geraniums from pots into a freshly dug flowerbed. 'Trying to create an English garden?' he asked with a grin.

She smiled up at him. She was wearing a halter top that had seen better days, and a pair of shorts that looked as if they had once been Alan's. There was a smudge of dirt on her cheek, and her hair hung in its usual untidy mess, cascading thickly over her shoulders.

'And why not?' she asked, rising to her feet to greet him, her full heavy breasts straining against the cotton of her halter top, a trowel still in her hand. 'I find the sight of familiar flame-red geraniums distinctly comforting. I only wish primroses and violets would flourish here as well.'

He didn't kiss her, although he wanted to. She had, very early in their relationship, insisted that no sign of physical intimacy be demonstrated between them in front of the children, in case it disturbed them. He had respected her fears but was becoming increasingly frustrated by them. His mouth twisted ironically. He knew the conclusion Tom had drawn when Helena had announced she was moving into a flat of her own. He had assumed it was because they wanted more privacy in which to conduct their affair. He had been wrong. Although Helena had become his lover with a hunger and abandon he had found unnerving, nothing on earth would have induced her to do so beneath her own roof, where the children would be in earshot and where, by some freak chance, they might not only be overheard, but also seen.

'I want to talk to you,' he said, swinging Jeremy to the ground.

'Oh, can't we go to the park?' Jeremy wailed disappointedly.

Alastair ruffled his blond curls. 'Later, Jeremy. I want to talk to Mummy for a little while.'

At the expression on his face and the determination in his voice, Helena felt her heart sink. Why, oh, why couldn't he be content with things as they were? He was the one who would be hurt by forcing matters to a head; the one who would feel rejected. And there was no need for it. She was happy in his company, he slaked her awful desperate sexual loneliness, but he wasn't a replacement for Alan, and never could be. Now he was going to force her to say so.

'Let's find Jung-lu, children,' she said wearily, 'and ask her to look after you for a little while.'

'Don't want to stay with Jung-lu,' Jennifer pouted, toddling at her side. 'Want to stay with you and Uncle Alastair.'

'Later, poppet.' Helena gave her a kiss on her chubby cheek and handed her over to the amah. 'Look after them for half an hour, Jung-lu. I shall be in the sitting-room with Major Munroe and I don't want to be disturbed.'

She led the way into the sitting-room and lit a Du Maurier, inhaling deeply. 'I know what you're going to say to me, Alastair, and I don't want to hear it. Why can't we continue as we are?'

'Because the battalion may be moved soon and, if it is, I want there to be a formal under-standing between us before I have to leave.'

She looked across at him in affection and despair. He was so punctiliously correct, even now, when he was about to propose marriage. She knew that his reserved demeanour was occasioned by shyness, and it was one of the things she found endearing about him. He was so competent and in command in his professional life, and so vulnerable when it came to his personal life, She said, trying gently to steer the conversation away from themselves and on to a more general topic: 'Why do you suppose the Royal Scots are to be moved? There won't be many troops left for defence if they do go.'

'The general opinion is that we've been here too long and that it's a waste of our time. If war breaks out, it's going to be in Europe, and that's where the action will be. Not here. We've been warned to stand by for a return to England.' He took the cigarette out of her hand and crushed it out in a nearby ashtray. 'I want you to marry me,' he said, a faint touch of colour on his cheeks betraying his inner agitation. 'I know that you think it's too soon for you to make such a decision, but circumstances aren't normal, Helena. I don't want to find myself whisked back to England with no idea when I will see you again. I want to *know* that I will see you again.' He took her hands. 'Please, Helena,' he said gruffly, 'I'm not very good with words, but I love you and I want to look after you.'

A lump rose in her throat, and she felt her eyes begin to sting with tears. He was so good and so honourable, and she hated knowing she was going to hurt him. 'I'm sorry, Alastair,' she said,

207

and her eyes weren't on him but on the silver-framed photograph that stood on the lacquered cabinet. 'It's too soon for me. Please try to understand.'

He swallowed hard. He had been speaking the truth when he had said that words did not come easily to him. He wasn't a man who felt at ease in female company and, although he was thirty-two, there had been very few women before Helena, and none that he had considered marrying. It was Helena's lack of strived-for glamour that had first attracted him. She was so fresh and open, so totally without guile. 'I'm not asking for an early marriage, Helena,' he said stubbornly. 'I know that it would be too soon for you, but I want a commitment from you that we *will* marry some day.' He took a ring box from his pocket and added awkwardly: 'I don't know whether the size is right, but...'

It was a solitaire diamond. The tears fell down her face. It was so typical of him that he should have bought it, striving to please her, and that it was the very worst thing he could have done, for to be able to wear it she would have to remove Alan's ring. She shook her head. 'No,' she said, her voice strangled in her throat. 'I couldn't...'

And then he took her right hand, and said: 'On this hand, my love, just for a little while...'

His understanding shattered her, and she crumpled against him, crying unrestrainedly. He knew that she was crying for Alan. He rocked her against him, and when her tears subsided and he lifted her right hand and slipped the ring on to her fourth finger she allowed him to do so.

'We'll move it to the left hand later,' he said, 'whenever you are ready to do so.'

She gulped and nodded, and wondered for the first time whether she really was a fool for refusing him. 'Let's have a cup of tea,' she said thickly, and went into the kitchen to make it. Strong and sweet, and with milk, just the way he liked it.

Julienne arched her spine, her spicy red hair curling damply around her face, her eyes closed, her lips parted as she cried out with pleasure.

Derry Langdon lay naked beneath her, his large strong hands on the pale flesh of her buttocks. She was straddling his face, the glossy mat of her pubic hair skimming his nose and mouth as her hips moved with increasing speed. His mouth was open, hungry for her sweet juices, for that tiny pearl embedded in the velvety soft flesh. She moved faster, her eyes tight shut, her pretty, feline face contorted with pleasure. His fingers gouged into her buttocks, pulling her down, down, down on to his lips, his searching tongue, his nibbling teeth.

'Bon dieu! D'un bon dieu!' Julienne shrieked ecstatically as his rough hot tongue lapped her clitoris, his lips sucking, his tongue probing. Her hips gyrated frenziedly as she slipped and slithered over his sweat-soaked face and then, with a scream, she arched backwards, her orgasm stabbing victoriously through her.

His hand slid up to her hips and he twisted her beneath him frenziedly, his hard pulsating cock ramming deep within her throbbing moistness, his sperm shooting from him as he gave a long harsh cry of release.

'That was good, *n'est ce pas?*' she said, her eyes dancing as she leaned on one elbow, looking down at him.

Derry grunted, unable to speak, his heart slamming against his chest like a sledgehammer, his breathing that of a man who had just sprinted a mile in under four minutes.

Julienne giggled and wound a lock of his hair around her finger. It was not straight and sleek like Ronnie's hair, but crisp and curling and coarse-textured.

'Perhaps you would like to do it again?' she asked, her voice full of suppressed laughter.

He opened one eye and looked up at her. It was the first time they had made love. He didn't know what sexual athleticism her previous lovers had been capable of, but he was not going to try to compete with them. Death from a coronary in bed with another man's wife was not part of his plans for the future.

'You must be joking,' he said expressively, and Julienne gurgled with laughter, sliding down beside him, her head on his chest, her lips against his sweat-damp skin.

After a little while, when his breathing had returned to normal, he said: 'Where does Ronnie think you are?'

Her shoulders lifted against him in an expressive Gallic shrug. 'I don't know. The club ... shopping...'

He slid his arm from beneath her and pushed himself up against the pillows, reaching for the cigarettes and lighter on the bedside table. 'It's some hell of a marriage you two have. Does he never question where you've been or how you've spent your time?'

Julienne sighed. It was always the same. Sooner or later her lovers all became obsessed with curiosity about her marriage. Derry was simply displaying his interest much sooner than most. She kneeled up on the crumpled sheets and faced him, her breasts high and pert, her nipples a rich ruby red, her hands clasped in pagan demureness on her naked lap. 'I do not talk about my marriage with anyone,' she said with a seriousness so out of character that he raised his eyebrows. 'I am very happily married. I love Ronnie. Ronnie loves me. Whatever you and I do is fun, but it does not affect my marriage. Do you understand?'

'Not in a million years,' Derry said truthfully.

A tiny frown puckered her brow, and he reached out for her, drawing her close against him. 'OK, sweetheart. If that's the way you want it, that's the way it will be. No talk of Ronnie. Who the devil shall we talk about?'

'Melissa,' Julienne said promptly. 'Do you know yet where she is? Is Raefe really keeping her a prisoner and, if he is, why are you not doing something about it?'

This time it was Derry's turn to frown. Melissa was his sister, and he hated the trial and the sordidness that had been publicly revealed, almost as much as his father had done.

'Melissa is OK,' he said abruptly. 'She found the trial an ordeal, and who can blame her? She

211

doesn't feel strong enough to face people yet, not after some of the accusations Raefe's defence counsel threw at her.'

Julienne ran the tip of her finger down his sternum and on to the smooth hard flatness of his belly. 'You mean he isn't keeping her in the New Territories against her will?' she asked disappointedly.

'No.' Her fingers were feather-light in his pubic hair, and he felt his heavy flaccid sex begin to stir.

'That is a pity,' Julienne said regretfully, cupping his testicles in the palm of her hand, enjoying the feel of the weight of them, watching with satisfaction as his splendid cock began once more to stir and swell.

He closed his eyes. It was impossible that she could arouse him again and so soon but, all the same, it was pleasant to lie back and allow her to try. He had no intention of giving her any information about Melissa. Melissa would have to survive her own hell herself. He certainly wasn't going to cross swords with Raefe Elliot and demand that he bring her back to the Elliot home on Victoria Peak.

Julienne twisted on to her knees, not removing her hand from beneath the delicious weight of his scrotum. 'Did you know that there were rumours that the Royal Scots are going to leave the island?'

He didn't know and he didn't really care. He was a businessman, not a soldier. She was running the tip of her tongue lightly around the head of his cock, blowing softly on it, her hand firm

212

and warm on the shaft. 'How do you know?' he asked, his eyes closed, his voice strangled in his throat.

Julienne paused in her ministrations, looking down at his cock with satisfaction as it pulsed and hardened. 'A friend told me,' she said, and wondered whether she should terminate her affair with her Royal Scots major. To continue spending time with both him and with Derry might prove difficult, even for her. She sighed. Derry was really a most promising lover. It seemed as if her connections with the Royal Scots would have to be severed.

'Adam Harland thinks it will be a great mistake if they do go. He thinks the Japanese will attack us and that we should have more regiments stationed here, not less.'

'Then, he's a bloody fool,' Derry said thickly. 'Don't stop what you're doing, for God's sake!'

She bent her head again, her tongue running like a river of fire from the base of his penis to the tip, whorling around the blood-engorged head, her hand moving with slow and rhythmic expertise.

'Is Harland the middle-aged Englishman Stafford's been complaining about? One of the Semco directors out here for some kind of sabbatical?'

Julienne nodded, gracefully straddling him, one knee on either side of his tensed thighs, smiling to herself as she saw how his penis was straining upwards towards the tight glossy curls of her pubic hair, the moist hot lips of her waiting vagina.

213

'His wife is very young and very beautiful and very...' She paused, thinking of Elizabeth's curious untouched quality. 'Very inexperienced, I think.'

Derry was uncaring of Adam Harland's wife. 'By God, *you're* not!' he panted harshly as with her fingers she parted the dense mat of her pubic hair and opened the lips of her throbbing vagina.

'Now, *chéri*,' she whispered hoarsely, gently pulling his penis back from his stomach until it was pointing straight up in the air, still not plunging it into her hot moist depths. 'Let me show you how the second time can be almost as good as the first!' And as he moaned for her to hurry she slowly lowered herself on to the swollen tip, shuddering in ecstasy as the soft pillar of her flesh slid down on him and she was filled to the rim with his hardness and thrusting strength.

'Oh, that's good, *chéri*!' she whispered as his hands grasped hold of her hips, and she moved on top of him in voluptuous pleasure. *'C'est magnifique!'*

Tom Nicholson and Lamoon were laid on cushions on the floor of the Harland's summerhouse. Elizabeth had been prompt in inviting them to dinner, and many more dinners and suppers had followed. She had also kept her word about not gossiping about their affair. No one else knew of it, apart from Helena. Not even Alastair or Julienne.

'We can't go on like this, Lamoon,' Tom said fiercely. 'I have to speak to your father.'

'No!' Her dark eyes were enormous in the pale gold of her face. 'That would be the end of everything, Tom. He would send me away or marry me to a suitable Chinese. He mustn't know! Not ever!'

'He can't marry you off without your consent!' Tom said savagely, springing to his feet and pacing the wooden floor. 'It's 1939, for Christ's sake! Not the Middle Ages!'

'It is still the Middle Ages for Chinese girls of good family,' Lamoon said sadly.

He swore, knowing that she was right, knowing that nothing on earth would persuade her father to allow her to marry an Englishman.

She rose to her feet, walking with infinite grace towards him, her long black hair hanging sleekly down her back. 'Don't feel so violently about it, Tom,' she said gently, slipping her arm through his. 'It is the way things are, and we must learn to accept it.'

He pulled her into his arms with a groan. He loved her, but there were times when her Chinese placidity nearly drove him mad. 'How can you be so accepting of prejudices that are so crass?' he asked despairingly.

He was a foot taller than she was, and she stood on tip-toe, kissing the corner of his mouth. 'Because there is nothing we can do, Tom. We both know the rules and, whether we agree with them or not, we have to abide by them.'

'Damn the rules!' he said vehemently. 'Not everyone respects them! Raefe Elliot doesn't, and the world hasn't caved in around his shoulders!'

'Of course it hasn't,' Lamoon said with amusement. 'Raefe Elliot is a man. And the Chinese girls who are his friends are not upper-class respectable Chinese girls. He is not intent on marrying one of them.'

'If he wanted to, he would,' Tom said darkly.

Lamoon giggled. She thought perhaps Tom was right. But Raefe Elliot wasn't Tom, and she wasn't a Wanchai bar-girl. For girls like her, mixed marriages were out – there were no exceptions, no alibis, no discussions. As a businessman, her father conducted himself in a manner that his European customers regarded as enlighteningly westernized. In his home, western mores had no place. He was a rigid disciplinarian, as all Chinese husbands and fathers of his class were. If he once knew or suspected that his daughter was consorting with an Englishman, then Lamoon knew she would never see Hong Kong or Tom again.

'We must be grateful for what we have,' she said practically, her slender body pressed close against the long hard strength of him. 'If it wasn't for the nursing classes, we wouldn't be able to meet at all.'

'I am grateful,' he said huskily, bending his lips to the soft sheen of her hair. 'But one afternoon and one evening a week aren't enough.'

The war being waged on China by Japan had been to their advantage. When Lamoon had asked her father if she could attend nursing classes at one of the local hospitals, he had reluctantly agreed. It was an activity that did not lower the family status, and it would be as well for her to be useful if international affairs deteriorated.

Lamoon had enjoyed the classes immensely, but she no longer went to them. Instead she met Tom. At first, the difficulties had seemed insurmountable. They couldn't go for drinks at one of the many clubs that Tom's friends went to with their girls. They couldn't dance at the Peninsula, or hold hands across a candlelit table at the Parisian Grill. If they did so, they would be seen. The Chinese grapevine would hum into life, and her father would know of her activities within hours, possibly even minutes.

Instead of going to any of the normal venues, they had driven out into the New Territories, avoiding the more frequented roads, walking hand in hand along little-used tracks. It was on one such excursion that Adam and Elizabeth had seen them, and now they had somewhere else to meet.

This summerhouse was tucked away at the bottom of the sprawling garden, out of sight of the main house. Gradually, as their visits to the Harlands had become more frequent, it had become accepted that the summerhouse was their meeting-place, and inviolate. On a Thursday afternoon, when it was her nursing-class day, and if Elizabeth and Adam were out together, or with friends, the houseboy would open the door to them and they would walk through the house and out into the garden and down to the summerhouse.

'I don't understand why you will come here, but refuse to come anywhere near *my* house,' Tom had said in the beginning, bemused. 'It's only fifteen minutes away.'

'Because if anything terrible happened, and it was discovered we were meeting, my father would not lose as much face if it was discovered we were meeting in the home of a respectable married couple as he would if it became known that I had visited you in your home, alone.'

Tom was too well aware of how important face was to a Chinese to argue the point with her. Their afternoon meetings had continued, and the little summerhouse had become the centre of their world.

He lifted her up in his arms and turned back with her towards the cushions. They had met at a party for influential Chinese businessmen and their European counterparts at Government House. Her mother had been ill, and she had taken her mother's place at her father's side. He had never in his life seen a girl so beautiful. Her hair had shone like burnished jet, her dark almond-tilted eyes had flickered once in his direction and had then been demurely cast downwards, but he had seen the suspicion of a smile at the corner of her mouth, and he had known that she was as attracted to him as he to her.

He had known, right from the beginning, that to try to date her was crass and impossible. Chinese girls of her social background did not make assignations with *anyone* without their father's permission and certainly not Europeans. But he had persisted. He had driven out to her family's mansion at Shan Teng and had waited until he had seen her being driven from the grounds in a chauffeured Rolls. The Rolls had taken her to an exclusive hairdressing salon in Victoria. When she came out of the salon an hour later, he had been waiting for her on the pavement and, to his indescribable relief, she had agreed to meet him. That had been the first of her skipped nursing classes.

The following months had been the most tortured he had ever known. She had come to meet him willingly, her mouth parting shyly beneath his when they had kissed, but he had known that he couldn't make love to her with the same selfish lack of thought as he might have done to a European girl. If she became pregnant, there could be no hasty marriage to make matters right. She was running risks enough in merely meeting him. He couldn't ask her to run even greater ones. Ones that would destroy her life.

He wasn't accustomed to celibacy, especially when it was coupled with such raging physical longing. At first, he had been unable to sustain it. He had had a brief and not altogether unsatisfactory affair with Julienne, and there had been occasional forays into the bars and nightclubs of Wanchai. He had soon stopped such expeditions. The bar-girls with their long black hair and pale gold skin had been cruel reminders of Lamoon, so like her and yet so many light-years different from her.

At the beginning of the year, when he had left Hong Kong for a business trip to England, he had been relieved at their separation. It would enable him to think clearly, perhaps to find the strength of mind to end their affair once and for all. When he had seen Elizabeth Harland aboard the *Orient Princess*, he had been filled with hope. If any woman could banish Lamoon from his thoughts, surely the ethereally beautiful Elizabeth Harland could do so. But she had not been another Julienne, sexually indiscriminate and looking for fun outside her marriage. In the end, he had never even propositioned her. He had known that such a venture would end in failure and, by then, he had known that it was too late. That no woman, not even Elizabeth, could replace Lamoon in his heart.

'We *have* to be able to marry!' he said fiercely as he laid her down on the cushions. Christ! He had been in love with her for eight months, and for the last four months he had been totally celibate. It wasn't a situation that could possibly continue. She lay very still, her hair spreading around her shoulders like a pool of black ink. 'We cannot marry,' she said softly, her eyes holding his, the expression in them one he had never seen before. 'But we can be husband and wife to each other...'

His breath was coming short and quick, his heart slamming against his breastbone. 'No,' he rasped. 'There are too many risks for you.'

She slid her arms around his neck. There were too many risks for her if he did not make love to her. He was a handsome healthy thirty-five-year-old man, unaccustomed to celibacy. If he did not make love to her, the risks were that he would turn elsewhere for lovemaking. To the pretty, sensuous Mrs Ledsham, or to the bar-girls of Wanchai. And she wanted him to make love to her. She wanted to feel his strong hard body naked against hers. She wanted to take what happiness she could before their affair was discovered, and before her father sent her far away.

'I love you,' she whispered, and as she spoke she was unbuttoning her cheong-sam, her fingers trembling, but her eyes utterly sure as she stepped gracefully free of it.

He was a man of iron self-control, but that control had been exercised to the full for the best part of a year. He hesitated for one brief agonizing second and then, with a groan, he, too, began to scramble out of his clothes. Restraint was gone, and in its place a burning, savage hunger, demanding to be slaked.

'I love you ... love you...' he gasped hoarsely as he flung his trousers and shirt on top of her discarded cheong-sam.

He had always imagined that when they finally made love it would be with the utmost tenderness. She was a virgin; she would need time, gentleness. Never in his wildest dreams had he imagined it would be like this. A voracious scramble to free themselves of their clothes, an animal-like eagerness to transcend the bounds he had previously placed on them. She kneeled in front of him, her breasts pale and beautiful, the dark centres erect and taut. He cupped them in his hands, glorying in her beauty, bending his head to them, kissing, sucking, nibbling.

'Quickly,' she panted, her eyes urgent, her pupils dilated. 'Quickly!'

He pressed her backwards, his hand going to the small restraining panties she still wore. His

221

palm closed over her mount of Venus and she moaned, digging her nails into the flesh of his back. She was smooth and hairless, soft as a dormouse. He wrenched her panties down to her knees, to her ankles, knowing as she kicked herself free of them that he was going to be all the things he shouldn't be. Quick. Urgent. Brutal.

'Oh God!' he prayed, but it was no use. He had waited too long for her to be able to exercise restraint or tender loving care.

His fingers touched her and she gave a willing cry, the cry of a small wild animal on the verge of copulation. She was hot and moist, as ready for him as he was for her. With a groan that seemed to come from the soles of his feet, he guided his penis to the entrance of her vagina, his mouth bruising and grinding against hers, his tongue plunging deep as he thrust into her dark sweet centre, experiencing a cataclysm of relief that almost robbed him of his senses.

Afterwards, when he could breathe again, when his body had stopped shuddering with pleasure, he became conscious of the wetness of tears on his shoulder. He pushed himself up on to his elbows, looking down at her with horror. 'Lamoon ... sweetheart ... don't! It won't always be like that, I promise!'

Through her tears she began to laugh. 'Oh dear, won't it? And I thought it was so wonderful!'

Relief swamped him. Her tears were not because he had hurt or disappointed her; they were a release of her emotions, and he felt tears sting the back of his own eyes. 'Oh God, I love

222

you,' he said passionately, folding her once more in his arms, lying with her on the scattered cushions, delighting in the feel of her small, delicate, exquisite body next to his.

She turned her head slightly, kissing his shoulder. 'I have to be going,' she said regretfully. 'The class will be at an end in twenty minutes.'

He stifled his disappointment. Chu, her father's chauffeur, would be waiting for her at the front entrance of the hospital. He had to get her down to Victoria and to the rear entrance five minutes before the nursing class ended. Then she would walk through the hospital, emerging from the front entrance as if she had been to class, and no questions would be asked.

He sighed, reaching for his trousers. He knew that Lamoon thought that their becoming lovers was as far as they could take their relationship but, for him, today had been only the beginning. Snatched hours one afternoon and one evening a week were not enough. He had been speaking the truth when he had said that a way would have to be found to enable them to marry. He zipped up his trousers and fastened his belt buckle. Perhaps Raefe Elliot could help him. He knew how the Chinese thought. He would know the best way to approach Lamoon's father. He held out his hand to help her stand. He would see Elliot at the earliest opportunity. Lamoon might have accepted that they could never marry, but he would never do so. Not while he had breath in his body.

Ronnie Ledsham sat in the Peninsula Hotel's

Playpen Restaurant and watched the doors, a small smile crooking the corner of his mouth. Elizabeth Harland would get the surprise of her life when she asked for Julienne's table and found only him waiting for her. Julienne would be furious when she found out how he had enticed Elizabeth, but he was accustomed to Julie's fury and it never lasted. Within minutes she would be giggling, and he would, of course, tell her that his ploy had been in vain and that Elizabeth had rejected his advances. In reality, he was determined that she would do no such thing.

He had already had one double whisky and soda and he raised his index finger slightly to summon the waiter and to order another. The Playpen wasn't one of his usual haunts. He found the long narrow room, with its lush red carpeting and potted palms and red-shaded table lamps, far too colonial and prim and proper, but it was a rendezvous that would arouse no suspicions in Elizabeth's mind, and it had one mitigating factor in its favour: its windows afforded splendid views, looking out over the harbour and the cloud-wreathed majesty of Victoria Peak.

He glanced at his watch. She was five minutes late. He had thought women only kept men waiting, not their women friends. He wondered if he had been too confident in thinking that his wheeze would work. It would have been normal for Julie to have rung Elizabeth and have asked her to lunch, not to send a note. His smile deepened. He had been proud of that note. He had long ago perfected an imitation of Julie's hasty scrawl and he thought that he was now beginning

224

also to capture the flavour of her breathless messages. 'Darling Elizabeth,' he had written, 'I saw this dog collar in Lane Crawfords and thought it *perfect* for your little dog and please, please, please do me a favour and meet me for lunch at the Playpen tomorrow at 1 o'clock as I'm in the most *awful* trouble and Ronnie is going to kill me! Please, please, please! Love and kisses, Julienne.'

Elizabeth would be furious, of course, when she was led to his table, but he was confident that she wouldn't walk away. That she would, at least, stay and have lunch with him. It would be the first time that he had been able to arrange matters so that they were on their own. His drink was finished, and he ordered another. It had been a long time since he had been in such determined pursuit. Women were to be enjoyed and not taken too seriously. The last thing he wanted was a heavy-weather love affair. He usually knew, instantly, whether a woman would be trouble-some or not, and if his sixth sense gave out alarm bells, then he left her well alone. He wanted fun, not a divorce or a rift with Julie.

He sipped his whisky and soda thoughtfully. It was hard to tell whether Elizabeth Harland would be trouble or not. There was something about her that teased and tantalized him, some-thing he couldn't quite define. There was a self-contained, untouched quality about her that he found sexually very disturbing. A woman so sensually beautiful had no right to carry with her such an air of unconscious innocence. Not for the first time he found himself wondering what

225

her sex life with Adam Harland was like, his penis swelling hot and hard against the tight line of his trousers. My God, but there were one or two things he'd like to do to her that would take that untouched look from her eyes! He wondered if her pubic hair was as silver-blonde as the hair she always wore so sleekly coiled. Why the devil did she never wear it down, loose around her shoulders? He imagined it sliding through his fingers, brushing across his stomach, his thighs.

The doors at the far end of the room swung open, and she stepped into the room. The *maître d'hôtel* was at her side instantly. He saw her ask for Julienne's table, her eyes flicking around the room in an effort to locate her. He saw the *maître d'hôtel* mouth the words. 'This way, madame,' and begin to lead the way between the white-naperied tables and carver chairs, to where he waited for her. As they approached the *maître d'hôtel's* eyes were expressionless. Ronnie's generous tip had ensured his wholehearted complicity.

Elizabeth's eyes met his, and he saw a pucker of puzzlement crease her forehead. A brilliant turquoise skirt swirled around her long sun-kissed legs; a silk shirt of palest mauve tantalizingly skimmed her breasts; her sandals were high and delicate, tiny gold straps so insubstantial he wondered how on earth she could possibly walk in them.

He rose to meet her, his smile wide. 'I'm glad you could make it, Elizabeth. You look fantastic.'

Her green-gilt eyes were uncertain. 'I'm sorry,

226

I don't understand. Where is Julienne?'

The *maître d'hôtel* was pulling out her chair. Ronnie waited until she was seated, and then, sitting opposite her, said: 'Julienne was called away. She asked me to take her place. Are you familiar with the menu here? The seafood is out of this world.'

Elizabeth wasn't interested in the seafood. She said coldly: 'I don't believe you, Ronnie. You're lying.'

His grin widened. 'Of course I am,' he said with what he hoped was endearing charm. 'I always do.'

She pushed her chair back, about to rise to her feet, and he shot his hand out, circling her wrist restrainingly. 'Don't go, Elizabeth. I want to talk to you. Please stay.'

For once he looked and sounded sincere. She sank back in her chair. Perhaps he really did want to talk to her. Perhaps Julienne really *was* in trouble.

'All right,' she said reluctantly. 'Could I have a Martini, please? With lemon.'

He ordered her drink, ordering himself another whisky and soda. He was beginning to feel pleasantly inebriated, and his words were slightly slurred as he said: 'You really are the most difficult girl to speak to alone, Elizabeth. I had no choice but to resort to subterfuge.'

The waiter was impatient to take their order. 'I'll have the melon and a plain omelette,' Elizabeth said, without looking at the leather-bound menu. She was wrong in thinking that Ronnie wanted to talk to her about Julienne. He was making yet another pass, and the sooner she could decently take her leave of him, the better. 'I'll have the mixed hors-d'œuvres, the beef Wellington, and a bottle of burgundy,' Ronnie said, feeling eminently pleased with himself. As the waiter departed, he took her hands across the table. 'Elizabeth, Elizabeth, *beautiful* Elizabeth, don't look so cross. I only want to spend a little time with you.'

She tried to pull her hands free, but his grasp tightened. She wondered how much he had had to drink.

'We've been through this scene before, Ronnie,' she said with as much patience as she could muster. 'I like you a lot. I think you're amusing and good fun, and I definitely do not want to have an affair with you. Now can we let the subject drop? Otherwise we'll no longer even be friends.'

The wine waiter poured the wine. Ronnie tasted it and signalled him to fill their glasses. 'You have entirely the wrong idea about me,' he said, ignoring his hors-d'œuvres and drinking the wine appreciatively. 'I'm not at all the womanizer I'm made out to be. The fact is' – he imprisoned her hands once more, the slur in his words more pronounced than ever – 'that I'm *terrified* of women. What I need is a woman to be a friend to me, to understand me, to...'

She didn't hear the rest of his sentence. Over his shoulder at a nearby table was a familiar figure. She felt her cheeks flush scarlet as Ronnie continued to grasp her hands tightly and as Raefe Elliot's eyebrow quirked enquiringly.

'Ronnie! For God's sake let go of my hands!' she hissed, aware that it wasn't only Raefe who was casting a curious look in their direction.

Ronnie was reluctant to do so, but the impossibility of both holding her hands and drinking his wine prompted him to acquiesce. He reached out for his glass and accidentally sent it flying. A crimson stain flooded the virgin-white table-cloth, sprinkling her turquoise skirt with ugly dark spots.

Ronnie looked at the damage in bemusement. He was drunker than he had thought. Which was foolish of him when there was so much at stake. Elizabeth was pushing her chair away from the dripping table, a waiter was rushing over to them with a clean cloth, and Raefe Elliot was standing over them both, saying to Elizabeth in lazy amusement: 'Glasses are very unstable things in your vicinity, aren't they, Mrs Harland? Allow me.' And he took a napkin from the table and unceremoniously blotted the stains on her skirt while the waiter stood by superfluously.

'I think this lunch has come to its natural end, don't you?' he said in a matter-of-fact tone and, without waiting for her reply, took her hand, drawing her to her feet.

'Give my good wishes to Julienne,' he said laconically to Ronnie, who was gazing at him in open-mouthed bewilderment. 'Tell her I've escorted her friend home and that no damage has been done.'

'Just a minute... Ronnie protested. 'What the hell...?'

The expression on his face was so comic that

229

Elizabeth found herself laughing.

''Bye, Ronnie,' she said and, feeling as if she were drunk herself, she allowed Raefe Elliot to lead her from the room and out through the Peninsula's marbled lobby and into the street.

Chapter 9

He made no attempt to release his hold of her as they stepped out beneath the *portecochère*. She was aware of the doorman bidding him a respectful goodbye; of a long, low and sleek ice-blue Lagonda sliding to a halt in front of them; of the bellboy who had driven it from its parking-place stepping out and opening the passenger-seat door for her.

She tried to regain control of the situation; to behave with her usual cool dignity.

'Thank you for escorting me from the restaurant,' she began, her voice so shrill and cracked she barely recognized it as her own. 'I'm very grateful, but I have my own car and—'

'I'm sure you have.' There was a quirk of laughter at the corner of his mouth and utter assurance in his eyes. 'But as I couldn't help but notice that you had left your lunch untouched I thought we would rectify matters.'

'I'm sorry, I couldn't...' Her throat was so dry she could hardly speak. Dear God in heaven! If she couldn't sustain a rational five-minute conversation with him, how could she ever hope to survive lunch?

'I insist,' he said and, though his amusement at her resistance was naked, his dark rich voice brooked no argument.

'I have engagements...'

His hand was beneath her arm. He had replaced the bellboy at the door of the car and was standing so close to her that she could smell the faint tang of his lemon-scented Cologne, feel the warmth of his breath on her cheek. She was excruciatingly aware of his lean hard strength, of whipcord muscles beneath his lightweight jacket, of his fingers on the bare flesh of her arm burning like a brand.

'Break them,' he said, and she could see flecks of gold near the pupils of his eyes and a tiny white scar knifing down through his left eyebrow.

Her breath was so tight in her chest that she could hardly breathe. No one, ever before, had held her in quite such a way. There was ownership in his fingers. Utter assurance. She knew she couldn't possibly go with him. Adam would be furious. They would be bound to be seen, and she had told him that she was lunching with Julienne. The complications when she tried to explain to him would be endless. His fingers tightened fractionally on her arm, and she felt a sudden giddy surge of elation. She didn't care. It was only a lunch. She was doing nothing wrong. Nothing she need be ashamed of.

'All right,' she said, sitting down in the passenger-seat, her legs trembling violently. 'I will.'

He grinned down at her, white teeth flashing in his sun-bronzed face. He had never had the slightest intention of allowing her to refuse. He strode round to the other side of the car, opening the driver's door and slamming it behind him.

'Now,' he said, as he punched the engine into life, 'tell me what the hell you were doing having lunch with a womanizer like Ronnie Ledsham?'

Never had she believed it possible for anyone to drive down Nathan Road at such speed. Rickshaws, taxi-cabs, bicycles, hawkers, all were circumnavigated with a skill and dexterity that left her breathless.

'It was unintentional,' she said as they rocketed past Kowloon Park and the road that led to Helena's little flat. 'I thought I was going to meet Julienne.'

He shot her a swift glance, and she looked away from him quickly, disconcerted by the immediate understanding she saw in his eyes. It was as if there was already a bond between them, as if they were already speaking in the verbal shorthand of long-married couples. But not all couples. Adam would not have understood her so completely. He would have been puzzled. He would have asked her what she meant. Why she hadn't met Julienne as she had intended. Why Ronnie had been there in her place.

She said, trying not to think of Adam, hating her feeling of disloyalty: 'Where are we going?'

'To a small restaurant I know near Sham Tseng.'

His hands on the Lagonda's wheel were sure and strong. She wondered what such hands would be like on her naked flesh, and was appalled at her lasciviousness. Panic swamped her. She shouldn't have come. She should have thanked him for extricating her from Ronnie's company and she should have declined his invitation to lunch and driven straight home by herself. She wasn't Julienne, she wasn't accustomed to dealing with a man as fast and sophisticated as Raefe Elliot. A man who kept his own wife a prisoner. A shiver ran down her spine. Who was to say what he would do with her if she was to disappoint him?

'We're nearly there,' he said, and as he shot her a down-slanting smile her panic ebbed. She was behaving like a sixteen-year-old on a first date. Nothing was going to happen to her. She wasn't going to disappoint him, because he wasn't going to ask anything of her. They were going to have lunch together. They were going to exchange the kind of conversation they would have exchanged if they had met at one of the Nicholsons' or one of the Ledshams' parties. And afterwards she would tell Adam and they would laugh about Ronnie's idiocy and its unexpected consequences and she would probably never see Raefe Elliot again, not on his own.

The Lagonda slid to a halt outside a small plain-fronted building, its windows covered by blinds. 'It's all right,' he said as he saw the expression on her face. 'It's not a Triad-run gambling den. It's a very respectable restaurant.'

When they stepped inside she wondered if she were dreaming. Small tables were covered with white damask tablecloths; glasses sparkled; silver gleamed. It was like being in a small restaurant on the Left Bank in Paris, not a Chinese restaurant fifteen miles from the centre of Kowloon.

He ordered dim sum and an ice-cold bottle of Mou Tai, and it was obvious that he was as well known to the head waiter as he was to the head waiter at the Peninsula and at the Repulse Bay.

'It's little known but patronized heavily by those who do know it,' he said as the waiter hurried away with their order.

'And who is it that knows of it?' she asked curiously.

'Government officials, high-ranking civil servants, people who want to get away from the tumult of Victoria and Kowloon for an hour or two.'

She nodded. She could see at a glance that it was both exclusive and expensive. She had asked for a Cinzano, and as she sipped her drink he said: 'Until now, you've never given me a chance to say how sorry I am for hurting your feelings, but I am. However' – his eyes held hers steadily – 'I'm not sorry for what I said. It still stands. If your husband thinks he can come out here and enjoy a skirmish with the Japs that will enable him to return to England a hero, he's badly mistaken.'

She wondered why she felt no anger. She said, returning his gaze unflinchingly: 'My husband was awarded the Military Cross in the Great War. He is already a hero.'

'I never said he wasn't a brave man,' Raefe said placatingly. 'Only that he was ignorant of the situation out here, and that his view is a foolish one.'

The dim sum were wheeled to the side of their table on a trolley. As the steaming bamboo baskets were transferred to their table, she said stubbornly: 'Maybe so, but it's a view that is held by a lot of people who have far more experience of the Orient than Adam. Sir Denholm Gresby is in agreement with him, and Alastair Munroe, and no one could accuse Alastair of being a fool.'

'I could,' said Raefe with annoying equanimity. 'Alastair is a military man, and like most military men he isn't over-blessed with imagination. He's been told by his company commander that the Japanese pose no real threat, and he accepts what he is told. But he's wrong.'

'And Sir Denholm?' she asked, knowing very well what he would think of Sir Denholm.

He snorted in derision. 'Denholm Gresby is a classic example of British obdurateness. He actually believes that the Japanese can't see in the dark and that we need never fear any night attacks from them! He's an old buffer who should be pondering the mistakes his kind made in the last war, not seeking to repeat them if there's another!'

She suppressed a smile. He was almost as vehement about Sir Denholm as Sir Denholm was about him. She said with genuine curiosity: 'Have you lived in Hong Kong all your life?'

'I was born here, but I was educated in the States.'

'And you've never considered returning to America to live and work?'

The grin was back. 'No. Hong Kong is in my blood and in my bones. It's where I'm happy and it's where I belong.'

She suppressed a smile. Ronnie had said that

236

the Elliots were an old New Orleans family and, although Raefe was adamant that Hong Kong was where he belonged, she could quite easily imagine him strolling down the Vieux Carré, his hair curling low in the nape of his neck, as swashbuckling and as handsome as a legendary riverboat gambler. There was a fearlessness about him, a daring, an insolence towards life that both excited and intrigued her. She couldn't imagine him ever compromising, ever settling for less than he wanted. Raefe Elliot wouldn't have abandoned his studies at the Royal Academy to please anyone. Nor would he have left London for Hong Kong if it was in London that his future career was being forged.

His hands reached out across the table and took hers, and at his touch an impulse of sensuality went up inside her like a flare.

'What are you thinking about?' he asked disconcertingly. 'Your eyes are unhappy. I want to know why.'

She said, with an ease that stunned her: 'I was thinking about my music. About how much I long to be back on a concert platform again. How desperately I resent the opportunities I am missing!'

'You're a pianist?' There was surprise in his voice, and then he looked down at her hands. At the long, slender, supple fingers, the short oval-trimmed nails, and he said: 'Tell me about it. Tell me all about yourself. Your dreams. Your wishes. Your fears.'

She made no attempt to free her hands from his. She said: 'For as long as I can remember, I

237

have played the piano. It is so much a part of my life that I cannot imagine existing without it. It is what I am. A pianist. And when I am deprived of the opportunity to develop my talent and to progress, as I am now, then I feel...' She opened her hands expressively. 'Then I feel as if I'm being bodily starved.'

He nodded, and she knew that he did not think she was being histrionic. That he understood. She said: 'I think I was born with the ability to play the piano. My mother was very musical and she taught me from when I was very small. Later, when I was six, I was professionally taught, and once it was explained to me how the lines and dots worked I was able to read music very quickly, and by the time I was seven I could sight-read. I learned so fast once I had started that it was as though it was something I already carried inside me, as though I knew how to play without needing to be taught.'

'What happened?' The dim sum was forgotten. The waiters were watching them with resignation, sensing that it was going to be a long time before they took their leave.

'I won a scholarship to the Royal Academy of Music in London and then, when I was ten, my mother died.'

'And?' he prompted gently.

'And my father needed me to be with him.' There was no resentment in her voice, and he noticed how her eyes softened as she spoke of him.

'He was a gypsy at heart.' An impish smile touched the corners of her mouth. 'Though a

238

luxury-loving gypsy! We spent our time travelling between Paris and Nice, Geneva and Rome. There wasn't much time for piano tuition, although I had a Steinway in our permanent suite at the Negresco.'

'What happened then?' he asked, intrigued, wondering how the hell she had come to be married to Adam Harland.

'Daddy died when I was seventeen. I moved back to London, began to study once more at the Royal Academy, and six months later I married Adam.'

'Where did you meet him? Was he at the Academy, too?' He couldn't imagine it in a million years.

'Oh, no.' Her eyes widened in surprise, as if she were amazed that he hadn't realized she had always known Adam. 'Adam was Daddy's closest friend. I've always known him, ever since I was a little girl.'

So that was it, he thought intrigued. No parties. No boyfriends. Just a bereavement that had left her entirely alone in the world, and a man she had always known as her father's friend and whom it had seemed quite natural to her to marry.

He said: 'When I was at school in the States, my closest friend was Roman Rakowski, the Polish conductor. He was there because his parents were Jewish and admired the American way of education. He was a brilliant musician, even then. Nothing else mattered to him. Not food; not girls; nothing. I learned quite a lot about musicians through my friendship with

Roman. I learned that their duty is first and foremost to their music. Not to parents, lovers or friends.'

'But most parents, lovers and friends cannot understand that,' she said, and the pain in her voice sliced through him. 'Daddy didn't. Adam doesn't.'

'Then, as much as you love them, you must hurt them,' he said, his lean-boned face hard and uncompromising. 'Talent, to survive, has to be exercised.'

A shiver ran down her spine. She knew that what he said was true, and that there was only so much time she could allow Adam and that already she had allowed him too much.

'Tell me about Roman Rakowski,' she said. 'He's in Australia now, isn't he?'

Her hands were trapped once again by his. They were strong hands, olive-toned and well shaped. Hands that gave a feeling of security and safety.

'Yes. As a Jew he found the doors of many of the great European orchestras closed to him. For a time he had been with the Berlin Philharmonic, but Hitler's racist policies made his position there impossible. He was not allowed to play or to conduct, or even to teach. He's in Sydney now, and he's composing and conducting and doing everything in his power to persuade the Australian government to give more assistance to Jews desperate to leave Germany and eastern Europe.'

She looked down at her wristwatch and saw with disbelief that it was nearly four o'clock.

'It's late,' she said, knowing that she must go

240

and that she did not want to. 'I must be going home.'

He didn't argue with her. He would see her again, and when he did she would not have to hurry away from him.

They sat side by side in his car, and it was as if something unspoken had been stated between them, making words unnecessary. 'My car is parked at the Peninsula,' she said as they entered the crowded noisy streets of Kowloon.

He drew to a halt outside the Peninsula Hotel, and she was appalled at the prospect of leaving him. He made no attempt to touch her, to arrange another meeting.

She stepped from the car hardly able to believe that four hours previously she had driven to her luncheon appointment with no sixth sense of the events that were to follow.

'Goodbye,' she said. 'Thank you for the lunch.'

'You didn't eat a mouthful,' he said in amusement, and then Lady Gresby's voice could be heard exclaiming: 'Elizabeth! What a lovely surprise. Is Adam with you?'

'This is where I leave you to your fate,' Raefe said as she bore down on them and, grinning devilishly, he pressed his foot down hard on the accelerator, sweeping out into the maelstrom of late-afternoon traffic.

'Who was that?' Lady Gresby asked curiously, squinting her eyes against the sun, and then, not waiting for Elizabeth to reply: 'For one moment I thought it was that terrible Mr Elliot!'

Elizabeth did not enlighten her. She was suddenly tired and she wanted desperately to find

241

somewhere cool and quiet where she could think. She excused herself from Lady Gresby as quickly as she could and then, instead of returning straight home, she drove right to the top of Victoria Peak and parked her car. Folding her hands on the wheel, she leaned forward on them, staring out over the vista of sea and sky and distant mountain peaks.

It really had been the most extraordinary afternoon. She had been out with the most notorious man in Hong Kong and she had not had so much as a finger laid on her. And she had wanted him to. Oh, yes, if she was honest, she had wanted him to. Despite the heat, she shivered. She was twenty-five and for the first time in her life she had met a man that she wanted to go to bed with. And she couldn't do so, for she was happily married to Adam.

She hugged her arms. He would ask her to meet him again, and she would have to refuse. She wasn't capable of the kind of affairs that Julienne indulged in. Affairs that seemed to have very little effect on her marriage. If she was unfaithful to Adam, the very foundations of her life would crumble. She would never be able to look into his dear kind face again. And, if he ever came to know of it, he would not be able to shrug the knowledge off as Ronnie Ledsham would. He would be devastated – utterly destroyed.

Slowly she leaned back and turned the key in the ignition. Raefe Elliot had revealed to her a side of her nature she had never previously believed existed. As she began to drive back down the Peak towards her home and her husband, she knew that she wasn't grateful to him. That she would far rather have remained in ignorance.

'Did you have a nice day, darling?' He was sitting out in the garden, reading the *Hong Kong Times* and drinking a cold beer.

'Yes.'

He raised his hand towards her, and she gave it a loving squeeze before sitting down on one of the cane chairs next to him.

'How was Julienne? Still miffed at Ronnie?'

'Yes. No. I don't know.'

He put down his paper and looked across at her queryingly. She felt her stomach muscles contract sickeningly. She had never lied to Adam, and there was no need for her to lie now. Her disloyalty to him had not been physical. It had merely been mental. She said, with a quick bright smile: 'I didn't have lunch with Julienne. There was a mix-up over the dates. I'm lunching with her next week.'

'You should have come down to the tennis club. I beat Stafford six-two, six-one in straight sets.'

She smiled, and he waited expectantly. She said: 'I ran into Raefe Elliot at the Peninsula and he insisted on taking me to lunch so that he could apologize over the drinks incident.'

He had been looking at her with unfettered pleasure in his eyes. Now the pleasure died, to be replaced by incomprehension. 'But I thought *you* spilt the drink on *him*? It isn't his position to apologize, surely?'

'Oh, he was quite cross at the time,' she said,

243

trying to sound carelessly indifferent and failing miserably. 'I think it was that he really wanted to apologize for.'

'I see.' His brow was furrowed, and he plainly did not see at all. 'So what did you do? Have lunch with him at the Pen?'

'No.' She didn't turn her head to meet his eyes. Instead, she studiously watched a blue magpie as it darted down through the trees. 'We went to a restaurant out near Sham Tseng. It was very nice, darling. We must go there ourselves some time...'

'Sham Tseng?' he asked incredulously. 'That's miles away!'

'Only about fifteen miles,' she said, her eyes still on the magpie's glossy plumage. 'He dropped me off at the Pen and I saw Miriam and she invited us for drinks on Sunday...'

'Good God! She didn't see you with Elliot, did she?' Adam expostulated, jumping to his feet. 'I *told* you not even to contemplate having lunch with him!' He ran his fingers through his still thick hair, seriously perturbed. 'It will be all over the Club by tomorrow!'

'No, it won't,' she said soothingly, rising to her feet and taking his hand. 'The sun was in her eyes and she didn't recognize Raefe. There won't be any talk and, if there is, why should it matter? I was having a perfectly respectable lunch, just as I often have with Tom...'

'Raefe Elliot isn't Tom Nicholson!' Adam said savagely, disliking the easy familiarity with which she uttered Elliot's christian name. 'Any woman seen out alone with Elliot automatically risks her reputation!'

'I can't imagine why,' she said crisply, letting his hand go and picking up the newspaper and his empty glass. 'He was perfectly charming and he didn't make a pass at me, unlike Ronnie Ledsham who *always* makes a pass! And who you count as your friend!'

'You never told me Ronnie had made a nuisance of himself to you,' he said, his voice dangerously harsh. 'What happened? When? Where?'

They were on the verge of a furious row, and she said, desperate to avert it: 'Oh, goodness, it doesn't matter, darling. Ronnie makes a pass at *everyone*. All I'm trying to say is that we should make up our own mind about people. Not simply believe everything that we hear. I had lunch with Raefe Elliot; he made his apology. He didn't make a pass at me, and I certainly shan't be having lunch with him again. Now, let's go indoors and have a drink and forget all about it.' She tucked her hand into his arm. 'Miriam says the rumours about the Royal Scots being transferred to Europe are untrue. They are going to be here for another year at least. Perhaps by the time they do go Helena and Alastair will be married.'

She had expected that Raefe would telephone her next morning. He telephoned her that night. She was in her bedroom putting the finishing touches to her hair and make-up. They were going to a Russian-style nightclub in Wanchai with a party of friends from the tennis club.

There was a light knock at her bedroom door

and Mei Lin entered, saying in her bird-soft voice: 'Mr Elliot is on the telephone, missy.'

Elizabeth's hand faltered as she put down her hairbrush. 'Thank you, Mei Lin.' She walked quickly out into the wide cool hall, grateful that Adam had not been in the room and had not overheard Mei Lin's message.

His dark rich voice sent a ripple of pleasure down her spine. 'I'll meet you at one o'clock tomorrow at the ferry.'

'No!' she had meant to sound cool and detached and was furious with herself at the panic she could hear in her voice. Her hand tightened on the receiver. 'No,' she said again, this time with more control. 'I can't see you for lunch again.'

'How do you know it was lunch I had in mind?' he said with amusement. She could imagine the smile tugging at the corners of his mouth, the dark sheen of his blue-black hair as it tumbled low over his brows.

'Whatever it is, I can't come,' she said stiffly.

There was an infinitesimal pause, and then he said softly: 'Why? Because you didn't enjoy yourself this afternoon? Or because you enjoyed yourself too much?'

'Because I enjoyed myself too much,' she whispered and put the receiver down unsteadily on its rest, not wanting to hear his voice for a moment longer, terrified that she would weaken, that she would tell him she would meet him any place, anywhere, any time.

When he rang back again in five minutes, she instructed Mei Lin to tell him that she was no longer at home. And all through the next few

246

days she adamantly refused to answer his calls.

Two weeks later they joined the Ledshams, and Helena and Alastair, at a beach-party at Tsuen Wan in the New Territories. 'This is the beginning of the Gin Drinkers' Line,' Alastair said to Adam, pointing up into the hills to a distant line of recently constructed pillboxes. 'Work began on those in nineteen thirty-seven when there was talk of a division from Singapore reinforcing the garrison. They never came, and so work was halted. Not much use having a defence line this far forward if there aren't enough troops to man it.'

'How far does it stretch?' Adam asked curiously.

'Eleven miles. It zig-zags all the way from here round to Ma Lau Tong on the east side of Kowloon. In some places they did quite a lot of work. For example, near the Shingmun Redoubt, a mile or so east of here, trenches were dug, cement overhead protection added, and fields of fire studied.'

'Why did they call it the Gin Drinkers' Line?' Elizabeth asked, intrigued.

'Look at the glass in your hand,' Alastair said, laughing. 'It's because this spot, where it starts, is so popular for parties.'

'Do you think they'll reactivate work on the line if plans go ahead for a civilian Volunteer Force?' Ronnie asked, lying flat on his back on the sand, Julienne's sun-hat over his face.

'I shouldn't think so. Even if every civilian in Hong Kong was trained and armed, there still wouldn't be enough men to hold a line so far up-country. The best line of defence is the strait between Kowloon and the island.'

'Gee, thanks,' Helena said drily. 'And what happens to people like me, living in Kowloon, if yellow hordes come thundering across the border and the British army is tucked safely away across the straits?'

'They catch the ferry, my love,' Alastair said easily. 'And the chances of such an event ever happening are extremely remote. Japan is in no position to attack us or, apart from China, anyone else.'

Julienne removed a bottle of gin and a bottle of tonic from a capacious picnic-hamper and poured a generous amount of each into a glass. 'I have heard you have lots of men sick at the moment,' she said to Alastair. She had terminated her affair with her major, but it had been done in a satisfactory manner. In bed, with a lot of laughter and gossip.

'You mean malaria?'

Julienne nodded. 'I don't understand why anyone should be sick of it. Not when the Army gives out quinine tables and mosquito-repellent cream.'

'The Royal Scots think they are under divine protection,' Ronnie said with a grin. 'No creams and tablets for our brave Lowlanders, eh, Alastair?'

'If men do scorn the medication they're given, then they're fools,' Alastair said, refusing to be riled. 'Mosquitoes are not respecters of persons. They'll bite a Royal Scot just as soon as they'll bite an Englishman.'

'I won't let them bite you, *chéri*,' Julienne said to Ronnie, rubbing sun oil into his shoulders. 'Mosquitoes, ugh, nasty vicious little creatures!' She began to hum happily under her breath. Her affair with Derry was going very well. She smiled to herself, remembering their lovemaking of the previous afternoon. Derry possessed what her major had lacked – sexual imagination nearly as inventive as her own.

Helena, helped by Alastair, began to spread out picnic food on a crisp white cloth. Yoghurt cheese balls in a jar of golden olive oil, smoked eel pâté with crackers, a crunchy apple salad, fennel and salami and black olives, a raised pork and apple pie that she had made herself the previous night, sesame bread sticks, grape tartlets, a melon crammed with raspberries, rum and raisin fudge squares, and, for Alastair, an almond-encrusted Dundee cake.

'Good girl,' Alastair said with relish; and, seeing the swift deep smile that Helena gave him, Elizabeth wondered if perhaps Helena had changed her mind about not loving him enough. They certainly seemed to be very happy together, and there was a contentment about Helena that had been conspicuously lacking when she had first met her.

'I think I might take a stroll and have a look at those pillboxes,' Adam said, rising to his feet and brushing the sand from his trousers.

'It would be much more sensible to have a swim,' Julienne said suggestively, her eyes telling him that if he accepted it would also be a lot more fun.

'Later,' he said, unaware of the unspoken invitation behind her words. 'When I come back.'

Julienne sighed and then giggled at his preferring a climb in the hills to a swim alone with her. She had been flirting shamelessly with him for the last two months and there were times when she wondered if he were even aware of it. Whatever else Adam was, he was not a romantic. She looked across at Elizabeth and wondered if she minded. She was wearing white shorts and a pink cotton halter top, her long legs seeming to stretch for ever, her skin honey-gold, her hair coiled high in a loose knot, so blonde that it looked like spun silver.

'Why do you never wear your hair down, Elizabeth?' she asked as she wriggled provocatively out of her dress, revealing a daringly cut French bathing costume.

'It's cooler like this,' Elizabeth said, plunging two bottles of champagne into a chilling bucket of sea-water.

'If I had hair that colour, I would wear it down all the time,' Julienne said, sweeping her own vibrant red curls up beneath her bathing-cap. 'It would be like a sheet of gold hanging to your shoulders and would make you look even younger than you do already.' Her eyes widened, comprehension dawning suddenly. *'Tiens!'* she said as she fastened her bathing-cap. 'So *that* is why you wear it always so sleek and so prim and proper.' And she laughed delightedly. 'I promise I will not tell!' she said mischievously as Ronnie raised himself up on one elbow, demanding to know what all the hilarity was about. 'I shall be as quiet as the little mouse.' And, still laughing, she ran down across the beach, plunging into the foam-flecked waves.

Ronnie looked across at her. Adam was a good hundred yards away, climbing a rocky gulley that led to the first of the pillboxes. Helena and Alastair were sitting, heads close together, deep in conversation. It was the first time since the débâcle of their lunch at the Peninsula that he had had the opportunity to speak to her alone.

'I rather ruined things the other week, didn't I?' he said regretfully. 'Too much to drink too soon, that was the problem.'

'There wasn't a problem at all,' Elizabeth said easily. 'You simply made an error of judgement.'

'Meaning that you're not remotely interested in helping me to while away the long hot days of a Hong Kong summer?' he asked and, though his voice was teasing, there was unmistakable heat in the electric-blue depths of his eyes.

'None at all,' she said lightly.

He sighed an exaggerated sigh of disappointment and then said curiously: 'You didn't tell Adam about my ... er ... error of judgement, did you?'

'I didn't tell him how you lured me to the Peninsula, but I did tell him that you had made a pass at me. It came out in the course of a conversation about someone else entirely.'

'I see.' He rolled over on to his stomach, squinting at the small figure that had nearly reached the top of the gulley. 'I thought he'd been a bit cool towards me lately. That's a pity. I

251

like old Adam.' He turned back to look at her. 'I don't suppose you will tell me who the person was you were discussing when my name was mentioned?'

She grinned. 'No,' she said, drawing the champagne out of its makeshift ice-bucket and feeling it speculatively.

'Is that cold enough?'

'Nearly.' She plunged the bottle back into the water, and he said: 'I hadn't realized till our lunch at the Pen just how very friendly you were with Raefe Elliot.'

'I'm no more friendly with him than I am with you or Tom or Alastair. In fact, not nearly so much.'

He grinned. 'You're a damned sight more friendly with him than anyone realizes. I imagine Julienne would be *very* intrigued if I told her that the last time I saw you Raefe Elliot was leading you in an iron-strong grasp from the Playpen Restaurant!'

'But you can't tell her any such thing,' Elizabeth said, laughing, 'not without revealing what you were doing there and *why* Raefe was escorting me away.'

He thumped the sand in mock anger. 'Damn me, if you're not right again. However, take a word of warning from one who knows.' His eyes were suddenly grave, his voice no longer bantering. 'Raefe Elliot isn't a man to tangle with lightly, Elizabeth. I'd steer far clear of him if I were you. Even for a woman like Julienne, Raefe Elliot would mean trouble, and for you and for Adam...' He shrugged expressively.

'Don't worry about me and Adam,' Elizabeth said with sudden fierceness, hugging her knees close to her chest. 'I would never let anything hurt Adam, not ever!'

'I'm glad to hear it,' Ronnie said with sincerity. 'Now, pass me one of those bottles of champers and let's have a decent drink.'

It was eight in the evening before they left the beach for home, Ronnie and Julienne in Julienne's little Morris, the rest of them squeezed tight in Alastair's larger car. By the time they reached Kowloon the shadows were lengthening beneath the banyan trees that lined Nathan Road and Elizabeth was on the verge of sleep.

Suddenly her eyes flew open. There was no mistaking the pale blue Lagonda in front of them, or the virile broad-shouldered figure at the wheel. She looked quickly across at Adam, but he was talking to Alastair and no one else seemed to have realized that the car in front of them was being driven by Raefe Elliot.

She looked again, and this time she sucked in her breath sharply. He wasn't alone. A small, sleek, dark head was resting lovingly against his shoulder. She could see the gleam of earrings, the rich brocade of a cheong-sam. As she watched, he turned his head, laughing down at the delicately featured, pale-gold face at his side, and then Alastair turned right towards Helena's flat and the Lagonda continued on down Nathan Road.

There was a pain in her chest as if a dagger had been driven between her shoulderblades. She wondered where they were going. To the Peninsula perhaps, to a dinner-dance? To the Parisian Grill? Wherever it was, it was none of her business. She hadn't, surely, expected him to sever all romantic ties merely because he had once taken her out for lunch? Her nails dug deep into her palms. Dear heaven! He hadn't even made a pass at her! She hadn't allowed him on the telephone to say why he wanted to see her again. It was probably only to give one of his girl-friends cut-price piano lessons!

'Here we are, home again,' Helena said to her as they slid to a halt. 'Hasn't it been a glorious day?'

But Elizabeth didn't answer her. She was sick and tired, appalled at the ferocity of her jealousy, confounded by the depth of her physical longing.

'Let's go straight home,' she said to Adam as Julienne's little Morris swerved to a halt behind them.

He looked down into her face, shocked at how tired and drawn she suddenly looked. 'OK, sweetheart,' he said, his arm tightening around her shoulders. 'We'll go home and have an early night. It's been a long day.'

Chapter 10

Raefe rolled over in bed, feeling for his wrist-watch on the bedside table. He looked at it and groaned. Five-thirty. He had thirty minutes to reach Kai Tak and the Northrop waiting to fly him to his meeting with Colonel Landor in Singapore.

By his side Alute began to stir, moving towards him, her hands lightly caressing his chest, beginning to move enticingly lower. Regretfully he swung his legs from the bed, striding towards the shower.

'Oh!' At his abrupt departure Alute's eyes shot open in disappointment. 'You are going so soon?'

Steaming-hot water gushed down over his head and shoulders. 'It's five-thirty,' he shouted. 'Go back to sleep.'

'Sleeping alone is no fun,' she protested sulkily. She hated his business trips to Singapore. There were so many girls there, and she lived in fear that he would find one he preferred to her and bring her back with him. Perhaps – horror of horrors – he would even install her in his house on Victoria Peak.

Alute had never been inside the house that Raefe had shared with his wife. He no longer

255

lived there, preferring his luxury apartment in Central; and, although Alute had often stayed the night in the apartment as she had last night, she had still not managed to fill the wardrobes and drawers with her dresses and lingerie. To her chagrin, she was still not his number one girl and there were times when she wondered if she ever would be.

He strode back into the bedroom, magnificently naked, rifling through a drawer for underpants and socks, water glistening in his hair and gleaming on his strong shoulders.

She wound the sheet seductively tight around her slim body and kneeled up on the bed. 'Can't you spare just ten minutes?' she wheedled, letting the sheet slip down to expose a small, tip-tilted breast and dark-gold nipple.

He grinned, dressing with practised speed. 'No,' he said, and there was no regret in his voice. He had more important things to think about than sex.

For the past two years, unknown to anyone, even Melissa, whenever he had visited Singapore on a necessary business trip, he had also visited military headquarters at Fort Canning, reporting to British Army Intelligence on any suspicious Japanese activity.

He strode into the sitting-room, unlocking his wall safe and removing two thin files. There were times when he wished that the British had never approached him. They asked for information, they received information, and, in Raefe's eyes, they did bugger all with it. He slammed the wall safe shut, grabbed a small overnight bag from a chair and was out of the apartment before his sleepy houseboy could even ask if he wanted coffee.

Colonel Landor finished reading Raefe's report and then laid the file back on his desk, his mouth tight-lipped. 'Do you really believe in the accuracy of this report, Mr Elliot?'

Raefe met his eyes unflinchingly, his face grim. 'Yes, I do.'

Landor drummed his fingers on the file and then pushed it away abruptly. 'Even if you are right, and these men *are* Japanese intelligence officers, we can't expect the Foreign Office to expel them, as you suggest. *We're* not at war with Japan. It's the Chinese who are at war with them. Such an action on our part would cause no end of a diplomatic row!'

Raefe's nostrils flared. 'Sooner or later Japan is going to attack Hong Kong and Singapore,' he said, keeping control of his fury with difficulty. 'When she does, we don't want her having access to every detail of our defence strength! At the moment, there are five Japanese army personnel in Hong Kong, seconded from the Japanese army for the alleged purpose of learning English. All five are intelligence officers, their sole reason for secondment being to build up a finely detailed picture of our present defences and our proposed defences. They must be expelled immediately! To allow them to remain, knowing what we do, is insanity!'

Two angry spots of colour touched Colonel

Landor's cheeks. 'Your task is to ferret out facts and report on them, Mr Elliot. It doesn't extend to commenting on action that is or isn't taken!'

Raefe suppressed his fury with difficulty, hoping he would have the pleasure of seeing Landor's face when the Japanese poured south, battle-maps of the island's defences in each and every pocket.

'The other Japanese you've named – are you convinced of your facts?'

'Positive,' Raefe said through clenched teeth. 'The Japanese barber at the Hong Kong Hotel holds the rank of lieutenant-commander in the Japanese navy. At the moment he cuts the hair of the Governor, the Commissioner of Police, the officer in charge of the Special Branch, and the chairman of Hong Kong and Shanghai Bank!'

Colonel Landor's face was pale. It was one thing to be told that the barmen and masseurs of Wanchai were listening assiduously to the gossip of British troops and reporting anything of interest back to Tokyo. It was quite another thing to think of men like the Governor and the Commissioner of Police being lured into unsuspecting gossip by their barber. A shiver ran down his spine as he remembered his own trim and shave earlier in the day. He had been bowed from the chair by his Japanese barber, feeling as if he were a million dollars. Under those relaxing conditions it was very easy for even the most careful of men to talk carelessly.

'What about the Italian waiter at the Peninsula Hotel? Are you sure of him as well?' he asked tersely.

'As sure as I can be. And the jeweller in the Queen's Arcade.'

Landor grunted. The prospect of Japanese spies in the hotels, bars and shops of Hong Kong was not a cheering one. Even less cheering was Elliot's second report.

'How long do you think this Chinese fifth column, as you style them, have been infiltrating into Hong Kong?'

'Probably ever since the Japanese installed a Chinese as puppet leader over the parts of China they have conquered. It's Wong Chang Wai's followers who will be helping the Japs if and when they attack. They are being recruited by the Japanese in Formosa and then brought over to the China–Hong Kong border. Entry is easy. All they have to do is mingle with the refugees entering the island every day.'

'And you think that the Japanese have armed them?'

'I'm sure they will have partially armed them,' Raefe said grimly, 'and I'm also sure that they will be well primed as to what acts of sabotage would most damage us.'

Colonel Landor passed his hand over his eyes. He could imagine the damage they could do all too well. Sniping at isolated and vulnerable posts, acting as despatch riders, spreading false rumours and signalling to their Japanese masters the positions of guns and pillboxes. Dear God, it would be mayhem. It was hard enough for British troops to differentiate between Japanese and Chinese, without expecting them to be able to differentiate between Chinese sympathetic to them and Chinese prepared to stab them in the back.

He hoped devoutly that Elliot's assessment of the situation was wrong and had a sickening feeling that it wouldn't be. When it came to the Chinese and Japanese, Raefe Elliot's instinct was unerring. He picked up the files. It was up to the Foreign Office to deal with the Japanese seconded from their army on the pretext of learning English. They, at least, should be easy to get rid of. As for weeding out Wong Chang Wai's followers... He doubted if even Elliot himself could accomplish that task.

Raefe slammed out of military headquarters, small white lines etching his mouth. Both the reports he had submitted were damning, and he doubted if action would be taken on either of them. There would be those amongst the high command who would regard Japanese spies in Hong Kong as a joke. 'What harm can they cause?' he could imagine them saying. 'The Japs will never have the nerve to attack. Another gin and tonic, old boy?'

He stormed out into the blistering heat of early afternoon. The British didn't want the bald truth. They wanted innocuous reports they could write memos about, shuffling them from department to department, theorizing and temporizing over them. His car was waiting at the gates, and he yanked open the rear door.

'Raffles,' he said curtly to his Malay driver, sinking back against the cracked leather upholstery. He had other business to conduct whilst in

Singapore, but first he needed a long cold drink.

As the car sped down wide avenues flanked by trim grass verges and frangipani trees, he wondered why it was Hong Kong that he, his father and his grandfather had preferred. Their business interests had always had firm roots in Singapore. It was Singapore godowns, as well as Hong Kong godowns, that bore the name 'Elliot & Sons' in large black lettering. A mirthless smile touched the corners of his mouth. The '& Sons' no longer had any meaning. He had no son and, as long as he remained married to Melissa, there wouldn't be one. Not one he could acknowledge.

The car sped past the slim spire of St Andrew's Cathedral and down to the waterfront. Perhaps he had never settled here because such large parts of the city were so very English. There was something gentlemanly about Singapore that was lacking in the hurly-burly of Hong Kong. The Malay driver slowed down reluctantly for a traffic policeman, basketwork wings strapped to his back so that he did not need to wave his arms in the heat, but merely had to turn his feet in order to direct the cars. The heat was stifling, and a trickle of sweat ran down Raefe's neck as they picked up speed, cruising past the green padang of the Cricket Club, with its football and cricket pitches, tennis-courts and bowling greens. He had no time for a game of tennis on this trip.

Two years ago the International Rubber Regulation Committee had raised the output quota to 90 per cent of what Elliots were capable of producing. The reason had been the increased demand by America for rubber, and it had meant vast profits. Extra labour had been employed, and very few people, apart from Raefe, had stopped to wonder *why* the Americans were suddenly stockpiling rubber. He had seen it as an indication that the American government was increasingly apprehensive about a war in the East that would cut off their supplies. When he had suggested this in an official report, it had been politely discounted.

A year ago the boom had come to an abrupt end. Rubber stocks were so high that the price had slid to rock bottom, and now Elliots were handling more rubber than ever, and losing money at the same time. New markets had to be found, and Raefe was on the verge of closing a deal with an Australian company. But first he needed to know if he had the shipping available to deliver. And that meant a detailed discussion with his general manager at his head office in Robinson Road.

The car sped up the palm-flanked drive to the rambling ornate Victorian splendour of Raffles Hotel, and he felt his fury at Colonel Landor's negative attitude begin to dissipate. With luck his report would reach Whitehall and, with even greater luck, someone, somewhere would take note of it.

The tables beneath the vast roofed-over veranda were full but, as he entered, a waiter scurried over to him, a table was cleared, and as he crossed to it, acknowledging people he knew, he stopped short, his heart hammering violently.

She was sitting near a tall fan-like fern, her head averted, her wheat-gold hair knotted high at the back of her head. He felt his mouth dry and then he moved towards her and she turned to her companion, laughing at a remark that had been made, and he saw that it wasn't Elizabeth at all. Just an exceptionally pretty woman who had none of Elizabeth's grace, or sensuousness, or sexually arousing fragility.

He continued to his table, ordering a double Scotch and soda, thunderstruck at the depth of his disappointment. At this moment in time the last thing he needed was an emotional involvement with a married woman. Despite his very strong physical attraction to her, he had felt an element of relief when she had adamantly refused to have any further contact with him. But he hadn't, for one moment, forgotten her. She was impossible to forget.

The waiter was at his elbow, and he ordered a curry tiffin. Had he really believed he was going to accept her refusal to speak to him on the telephone, to meet him again? The woman who was a pale caricature of her rose to her feet and left the room. He knew that if it had been Elizabeth who had left the room, no matter how crowded, it would have been as if a light had gone out or the sun had gone in. There was a luminous radiance about her, a gentleness that he had never encountered in any woman before. And yet she was tough. He remembered the way she had spoken to him about her music, the passion that had entered her soft smoky voice. A smile crooked the corners of his mouth. He doubted that her passion had ever been unleashed on her dull and steady husband.

* * *

When his plane touched down at Kai Tak two days later, Derry Langdon was waiting for him, sitting at the wheel of a jeep, a battered sun-hat on the back of his head, a cigarette between his fingers.

Raefe ignored his own car and walked across to his brother-in-law. He liked the easygoing and affable Derry and found it hard to believe that he had been spawned by the same genes that had spawned Melissa.

'How was Singapore?' Derry asked as Raefe swung himself into the jeep beside him.

'Hot and colonial,' Raefe said briefly. 'What's the matter, Derry? Fresh trouble?'

Derry took a last puff at his cigarette and then dropped it to the floor of the jeep, crushing it out beneath his sandalled foot. 'Pa insists that Melissa returns to Victoria. He's going to take a court order out claiming that you're holding her against her will.'

'Your father's a fool!' Raefe said savagely. 'Damn it all, can't he get it into his thick skull that I'm trying to save Melissa's life?'

Derry shrugged helplessly. 'He doesn't believe things are that bad. He thinks it was unhappiness which drove her to drugs and Jacko, and that you are the cause of her unhappiness. His reasoning is that if he takes her away from your control, then she's bound to start recovering.'

'If he believes that, he'll believe anything!' Raefe said explosively, running his fingers through the thick tumble of his hair. 'Christ! If she comes back to Victoria now, no one is going

264

to believe she was an innocent victim!'

'Pa doesn't see it that way. He says if she returns to Victoria everyone will be able to see that she is fine and it will confirm the belief that she was only labelled a drug-taker in order to provide you with a defence.'

'Well, we both know that's not true, don't we?' Raefe said wearily.

They were silent for a minute or two, and then Derry said: 'How is she?'

'A mess.' His voice was curt, but Derry could hear the underlying pain and despair.

Derry stared moodily out over the airfield. His sister had always been headstrong and self-willed – and heart-breakingly pretty. Their parents had been divorced when he had been twelve and Melissa ten. Their mother's new lover had not relished being encumbered with her children, and so custody had been awarded to their father and he had compensated for the disruption of their lives by spoiling them both to excess. Derry had enjoyed the spoiling and, as far as he was aware, it had left no long-lasting ill effects on him. But Melissa ... He sighed. All the spoiling in the world would not have been enough for Melissa.

As a child she had demanded, and received, instant gratification of all her needs. And she had continued to do so as an adult. Her feline seductive prettiness had ensured that she rarely received any obstruction to her wishes. Her father had said it was a pleasure to indulge her, and her many boyfriends had all seemed to think likewise.

And then she had married Raefe. The match had alarmed his father, who, despite Raefe's wealth, regarded him as being socially dubious. If the fellow had a touch of the tarbrush about him, he didn't want it showing in *his* grandchildren. Derry had grinned at his father's fears and had thought that at last Melissa was showing good sense. Raefe Elliot was a distinct improvement on the chinless wonders she had previously favoured.

Even now he didn't know what had gone wrong. He suspected that Raefe had tried to curb Melissa's childish selfishness and that Melissa, unaccustomed to restraint, had rebelled by indulging in flagrant flirtations with Raefe's friends. If she had hoped that the fear of losing her would bring him to heel like a pet dog, she had been very wrong. His friends had been embarrassed, and Raefe had been, outwardly at least, indifferent.

Furiously, Melissa had cast her net wider, and from the minute that Derry had known of her affair with an officer serving with the Middlesex he had known that her marriage to Raefe was doomed. He didn't know when the drug-taking had started. Heroin was easily available in Hong Kong, and it had been her lover in the Middlesex who had introduced her to the habit. She had begun by using it with what she thought was sophisticated carelessness and had plunged with hideous speed into desperate addiction. It had been then that his liking for his brother-in-law had turned into respect.

When Melissa had confronted Raefe with the

truth of her affair, she had also maliciously told him that she was pregnant. That, though he was the father of her child, he would never know for sure whether she was telling the truth or not. Raefe had taken one look at the blond, blue-eyed, pale-skinned specimen she had broken her marriage vows for and had known immediately that there would be no doubt as to the parentage of the child once it was born. Until it was, there would be no divorce. And no scandal. Melissa discovered that her lover, who had promised to love her for eternity, was not quite so constant when faced with an ultimatum that he either stopped seeing her or received the thrashing of his life. It was then that they had become aware of her growing heroin addiction.

Raefe had taken her to Perth, to a doctor who specialized in conquering drug dependence, but Melissa had no desire to be freed of her craving and he had been unable to help her.

Raefe had brought her back to Victoria, and a week later she miscarried the baby. It was dark-haired and brown-eyed, and it had died of heroin poisoning before it had even been born.

It was a month later when Raefe had returned home from a trip to Singapore and found Jacko Latimer in her bed. Derry didn't know if Raefe had meant to kill Latimer. He wouldn't have blamed him if he had done. But, with or without intent, Jacko Latimer had died and they had all had to endure the long-drawn-out agonies of the trial. Melissa had been the least concerned. She was supremely indifferent to Latimer's death, and seemed almost as indifferent to the sentence

Raefe would receive if he was convicted of his murder. It was while they were in court, Raefe tense and strained, his father hunched and suddenly old, that Derry had come close to hating his sister. He said now: 'Is she still on it?'

Raefe nodded. 'In decreasing amounts. And the stuff she is getting is clean, unlike the dirt that Latimer was feeding her.'

'But how long can you keep it up? She won't stay in the New Territories against her will for ever.'

A mirthless grin touched Raefe's mouth. 'She isn't there against her will, Derry. She's there because she wants to be. She doesn't want to be in Victoria with your father fussing around her, watching her every move. She wants to be where she has access to heroin, even if it is in decreasing amounts.'

'And will it work?' Derry asked bewilderedly.

'It's got as good a chance of working as anything else. The household staff are one hundred per cent loyal to me. She's receiving her heroin under almost medical conditions and she's being weaned, very gradually, off it.'

'And when she is?' Derry asked curiously. 'Will you both move back to your home on the Peak?'

'Good God, no! I shall never live with her again!'

'Then, why not divorce her now? Why persevere with trying to cure her when all you get for your pains is the accusation that you're keeping her a prisoner and mistreating her?'

'Because she's my wife,' Raefe said tightly,

268

'and my responsibility. Because when I divorce her I want her to be fit and physically able to start a new life on her own.'

'And if she isn't?'

The lines around Raefe's mouth deepened. 'She will be,' he said vehemently, swinging himself down from the jeep. 'Just tell your father she's better off where she is than in Victoria, where every petty drug-pusher in town can find her and proposition her.'

He strode across to his Lagonda, grateful that Derry hadn't asked to visit Melissa. Derry slammed his jeep into gear, giving him a wave, and then disappeared in a cloud of dust down the road leading towards Kowloon. Raefe wondered if he was still enjoying an affair with Julienne Ledsham and grinned. If the affair was still in progress, he would be enjoying it. Julienne would see to that.

He was at the intersection of Chatham Road and Salisbury Road when Tom Nicholson, driving his sleek-looking Packard, slammed his hand on the car's horn, waving for him to pull over.

He sighed. He was hot and tired, and he wanted nothing more than to get home and shower and sleep. He pulled over, and Tom screeched to a halt in front of him, vaulting from the Packard and striding towards him. 'You're just the person I want to see. I've been ringing you for the past two days, but your houseboy said he didn't know when you would be returning. How was Singapore?'

Raefe knew it wasn't a question he was interested in receiving a reply to and he ignored it, saying: 'I only touched down an hour ago. Whatever it was you wanted to see me about, can't it wait?'

'It can,' Tom said reluctantly, 'but I'd appreciate it if you could spare me ten minutes, Raefe. I've got problems and I don't know who else can advise me.'

They were only a hundred yards or so away from the Peninsula. 'OK,' he said wearily. 'Let's go down to the Long Bar and talk over a couple of drinks.'

'Thanks,' Tom said briefly, his eyes showing his gratitude. 'I'll follow you on.'

He strode back to his Packard, and Raefe once more put his Lagonda into gear and cruised down the remaining stretch of Salisbury Road and into the Peninsula's luxurious forecourt.

'What's the problem?' he asked Tom when they were sitting with their drinks, fans whirring coolingly above their heads.

'Prejudice!' Tom said succinctly.

A glimmer of a smile touched Raefe's mouth. 'Who is she?' he asked, as a waiter removed their glasses and replaced them with two more.

'Lamoon Sheng.'

Raefe's brows rose expressively. No wonder Tom had problems. 'How the devil have you been managing to meet?'

'Deception,' Tom said distastefully. 'She goes to nursing classes every Monday and Thursday. The family chauffeur drops her off at the front entrance of the hospital and picks her up.'

'Only she never goes to classes?'

'She used to. Before we met. Now she simply walks straight through the hospital to the rear entrance, and those few hours are the only time we have together.' His voice was bitter, and Raefe, knowing the impossibility of Tom taking Lamoon Sheng anywhere publicly without knowledge of it reaching her father, said curiously: 'Where do you go?'

'To the Harlands. They are the only people who know about us, and Adam Harland has been very supportive.'

'He would be,' Raefe said drily, a nerve beginning to twitch at the corner of his jaw. 'He knows damn all about the Chinese or what would happen if Lamoon's deception were discovered.'

'At least he's free of the stinking racial prejudice which seems to afflict everyone else!' Tom said explosively. 'It isn't as if it's only the whites! The Chinese are just as bad. Smiling at us and deferring to us, and scorning us behind our backs! The hypocrisy of it drives me wild!'

Raefe's smile was cynical. He knew damn well that Tom had never previously given a thought to the racial undercurrents that divided Hong Kong. Before he had fallen in love with Lamoon Sheng, he would have been as horrified as anyone else if a Chinese had stormed the gates of his favourite club. He said mildly: 'It's changing. If there's a war in Europe, it will come over here, and then everything – even Hong Kong – will change.'

'Christ! I can't wait for a bloody war to change things! I want things to change now!' He leaned

271

towards Raefe, his hands clasped between his knees, his eyes urgent. 'I want to marry her, and I want you to tell me the best way of approaching old Sheng in order to ask for his consent.'

Raefe shook his head. 'There isn't *any* way you can approach Sheng and ask for his daughter's hand in marriage. Lamoon isn't a Wanchai bar-girl with no family to protect her. She's the only daughter of a very rich man. A very rich *Chinese*. He'd have your balls if you even suggested that you wanted to marry her.'

'It's nineteen thirty-nine, not *eighteen* thirty-nine,' Tom said persistently. 'He's a business-man. He deals with Westerners every day. There must be *some* way of approaching him!'

'He's a leader of the Chinese community, Tom. He's a respected man, and in his eyes his honour would be shamed if it was known that his daugh-ter was in love with a European. If you persist in seeing her, sooner or later you'll both be found out and then you'll never see her again.'

Tom groaned and ran his fingers through his hair. 'She isn't a minor. She's twenty-one, for God's sake...'

'It would make no difference if she was forty-one,' Raefe said, looking across at him pityingly. 'She's subject to the rigid discipline of a Chinese family bound by autocratic rules impossible to violate, subject to the will of a father whose authority, by Chinese custom, is absolute. It's a system that can't be bucked, Tom. Not yet. Not till European and Chinese ideas about colour and culture change dramatically.'

'Fuck the bloody system!' Tom said savagely,

the skin tight across his cheekbones, his well-shaped mouth thin and straight and bitter with pain. 'If the only way I can live with Lamoon is by kidnapping her and taking her away from this caste-ridden place, then, by God, that's exactly what I'll do! At least in America we could live together openly and not be socially ostracized!'

'Would Lamoon be happy living like that?' Raefe asked quietly. 'She's been brought up as a dutiful daughter, deferring to her father in all things. The fact that she risks so much to meet you as she does is remarkable, but would she be able to face the thought of never seeing her family again? Of being the cause of their loss of face? Family honour, to a Chinese, is more important than life itself. I don't see how she could make the adjustment. No matter how much she loves you.'

Tom drained his glass, the set of his jaw determined. 'When I need your help with Sheng, can I depend on having it?'

'Yes,' Raefe said, rising to his feet, and then, as they left the bar together, he added with grim humour: 'When you do face him, you're going to need all the help you can get!'

He left Tom outside the Peninsula's front entrance and drove with unaccustomed tiredness the short distance to the vehicular ferry. The crossing took only eight minutes, and a quarter of an hour later he was in his flat in Central, standing, his face upward, beneath a gushing shower, one of his house-boys busily preparing a meal, the other one pouring him a large Scotch on the rocks.

There was still a lot of work to do for Intelligence. Apart from the Japanese army of officers who had infiltrated the British armed forces on the pretext of peacefully learning English, he had uncovered two other Japanese spies he was convinced were of paramount importance. His personal underground information network had reported that the barber at the Hong Kong Hotel was no small-time agent, but a lieutenant-commander in the Japanese navy. God knew what other ranks were in positions of trust inside Hong Kong, listening to the conversations of generals and brigadiers.

He stepped from the shower, shaking water from his hair, swaddling a towel around his hips. He was in a unique position to ferret out information for British Intelligence. He spoke Cantonese and he commanded Chinese respect on a far deeper level than the day-to-day smiling obsequiousness habitually accorded Europeans. His grandmother had been Eurasian and, though he could quite easily have denied it, he never had. He was in the rare position of being acceptable, with only slight reservations, in both Chinese and European society.

He lit a cigarette and strolled across to the huge window that looked out over the streets and squares of Central, and the piers and densely packed harbour.

His wealth cocooned him from the worst aspects of prejudice. Englishmen wishing to do business with Elliots conveniently forgot that old man Elliot had married a girl whose skin was pale gold and not white. Besides, apart from the dark hair there was nothing very Eurasian about the Elliots. Both Raefe and his father had been educated at prestigious American universities. They were American and they were rich, and old man Elliot's peccadillo was conveniently forgotten. At least it was forgotten unless there was a question of Elliot marrying one of their daughters. Then prejudice reasserted itself with a vengeance. No one wanted a dark-skinned throwback as a grandchild. It was a risk best not taken. When Melissa Langdon had married Raefe, there had been sighs of relief from anxious fathers, and Colonel Langdon had been, and still was, a man much sympathized with.

A grim smile touched the corner of Raefe's mouth. He was well aware of their fears, and of how groundless they were. His grandmother had been Polynesian, not Chinese. Her skin, and the skin of her forebears, had held only the merest hint of colour. The chances of a child of his being born dark were infinitesimal. Not that he cared. His grandmother had been a princess whose line of breeding went back much further than any of the Englishmen who murmured askance about his being allowed into their bars and clubs. She had been beautiful and courageous, working alongside his grandfather in up-country Malaya and in Sumatra, as responsible for the founding of Elliot wealth as his grandfather had been. If she had been as black as coal, he would have been equally uncaring and just as proud of her.

Across the Kowloon Peninsula the sky was flushed, the swift pink twilight of the tropics fall-

ing swiftly. Whisperings about his racial background had long since ceased to perturb him
even faintly; but they had made for inner loneliness when he was a child, and that inner loneliness still remained. He crushed his cigarette out
in a jade ashtray. He had thought that his sense of
separateness had been over when he had married
Melissa. He had thought he was gaining a
beautiful wife who would also be his lover and
his friend. The bitterness of his disappointment
still seared.

Melissa was incapable of offering loyalty or
the kind of companionship on which a marriage
could be built. She had only her body and her
face, and they had both been so enticing that,
God help him, he had paid no attention to her
other qualities until he had got his ring safely
on her finger and had enjoyed her tantalizing
sexuality at his leisure.

Realization had been torture. She had wanted
him to treat her as her father had done. To indulge and flatter and pamper, and to seek nothing
back in the form of companionship at all. He had
indulged her financially to the best of his not
inconsiderable ability, but he had refused to
allow her to shout and be physically abusive to
the amahs and houseboys who had served him
since he was a child. There had been tantrums,
sulks. And then the flirting had begun. He had
exercised a patience he had never known he
possessed. Knowing that he no longer loved her,
he had lovingly tried to make her see how need-
lessly foolish she was being. Because he had not
flown into the jealous rages she craved, her

276

flirtations became wilder and more socially embarrassing. His friends made excuses and no longer visited them, and then Melissa, unable to arouse the attention she sought on home ground, sought it elsewhere. At the Cricket Club and the Swimming Club. And men like her major in the Middlesex were only too happy to oblige her.

He stared broodingly out over the harbour. His own behaviour had not been blameless. After she had lost his son he had had as many women as he chose to reach out for. Sophisticated, clever, decorative women. Women whose husbands and fathers were the backbone of Hong Kong society. And there had been other women, too. Women like Alute. Practised women of great grace and beauty. And not one of them had touched his heart or his emotions. Until he had met Elizabeth Harland.

He swung away from the window, his frown deepening. What the devil was it about her that so intrigued him? He was accustomed to beauty in the women who graced his arm. It wasn't only her pale blonde beauty that intrigued him. It was something else. Some quality he had felt instantly in accord with. Beneath her smiles and her husky laughter she was as desperately lonely as he was, as out of touch with those around her, as untouchable, as unreachable. But not with him. She had felt the same instant recognition as he had done. He had seen it in her eyes, heard it in her voice. And she thought that by refusing to speak to him or to meet him she could escape the consequences of that recognition.

A smile quirked the corners of his mouth. She was wrong. There were some things in life that were inescapable. As she would very soon discover.

Chapter 11

'Mrs Harland is not at home,' Mei Lin said nervously as Elizabeth stood three feet away from her, every line of her body taut with tension.

Raefe gave a disbelieving chuckle. 'You make a bad liar, Mei Lin. Tell Mrs Harland that if she won't speak to me I'm coming round. I'll be there within ten minutes.'

Elizabeth's hand shot out for the telephone. 'No!' she gasped, appalled at her physical reaction to his voice, knowing that the last thing on earth she wanted was to confront him beneath her own roof.

The tone of his voice changed. 'I'll meet you at the foot of Peak Road,' he said gently.

She opened her mouth to protest, but no sound came, and then she heard him replace his telephone receiver and she knew that she didn't want to protest. She wanted to see him more than she had ever wanted to see anyone in her life.

'I'm going out,' she said unsteadily to Mei Lin. 'When Mr Harland returns from his game of golf, please tell him that I've gone for a drive and that I'll be back in time for dinner.'

'Yes, missy,' Mei Lin said, but her eyes were worried, her voice unhappy. She liked Mr Elliot, but he had a bad reputation where women were concerned, and she knew that Mr Harland would not like it if he knew that his wife was surreptitiously meeting him.

Elizabeth ran upstairs to her bedroom, taking a white linen jacket from her wardrobe, picking up her leather clutch-bag with the ivory clasp from her dressing-table. She paused for a moment looking at her reflection in the glass. Her hair was glossy and sleek, coiled low in the nape of her neck; her face was pale, almost ashen; her eyes enormous, the pupils large and dilated. It was the face of a woman on the edge of some dreadful abyss. And all she was doing was meeting Raefe Elliot at the bottom of Peak Road.

She took a deep steadying breath. She was being a fool. He wasn't interested in her. He was more than happy with his petite fragile-boned Malay girlfriend. And, if he were interested in her, it would make no difference. She was happily married to Adam. She was doing what women and men did in Hong Kong every day of the week. She was meeting an acquaintance of the opposite sex for a chat and possibly lunch. It was all perfectly harmless, and she was revealing a pathetic lack of sophistication by behaving as if it were an event of earth-shattering importance.

Having suitably scolded herself, her hands were steadier as she reversed her Buick out of the large double garage. She would talk to him about Roman Rakowski. She had read in a London newspaper that he had been instrumental in helping the Polish violinist, Bronislaw Huberman, establish a first-class orchestra in Palestine, composed entirely of Jewish musicians who had fled Nazi persecution. It would be interesting to find out more about it. Toscanini had conducted the inaugural concert, and she remembered Professor Hurok saying that the programme had been a large and demanding one, including works by Brahms, Rossini, Schubert, Mendelssohn and Weber.

Her hands tightened on the wheel. She couldn't remember the last time she had been able to talk intelligently about music with anyone. Adam listened to her politely when the London papers arrived and she was able to read the latest concert reviews. But he only listened to her, he didn't enter into any discussion, and she knew that he was always relieved when the conversation turned to other subjects.

The road twisted down between forests of bamboo and fern and stunted Chinese pines. Raefe Elliot wasn't a musician. Why did she feel that she could talk to him about music? Why did she feel that she could talk to him about any subject under the sun? She sped past a traditional four-storey Chinese house that had been built by a rich merchant in age-old Chinese chauvinistic style, with one storey apportioned to each of his wives. Why did she feel so alive when she was with him? So aware of all her senses? She had looked at his hands on the wheel of his car when he had driven her to Sham Tseng and she had physically ached with the need to have them on her naked flesh. A wave of guilt surged up towards her throat. Why had she never felt like that with Adam? Why, oh, why could she not yearn for Adam in the shameless way that she did for this man she barely knew? This man she was not in love with, never would be in love with, but who by the mere tone of his voice awakened a sensuality in her that had previously lain dormant.

She sped round the last bend and saw his Lagonda parked beneath the trees. For a split second that she was to remember all her life she was tempted to speed past him. Her foot hovered over the accelerator, and then he opened his car door and stepped out on to the side of the road, tall and broad-shouldered in an open-neck silk shirt and white flannels, and her foot came down hard on the brake.

She squealed to a halt in a cloud of dust, and he walked across to her and grinned. 'That was quite an entrance. I could hear you coming for the last two miles.'

She stepped out of the Buick feeling foolish, wondering if he thought she had driven at high speed out of burning impatience to be with him again, and then she saw the dark tilt of his brows and the line of his jaw, and the curve of his mouth, and she didn't care what he thought.

'It's the car,' she said with an answering grin. 'It was made for America and wide open spaces. It doesn't like cautious driving.'

He took her arm lightly, proprietorially, and every sexual nerve-ending in her body screamed into life. 'We'll drive the rest of the way in the Lagonda,' he said in amusement. 'It's British and much better behaved.'

'Where are we going?' she asked as he opened

the Lagonda's door for her.

'Somewhere quiet. Shek-O or Big Wave Bay.'

'I haven't brought a bathing-suit with me.'

He walked round the car and slid into the seat next to her, punching the engine into life. 'It doesn't matter,' he said, and there was a wicked gleam in his eyes. 'Neither have I.'

He drove with swift expertise to Wong Nai Chung Gap and then, instead of plunging down the steep road towards the south side of the island and the golden sands of Repulse Bay, he turned left on to a narrow road she had never travelled on before; it curved through densely wooded country, past a magnificent reservoir, and then it skirted the foot of Mount Collinson and wound down through giant banks of purple daphne and oleander, to the tiny village of Shek-O.

The sea was azure, and beyond the headland two small islands lay, bathed in a heat haze, insubstantial as mist. He drove on another mile or so, until the rough and unmade road petered out into the hills. They were at Big Wave Bay. The mountains soared up behind them, the bay was tiny and secluded, and there wasn't another human being within sight.

As she stepped out of the car, happiness struck through her like an arrow. It was a shock of joy so physical, so precisely marked, that she was to know, ever afterwards, the exact moment at which her world changed.

'Let's swim.' He was already pulling off his shirt, kicking off his shoes.

She hesitated only for a second and then she

shrugged herself free of her jacket, unzipping her skirt and letting it fall to the sand.

Naked, he was even more hard-muscled and magnificent than she had imagined. His broad chest was covered with a light mat of crisply curling dark hair, his hips were narrow and he was as assured, as unselfconscious naked as he was when dressed in a white dinner-jacket summoning the waiter at the Peninsula or the Hong Kong Club.

She unbuttoned her blouse, letting it fall at her feet, and then he reached out his hand for hers and, dressed only in her bra and panties and lace-edged underslip, she ran with him over the silver sand and plunged into the azure waves.

The first shock of the water made her gasp aloud. A wave broke over her head, and then she struck out strongly, shaking the salt from her eyes, laughing with pleasure. He trod water for a second, white teeth flashing in his sun-bronzed face as he grinned across at her, making sure that she was at home in the water before he struck out in a smooth crawl.

After the heat of the sand the water was blissfully cool and silky, the waves lifting her buoyantly, filling her with exhilaration. There was a faint breeze blowing off the land, its heady mixture of oleander and pine, sweet and sharp, coming in warm puffs through the salt smell of the sea.

'Happy?' he shouted across to her as they breasted the curve of the bay.

An avalanche of foam crashed down on her, the next wave lifting her high and clear. 'I feel as if I've died and gone to heaven!' she shouted back exuberantly, twisting over to float and letting the waves lift and carry her, closing her eyes against the brilliance of the sky.

He trod water, watching her, knowing that the whole course of his life had changed. He had thought himself in love once before and he had been grievously mistaken. He was not mistaken this time. At thirty-two, when he had thought himself too hardened ever to feel love for a woman again, he was experiencing the *coup de foudre*, the thunderclap of unreasoning instant infatuation. An infatuation he knew would endure. He swam across to her, his strong hands gently circling her waist.

Her eyes shot open, a moment's panic flared through them, and then she was treading water, facing him, her body pressed close against his, and as the heavy swell of the sea continued to lift them and let them fall he said harshly: 'I want you! I've wanted you from the first moment I saw you.'

Spray fell over them in a glittering sheet.

'You're crazy!' she gasped, shaking her face free of water, her hands hard against his chest, Excitement spiralling through her.

'I know!' White teeth flashed in a sudden grin. 'But it's true. And this is one place where you can't run away from me!'

She could feel his heart hammering beneath the palm of her hand, their legs were intertwined as they trod the green-blue water, spray cascaded from his hair, running in rivulets down his sun-tanned neck and on to his powerful shoulders.

She felt herself groan, a deep agonized groan almost of pain, and then her arms slid up and around his neck, and as his mouth came down on hers in swift unfumbled contact her lips parted, her tongue slipping feverishly past his.

A wave broke over them, forcing them apart. Water drummed in her ears, spray streamed down her face, and then she was above the surface once more and in the circle of his arms and his hands were on her breasts and her thighs as they swam and twisted and turned and touched like two sea-creatures, without restraint or inhibition.

When they made for the shore she swam there on her back, her arms rising and falling with supple grace, her nipples dark and erect and taut against the saturated silk of her lingerie. He swam easily and strongly at her side, his dark eyes afire with what had previously only smouldered, constantly reaching out to her, sliding his hand along the satin smoothness of her leg, skimming her breasts, twisting on to his back and enjoying the touch of her body next to his as they effortlessly neared the shore.

She felt the soft sand beneath her feet and stood, the waves foaming around her waist. She no longer felt sober or sane or remotely the person she had always believed herself to be. He stood naked at her side, like a magnificent animal, water pouring from the blue-black sheen of his hair, the lean tanned contours of his body rippling with strength and virility.

As their eyes met and he seized hold of her

hand, running with her up the sand, she felt a moment's blind panic. What if her body betrayed her – denying her, as it had always done, the pleasure she had merely glimpsed?

'What's the matter?' he asked, his brows flying together in concern as he pulled her down beside him.

'Nothing...' she gasped as he rolled his weight on top of her, imprisoning her beneath him. She couldn't continue. She couldn't tell him that she was terrified. That lovemaking had never been more than warmth and comfort and gentleness. That the fury and splendour of it had always been beyond her grasp.

'You taste of salt,' he said, and then, as his hands circled her wrists, holding her fast, he lowered his head to her breasts, taking a nipple into his mouth, and every sexual nerve-ending in her body screamed into life.

There was no hesitancy about his movements, none of the near-apologetic reverence with which Adam approached her. He was utterly sure, dominantly masterful, and her response to him was instant.

'Quickly! Quickly! Please!' she moaned, spreading her legs wide, consumed by sexual passion, strung on exquisite chords that reached deep within her vagina, demanding satisfaction.

He released her wrists, his hands like fire on her flesh as they ran down the flatness of her belly, the curve of her inner thighs, skimming the sea-wet golden curls of her pubis, the engorged lips pink and moist, craving for his touch.

'Not yet, Lizzie,' he whispered hoarsely as her

287

hands tightened in his hair and her hips thrust upwards towards him. 'Not yet, my darling...'

His mouth ground on hers, his tongue plunging deep as his hands ran down to her knees, back up the smoothness of her thighs, until at last when she thought she could bear no more his fingers slipped inside her and a low animal cry choked her throat. She could feel herself slippery and wet as the heel of his hand moved with devilish expertise over her clitoris and then, as her nails gouged his back, as she pleaded with him to take her, his hands were once more on her breasts and he thrust deep inside her, filling her until she thought she would die with the pleasure of it.

It was like nothing she had ever known. They moved together in a frenzy of passion, ascending together towards an unbearable summit. A summit she had never climbed before, never even imagined existed. Her hands tightened con-vulsively around him, her voice cried his name again and again and again as the ecstatic point of physical and emotional explosion was reached.

Afterwards she lay gasping beneath him, wondering if, in the last few seconds, she had lost consciousness. The reverberations were still beating through her body, singing along her blood as though they would never end.

He was panting harshly, looking down at her with almost ferocious triumph. He had known she had been scared. He had sensed, too, that despite being married she was almost virginally inexperienced. There had been a moment, right at the beginning, when he had felt her panic, her resistance, and he had overcome it as he would have done a filly that needed breaking. A smile touched the corners of his mouth, and then, with utmost tenderness, he lowered his head and kissed her gently on the mouth.

'You're very special, Lizzie,' he said huskily, tracing the line of her cheekbone and jaw with the tip of his finger. 'So special that I'm never going to let you go.'

She gazed up into his dark gold-flecked eyes, so languorous from his lovemaking that she could hardly move. Slowly she shook her head against the sand.

'No,' she said, and there was the regret of a lifetime in her voice. 'I'm not yours to keep or to let go, Raefe. I'm Adam's, and what happened today...' Her voice thickened, as if it were full of smoke. 'What happened today can never happen again.'

She saw disbelief flash through his eyes, and then he rolled away from her, sitting up and grasping hold of her upper arms, pulling her towards him. 'Don't start being consumed by guilt!' he said savagely. 'I'm not wanting a couple of one-night encounters – a shallow little affair conducted at the Hong Kong Club and the Peninsula and interminable lunchtime cocktail-parties! When I say you're going to be my lady, that's exactly what I mean! Mine! For good. For keeps. Christ!' His fingers tightened on her arms so that she cried out in pain. 'I'm old enough to know that this sort of thing doesn't happen twice in a lifetime! At my age there's no such thing as infatuation. It's love, and I'm damned well not going to squander it on a furtive cheap affair!'

289

Through the depth of her pain she was aware of a deep all-pervading joy. He wasn't a man who used words lightly. The cataclysm of passion which had overwhelmed her had overwhelmed him also. He believed himself to be in love with her, and she knew with a shock that left her almost senseless that against all reason she was deeply, irrevocably in love with him. But she would not see him again. Her loyalty lay elsewhere. Adam had given her his love for as long as she could remember. Together, slowly and with care, they had built something of value. She wasn't going to jettison it because she had, at last, discovered the depths of her own sensuality.

'I don't want a furtive cheap affair, either, Raefe,' she said gently, 'and there is no alternative.'

'There is!' His eyes blazed as he sprang to his feet, pulling her up against him. 'I want you to come and live with me! I want you to be divorced and I want to marry you!'

She shook her head again, and the last remaining pin fell free. Her hair tumbled wetly to her shoulders, the sun burnishing it to silver.

'No,' she said again, and though her voice was low there was no equivocation in it. 'My marriage is not like yours, Raefe. I'm not tied to a person I no longer love or respect. Adam has never done anything to harm or hurt me. All he has ever done is to give me his love, and I would never, ever hurt him.'

He took her chin between his fingers, tilting her face to his with almost brutal strength. 'But you're not in love with him, are you?' he rasped.

'What we just experienced isn't what you experience with him, is it?'

She twisted away from him, refusing to reveal to him the barrenness of her marriage bed, knowing that Adam deserved that, at least, from her. Her clothes lay scattered on the sand. She began to dress hastily, her hands trembling as she zipped up her skirt and fastened the buttons on her blouse. He watched her silently for a few minutes and then strode across to where his trousers and shirt lay in a discarded heap. She pushed her blouse into the band of her skirt, appalled at the rift that was yawning between them. A rift that was of her own making. He dressed with the speed and panther-wary grace that characterized all his movements. It had never occurred to her before that a man could be beautiful. She could have watched him for hours, riveted by his slim suppleness, his athletic muscular coordination, the blue-black tumble of his hair as it curled thickly at the nape of his neck.

'I'm not going to take no for an answer,' he said, fastening his belt-buckle and picking up his shoes, walking across to her and sliding his free hand around her waist. She tried to pull away, but he held her easily. 'I want you, Lizzie,' he said, and there was such burning desire in his voice and in his eyes that she felt her throat dry and the blood begin to roar along her veins. 'And, to prove to you how much, I'm going to start divorce proceedings immediately against Melissa.'

She leaned against him as they walked back to the car, only the knowledge of how her action would devastate Adam preventing her from flinging her arms around his neck and telling him that she would live with him anywhere, uncaring of the scandal; uncaring of anything if only they could be together.

She said, her voice oddly flat as she stepped into the car: 'Tell me about Melissa. All I have heard are the rumours. That you treat her appallingly. That she turned to Jacko Latimer for comfort.'

'She turned to Jacko Latimer for heroin,' Raefe said drily, gunning the Lagonda's engine into life. 'Comfort she gained elsewhere. Mostly with a major in the Middlesex. Sometimes with a junior diplomat at Government House. Sometimes, before she saw fit to tell me about her major, with me.'

There was such bitterness in his voice that she hesitated before saying: 'Did you love her very much?'

'I thought I did.' There was a sudden flexing of muscles along his jawline. 'She soon disabused me of the idea.'

The sky above Mount Collinson was flushed a deep rose as they sped out of Shek-O village and back along the road leading to the Gap.

'Will a divorce distress her?' she asked curiously.

His shoulders shrugged imperceptibly. 'I doubt it. The only thing that distresses her these days is the thought of having her heroin supply cut off.'

She was silent. She knew nothing at all about drugs. After a little while she said: 'How does she manage ... now that Jacko Latimer is dead?'

He turned his head, his eyes meeting hers unflinchingly. 'I supply her,' he said with a harshness that made her wince. 'If I didn't, she would get adulterated muck from Chinese dealers and be dead within six months. As it is, I can regulate the amount she receives. It's impossible to bring her off it overnight. I tried once, in Australia, before I knew about Jacko, and failed. This way takes time, but at least there's a chance it will succeed eventually. And at least she's still alive.'

There were tight white lines around his mouth. She remembered Sir Denholm Gresby saying that he was a blackguard who had ruined his wife's life and done his best to ruin her reputation. He had done neither. He had tried to save her life once before and even now, after her behaviour had led to him standing trial for his life, he was still trying to save her and to help her.

The daffodil sky of evening engulfed them as they crowned Wong Nai Chung Gap and began to descend towards Victoria.

'I haven't the slightest intention of taking any notice of what you've said,' he said forcefully as he pulled up at the isolated spot at the foot of the Peak Road where she had parked her Buick. 'I don't give a damn about your husband or your feelings of loyalty. Your life with him is in the past. It's your life with me now that matters.'

She turned away from him, opening the car door, barely trusting herself to speak. He strode round to her, trying to take her in his arms, but she resisted with such passion that he released his hold.

'I can't do as you ask!' she cried vehemently. 'I've behaved disgracefully enough already and I can't behave like that again.'

'Then why did you let me make love to you?' he demanded, his eyes burning, his brows flying together satanically.

She looked up at him for one last time. 'Because I needed to prove something to myself,' she said quietly and then, her voice choked: 'Because I wanted to.' Quickly, before he could reach out for her, she spun on her heel, running towards her car, not looking behind her as she wrenched the door open, turning the key in the ignition with trembling hands, pressing her foot down hard on the clutch and accelerator.

He made no attempt to restrain her. She was on the verge of an emotional collapse, and he knew that he could achieve nothing by putting more pressure on her. She had to have time to come to terms with what had happened between them. Time to see that her heart, and future, lay with him and not with Adam Harland.

Elizabeth sped up the darkened twists of Peak Road, the lights of Victoria glittering exotically to her right, the dark bulk of the mountain towering up on her left. It was nearly seven o'clock. She had been away from the house for nearly five hours. She tried to remember if they were going out to dinner that evening, if guests were coming to them, and couldn't. She could still feel the heat of Raefe's hands on her inner thighs, taste the heat of his mouth, feel the hard strength of his body. She had never imagined that lovemaking could be so ferocious, so exquisitely joyous. She slewed off the road on to the secondary road that led her home. And then there had been that moment afterwards, that moment when he had traced her face with his finger and kissed her with all the tenderness of absolute love. She began to shake. It would be so easy to turn her back on everything and live with him as his mistress. So easy and, for her, so very, very wrong.

She slammed the car into the garage. Adam's Riley was already parked, his golf bags still on the rear seat. She caught sight of herself in the dim light of the driving-mirror. Her hair hung dishevelled to her shoulders, her face was bereft of make-up, her clothes looked as though they had been flung on. She stepped out of the car, closing the door behind her. She couldn't allow Adam to see her like this. He would think she was ill; that she had been in an accident. She hurried round to the rear of the house, entering by the kitchen door as quietly as she could.

'Mr Harland is waiting dinner for you, Mrs Harland,' Chan, her number one houseboy said, staring at her in surprise as she walked quickly through the kitchen towards the back stairs.

'There's no need to tell him that I'm home. I'll tell him myself,' she said, bewildering him even more.

'Is there anything I can get you, missy?' Mei Lin asked breathlessly, running after her as she walked quickly towards her bedroom.

'Run me a hot bath, Mei Lin, and lay out fresh underclothes and a dress for me,' she added, her heart pounding in case Adam should have heard her enter the house; should see her before she had time to compose herself, to bathe and change.

'Mr Harland has been very worried,' Mei Lin said, pouring Cologne into the bathwater as Elizabeth scrambled out of her clothes. 'There has been some bad news, I think.'

Elizabeth stepped into the bathwater, reaching for her bottle of Elizabeth Arden shampoo. The news was probably about Semco. Adam had been spending an increasing amount of time down at the office, and she knew that he had intended lunching with Leigh Stafford before going on to the golf club. She lathered her hair furiously. Whatever his news, it could scarcely be as bad as the news she had so very nearly brought home to him. The news that she had fallen in love with Raefe Elliot and intended spending the rest of her life with him.

She stepped out of the bath, wrapping a towel around her head and another around her chest. There were bruises on her arms where Raefe had seized her when she had told him that she was not leaving Adam.

'Not the short-sleeved dress,' she said to Mei Lin as she hastily put on fresh underclothes. 'The turquoise silk with the wrist-length sleeves.'

She towelled her hair dry, sweeping it up into a smooth chignon, securing it with ivory pins. The turquoise silk dress was cool and elegant. She put on high-heeled, delicately strapped sandals, sprayed herself with perfume and took one last look at herself in the mirror. She didn't look like an adulteress. Nothing showed outwardly. Her hair, her eyes, her skin were just the same. But she had changed inwardly. She was no longer the same woman who had left the house only hours earlier. That woman had been an emotional virgin, and she was a virgin no longer.

He was sitting on the veranda, reading the *Hong Kong Times*, a sundowner on the table by his side. At her approach he turned, his usual smile absent, his face grave.

'Hello, darling, I'm sorry I'm late,' she said, slipping her arm around his neck and dropping a kiss on his forehead. 'I went for a drive and forgot the time...'

He rose to his feet slowly and took both her hands in his. 'It's happened,' he said, the lines around his mouth grim. 'The news was broadcast today.'

'What's happened?' She was momentarily disorientated, so sickened at the necessity of her cheap lie that her usual perceptiveness deserted her.

'The inevitable,' he said sombrely, drawing her close into the circle of his arms. 'Great Britain is at war with Germany.'

Chapter 12

In Tom Nicholson's driveway, Chinese chauffeurs leaned against sleek and gleaming Buicks and Packards and Chrysler limousines. It was Jeremy Nicholson's sixth birthday, and Helena, realizing the limitations of her small Kowloon flat, was holding his birthday party in Tom's large house on the Peak.

'Oh, goodness,' she said to Elizabeth, pushing a thick fall of hair away from her face, 'I'd forgotten that children's parties were such hard work. Are there really only twenty children here? It sounds like a hundred and twenty!'

'The conjuror wants to know if you want him to perform now or after the cake has been cut,' Elizabeth said, picking up a small boy who had fallen over part of a train set, a present temporarily discarded.

'Now,' Helena said unhesitatingly. 'It may keep the sound level down. He's going to perform in the garden, so we had better usher them all outside.' She turned towards the amahs who were endeavouring to maintain some kind of control over the proceedings. 'Jung-lu, could you lead the children out into the garden and ask them to sit quietly for the conjuring show? Mei Lin, that little girl is trying to put six chocolate cakes into her mouth all at the same time. Please take them away from her, she's going to make herself sick.'

Her warning come too late. Mei Lin, accustomed to the childless order of the Harland household, gave Elizabeth a look of pained reproach at having been brought along to assist and then led the offending child towards the nearest bathroom.

'Oh God, oh hell!' Helena said as the word 'conjuror' went from mouth to mouth and there was a stampede towards the garden that nearly knocked her from her feet. 'What I need is a stiff gin and tonic, but it looks such bad form to be clutching a drink in the middle of a children's party!'

Elizabeth giggled and removed a paper streamer from her hair. 'There's respectability in numbers. I'll have one with you.'

'Two *very large* gin and tonics, Lee,' Helena said to her houseboy as they walked outside to the veranda, collapsing on the cane chairs that overlooked the garden and the conjuror and the exuberant children. 'Oh, gosh, that child who was sick is still eating! Who on earth is she? She must have a tummy made of steel!'

Elizabeth accepted her drink from the houseboy, sipping it gratefully. 'She's Lady Gresby's grandchild,' she said with a grin. 'Don't you remember? She's out here until Christmas.'

'So that's the "dear sweet little thing" Miriam Gresby described to me,' Helena said, marvelling as a fistful of crushed macaroons followed an éclair and two raspberry-jam tarts. 'Tom says

299

the Gresbys may have her for longer than they had anticipated. Travel to and from Britain is no longer safe now that the cards are on the table. If things get sticky here as well, I imagine that the Gresbys will have to send her on to Canada. That's where most of the children are being evacuated to.'

The conjuror was now in his stride, and the noise level had fallen as the children sat cross-legged before him in rapt fascination.

'It seems hard to think of a war as a reality,' Elizabeth said, gazing out over the smoothly manicured lawn and the painted Chinese lanterns bobbing gaily between the trees. 'Nothing has changed here at all.'

'It's only been a week,' Helena said, swirling the ice cubes meditatively around in her glass. 'Give it time. Have you heard of the suggestion that a volunteer force be formed? It's to be something on the lines of the Territorials. Regular drill and training and open to any man who wants to join. Alastair thinks it's a good idea. He's beginning to alter his opinions, I think.'

'In what way?'

'He doesn't seem to think the Japanese quite the joke that he used to.' Her expressive animated face was suddenly sombre. 'And I don't think them a joke at all. Jung-lu has family who have just arrived in Hong Kong from mainland China. The stories they have brought with them, of Japanese rapes and murders, are horrific. If the Japanese *do* invade, it will be the Chinese who will suffer the worst, people like Jung-lu and Mei Lin.'

'*Bonjour!*' Julienne called gaily, swinging towards them with an enormous teddy bear in one hand and a glass of white wine in the other. '*Alors!* What is the matter? Has someone died?'

'We were talking about the Japs,' Helena said with a grin. 'Not a very jolly conversation, unfortunately.'

'Oh, the Japs...' Julienne said dismissively, sinking into a luxuriously padded cane-backed long chair and holding the teddy bear up for inspection. 'Isn't he adorable? I couldn't resist him. Ronnie said I was crazy. That no little boy of six years old would thank me for giving him a teddy, *mais, je ne le croix pas.*' She gave a gurgle of impish laughter. 'He has a very naughty look that reminds me of someone I know very well! If Jeremy doesn't fall in love with him *immédiatement*, then I will keep him for myself!'

'Jeremy will adore him,' Helena said, trying to see any similarity between the cheeky-looking teddy bear and Julienne's friend in the Royal Scots. There was none. Alastair had told her that he thought the affair was over and that Julienne had a new boyfriend. Helena wondered who it could be. There had been a time when Julienne had flirted outrageously with Adam Harland, but she was quite sure that Adam had never responded. Even if he had, Helena was sure that the affair would have been short-lived. Adam was too steady and staid for a woman of Julienne's exotic tastes. Which left plenty of other people and one in particular.

Raefe Elliot had been having a drink with herself and Alastair the previous Tuesday, and

301

she had mentioned Jeremy's forthcoming party, and the fact that Julienne and Elizabeth would be helping her survive it. She had been surprised when, as they parted, he had said laconically that he would drop in for five minutes or so to wish Jeremy a happy birthday. She had wondered then if he had had an ulterior motive. Now she was sure of it.

'Is Tom not here?' Julienne asked, shielding her eyes from the sun as she looked out over the lawn and the throng of children.

'Good heavens, no!' Helena said, amused. 'He allowed me the use of the house on the strict understanding that he wasn't to have a thing to do with it.'

Julienne sighed. Her affair with Tom was long over, and she had no desire to rekindle it. Nevertheless, he would have been welcome company. To Julienne, a social gathering without a male present was like a gin and tonic without the gin. A slight frown furrowed her brow. 'He isn't going to return to England, is he? To – how do you say it in English? – join up.'

Helena shook her head, a slight frown furrowing her brow. Julienne had an uncanny knack of knowing what people were going to do even before they knew it themselves. 'No. Why do you ask?'

Julienne shrugged. 'There's been quite a rush for the boats since the broadcast. Three of Ronnie's friends have booked passages home. They want to enlist and give Hitler a bloody nose.' A smile hovered at the corners of her pink-painted mouth. 'And I know of one or two bored husbands who are using patriotism and Monsieur Hitler as an excuse to escape from their *very* dull marriages!'

'Tom couldn't go, even if he wanted to,' Helena said practically. 'As a junior diplomat he's in Hong Kong until he's posted elsewhere.'

'Is there any further talk of the Royal Scots being moved?' Julienne asked, confirming Helena's belief that her affair with her Royal Scots major was over and finished.

Helena shook her head. 'No. Alastair says most of the men are impatient for a posting where they will see some action, but it doesn't look as if they're going to get one. There's even talk of the garrison here being strengthened.'

'That could be fun!' Julienne's eyes sparkled wickedly at the thought of a fresh input of handsome young officers.

The conjuror came to the end of his performance, producing two doves amid a cloud of smoke. The children clapped and shouted noisily and then, when it became apparent that nothing else was to follow, began to charge back towards the house and the tea-table.

'*Tiens*!' Julienne cried, seizing her drink as the table beside her was rocked beneath the stampede. 'I think I must go now!'

'You will do no such thing,' Helena said mercilessly. 'You can help hold the dear little things at bay while Jeremy cuts his cake.'

With a horrified expression on her face, Julienne followed Elizabeth into the large, airy, balloon-filled dining-room. '*Merde*!' she said expressively as she was surrounded by sticky

faces and sticky fingers. 'What on earth possessed Helena to invite so many children? There
must be hundreds here!'

'Twenty,' Elizabeth said with a grin, removing
a brightly painted *papier mâché* figure from a
child who was trying to eat it.

Julienne trod into a cream cake that had been
inadvertently dropped to the floor. 'I don't
believe it!' she moaned, looking down in horror
at her ruined suede shoes. 'They are like an
invading army! Who on earth is that child trying
to eat an almond slice and a fairy cake and a
brandy-snap curl all at the same time?'

Elizabeth giggled. 'Lady Gresby's grand-
daughter. She's quite talented at getting several
things into her mouth at the same time.'

Julienne shuddered and, following Elizabeth's
example, reluctantly joined hands with the
children at either side of her as the candles were
lit on the cake and everyone began to sing
'Happy Birthday' to Jeremy.

It was Mei Lin who saw him enter the room.
Her eyes flew to Elizabeth, but she was lifting a
child up to see the cake and the candles as
Jeremy began to huff and puff ready to blow
them out. He strolled towards the laden buffet-
table, a lavishly wrapped present tucked beneath
one arm, a white silk shirt open at the throat,
white flannels hugging his hips. Julienne, immediately sensing the presence of a member of
the opposite sex, looked away from the cake, her
eyes meeting his, her eyebrows lifting in surprise
and pleasure.

'Happy birthday to youuuu, happy birthday to

youuuu,' the children chorused gustily. 'Happy birthday, dear Jeremy, happy birthday to youuu.'

To Julienne's chagrin he did not accept the invitation in her eyes to come and stand beside her. Instead he weaved his way imperturbably between the rioting children, towards his hostess.

With a great exhalation of breath, Jeremy succeeded in blowing out the last candle, and amidst frenzied cheering Helena hugged him tight and then looked up and saw Raefe. Her mouth widened into a welcoming smile. 'My goodness! You actually came! How brave of you! There isn't money enough in the world to tempt Tom to a children's party!'

'It is a bit fearsome,' he said with a grin, handing Jeremy his present, not looking as if he found it at all fearsome.

Jeremy tore the paper off his present, revealing a magnificent clockwork sports-car. He whooped in delight, and Helena said promptingly: 'Say "thank you" to Mr Elliot, Jeremy.' As she did so, she turned towards Jung-lu. 'I think it's time for the children to be given their kites now, Jung-lu. They can take them outside to fly them and, Lee...' Her houseboy moved forward. 'Drinks, please. A whisky and soda for Mr Elliot and two gin and tonics and a glass of white wine, please.'

Relieved that the end of the party was in sight without any accidents material or physical, she pushed her hair once more away from her face and said to Elizabeth: 'Gosh, and to think there'll have to be another one next year, and another one the year after that, until he's at least twenty-one!' She was laughing, but as she looked across

305

at Elizabeth her eyes widened and her laughter faded.

Elizabeth hadn't moved from her position near the table, only now there were no children crowding round her. Her eyes were wide and dark, her finely etched face so pale that Helena thought she was about to faint.

'Elizabeth, are you all right?' she began in concern and then she became aware of Raefe, his eyes holding Elizabeth's, the expression in them of such burning, blazing desire that she fell back in stunned shock.

The children had surged into the garden, Junglu and Mei Lin in their wake. Lee had handed both herself and Julienne their drinks and was standing beside Raefe and Elizabeth, his silver drinks tray proffered deferentially. Neither of them made the slightest move towards removing their glasses. Helena doubted if they were even aware of his presence.

'Why won't you speak to me on the telephone?' he asked her harshly. 'Why won't you at least talk to me?'

Her hands opened and closed at her side as if seeking for a support that was absent. She was wearing an amethyst silk shirt and a white linen skirt, little gold sandals and not much else. With a fresh wave of shock, Helena realized how sexy and effortlessly chic her friend was, how unknowingly provocative.

'I told you that I wouldn't see you again...' Her voice was barely audible, her eyes bruised with pain.

'*Mon Dieu...*' Julienne whispered beneath her

breath, staring from one to the other in disbelieving comprehension.

Helena raised her eyebrows sharply in Lee's direction, indicating that he remove himself with all speed. The less he heard the better. As it was, Jung-lu and Mei Lin would be treated to a highly descriptive account of what had happened, and before the end of the day, the Chinese love of gossip being what it was, the staff of every household on the Peak would be cognizant of the facts. Including Adam's.

'This is ridiculous...' His voice was brusque, full of such deep need that Julienne felt a shiver run down her spine and a flush of heat surge through her groin. 'I must see you, must speak to you!'

She shook her head stiffly, as if she could barely force herself to move. 'No,' she repeated, through parched lips. 'We have nothing to talk about, Raefe. Nothing to discuss.'

'*Like hell we have!*' His hand shot out, encircling her wrist, and as Elizabeth cried out like an animal in pain Helena stepped forward, saying urgently: 'For God's sake stop it! The children will be back at any minute.'

Elizabeth sucked in a deep shuddering breath and with sudden strength wrenched free of his grasp. 'You shouldn't have come here!' she flared at him, her eyes brilliant with anguish. 'You shouldn't have come!' She pushed past Helena, running from the room, tears pouring down her face.

'Lizzie!' He sprang after her, catching up with her in the mosaic-tiled hall, seizing her wrists in a grasp she couldn't escape. 'Listen to me, for God's sake! I telephoned Roman last night. He's given me—'

'Did you tell *him* we were lovers, as well? Just as you've so publicly told Helena and Julienne? Just as you might as well have told Adam!'

'I told him you were a brilliant pianist,' he rasped, his hawk-like face as agonized as hers. 'I told him you needed a teacher! A great teacher.'

'Did you tell him that you've never heard me play?' she sobbed in fury, tears of rage and grief mixing inextricably. 'Did you tell him I was a married woman who was bored with her husband and wanted a little diversion?'

'I told him I loved you!' he shouted at her, his fury demonic. 'I told him you were dying inside by inches because your fool of a husband had cut you off from your musical life-blood! I told him—'

'Adam's not a fool!' If she could have clawed his face, she would have done. She hated him; hated herself; hated the spectacle they were making of themselves in front of Helena and Julienne. 'He's good and he's kind and he's twice the man that you are!'

'There's a man in Kowloon,' Raefe continued, not deigning even to respond to her last, furiously flung words. 'His name is Li Pi, and Roman says he's one of the greatest piano teachers alive today. He's in retirement now, but Roman has spoken to him and he's willing to see you—'

Her hand at last twisted free, and she slapped him across the face with all the force she was capable of. 'Never! I shall never take anything

308

from you, Raefe Elliot! Not ever again!'

As she broke free of him, running from the house, the children surged out into the hall, kites and carefully wrapped slices of birthday cake in their hands. He took a step after her, and Helena rushed forward grabbing hold of his arm. 'For God's sake, no!' she hissed. 'It will be all over the island!'

He stopped short, his hands clenched, a nerve twitching furiously at his jawline, watching as she hurled herself into her Buick, ramming it into gear, disappearing down the drive in a cloud of dust.

Other cars began to motor slowly towards the open door. 'Timothy, your car is here,' Helena said in a cracked voice, forcing a smile and despatching one of her guests with relief. 'Jonathan, your chauffeur is waiting. Lydia ... Rosalind...'

'I'm sorry,' Raefe said to her tautly, the abrasive masculine lines of his face harsh as the children tumbled out into the drive. 'I didn't intend there to be such a scene.'

'I don't know what has happened between the two of you, Raefe,' she said bewilderedly. 'But, whatever it was, there can be no future in it. Her marriage is a good one. She won't throw it away. Not for you or for anyone.'

A mirthless smile touched the corner of his mouth. 'She will, Helena,' he said with utter certainty. 'Just give her time and she'll leave him and come to me and she won't ever regret it!'

'*Ce n'est pas possible! I* could hardly believe it!' Julienne said, rolling away from Ronnie and lying on her back in their big double bed. 'I thought he was forcibly going to pick her up and carry her away!'

Ronnie pushed himself up against the pillows and reached towards the bedside table for his cigarettes and a lighter. 'What the devil does Elliot think he's playing at? The news will be all over the Peak by sundown.'

'*Mais oui*,' Julienne said admiringly, turning towards him, leaning her weight on her elbow. 'But he obviously does not care.' She took his cigarette from between his fingers and drew on it meditatively. 'What *I* want to know, *chéri*, is when did this all start? I had no idea, and I could see from Helena's face that Helena had no idea, either.' She handed him back his cigarette and leaned her chin on her hand. 'Raefe Elliot and Elizabeth! It is incredible, is it not? I always thought her so calm, so sensible, so ... so very English.'

Ronnie grinned. There were times when Juli was not half as perceptive as she believed herself to be. 'Still waters run deep,' he said, pulling her close against his chest. Above her tousled red curls his eyes were speculative. Had Raefe and Elizabeth already been embroiled in an affair the day he had lured her to lunch at the Pen? Or had that been the beginning? Had he, Ronnie Ledsham, been inadvertently responsible for this most intriguing turn of events?

Julienne's fingers ran lightly and arousingly over the smooth hard contours of his chest and down to the heavy weight of his sex. 'I always thought that you were more than a little interested in *la belle Elizabeth* yourself,' she said coaxingly. 'Perhaps you were, *chéri*, and perhaps *she* was not interested?'

'Rubbish,' Ronnie lied good-naturedly, his penis throbbing and hardening in the warm grip of her hand. '*La belle Elizabeth* is too cool and contained for my taste.'

Julienne giggled as he rolled his weight on top of her, taking a small erect nipple into his mouth. 'I think you are wrong, *mon amour*,' she said, sliding her legs around his waist, arching herself towards him with pleasure. 'Yes, where Elizabeth is concerned, I think you are very wrong!'

'I've never been so devastated in my whole life,' Helena said to Alastair, her eyes dark with worry. 'It wouldn't have mattered where they had been; they could have been at a reception at Government House and it wouldn't have made an iota of difference! He would still have thundered at her that he loved her; that he had to see her; had to speak to her.'

'And Elizabeth?' Alastair asked with interest. 'What did she say in return?'

'I thought she was going to faint. She was so white, so still. She said that they had nothing to talk about. Nothing to discuss.'

'Then, whatever there has been between them is all over,' Alastair said dismissively, regarding Helena's wide-hipped, ripe, lush body with satisfaction.

They were in bed at her Kowloon flat. Tom was taking Jeremy and Jennifer to the zoological gardens the next day for a birthday treat, and so

Helena had left them with him for the night and had returned home alone.

Helena shook her head. 'No,' she said, pleasantly comfortable in the circle of his arms. 'If you had heard the passion in their voices, seen the expression in their eyes, then you would know that despite all her protests to the contrary it was far from over.'

Alastair's forefinger traced the line of her neck down to her shoulder, to her breast, to the full dark aureola of her nipple. 'The man's a bastard,' he said succinctly. 'I don't know why you bother with him.'

'I like him.' She shifted her position so that he could reach both her breasts, loving the slow unhurried deliberation of his hands. 'I like his go-to-hell attitude that takes no account of what people say or think. I like the way he takes his Malay girlfriend with him to all the places he would take a white girl. There's something very feral and primitive about him, something barely veneered by the politeness civilization demands.'

'Good grief,' Alastair said, sitting bolt upright and staring at her in shock. 'You wouldn't like it if *I* behaved in the same manner! Squiring other women around when he has a perfectly sweet wife at home. Thrashing Jacko Latimer so that the man dies of his injuries! Gambling tens of thousands at Happy Valley! Racing around in that damned Lagonda of his as if the island were his personal racetrack!'

Helena slid her hands up and around his neck, pulling him affectionately back down against her. 'Of course I wouldn't, silly,' she said agreeably. 'I like you just the way you are.'

His light blue eyes darkened fractionally. It was still 'like' and not 'love'. He said, with a trace of harshness: 'The fellow is a rogue. He doesn't give a damn about anyone but himself.'

'I think you're wrong there,' Helena said as he rolled her gently over on to her stomach and she raised herself up on her hands and knees, her heavy mane of hair swinging down on to the bed, her breasts hanging like full rich fruit, her legs apart as he kneeled behind her. 'I think he cares very much about Elizabeth. He mentioned a teacher he had found for her. A piano teacher...'

He was no longer listening to her. The firm head of his penis pushed hard into the entrance of her vagina, his hands tightening convulsively on her buttocks. 'Oh God!' he groaned, thrusting deep inside her in an agony of relief. 'Oh God, but I love you, Helena! Jesus, but I love you!'

For the second time, Elizabeth slammed the Buick into the double garage beside Adam's Riley. Her hands were trembling when she took them from the wheel. Damn him! Damn him! Damn him! How *dare* he compromise her in such a way in front of Julienne and Helena and God alone knows how many servants and children?

There was a piece of paper tucked securely beneath one of her windscreen wipers, but she did not bother to remove it. Several of the cars parked in the Nicholson drive had been littered with party streamers. Her houseboy could

313

remove it when he cleaned the car.

She entered the house, knowing very well what it was she had to do. She should never have come to Hong Kong, never have abandoned her musical studies in London. She was twenty-five, for God's sake. In musical terms that was old. If she wanted to make an international name for herself as a pianist, then she had no time to lose. She had already won two major prizes, and for a short time they had placed her where she wanted to be – on the concert platform. But they had not been enough to establish her. There had been no frantic letters from promoters, demanding that she return to England and undertake engagements for them. She was out of sight and out of mind. To save her sanity – and her marriage – she had to win another major prize and so make a triumphal return.

'Hello, my love. Was it a good party?' Adam asked, stuffing tobacco down in his pipe as he walked towards her.

'Yes ... no...' she replied, appalled at how distressed she still felt.

He laughed, putting his arm around her shoulders. 'Make up your mind, love. Either it was or it wasn't.'

She forced a laugh. 'Oh, you know what children's parties are like. The noise was indescribable.'

'It was far too quiet here,' he said, smiling down at her. 'I hate it when I come home and you're not in.'

'That's what I'd like to talk to you about,' she

said, knowing that this time she couldn't be a coward; that this time she had to tell him exactly how she felt. 'I want to go back to London, Adam.'

They had walked through the downstairs rooms to the long veranda that ran the length of the house at the back. It was Adam's favourite retreat at dusk. He liked to sit with a sundowner at his side, looking out over the garden and the hillside beyond and the magnificent views of Victoria and the harbour and the distant hills of the Kowloon Peninsula.

He sat down in his cane long-chair, saying good-temperedly: 'We've been through all this before, Beth. There can be no question of you returning to London now that war has broken out. Good heavens, children are being evacuated *away* from London in their thousands.'

'I'm not a child, Adam,' she said, sitting down beside him, struggling for calm and control. 'And it isn't because of the war that I want to return. It's a far more selfish reason.'

A closed shuttered look came down over his face. It was a look that she had grown familiar with. These days, whenever she spoke of her music, he would be conscientiously polite, but the same shuttered expression came into his eyes. He no longer wanted to hear about it. As far as he was concerned, her music had begun to be an intrusion. He had encouraged her in the early days of their marriage, taking pleasure in indulging her, but when it had come to a choice between moving to Hong Kong, which he wanted to do, or remaining in London so that she

315

could pursue her career, then there had been no choice at all. Just as there had been no choice when her father had wished to live in Nice.

'I'm twenty-five, Adam,' she said forcefully. 'If I want to continue my career – and I *do* want to continue it – then I have to win a major international prize. You know as well as I that it's the quickest and most effective route to a concert career, not only because of the publicity and prize money involved, but also because important orchestral engagements are guaranteed to the winners.'

'You can practise here,' he said obstinately. 'You already spend six hours a day at the piano. I can't see how you can expect to spend any more, no matter where you are.'

'Practising alone isn't enough. I need a critic, a teacher. Someone like Professor Hurok who will help me to interpret, to look for new insight.'

'No.' The lines around his mouth hardened. 'It's impossible, Beth. There's a war on, for God's sake! There won't *be* any international piano competitions this year – or next year, either, if the war continues. The world has got more important things to think about!'

'*I* haven't,' she cried passionately. 'There *isn't* anything more important to me than my music!'

She had risen to her feet, and he looked up at her steadily. 'Not even me, Beth?' he asked quietly.

She felt a sob rise up in her throat, remembering the time he had come to her and comforted her when her mother had died, remembering how he had always been there when she had

316

needed him, remembering how very much he had always loved her. 'Oh God, Adam! Why can't you see how much it means to me? Why can't you see how forcing me to choose is driving a wedge between us?'

He rose to his feet, taking her hands in his. 'It is you who are driving the wedge, Beth,' he said gently. 'Not me. You can continue your musical studies here, just as well as you can in London. And later, when we've put paid to Hitler and the world is sane again, then will be the time for you to think about pursuing a career on the concert platform. Until then, there is no point in returning to London. Yours will not be the only promising career to be put in cold storage till the war is over. Musicians will be entering the forces, just as men from every other walk of life are doing. It is the war that is robbing you of London and an international prize, Beth, not me.'

She looked despairingly into his eyes. Everything he said was common sense. The war would have affected international competitions; there would be other aspiring concert pianists, besides herself, whose careers had been brought to an abrupt halt. And yet ... And yet ... She closed her eyes, sick with longing, knowing that Raefe would not have taken such an attitude. That Raefe would have understood the depth of her need. That Raefe would not have allowed Hitler to interfere with any of his plans for the future.

'I love you very much, Beth,' Adam was saying, folding her into his arms and holding her close. 'Please be patient. Wait until the war is over, and then I'll give you all the support that I can.'

Defeated, frustrated tears pricked the back of her eyelids. Till the war was over. How many years would that be? And how many other reasons would he then find for a further postponement, and a further one?

'If it isn't possible for me to return to my studies with Professor Hurok,' she said tenaciously, 'I want to return to London anyway, Adam.'

He pulled away from her, looking at her white set face in bewilderment. 'But why? There's nothing I could do there. Here, if the Japs attack, I will at least be able to fight!'

'We've been here for six months,' she said, knowing that this was one battle she could not concede. 'I'm tired of it, and—'

'Tired of it?' He began to laugh indulgently. 'Good heavens, Beth. How can you tire of it? Sun, magnificent beaches, superb swimming, tennis, riding, the best lot of friends we've ever had. Don't be ridiculous darling. You're suffering from a wave of guilt at not being home and suffering all the agonies of the blackout and evacuation.'

'No, I do feel guilty, but it isn't just that. I need to get away, Adam. Have a complete change.' He wouldn't return to London, she knew, but there were other places in the world. Places where she would not run the risk of meeting Raefe, of having her defences stormed, of leaving Adam and never returning to him. 'Couldn't we go to Singapore for a while? Helena says it's even more fascinating than Hong Kong.'

'I suppose we could go for a week or two if you really want to,' he said reluctantly. She squeezed his hand. A week or two would be a start. She could always encourage him to prolong their stay once they were there. 'Then, let's go, Adam! Please. Quickly.'

He laughed, too relieved that an awful scene had been averted to read anything odd into her sudden enthusiasm for a visit to Singapore.

'OK,' he said, 'I'd quite like to see Singapore myself. We'll go at the end of next month, when the dry season starts.'

'No!' she said fiercely, and this time he was surprised by her vehemence. 'I want to go now, Adam. This week if possible.'

'And miss Tom Nicholson's party?'

Her nails dug deep into her palms. Raefe would be at the party. If he looked at her as he had looked at her in Helena's, then Adam would guess. The whole room would know. 'Yes, darling,' she said stiffly, 'and miss Tom's party.'

'All right, Beth, if that's what you want,' he said with the air of a man who was being more than reasonably patient. 'We'll sail there; it will be more pleasant than flying. I'll call in at the agency and book a couple of berths tomorrow.'

Chapter 13

By six o'clock the next morning she was at her piano, wrestling with the Schubert B-flat Sonata. She had had a sleepless night, lying beside Adam, tortured by how easily she had been unfaithful to him. A week ago her life had seemed so ordered and secure, so predictable. Now nothing was predictable any longer. She had slipped out of bed quietly, so as not to disturb him, making herself a drink of lime juice and carrying it out on to the veranda. There was nothing she could do to wipe out what had happened. It was something she would have to learn to live with. And to forget.

She had turned away from the view of the distant harbour and the hills of Kowloon, her head hurting and her heart aching, knowing that she did not want to forget. Her betrayal of Adam had not only been physical; it had been, and continued to be, a mental betrayal that she could find no release from. She had sat down at the piano, grateful for the salvation it offered her, launching into the first movement, playing it far quicker than she usually did. It changed the entire character of her performance, and she forgot about Adam, forgot even Raefe, as she began to play the second movement, intrigued at the way that, too, was affected and changed.

It was ten-thirty by the time she had played the third and fourth movements to her satisfaction. She rose reluctantly to her feet. She couldn't remember what Adam's plans were for the day, but he hated having to leave the house without having said goodbye to her. She stretched her fingers, pleased with her new insights into a score she was deeply familiar with. She would return to it after she had had a late breakfast. She would play all four movements through again and then perhaps she would turn her attention to Bartók's Second Piano Concerto. It was a piece of music that had, so far, defeated her. The score looked as if a printer had just thrown a million black notes on the page, and she had always thought of it as being utterly impossible.

As she walked towards the drawing-room, Chan hurried to meet her, his face anxious. 'I found this beneath the wind-screen of your car, missy. Perhaps it is important?'

It was the piece of paper she had ignored when driving away from the party. She could see now that it wasn't a piece of streamer, and she took it from him. 'Thank you, Chan. Is Mr Harland still in the house?'

'Yes, missy. He's down at the tennis courts checking the nets.'

She thanked him again and looked down at the piece of paper in her hand. 'Li Pi, 27 Stonewall Mansions, Kimberley Road, Kowloon.' The handwriting was firm and strong. He must have slipped it under the windscreen-wiper before he had even entered Tom's to see her. Which meant that he had anticipated her reaction and had not been surprised by it.

From beyond the open windows, the only sound was the *chip-chop* of the gardener trimming the lawn around the flowerbeds. The air was heavy, as if a storm was due, the scent from the frangipani trees heady and sweet. She stood for a long time, staring down at the note in her hand. Li Pi. She had heard of him when she had been at the Royal Academy. He was one of the great teachers, and he was now in Kowloon, and Raefe had said that if she went to him he would see her.

The gardener continued to trim the lawn. Through the window she could see Adam down at the tennis courts, his hands deep in the pockets of his white flannels as he surveyed the nets.

Li Pi: he had taught at the Moscow Central Music School. His recordings of the Chopin Barcarolle and B-minor Sonata and the Schumann Concerto were incandescent interpretations that had become classics. She stared once more from the piece of paper in her hand to Adam, and back again. Would it be a further betrayal to him if she were to accept Raefe's introduction? And if she didn't? Wouldn't that be an even greater betrayal? A betrayal of her talent and all her years of work?

Mei Lin approached her and said in her sing-song voice: 'I have made fresh coffee for you, missy.'

'Thank you, Mei Lin.' She looked down once again at the piece of paper in her hand and then said decisively: 'I'm going out for a little while, Mei Lin. Tell Mr Harland that I'll be back for lunch.'

'Yes, missy,' Mei Lin said unhappily. Mr Harland did not like to be brought such messages. He did not like it when she left the house and he did not know where she was. He did not even like it when she was in the house and playing her piano. She had seen his frown of annoyance only hours ago when he had emerged from their bedroom and heard the music filling the downstairs rooms. And now she would have to tell him that Mrs Harland had finished playing and had left the house without even waiting to speak to him. Reluctantly she stepped out into the garden and began to walk down past the flowerbeds and the gardener, towards the tennis courts.

Elizabeth backed the Buick out of the garage, filled with the comforting certainty that she was doing the right thing. Adam had no need to know that it was Raefe who had introduced her to Li Pi and, even if he did know, there was no reason why he should be hurt or offended. Perhaps, if her professional life once more had direction and purpose, their personal life would regain the harmony it seemed to have lost.

She sped down the curving road towards Victoria, her stomach muscles tightening at the thought of the interview ahead of her. What if he did not consider her playing good enough? She had brought no music with her. Not even the Schubert score she had worked on all morning. She entered the crowded colourful streets of

Wanchai. Lacquered ducks as flat as pancakes, birds' nests, and sharks' fins hung from shops that were little more than holes in the wall. Coloured washing on poles jutted out like flags from the windows of the tall flimsy buildings. In the harbour sampans were packed so close together that she could see an agile Chinese boatman using them as stepping-stones, hopping across the water without wetting a foot. She drove down to the car ferry, driving the Buick aboard, getting out of it and standing at the deck-rail for the eight-minute crossing.

Professor Hurok had believed in her talent. She already had a remarkable list of achievements behind her. The Chopin Competition. The Brussels and Vienna Competitions. The Bartók recital at the Albert Hall.

The ferry docked in Kowloon, and she drove through the gaudy streets, wondering why a man who had spent so much of his life in the grey grandeur of Moscow should choose such an unlikely place for his retirement.

Stonewall Mansions was an old distinguished block of flats with a doorman on duty at the entrance. She asked for Li Pi, gave her name, and waited while he telephoned and received confirmation that she was expected.

The lift was small, and as it carried her upwards her stomach was cramped with nerves. She had been five months without a teacher. Roman Rakowski, who had recommended her to him, had never heard her play. Li Pi was seeing her out of politeness and had probably not the slightest intention of accepting her as a pupil. He was merely being kind, doing a favour to Roman Rakowski, who was in turn doing a favour to Raefe.

The lift stopped, and she walked along the corridor, stopping before number 27, her heart racing, her stomach tight. She raised her hand to knock, but before she could do so a small black-clad Chinese opened the door.

'My name is Elizabeth Harland. I have come to see Li Pi...' she began, thinking that she was speaking to an elderly houseboy, and then she saw the fierce intelligence and the flicker of amusement in his eyes and flushed crimson.

'Please come in, Mrs Harland,' Li Pi said graciously, opening the door wide. 'I have been expecting you to call.'

The room was huge and white-walled, the floor covered with sharply coloured rugs, the sparse furniture, dark and heavily carved, dominated by a magnificent Steinway concert grand.

'It's very kind of you to see me ... I didn't bring any music with me...'

'Please don't be so anxious,' Li Pi said smilingly. 'Would you like iced tea or coffee, or perhaps a lime juice?'

'Lime juice, please.' She could feel her stomach muscles beginning to relax. It was going to be all right. She could sense it, feel it in her blood and in her bones.

He made the drinks himself, pouring the ice-cold lime juice from a vacuum flask, saying as he handed hers to her: 'So you are a pianist, Mrs Harland?'

Her eyes met his, and she was no longer

nervous or unsure of herself. 'Yes,' she said fiercely. 'And I want to be a great pianist.'

'Ah, yes,' he said understandingly. 'The dream of so many thousands...'

She put down her glass of lime juice and said, her voice throbbing: 'Let me play for you.' She had to show him that she was not one of the thousands who merely dreamed. That she had the talent and the determination, the stamina to make her dream come true.

He nodded, giving her no suggestions, no guidance. She crossed to the beautiful piano and sat down before it, her throat dry, her heart slamming hard against her chest. The next few minutes were going to be far more important than her concert débuts at the Central Hall and the Wigmore Hall. More important even than her Liszt and Chopin competition performances. She sat quite still for a few minutes, composing herself, and then she lifted her hands, bringing them down on the keys with deft sureness, and the sombre, rich notes of Schubert's B-flat Sonata filled the sundrenched room.

When she had finished, he handed her the score of Brahms's F-minor Sonata and then, when the last notes had died away, the score of Debussy's 'Des pas sur la neige'. It was a piece she had never played before, and at first she was unsure of herself; and then, instinctively, she captured the melancholy atmosphere, the sadness, the intolerable dilemma that was present in it.

She waited tensely for his opinion, the adrenalin produced by her intense concentration singing along her veins. He was silent for what seemed like an age and then he said, with a nod of his head: 'You have talent. Indisputably, you have talent. But for the concert platform mere talent is not enough.' He crossed the room towards her, taking her hands, examining her fingers, her wrists, saying: 'The concert pianist must have many other qualities, Mrs Harland. He must possess unusual intelligence and culture, feeling, temperament, imagination, poetry and, finally, a personal magnetism which enables him to inspire audiences of thousands of strangers whom chance has brought together with one and the same feeling. If any of these qualities is missing, the deficiency will be apparent in every phrase he plays.'

'And if he has them?' she asked urgently.

'Then he must work, work, work. Practising must be a relentless occupation with countless monastic hours each day devoted to its perfection. Nothing and no one must be of greater importance!'

Her eyes held his, their sea-green depths no longer cool but burning with passion. 'Will you accept me as a pupil?'

He paused for so long that she thought she would faint. 'Yes,' he said at last. 'You have the necessary demons within. They are buried deep, and are not immediately noticeable, but they are there. However, understand this. The energy I shall demand you to expend upon that piano in any one lesson will be equal to the energy a boxer expends upon his antagonist at a prize-fight. It will be equal to a matador killing three large bulls. Never ask for mercy, for none will be given. At the end of every lesson, you will be ready to drop with exhaustion and you will weep with exhaustion. Then, and only then, will I be satisfied.'

Her smile was incandescent. 'I'm ready for my first bull, maestro,' she said zestfully.

Li Pi smiled. 'The Schubert B-flat Sonata,' he said. 'It was terrible. There were no shadings. The modulations from major to minor were too sudden. The tension must be kept alive in those long melodies and within those long movements. Schubert can present an idea, a subject, from so many different angles. For that you need a particular kind of sensitivity. Now, once again, from the beginning.'

'Did Mrs Harland say where she was going?' Adam asked Mei Lin, the lines running from his nose to his mouth seeming deeper than usual.

'No, sir. She said she would be back for lunch.'

Adam glanced down at his wristwatch. It was already ten-fifty. 'All right. Thank you, Mei Lin.'

He gave the courts a last, critical check, wondering if Beth had forgotten that they had invited the Ledshams for a game of doubles on Thursday evening. Perhaps she expected that by Thursday they would be aboard a boat bound for Singapore. He still hadn't been down to the shipping line to book a passage. He began to walk desultorily back towards the house.

The truth of it was that he had no real desire to jaunt off to Singapore. Not just at the present moment. Ever since war against Germany had been declared, there had been talk in Hong Kong of forming a volunteer force, just in case war in Europe triggered off one in the East. If a volunteer force were formed, he wanted to be in at its inception, not lounging on a boat in the South Pacific.

The house seemed empty and bare without Beth in it. He stood at the music-room door, staring moodily at the piano that had been specially shipped from Perth. He had always been tolerant about her need to play. He had taken her to concerts night after night in London. Even here in Hong Kong, he lived like a bachelor for most of the day, apologizing for her absence at bridge parties, at tennis matches, at the racecourse, in order that she could indulge in long hours of self-imposed practice. He felt a prick of irritability. She hadn't been as tolerant in return. Wanting to return to London was sheer idiocy. He sometimes wondered if she had any idea of the realities of war and was aware, as he had been lately with increasing frequency, of the twenty-four years that divided them.

He looked at his watch again. It was eleven o'clock. He doubted very much that she would be back for lunch and had no intention of wasting the rest of the day by waiting around for her. He crossed the cool marble-tiled entrance hall, picked up his golf-bag and strode out of the house towards the garage. He would go to the golf club and have lunch there. And, because he loved her more than he loved anyone or anything, he would call in at the shipping office and book a double berth on the earliest possible sailing to Singapore.

'I didn't expect to see you here today,' Alastair said pleasantly as he walked into the club bar. 'I thought Fridays and Mondays were your days for a round?'

Adam slid on to a bar-stool alongside him. 'I didn't expect to find you here during the week, either. What's the matter? Has the Army dispensed with your services?'

Alastair laughed. 'Not yet, they haven't. I'm back on duty at six. What do you want? A stengah or a G. and T.?'

'A stengah, please,' Adam said as the Japanese barman approached. 'I don't suppose there's any chance now of you being posted to pastures new?' he said as Alastair ordered their drinks. 'Not now the government is exercising caution and putting the island on a war footing.'

The barman filled two long, iced glasses to the brim with a thirst-quenching mixture of whisky and soda water and pushed them across the bar towards them.

Alastair took a sip of his drink and said reflectively: 'I shouldn't read too much into the government's action, Adam. It's a formality, that's all.'

Adam looked across at him sharply. 'You don't still hold to the view that the Japs are harmless, do you?'

The barman had turned his back on them, but was still within earshot as he began to polish glasses meticulously.

330

'No...' he said slowly, his eyes on the barman. 'I don't think I do. Not when they are so flagrantly in sympathy with Hitler and Mussolini.'

'Makes no difference who the Japs are in sympathy with,' Denholm Gresby said knowledgeably, walking up to the bar behind them and overhearing them. 'Japan's best intentions can only be served by her remaining neutral.' He clicked his fingers in the direction of the Japanese barman. 'She'd be a fool to be anything else,' he snorted as the barman waited for his order. 'The short-arsed yellow bastards might fight well against a third-rate Chinese force, but they'd get a bloody nose if they ever met with the British army!'

Adam slid off his bar-stool and carried his drink over to the far corner of the room where he had a good view of the golf course. Alastair joined him.

'He's a bit overpowering, isn't he?' he said to Adam. 'I can't understand why Tom is so friendly with him.'

'It's probably professional necessity,' Adam replied, wondering if it mightn't have been wisest to have booked the later sailing to Singapore rather than the earlier one. He frowned. He would have to telephone Tom and say they wouldn't be at his party, and he would have to telephone the Ledshams and say the tennis was off, and he would have to cancel a hundred and one other things that he had no wish to cancel.

'Don't let him get to you,' Alastair said comfortably, seeing the fierce pull of his brows.

'I wasn't thinking of Gresby. I was thinking of

Beth,' Adam said in a moment of rare candour.

Alastair raised his eyebrows and remained silent. He had no particular wish to be made a confidant to Adam's marital difficulties, but if it helped Adam to talk about them, he would willingly listen. 'What's the matter?' he asked delicately. 'Is she ... er ... having problems?'

'Yes.' Adam's voice was unusually tight. He had had no intention of talking to anyone about Beth, but he knew that whatever he said to Alastair would go no further, and he badly needed to give vent to his feelings. 'I'm having to take her away. God knows, I don't want to. There's the volunteer force to consider and a score of other things.'

'Where are you taking her?' Alastair asked awkwardly. He wondered if this particular problem had ever hit the Harlands' marriage before. In the strong cruel light of the sun, Adam looked every one of his forty-nine years. And Elizabeth was only twenty-five. It was an age difference that many marriages bridged quite happily. Obviously the Harlands were not one of them.

'Singapore,' Adam said with more bitterness than he had intended. 'We'll be there for a few weeks, I suppose. Until she gets it out of her system.'

Alastair cleared his throat and wondered what was the right thing to say. He couldn't imagine how he would feel if, after several years of marriage, Helena were to be unfaithull to him. He doubted that he would be quite as rational about it as Adam was being.

'Best thing to do,' he said at last. 'She'll soon

forget him. It isn't as if Elliot's intentions towards her are honourable. I doubt if the bastard knows what the word "honour" means.'

Adam had turned towards him, and Alastair carefully avoided his eyes.

'If it's any comfort to you, Elizabeth isn't the first and she won't be the last. Women fall for him like flies. It was the little Chesham girl a few weeks ago, and Mark Hurley's wife a few weeks before that.'

Adam was still silent, and Alastair drained his glass, wishing to hell that the conversation had never been started.

'You're crazy,' Adam said at last, his voice scarcely recognizable. 'Beth isn't involved with Elliot! She hardly knows him!'

Alastair felt the blood leave his face. Slowly and stiffly he turned towards Adam and knew that he had made the most God-awful error. Whatever Harland had been talking to him about, it hadn't been about his wife and Raefe Elliot.

'God, no!' he said, forcing a laugh, trying to remember what the hell he had said. 'You've misunderstood me, Adam. What I was saying is that Elizabeth isn't the first woman to make excuses for Elliot's behaviour. The Chesham girl and Mark Hurley's wife both did the same thing when he was awaiting trial for Jacko Latimer's murder.' He ran a finger along the trim line of his moustache.

'And Beth?' Adam asked, the lines around his nose and mouth pinched and white. 'What has he done that she needs to make an excuse for him?

What the devil did you mean when you said that she'd soon forget him, that his intentions towards her weren't honourable?'

'I thought you realized he was making a play for her that day we were all at the Repulse Bay Hotel,' Alastair said smoothly, cursing himself for being the biggest fool in Christendom. 'Instead of being offended, Elizabeth excused him by saying we were all reading more into it than there was. Give a dog a bad name and all that sort of tosh. And his intentions certainly *weren't* honourable. They never are. You're lucky that Elizabeth paid him so little attention. Now, what do you want? Another stengah?'

Adam was aware that he was on the verge of making himself look a fool. The trouble was he hadn't been listening to Alastair very carefully. He had been thinking of the booking he had made for the *Blantyre Castle* and the numerous arrangements he would have to make before they left. It wasn't possible for Alastair to have meant what he had thought he meant, and to pursue the conversation would only be to arouse preposterous suspicions in Alastair's mind.

'No, thanks,' he said shortly. 'I must be getting on. Give my love to Helena. 'Bye, Alastair.'

He walked abruptly away from him, and Alastair wiped his forehead with the back of his hand, letting out a huge sigh of relief. God, but he'd walked into that one with both feet! He walked across to the bar and ordered another stengah. With a bit of luck he had successfully talked himself out of it, but it hadn't been easy. Gresby came up to him and asked if he'd heard if Ronnie Ledsham's horse was running again on Saturday. Alastair said he thought so, but his thoughts weren't on Saturday's race. Because of his clumsiness, he realized that he still didn't know why Adam was so concerned about Elizabeth, or why he was having to take her away.

'Might have a little flutter, then,' Sir Denholm was saying.

Alastair ignored him. He was still thinking about Elizabeth Harland. If Adam was unaware of her relationship with Raefe Elliot, what the devil else was she up to that was concerning him so much?

Adam walked swiftly out of the club, throwing his golf-bag into the rear of his Riley. He no longer had any desire to play. Damn Alastair and his rambling remarks about Beth and Raefe Elliot. What the hell had he meant about her soon forgetting him? He slammed the Riley into first gear and eased down the drive towards the road. He'd *said* he was only referring to the way Beth had excused Elliot when he had made that unpardonable pass at her at the Repulse Bay. He pushed the Riley's nose out into the stream of traffic heading towards Victoria. The damn trouble was that he hadn't really been listening, and Alastair had certainly looked uncomfortable enough when he had rounded on him.

It was lunchtime, and the traffic was heavier than normal. He overtook a bus and a clutch of Chinese schoolgirls on bicycles. Beth and Raefe Elliot indeed! The whole idea was so patently ridiculous that his anxiety began to ebb. He had

335

misheard. Alastair always was a waffler, never getting to the point of his conversations. He had been talking about Elliot's notorious popularity with women, and citing Beth as a case in point of a sensible woman who, even so, made excuses for his disgraceful behaviour. He certainly hadn't been suggesting anything more compromising than that.

He slewed into Peak Road, travelling far faster than he normally did. He'd been a bloody fool to have reacted in the way he had. Alastair must have thought he had taken leave of his senses. He parked the car in the garage and stared at the empty space where Beth's Buick normally stood. She had said that she would be home by lunchtime, and it was one-thirty and she was still out. He frowned as he stepped out of his car, slamming the door behind him. The idea of Beth indulging in a wild affair with Raefe Elliot might be ridiculous, but she was certainly spending far too much time away from him and away from home. His shoulders were hunched as he walked into the house. He didn't relish the thought of having lunch alone. And he didn't relish the thought of spending long hours wondering where the devil Beth was, and what she was doing.

When he heard the sound of the car engine chugging to a halt, he threw down his newspaper and hurried to the porch to greet her. It wasn't Beth. It was Helena, her open-top little Morgan parked diminutively where Beth's Buick should have been.

'Hello,' she said cheerily, walking across to him, her mass of dark auburn hair bouncing glossily on her shoulders. 'Is Elizabeth in? I wanted to know if she fancied an afternoon's shopping. There's a sale on at Lane Crawfords and lots of goodies to be had.'

In actual fact she had absolutely no intention of spending the afternoon jammed amidst a crush of shoppers. She had driven round expecting to find Elizabeth in by herself, practising on the piano, and Adam at the golf or cricket club. Elizabeth had not contacted her since the dreadful scene that had taken place between her and Raefe at the children's party, but Helena was sure that she must want desperately to talk to someone. As the only person she could possibly talk to was herself or Julienne, Helena had decided to make herself speedily available. Julienne as an adviser, in the kind of situation that obviously existed between Elizabeth and Raefe, would be a disaster.

'She's out, I'm afraid,' Adam said, not succeeding in disguising his gloominess. 'Probably already down at the sale.'

Helena did not think so and, by the tone of Adam's voice, was sure that he didn't either.

'That's a pity,' she said, wondering whether to take her leave or not, and then, seeing the droop of Adam's shoulders, she said impulsively: 'Perhaps I could stay and keep you company until she returns. Alastair has begun dropping hints about civilian wives being encouraged to return to Great Britain in case there's a flare-up of trouble with the Japs. I haven't the slightest desire to go. You don't think it will come to that, do you?'

Adam led the way into the large white-carpeted drawing-room. 'Not a chance,' he said with a return of good humour. 'Alastair never does get his facts right. What will you have, Helena? A gin and tonic, or a Martini?'

'Gin and tonic, please,' Helena said, sitting herself comfortably on the deep-cushioned sofa, amused to see that her ploy had been successful. Once the conversation had been turned to the Japanese and the threat, or the lack of a threat, of war, Adam would talk happily *ad infinitum*.

'...so the Japs will chance their arm,' Adam said as they continued the discussion over a light lunch of scrambled eggs and prawns and a chilled bottle of Graves. 'But we'll soon shove them off.'

'I'm pleased to hear it,' Helena said with a laugh as he refilled her glass. 'Have you any hope of being placed in the tennis championships next month? I strained my shoulder a week or so ago, and it's letting me down. Otherwise Julienne and I were safe favourites for the doubles.'

They talked of the tennis championships, the horse Ronnie was running at Happy Valley on Saturday, the staggering way anything planted in a Hong Kong garden flourished and spread. To her surprise, Helena found herself not only pleased that she had taken Adam's mind off Elizabeth's absence, but also effortlessly enjoying herself.

He was an easy companion. He never seemed to think it necesssary to bolster up his masculinity by flirting or making the kind of double-

338

edged remarks that Ronnie would have found obligatory in the same circumstances. There was something sweetly old fashioned about him, a gallantry and dependability that was oddly attractive.

They took their coffees out on to the terrace, and to her amazement Helena found herself talking to him about Alan. She had never done so before to anyone. Not with the same ease. It had been something in the way they had sat down together after their lunch. Something in the way he had handed her her coffee cup, after stirring the sugar in for her. Memory had stirred. Alan passing her the toast rack, the marmalade...

'And so you don't feel that you can ever marry again?' Adam was saying to her.

She shook her head, her square-jawed high-cheekboned face beautiful and pensive. 'No. What was between me and Alan was a real thing that we built very carefully for ourselves and, when we built it, it was perfect and satisfying. Just because it was blasted to bits by a drunken driver doesn't mean that I'm never going to try to build anything else among the ruins. Alan isn't a ghost, tagging along at my elbow. He would have encouraged me in my affair with Alastair, and if I wanted to marry Alastair, why, Alan would have encouraged me in that, too.'

'But you don't want to marry Alastair?' Adam prompted gently.

Her usual grin was back on her face. 'I don't know, Adam. I truly don't know.'

From behind them they could hear Mei Lin greeting Elizabeth in the drawing-room, and then the french windows opened and she stepped out on to the terrace, her eyes shining, her whole demeanour exultant.

Helena felt shock stab through her. If this was the way she returned from an assignation with Raefe, then it was beyond belief that Adam had still not guessed about it. As Elizabeth walked swiftly over to them, taking hold of Adam's hands and giving him a loving kiss on his cheek, she felt a spurt of anger as well as shock. Up until now her sympathy had been with Elizabeth. She had never, for one moment, imagined that it was an affair that was causing her anything but agony and mental torture. Now she was not so sure, and the thought of Adam being betrayed so brazenly enraged her.

'Hello, darlings, I'm sorry I'm so late. I've had the most *fantastic* morning.'

'And afternoon,' Adam said drily, glancing at his watch.

She hugged his arm. 'Please don't be cross. I really did think I would be back for lunch. I don't know where the time flew to. It simply vanished.'

Helena's eyebrows rose. No doubt it had done. It hardly seemed sensible to admit to it, though.

'I discovered that Li Pi, *the* Li Pi, who used to teach at the Moscow Central School, is living in Kowloon.' Her whole face was lit with an inner radiance. 'I went to see him this morning, and he's agreed to take me on as a pupil! Isn't that the most marvellous news, Adam?'

Helena felt the tension leave her body. Elizabeth wasn't as insensitive as she had begun to believe. She hadn't been out with Raefe after all. She doubted if even he could have put such elation into her voice and eyes.

'That's wonderful news, my love,' Adam said guardedly. 'But was there any point in going to see him now, when you are just about to leave for a holiday in Singapore?'

Helena looked at him in surprise. He hadn't mentioned one word to her about leaving for Singapore.

Elizabeth sat down on one of the cane chairs, pouring herself a coffee from the percolator standing on an adjacent table. 'I thought about that,' she said, her eyes carefully avoiding his as she added cream to her cup. 'The important thing is that I've made the contact and that he has agreed to teach me. I told him I would be away for three or four weeks, perhaps longer. It isn't a problem. And he will still be here when I return, and I now have someone to work *for*! There's a purpose to everything again!'

When she had finished stirring her coffee and raised her eyes, she looked not at Adam but at Helena. Everything that she wanted to say and could not say was explicit in her look. They were going away. She was going to get Raefe Elliot out of her system in the only way she knew. When she returned, Li Pi and her piano would be waiting for her, but Raefe Elliot would not be. Helena nodded her head slightly, to indicate that she understood.

'You'll enjoy Singapore,' she said, rising to her feet and judging that a tête-à-tête was no longer necessary. 'When do you leave?'

341

Elizabeth looked questioningly at Adam, and he turned to her, giving her his slow smile, all the love he felt for her vividly apparent.

'On Wednesday,' he said, and was rewarded by a tight hug.

Looking at them both, Helena felt a lump in her throat. They *were* happy together, and they deserved to continue to be happy together. She prayed to God that Raefe would have the sense to leave Elizabeth alone when she returned from Singapore.

'I'll be going now,' she said, knowing that if *she* were Elizabeth she certainly wouldn't risk losing a man of Adam's worth for a brief sexual frolic with a rogue like Raefe.

With her arms still tight around Adam's waist, Elizabeth looked towards her. ''Bye,' she called, knowing full well why Helena had come to see her and deeply touched by her concern. 'Everything's going to be fine, Helena. Really it is.'

Helena grinned, blew her a kiss, and walked with Junoesque grace through the house and out to her little Morgan. She hoped Elizabeth was right, but she couldn't help remembering that it was Raefe who had given her Li Pi's name and address. Raefe who had gone to the trouble to find a teacher worthy of her. And he had said he loved her. She doubted if he had said that very often in the past. And she doubted, very much, that he would let her go easily.

Chapter 14

'But why the hell have they gone? And for how long?' Ronnie asked, mystified, as he perched himself on the end of their double bed and watched Julienne as she scooped her spicy red curls up and away from her face, securing them in a neat twist on the top of her head before she began applying her make-up. 'We were supposed to be playing tennis with them tomorrow!'

'I have no idea,' Julienne said with a little shrug that sent her bathrobe slipping off one creamy-smooth shoulder. 'Elizabeth telephoned me yesterday and said that they were leaving for Singapore this morning. She said they didn't know when they would be coming back. In three weeks' time, perhaps. In a month. They really had no idea.'

'Bloody odd, if you ask me,' Ronnie said, eyeing Julienne's bathrobe as it slipped provocatively lower. 'I've never heard old Adam express any wish to go jaunting off to Singapore.' He grinned suddenly. 'He's not going to inspect its fortifications against the Japs, is he?'

Julienne giggled and applied tiny dabs of foundation cream to her forehead and nose and cheeks. Adam's preoccupation with Hong Kong's defences was a well-known joke between them.

'*Peut-être*,' she said, smoothing the foundation cream into her skin with practised fingers. 'Maybe.'

The bathrobe had slipped further, and a pleasingly pert breast with a dark, almost russet-coloured nipple was now magnificently displayed.

Ronnie rose to his feet and stood behind her, his hand sliding down and caressing the exposed part of her anatomy appreciatively.

'*Arrêtes!*' she said, with no ill-humour. 'Stop it, *chéri*. I am in a hurry.' She had just showered and in half an hour she was meeting Derry for drinks at the Peninsula. She added a slight touch of colour to her cheeks and sucked them in, regarding her heart-shaped face in despair. '*Quelle horreur!* Why can I not have cheekbones like the beautiful Elizabeth? All high and classical and wonderfully, wonderfully photogenic?'

'Because you have a face like a little kitten,' Ronnie said lovingly, his hand moving reluctantly away from her breast and resting chastely on her shoulder. He lowered his head and kissed her on the temple, hesitating for a moment and then saying: 'Don't go out this evening, Juli. Stay in and keep me company.'

Her violet-dark eyes shot open wide. '*Alors, chéri!* What is it? Are you not feeling well? Are you not going to the club to meet Alastair?'

It was Thursday night, and it was a fond fabrication on both their parts that on Thursdays Juli had a meal out with her girlfriends, and Ronnie met up with Alastair or Tom at the club. Both of them were well aware that in fact neither of them spent the evening in quite such a decorous manner and, until now, neither of them had very much minded. It was a mutual deception containing very little real deceit.

Ronnie looked at her pretty, concerned face in the dressing-table mirror. He was supposed to be going to Wanchai to meet a Chinese girl he had been seeing for over two months now. Stray tendrils of curls were escaping from the knot on top of Julie's head and curling forward on to her face. 'No, I'm not ill,' he said, wondering where it was she was going and if she was still seeing her major in the Middlesex. 'To tell you the truth, I just fancied a Thursday night at home for a change.' He cleared his throat, almost embarrassed by the confession. 'Together.'

She had been in the process of applying mascara, and her hand stayed for a moment in mid-air. She hadn't seen Derry for five days, and the mere thought of him sent an anticipatory tingle down her spine and a flush of heat to her vulva. 'Oh, *chéri* ... If I had known sooner...' she began, not wanting to hurt him.

He gave her a quick – too quick – smile. 'It's all right, Juli,' he lied. 'Perhaps next Thursday...'

She put down her mascara-brush and twisted round on the dressing-table stool to face him. His smile hadn't reached his eyes, and his voice had sounded distinctly wistful. '*Non*, not next week,' she said decisively, taking hold of his hands and twisting her fingers through his. 'We will both stay home tonight.' Derry could wait. He was, after all, only her lover. It was Ronnie who was her husband and her friend. Ronnie who came

345

first and always would do.

She flashed him her wide brilliant smile. 'It will make a nice change, *non*?' she said, hoping that he wasn't suddenly approaching middle age and respectability. If he was, there would be no more Derrys and that would be a pity. Also, she could not imagine Ronnie being respectable. He *enjoyed* philandering. It came almost as easily to him as it did to her.

She giggled and wound her arms about his neck. 'Perhaps we should give the houseboys the night off?' she said, her eyes sparkling wickedly. 'And then we can enjoy some really *noisy* sex, *chéri*!'

'...and so I thought that Elizabeth had talked Adam into leaving for Singapore because she wanted to put an end to her affair with Raefe,' Julienne said to Helena the next day as they were having lunch in Gripps at the Hong Kong Hotel. 'But now, after what Derry has just told me, I don't know what to think!'

'And just what *did* Derry tell you?' Helena asked, keeping her opinions about Elizabeth's motivations to herself.

Julienne picked up her wine glass, and half a dozen gold bracelets cascaded glitteringly down her arm. 'He said that Melissa was spending a few days in Victoria and that on Saturday Raefe was taking her to the Gold and Green ball.'

'You mean that there has been a reconciliation?' Helena asked, not believing it in a hundred years.

346

'No—o,' Julienne said cautiously. 'He didn't exactly say that. He just said that Melissa was bored and wanted to go to the Gold and Green, and that as she didn't have a suitable escort Raefe had agreed to take her.'

The dark sweep of Helena's eyebrows rose slightly. 'Well!' she said at last. 'He is her husband. He perhaps thinks that it's far safer for him to take her than it is for her to go with someone who may indulge her in her heroin habit.'

Julienne put down her wine-glass and began to toy with her asparagus. 'But, if Raefe had told Elizabeth that his wife was back in Victoria and that he was taking her to the Gold and Green, might that not be why she left for Singapore? Because she thought there had been a reconciliation between them?'

'No,' Helena said, with no trace of doubt at all. 'Believe me, Julienne. Where Raefe Elliot and Elizabeth are concerned, there are *no* misunderstandings. The only trouble between those two is that they understand each other too well!'

'*On verra*,' Julienne said, not totally convinced. 'We'll see.'

Helena looked at her in amusement. Julienne was always meticulously groomed. This lunchtime the mascara beneath one eye was ever so slightly smudged, and her gold-red curls looked suspiciously mussed. '*When* did you say you'd seen Derry?' she asked curiously.

Julienne had the decency to look slightly discomfited. 'This morning,' she said, avoiding Helena's eyes. 'Isn't that Kaibong Sheng, the Chinese industrialist, over there by the door?'

347

'Never mind Kaibong Sheng,' Helen said, her suspicions confirmed. 'Do you mean to say that you came straight here from Derry Langdon's bed?'

Julienne tried to look as if such a thing was unthinkable, and failed.

Helena shook her head in disbelief. 'My God, Julienne! It's barely one o'clock. Couldn't you have waited a bit longer? You only saw him last night!'

Julienne's Thursday nights were as well known to her friends as they were to her husband.

Julienne shook her head. '*Non,*' she said with commendable dignity. 'I did *not* see Derry last night. I hadn't seen him for *five* days!'

'So that is why he was pacing the Long Bar at the Pen. Alastair said he looked as frustrated as a caged lion.'

Julienne giggled. '*Pauvre petit,*' she said indulgently. 'I wasn't able to get a message to him and so, this morning, I drove over to his flat before he left for work.'

'And?' Helena asked promptingly, wondering how on earth the Ledsham marriage survived.

'And he did not leave for work,' Julienne replied, her eyes sparkling. 'Not for quite a while!'

They were still laughing when the waiter came with their bill.

'And just who were you with last night that drove the delectable Derry from your mind?' Helena asked as an afterthought as they rose to leave.

Julienne looked at her in surprise. 'Ronnie, of

course,' she said as if it should have been obvious. 'Who else?'

Melissa Elliot cast her eyes disinterestedly around the opulent drawing-room of her Victoria Peak home. It looked just the same as it had when she had left it. Glossy and immaculate and with as much warmth as a luxury hotel room. A slight frown puckered her brows. All the right ingredients were there and always had been. Ankle-deep carpets, lush settees, acres of flowers and piles of shiny new magazines on the long low coffee-table. Yet she was always aware that it was not quite right, and the knowledge irked her. She had an unfailing eye for colour and style where clothes were concerned, yet somehow the same flair did not extend to her home.

She walked moodily across the vast room to the windows that looked out over the mountainside and the distant city and the bay. At the moment she didn't give a damn whether the room looked like a hotel room or not. She would not be doing any entertaining here. Raefe's tolerance didn't extend *that* far. He would take her to the Gold and Green, and probably as many other functions as she wished to attend, but he had been adamant that he was not going to play happy families with her at Victoria Peak.

She drew deeply on a cigarette, her hand trembling slightly. God, but she needed something stronger than a cigarette, and there were over two hours to go before Huang would bring her her scheduled shot of heroin.

She hated Huang with implacable unadulterated hatred. Nothing on earth would make him unlock his blasted medicine cabinet and give her even a grain of heroin before the appointed time. Or a grain extra. She had tried everything: violence, sex, money. He had been, and still was, impervious to anything she could offer or threaten. 'Mr Elliot says...' he would repeat endlessly, and as far as Huang was concerned Mr Elliot's word was God-given law.

She ground her cigarette out in an onyx ashtray and continued to stare sulkily towards the distant hills of Kowloon. A sea mist was rolling rapidly landwards. The Peak, never slow at succumbing to cloud, was already wreathed in smoky-grey tendrils. Soon cloud and mist would meet and thicken into fog, and visibility would be reduced to a mere few yards. Raefe had said that he would drive up to see her that night. To discuss further their joint plans for her return to England.

The telephone on a low lacquered table some three feet away from her began to ring shrilly. She eyed it distastefully, making no move towards it, waiting till Kwan, one of the houseboys, ran into the room to silence it.

'Good morning, sir, Yes, sir. I will see, sir,' he said hurriedly and uncomfortably.

Melissa waited with a sudden feeling of expectancy. Perhaps it was Raefe. Perhaps he was telephoning to say the fog would be too heavy for him to drive up to the Peak later in the day. That she should ask the chauffeur to drive her down to Victoria now, before it grew any worse, and they would meet at his apartment.

'It is Colonel Langdon, Mrs Elliot,' Kwan

hissed, his hand firmly over the mouthpiece. 'He wishes to speak with you most urgently.'

Melissa's small-featured feline face tightened, the nostrils showing white. 'Damn and blast!' she said savagely. 'Tell the old fool I'm not here. That I'm still in the New Territories.'

'Yes, Mrs Elliot,' her number one houseboy said unhappily. Colonel Langdon was not a man who relished being lied to, and his temper was choleric when aroused. He began to lie to the Colonel with a smoothness born of years of practice, and Melissa threw herself petulantly down on to the nearest armchair.

Her father adored her. He indulged her every whim and thought she could do no wrong. It was all very gratifying but it was not what she wanted at the moment. She wanted the relief of being with someone who knew her for what she was, and accepted her for it without unnecessary pontificating. Her father had naturally expected that she would return to live with him after Raefe's trial. The very thought of it had filled her with horror. There would be the difficulty of obtaining heroin, the endless scenes and recriminations when he was at last forced to realize that the things Raefe had said about her in court were true. She didn't want that. She wanted one person, at least, to continue thinking of her as being perfect. And she wanted heroin. And so she had agreed to Raefe's conditions and gone to the farm Raefe's grandfather had bought fifty years ago, way out beyond Golden Hill.

At that time she had hated Raefe even more than she came to hate Huang. But even hating him she had to admit grudgingly to herself that he was treating her with surprising fairness. Their marriage was over, and had been over for nearly a year. After the revelations of the trial it was doubtful if any judge would award her decent alimony. And if she was to live in the style to which she had become accustomed, as Mrs Raefe Elliot, then she would need an exceptionally decent amount. Raefe's conditions had been blindingly simple. If she accepted his help in conquering her addiction, he would see to it that she returned to England with the kind of maintenance agreement that would keep her in luxurious comfort. If she didn't kick her addiction, then there would be no money, no future, nothing.

Her nails dug deep into her palms as she remembered. God in heaven, how she had hated him! He had made it all sound so simple, so easy; and for her, with her craving, it was all so bloody, bloody impossible.

The houseboy put down the telephone receiver and said apologetically: 'I don't think the Colonel believed me, Mrs Elliot. I think perhaps he will come to the house to see if you are here.'

Melissa merely glowered at him as if he were personally responsible for her father's actions, and he scuttled away, wondering how long she would remain in residence. How soon it would be before the house was once again empty, or occupied by Mr Elliot and, if the spirits were favourable, a new and more amicable mistress.

Melissa chewed her lower lip fretfully. Her houseboy was right. Her father would undoubtedly be on his way, and would probably still be there when it was time for Huang to give her the heroin she was waiting for so torturedly. She swore and closed her eyes. She knew that she wasn't very bright intellectually, but there were times when even she could not believe the mess she had got herself into.

She had never really wanted to go to bed with Paul Williams of the Middlesex; she had merely wanted to arouse Raefe's jealousy. Her eyes, cornflower-blue and still capable of looking surprisingly innocent, opened and narrowed. Even then, two years ago, their marriage had been in difficulties and she had not understood why. She still didn't.

She rose to her feet, prowling restlessly once more across to the vast window that looked out over the mountainside. There was very little to see now. The cloud and mist had fused, and Victoria and the bay were lost to view. She lit herself another cigarette and inhaled deeply.

Derry said that it was her own fault that Raefe had told her their marriage was over. That it would not have happened if she had not been so flagrantly unfaithful to him. Melissa knew that he was wrong. Somehow, for some reason that still eluded her, Raefe had fallen out of love with her long before she had embarked on her affair with Paul.

He had never given any indication of it by word or by action, but she had enough experience of her power over men to know when a man was no longer enslaved by her. And Raefe had not been. Not for a long while.

She removed a fleck of tobacco from her tongue and continued to stare sightlessly out into the swirling mist. She knew now, in retrospect, that she should have settled for what he had given her and would have continued to give her. His name, his protection and the remains of his affection. But it had not been enough for her. She hadn't wanted his affection, God damn it! She had wanted his passion. She had wanted him to be as crazy about her as she was about him. And he had not been, and nothing that she had done had altered the situation for the better. It had only made things indescribably worse.

She shuddered when she thought about Paul Williams. He had been fun for a time, and gratifyingly good looking, and she had thought herself marvellously in control of the situation. She wasn't in love with him, and so he couldn't possibly hurt her. She was only using him in order to arouse Raefe's jealousy. In order to make Raefe want her again. Only he hadn't, and Paul had hurt her catastrophically. He had introduced her to heroin, and almost instantly she had become agonizingly dependent upon it.

She hugged her arms tightly around her body as if she were suddenly cold. It was strange how supportive Raefe had been over her addiction. There were times when she could almost believe that, if it hadn't been for her unfaithfulness, her addiction alone would not have wrecked their marriage. He had no love left for her, but he had loyalty, and she knew now that as long as she had deserved that there would have been no other women, no talk of divorce. He would have been scrupulously fair to her, and even now, even after Jacko, he was still more understanding than anyone else she knew.

The throb of a car engine cut through the fog, and she glanced quickly at her wristwatch. There was another hour and forty minutes before Huang put her out of her misery. The prospect of enduring her father's anxious company for that length of time, and perhaps longer if she couldn't get rid of him, filled her with horror. She could hear one of the houseboys opening the door to him and low voices in the entrance hall. She took a deep steadying breath, wiped a trickle of perspiration from her forehead, and turned with a false smile to greet him.

It wasn't her father. It was Raefe. 'Kwan thinks your father is on his way here,' he said, striding into the room and immediately filling it with his presence. 'Which means we won't be able to talk.'

He slung his jacket on to a chair, his silk shirt open at the throat, his glossy black hair curling indecently low over the collar. She felt her throat constrict. God damn it, but he could still arouse feelings in her that no other man aroused. Only the knowledge that those feelings were no longer reciprocated prevented her from attempting charm on him. She had been a lot of things – a whore and a fool – but she still had a remnant of pride and would be damned before she showed a man who no longer desired her that she was still enthralled by him.

'He telephoned ten minutes ago,' she said curtly. 'Derry must have told him I was here.'

Raefe poured himself a Scotch and soda and gave his wife a long assessing look. For three months she had survived on a carefully regulated dosage of heroin, and she had coped with the situation far better than he had thought she would. Drug addiction was no picnic, and his rage at her stupidity in first falling prey to it was compounded by his pity for the suffering it was causing her. He said abruptly: 'You'd better go and see Huang. If your father arrives in the next half-hour, I'll tell him you're resting with a head-ache.'

Her eyes filled with tears of gratitude. 'Thank you,' she said thickly, and then, in despair; 'Bloody, bloody hell! Is it always going to be so bad, Raefe? Is it never going to get better?'

She looked very small, and very defenceless. For the hundredth time he wished Paul Williams into the darkest depths of a tormented hell. 'No,' he said gruffly, and to his surprise, and hers, he took her gently into his arms and held her trembling body close to his. 'It won't always be so bad, Melissa. You aren't aware of it, but it's getting better every week. You're on less than half the amount you used to be. Another three months and you'll be free of it.'

'But I won't!' she cried desperately. 'I still *want* more, Raefe. God in heaven, I *need* more.'

'No, you don't.' His voice was firm, his jaw hard as he looked down into her frightened face. 'Three months ago you didn't even *want* to be cured. You do now, and it's more than half the battle.'

She began to cry, and his arms tightened

356

around her, his voice deepening.

'I never said it would be easy, Melly. But it is possible. Trust me.'

At the diminutive use of her name, which she had not heard on his lips for over a year, she looked up into his strong face and wondered how she could have ever been such a fool as to have lost his love. 'I do trust you,' she said with childish simplicity.

He released his hold of her, and she walked unsteadily over to the door. She no longer had any bad trips on the heroin that Raefe obtained for her, but she still felt obscenely disorientated. 'Have you thought any more about when I can return to London?' she asked hesitantly, pausing at the door.

'Not yet, Melly. Not until there is no more need of Huang. Besides,' he said, as he saw the disappointment flare through her eyes, 'London isn't the best place in the world to be at the moment. Blackouts, gas-masks, the nightly waiting for Hitler's bombs. You're better off in Hong Kong.'

'And the divorce?' she asked in a small voice. 'Won't our appearing together in public prejudice it?'

If she had hoped that he would say that the divorce was no longer important, she was disappointed. 'No,' he said unequivocally. 'We're not sharing the same roof, and I damn well won't let anything prejudice it. There's no need to worry on that score.'

She looked at him curiously. She had never been able to understand him, never known what he was thinking. She said with a puzzled frown: 'What will you do when we are divorced?'

He grinned at her. The last few moments were the closest they had been in years. 'Marry again,' he said succinctly.

Her cornflower-blue eyes widened in disbelief. 'Who?' she asked incredulously. 'Surely not the little Chinese girl?'

The amusement in his eyes faded, and another expression took its place. An expression of such fierce intent that Melissa felt the jealousy she thought she had tamed surge through her once again. 'No,' he said, his voice clipped. 'Not Alute.'

'A European? Someone we know?'

The moment of closeness was coming to an end. He didn't want to talk to Melissa about Elizabeth. Not yet. Not until Elizabeth had left her husband. He had the irrational superstition that if he talked of it to Melissa fate would intervene and it would never come to pass. He said only: 'Yes, a European.'

She saw the tight lines around his mouth, the harsh set of his jaw, and said with sudden insight; 'She's married, isn't she?'

A nerve jumped at the corner of his jaw. 'You'd better go to Huang,' he said, his thoughts no longer on her and her proposed return to England, but on Elizabeth. 'Your father will be here at any minute.'

She knew there was no use in remaining. He had told her all that he was prepared to tell her. She hurried off in search of Huang, her mind working furiously. Who the devil could it be?

She knew he had had a brief affair with Mark Hurley's wife some months ago. Had the affair been resumed? And if it hadn't? If it wasn't the vivacious Mrs Hurley?

'Huang,' she called feverishly. 'Huang!'

There was Julienne Ledsham. She had always had an eye on Raefe, and the men Julienne Ledsham eyed nearly always succumbed. A wave of bitterness shot through her at the thought of another woman enjoying the wealth and comfort that was, by marital right, hers. Her nails dug deep into her palms. She damned well wouldn't sink into drug-addicted poverty while Julienne Ledsham, or someone like her, lived royally as Mrs Raefe Elliot. She would hold Raefe to his promise to provide generously for her. She would damn well free herself of her need for heroin. She would show them all just how strong the weak could be when they put their minds to it.

The Gold and Green ball was held in the Rose Room at the Peninsula Hotel and was attended by the élite of Hong Kong society. Julienne looked magnificent, her red-gold curls framing her face like a halo, her gown of starkly simple white velvet chic and very, very French. The top was cut halter-fashion, the skirt falling in total perfection from her tiny waist to her white satin-clad feet.

'I can't wait to see Melissa again,' she whispered to Ronnie as they greeted a crowd of friends and walked into the chandeliered splendour of the Pen's ballroom.

'Why? You were never bosom friends,' Ronnie said in amusement. 'Do you think she's going to have a placard around her neck, "Whore and Drug Addict"?'

'Of course not, silly,' Julienne chided, squeezing his arm. 'It's just that I would like to see if her looks have been affected. It is a reasonable curiosity.'

'It's ghoulish,' Ronnie said as the band began to play 'It's Only a Paper Moon' and he swung her out on to the floor in a pacy foxtrot. 'For my part, I hope to God her looks *haven't* been affected and that she's kicked the habit. I always thought Melissa Elliot a remarkably pretty girl.'

A tiny frown touched Julienne's brows. 'I do not think Melissa Elliot would be at all a good idea for you, *chéri*. I think, in fact, that it would make me quite unhappy.'

He looked down into her heart-shaped face and her pansy-dark eyes and grinned. He liked it when he aroused her jealousy. It was such a hard feat to achieve. 'Don't worry about Melissa Elliot,' he said, and for once he meant it. A woman with the kind of problems that beset Melissa was the last thing he wanted in his life. In fact, there were times lately when he wondered if he needed *any* women in his life. Apart from Juli. It was a thought that had made him wonder if he was ill at first, but to which over the last few weeks he had become accustomed. His only problem was how Julie would receive such an admission. If he began happily to practise monogamy, he would want Juli to do likewise. And Juli, he knew, was in the middle of a hectic

360

affair.

He looked around the crowded room. Who her present lover was he still wasn't sure. If he asked her, she would tell him, but the discovering of the identities of their respective lovers was part of the game they played and to ask outright would be to cheat. His eyes flicked from group to group. Whoever he was, he would be here tonight. And when he saw him with Juli he would know him.

'It's a pity Elizabeth and Adam aren't here tonight,' Alastair said to Helena as he danced her with stiff and correct expertise around the top end of the room. 'Adam enjoys full-blown affairs like this.'

Helena, seeing Raefe Elliot's distinctive dark head of hair, said drily: 'I don't think Elizabeth would have enjoyed this affair, darling. Have you seen who's over there? And who he's with?'

Alastair looked obediently in the direction she was indicating, and his brows shot high. 'Good God! He's brought Melissa with him!'

Helena, splendid in a gown of shot-green taffeta with huge puff sleeves and a skirt that crackled as she moved, said in amusement: 'She is still his wife. And I imagine that, whatever her reasons for hiding away in the New Territories, it must be pretty boring after a while. She always did enjoy the bright lights.'

'Yes, but...' Alastair struggled for words. 'I mean, they *are* divorcing, aren't they? There hasn't been a reconciliation?'

'Not that I know of,' Helena said as they waltzed past the Elliots, who were in conversation

361

with Major-General Edward Grassett, the General Officer Commanding British troops in China.

As she spoke, Raefe's eyes caught hers and his brows rose queryingly. She knew what he was intimating. Where the devil was Elizabeth? She lifted her shoulders in a barely perceptible shrug, indicating that she had no idea. He would find out eventually, no doubt, but not from her.

'Raefe Elliot is quite capable of finding happiness with a woman other than Elizabeth,' she said to Alastair as they danced out of his sight. 'But Adam Harland isn't.'

'And is that where your sympathy lies?' Alastair asked, aware that for the first time in his life, with Helena in his arms, he was actually enjoying dancing.

'Oh, yes,' Helena said with a warmth that took him by surprise. 'My sympathy is most definitely with Adam. He's one of the nicest men I've ever met.'

'Melissa Elliot looks no different now than she did a year ago,' Ronnie said to Julienne as the music came to an end and they walked from the floor. 'The only thing that's wrong with her is that she's too thin.'

'Silly,' Julienne said, amused. 'A woman *can't* be too thin!' She eyed Melissa appraisingly. She had always dressed well, with a flair more French than English. Her dress of shimmering blue silk emphasized the startling colour of her eyes, the neckline was softly cowled, the sleeves discreetly long, the back plunging spectacularly to her waist and a nestling gardenia.

'She is still very, very pretty, isn't she?' she whispered to Ronnie as they approached her. Her hair, golden blonde and sleek, was waved close to her head, skimming her ears, revealing tiny drop pearl earrings.

She was, but Ronnie still felt no desire to deepen his acquaintance with her. Women like Melissa Elliot were nothing but trouble and best given a wide berth. He tried to steer Julienne in another direction, but it was too late. She was already kissing Melissa effusively on the cheek.

'It's lovely to see you again,' she was saying, and there was no note of falseness in her voice. She *was* pleased to see Melissa again. The thought of any woman being cooped up in the New Territories with no opportunity for fun or gossip or dancing was anathema to her.

Melissa was momentarily disconcerted, looking quickly from Julienne to Raefe. There was nothing on either of their faces to indicate that they were playing out a charade and were, in fact, lovers who wished to marry as soon as it was possible.

'It's nice to be back,' she said cautiously. 'Nothing much changes, though, does it? I can't see any new faces; just the same old crowd.'

Julienne wondered if she knew about Elizabeth and hoped Ronnie wouldn't be so unfeeling as to mention the newly-arrived Harlands.

'One thing that hasn't changed is Miriam Gresby's dress sense,' she said naughtily. 'Have you seen her? She looks as though she is wearing a converted barrage balloon!'

363

Melissa began to laugh, and Ronnie glanced at Raefe and saw that his attention was focused fiercely on Julienne. It was obvious that he wanted to speak to her away from Melissa, and Ronnie could well imagine what it was he wanted to speak to her about. It was three days since Elizabeth and Adam had left Hong Kong, and Raefe obviously wanted to know where the devil she was.

The band launched into a quickstep, and he turned towards Melissa. 'Would you like to dance?' he asked gallantly.

'Very much,' Melissa said, stepping away from Raefe and towards him. There had been no dancing at all in the New Territories, and she had noticed the instant they had entered the ballroom that most men were steering clear of her, disconcerted by Raefe's presence at her side, the scandal of the trial still fresh in their minds.

The second they had gone, Raefe said fiercely: 'Where the hell is she?'

His white dinner-jacket flattered his dark good-looks magnificently. There was a raw edge to his voice that sent a shiver of pleasure down her spine. Not for the first time she wished that it was she who obsessed his thoughts and not Elizabeth.

She hesitated, feeling a surge of erotic pleasure at the temporary power she wielded over him. His voice took on a hint of menace, his eyes narrowing threateningly. 'For God's sake, Julienne,' he rasped through clenched teeth, *'where is she?'*

Her pleasure could be prolonged no longer. If she didn't tell him, he was quite capable of

364

laying violent hands on her. 'Singapore,' she said, noting how tense his powerful shoulders were beneath the exquisite cut of his dinner-jacket. 'They left on Wednesday morning aboard the *Blantyre Castle*.'

For Elizabeth, the journey to Singapore was emotionally the longest journey she had ever made. Though she hadn't yet broken the news to Adam, she had no intention of ever returning to Hong Kong. She couldn't do so, not if she was save their marriage.

For hour after hour she stood at the *Blantyre Castle's* deck rail, looking out over a glass-smooth sea, knowing she was forsaking the greatest passions of her life; her music and Raefe. Without Li Pi, she could see no future for herself as a world renowned concert pianist and the loss of that dream seared her heart in a way she knew Adam was incapable of understanding. Without Raefe, she barely knew how she was going to live. He was her soul mate in a way Adam, for all his decency and integrity and his love for her, could never be.

Her knuckles, as she gripped the deck rail, were white. She was doing the hardest thing she had ever done in her life – the hardest thing she hoped she would ever have to do. How Adam would react when she told him of her decision, she didn't know, but she knew that even if he insisted on returning to Hong Kong, she would not go with him. As for Raefe – how would he react when he knew she had gone – and gone for good?

The answer was instantaneous. He would come after her.

Tears streamed down her face.

He would come after her, but he wouldn't find her, for she had no intention of making Singapore her final destination. Only in London would she be safe from his finding her and safe from the temptation of hurtling back into his arms.

As darkness fell and the sea turned ink-black she knew that a part of her life she would remember for always, was over. Though Raefe would remain locked in her heart until the day she died, her future lay with Adam.

The night breeze was now chilly. Turning up the collar of her jacket she gave a last long look eastwards in the direction of Hong Kong and then, with a breaking but resolute heart, made her way back to the cabin where the husband who loved her was waiting for her.